TransAtlantic

by colum mccann

COLUM McCANN

TransAtlantic

BLOOMSBURY
LONDON · NEW DELHI · NEW YORK · SYDNEY

First published in Great Britain 2013

Bloomsbury Publishing Plc, 50 Bedford Square, London WC1B 3DP

www.bloomsbury.com

Bloomsbury Publishing, London, New Delhi, New York and Sydney
A CIP catalogue record for this book is available from the British Library

Hardback ISBN 978 1 4088 2937 0
Trade paperback ISBN 978 1 4088 4126 6

10 9 8 7 6 5 4 3 2 1

Title page art © Getty images/Hulton archive
Book design by Barbara M. Bachman

Printed and bound in Great Britain by CPI Group (UK) Ltd, Croydon CR0 4YY

This novel is dedicated to Loretta Brennan Glucksman.
For Allison, and Isabella too.
And, of course, for Brendan Bourke.

The author wishes to thank the John Simon Guggenheim
Foundation for a grant to help write and research this novel.

No history is mute. No matter how much they own it, break it and lie about it, human history refuses to shut its mouth. Despite deafness and ignorance, the time that was continues to tick inside the time that is.

– EDUARDO GALEANO

2012

THE COTTAGE SAT AT THE EDGE OF THE LOUGH. SHE COULD HEAR the wind and rain whipping across the expanse of open water: it hit the trees and muscled its way into the grass.

She began to wake early in the morning, even before the children. It was a house worth listening to. Odd sounds from the roof. She thought, at first, that it might be rats scuttling across the slate, but she soon discovered that it was the gulls flying overhead, dropping oysters on the roof to break the shells open. It happened mostly in the morning, sometimes at dusk.

The shells pinged first, silent a moment as they bounced, followed by a jingling roll along the roof until they tumbled down into the long grass, spotted with whitewash.

When a shell tip hit directly, it cracked open, but if it dropped sideways through the sky it wouldn't break: it lay there like a thing unexploded.

The gulls swooped, acrobatic, upon the broken shells. Their hunger briefly solved, they flapped off towards the water once more, in squadrons of blue and grey.

Soon the rooms began to stir, the opening of windows, cupboards and doors, the wind off the lough moving through the house.

Book One

1919

c l o u d s h a d o w

I T WAS A MODIFIED BOMBER. A VICKERS VIMY. ALL WOOD AND LINEN and wire. She was wide and lumbering, but Alcock still thought her a nippy little thing. He patted her each time he climbed onboard and slid into the cockpit beside Brown. One smooth motion of his body. Hand on the throttle, feet on the rudder bar, he could already feel himself aloft.

What he liked most of all was rising up over the clouds and then flying in clean sunlight. He could lean out over the edge and see the shadowshift on the whiteness below, expanding and contracting on the surface of the clouds.

Brown, the navigator, was more reserved – it embarrassed him to make such a fuss. He sat forwards in the cockpit, keen on what clues the machine might give. He knew how to intuit the shape of the wind, yet he put his faith in what he could actually touch: the compasses, the charts, the spirit level tucked down at his feet.

IT WAS THAT time of the century when the idea of a gentleman had almost become myth. The Great War had concussed the world. The unbearable news of sixteen million deaths rolled off the great metal drums of the newspapers. Europe was a crucible of bones.

Alcock had piloted air-service fighters. Small bombs fell away from the undercarriage of his plane. A sudden lightness to the machine. A kick upwards into the night. He leaned out from his open cockpit and watched the mushroom of smoke rise below. His plane levelled out and turned towards home. At times like that, Alcock craved anonymity. He flew in the dark, his plane open to the stars. Then an airfield would appear below, the razor wire illuminated like the altar of a strange church.

Brown had flown reconnaissance. He had a knack for the mathematics of flight. He could turn any sky into a series of numbers. Even on the ground he went on calculating, figuring out new ways to guide his planes home.

BOTH MEN KNEW exactly what it meant to be shot down.

The Turks caught Jack Alcock on a long-range bombing raid over Suvla Bay and pierced the plane with machine-gun fire, knocked off his port propeller. He and his two crewmen ditched at sea, swam to shore. They were marched naked to where the Turks had set up rows of little wooden cages for prisoners of war. Open to the weather. There was a Welshman beside him who had a map of the constellations, so Alcock practised his navigation skills, stuck out under the nailheaded Turkish night: just one glance at the sky and he could tell exactly what time it was. Yet what Alcock wanted more than anything was to tinker with an engine. When he was moved to a detention camp in Kedos, he swapped his Red Cross chocolate for a dynamo, traded his shampoo for tractor parts, built a row of makeshift fans out of scrap wire, bamboo, bolts, batteries.

Teddy Brown, too, had become a prisoner of war, forced to land in France while out on photographic reconnaissance. A bullet shattered his leg. Another ruptured the fuel tank. On the way down he threw out his camera, tore up his charts, scattered the pieces. He and his pilot slid their B.E.2c into a muddy wheatfield, cut the engine, held their hands up. The enemy came running out of the forest to drag them from the wreck. Brown could smell petrol leaking from the tanks. One of the Krauts had a lit cigarette in his lips. Brown was known for his reserve. *Excuse me,* he called out, but the German kept coming forwards, the cigarette flaring. *Nein, nein.* A little cloud of smoke came from the German's mouth. Brown's pilot finally lifted his arms and roared: *For fucksake, stop!*

The German paused in midstride, tilted his head back, paused, swallowed the burning cigarette, ran towards the airmen again.

It was something that made Brown's son, Buster, laugh when he heard the story just before he, too, went to war, twenty years later. *Excuse me. Nein, nein.* As if the German had only the flap-end of his shirt sticking out, or had somehow neglected to tie his shoelace properly.

BROWN WAS SHIPPED home before the armistice, then lost his hat high in the air over Piccadilly Circus. The girls wore red lipstick. The hems of their dresses rose almost to their knees. He wandered along the Thames, followed the river until it crawled upwards to the sky.

Alcock didn't make it back to London until December. He watched men in black suits and bowler hats pick their way amid the rubble. He joined in a game of football in an alley off the Pimlico Road, knocking a round pigskin back and forth. But he could already sense himself aloft again. He lit a cigarette, watched the smoke curl high and away.

WHEN THEY MET for the first time in the Vickers factory in Brooklands, in early 1919, Alcock and Brown took one look at each other and it was immediately understood that they both needed a clean slate. The obliteration of memory. The creation of a new moment, raw, dynamic, warless. It was as if they wanted to take their older bodies and put their younger hearts inside. They didn't want to remember the bombs that had dudded out, or the crash or burn, or the cell blocks they had been locked into, or what species of abyss they had seen in the dark.

Instead they talked about the Vickers Vimy. A nippy little thing.

THE PREVAILING WINDS blew east from Newfoundland, pushing hard and fast across the Atlantic. Eighteen hundred miles of ocean.

The men came by ship from England, rented rooms in the Cochrane Hotel, waited for the Vimy to arrive at the docks. It came boxed in forty-seven large wooden crates. Late spring. A whip of frost still in the air. Alcock and Brown hired a crew to drag the crates up from the harbour. They strapped the boxes to horses and carts, assembled the plane in the field.

The meadow sat on the outskirts of St John's, on a half-hill, with a level surface of three hundred yards, a swamp at one end and a pine forest at the other. Days of welding, soldering, sanding, stitching. The bomb bays were replaced by extra petrol tanks. That's what pleased Brown the most. They were using the bomber in a brand-new way: taking the war out of the plane, stripping the whole thing of its penchant for carnage.

To level out the meadow, they crimped blasting caps to fuses, shattered boulders with dynamite, levelled walls and fences, removed hillocks. It was summertime but still there was a chill in the air. Flocks of birds moved fluidly across the sky.

After fourteen days the field was ready. To most people it was simply another patch of land, but to the two pilots it was a fabulous aerodrome. They paced the grass runway, watched the breeze in the trees, looked for clues in the weather.

CROWDS OF RUBBERNECKERS flocked to see the Vimy. Some had never ridden in a motorcar, let alone seen a plane before. From a distance it looked as if it had borrowed its design from a form of dragonfly. It was 42.7 feet long, 15.25 feet high, with a wingspan of 68 feet. It weighed 13,000 pounds when the 870 gallons of petrol and the 40 gallons of oil were loaded. Eleven pounds per square foot. The cloth framework had thousands of individual stitches. The bomb spaces were replaced by enough fuel for 30 hours of flying. It had a maximum speed of 103 miles per hour, not counting the wind, a cruising speed of 90 mph and a landing speed of 45 mph. There were two water-cooled Rolls-Royce Eagle VIII engines of 360 horsepower and a turnover rate of 1,080 revs per minute, with twelve cylinders in two banks of six, each engine driving a four-bladed wooden propeller.

The onlookers ran their hands along the struts, tapped the steel, pinged the taut linen of the wings with their umbrellas. Kids crayoned their names on the underside of the fuselage.

Photographers pulled black hoods over their lenses. Alcock mugged for the camera, shaded his hand to his eyes like an ancient explorer. *Tally-ho!* he shouted, before jumping the nine feet to the wet grass below.

THE NEWSPAPERS SAID anything was possible now. The world was made tiny. The League of Nations was being formed in Paris.

W. E. B. Du Bois convened the Pan-African Congress with delegates from fifteen countries. Jazz records could be heard in Rome. Radio enthusiasts used vacuum tubes to transmit signals hundreds of miles. Some day soon it might be possible to read the daily edition of the *San Francisco Examiner* in Edinburgh or Salzburg or Sydney or Stockholm.

In London, Lord Northcliffe of the *Daily Mail* had offered £10,000 to the first men to land on one side of the Atlantic or the other. At least four other teams wanted to try. Hawker and Grieve had already crashed into the water. Others, like Brackley and Kerr, were positioned in airfields along the coast, waiting for the weather to turn. The flight had to be done in seventy-two hours. Nonstop.

There were rumours of a rich Texan who wanted to try, and a Hungarian prince and, worst of all, a German from the Luftstreitkräfte who had specialized in long-range bombing during the war.

The features editor of the *Daily Mail,* a junior of Lord Northcliffe's, was said to have developed an ulcer thinking about a possible German victory.

– A Kraut! A bloody Kraut! God save us!

He dispatched reporters to find out if it was possible that the enemy, even after defeat, could possibly be ahead in the race.

On Fleet Street, down at the stone, where the hot type was laid, he paced back and forth, working the prospective headlines over and over. On the inside of his jacket his wife had stitched a Union Jack, which he rubbed like a prayer cloth.

– Come on boys, he muttered to himself. Hup two. On home now, back to Blighty.

EVERY MORNING THE two airmen woke in the Cochrane Hotel, had their breakfast of porridge, eggs, bacon, toast. Then they drove through the steep streets, out the Forest Road, towards a field of grass sleeved with ice. The wind blew bitter blasts off the sea. They rigged wires into their flight suits so they could run warmth from a battery, and they stitched extra fur on the inside flaps of their helmets, their gloves, their boots.

A week went by. Two weeks. The weather held them back. Cloud. Storm. Forecast. Every morning the men made sure they were carefully shaved. A ritual they performed at the far end of the field. They set up a steel washbasin under a canvas tent with a little gas burner to heat the water. A metal hubcap was used as a mirror. They put razor blades in their flight kits for when they landed: they wanted to make sure that if they were to arrive in Ireland, they would be fresh, decently shaved, presentable members of Empire.

In the lengthening June evenings, they fixed their ties, sat under the wingtips of the Vimy and spoke eloquently to the Canadian, American and British reporters who gathered for the flight.

Alcock was twenty-six years old. From Manchester. He was lean, handsome, daring, the sort of man who looked straight ahead but stayed open to laughter. He had a head of ginger hair. A single man, he said he loved women but preferred engines. Nothing pleased him more than to pull apart the guts of a Rolls-Royce, then put her back together again. He shared his sandwiches with the reporters: often there was a thumbprint of oil on the bread.

Brown sat on the wooden crates alongside Alcock. He already seemed old at thirty-two. His bum leg forced him to carry a walking stick. He had been born in Scotland, but raised near Manchester. His parents were American and he had a slight Yankee accent that he cultivated as best he could. He thought of himself as a man of the mid-Atlantic. He read the antiwar poetry of Aristophanes and admitted to the idea that he would happily live in constant flight. He was solitary but did not enjoy loneliness. Some said he looked like a vicar, but his eyes flared a far blue, and he had recently got engaged to a young beauty from London. He wrote Kathleen love letters, telling her that he wouldn't mind throwing his walking stick at the stars.

— Good God, said Alcock, you really told her that?

— I did, yes.

— And what did she say?

— Said I could lose the walking stick.

— Ah! Smitten.

At the press briefings, Alcock took the helm. Brown navigated the silence by fiddling with his tie clip. He kept a flask of brandy in his inside pocket. Occasionally he turned away, opened the flap of his tunic, took a nip.

Alcock drank, too, but loudly, publicly, happily. He rested against the bar in the Cochrane Hotel and sang *Rule, Britannia* in a voice so out of tune that it was loaded with whimsy.

The locals – fishermen mostly, a few lumberjacks – banged on the wooden tables and sang songs about loved ones lost at sea.

The singing went on late into the night, long after Alcock and Brown had gone to bed. Even from the fourth floor they could hear sad rhythms breaking into waves of laughter and then, later still, the *Maple Leaf Rag* hammered out on a piano.

> *Oh go 'way man*
> *I can hypnotize dis nation*
> *I can shake de earth's foundation*
> *with the Maple Leaf Rag*

ALCOCK AND BROWN rose at sun up, then waited for a clear sky. Turned their faces to the weather. Walked the field. Played gin rummy. Waited some more. They needed a warm day, a strong moon, a benevolent wind. They figured they could make the flight in under twenty hours. Failure didn't interest them, but in secret Brown wrote out a will, gave everything he owned to Kathleen, kept the envelope in the inside pocket of his tunic.

Alcock didn't bother with a will. He recalled the terrors of the war, still surprised at times that he could wake at all.

– There's puff all else they can throw at me now.

He slapped the side of the Vimy with his palm, took a look at the clouds massing far off in the west.

– Except, of course, some more ruddy rain.

ONE GLANCE DOWN takes in a line of chimneys and fences and spires, the wind combing tufts of grass into silvery waves, rivers vaulting the ditches, two white horses running wild in a field, the long scarves of tarmacadam fading off into dirt roads – forest, scrubland, cowsheds, tanneries, shipyards, fishing shacks, cod factories, commonwealth, we're floating on a sea of adrenaline and – Look! Teddy, down there, a scull on a stream, and a blanket on the sand, and a girl with pail and shovel, and the woman rolling the hem of her skirt, and over there, see, that young chap, in the red jersey, running the donkey along the shore, go ahead, give it one more turn, thrill the lad with a bit of shadow . . .

ON THE EVENING of the 12th of June they take another practice run, this one at night so Brown can test out his Sumner charts. Eleven thousand feet. The cockpit is open to the sky. The cold is fierce. The men hunker behind the windscreen. Even the tip ends of their hair begin to freeze.

Alcock tries to feel the plane, her weight, her dip, her centre of gravity, while Brown works on his mathematics. Below, the reporters wait for the plane to return. The field has been outlined with candles in brown paper bags to make a runway. When the Vimy lands, the candles blow over and burn briefly in the grass. Local boys run out with buckets to douse the flames.

The airmen climb down off the plane to scattered applause. They are surprised to learn that a local reporter, Emily Ehrlich, is the most serious of all. She never asks a single question, but stands around in a knit hat and gloves, scribbling in her notebook. Short and unfashionably large. In her forties or fifties perhaps. She moves with a hefty gait across the muddy airfield. Carrying a wooden cane. Her ankles are terribly swollen. She looks like the type of woman who might be working in a cake shop, or behind a country-store counter, but she has, they know, an incisive pen. They have seen her in the Cochrane Hotel, where she has lived for many years with her daughter, Lottie. The seventeen-year-old wields a camera with surprising ease and style, a flirtation. Unlike her mother, she is tall, thin, sprightly, curious. She is quick to laugh and whisper in her mother's ear. An odd team. The mother stays silent; the daughter takes the photos and asks the questions. It infuriates the other reporters, a young girl in their territory, but her questions are sharp, quick. *What sort of wind pressure can the wing fabric withstand? What is it like to have the sea disappear beneath you? Do you have a sweetheart in London, Mr Alcock?* Mother and daughter like to stride across the fields together at the end of the day, Emily to the hotel room where she sits and writes her reports, Lottie towards the tennis courts where she plays for hours on end.

Emily's name banners the Thursday edition of the *Evening Tele-gram*, nearly always accompanied by one of her daughter's photos. Once a week she has a mandate to cover whatever she wants: fishing disasters, local disputes, political commentary, the lumber industry, the suffragettes, the horrors of the war. She is famous for her odd tangents. Once, in the middle of an article on a local trade union, she darted off on a two-hundred-word recipe for pound cake. Another time, in an analysis of a speech by the governor of Newfoundland, she strayed into the subtle art of preserving ice.

Alcock and Brown have been warned to be on their guard, since the mother and daughter have, by all accounts, a tendency towards nostal-gia and fiery Irish tempers. But they like them both, Emily and Lottie, the odd edge they give to the crowd, the mother's strange hats, her long dresses, her curious bouts of silence, her daughter's tall, quick stride through the town, the tennis racquet banging against her calf.

Besides, Brown has seen Emily's reports in the *Evening Telegram* and they are amongst the best he has read: *Today the sky was truant over Signal Hill. Hammer blows ring across the airfield like so many bells. Each night the sun goes down looking more and more like the moon.*

THEY ARE DUE to leave on Friday the 13th. It's an airman's way of cheating death: pick a day of doom, then defy it.

The compasses are swung, the transverse tables calculated, the wireless primed, the shock-absorbers wrapped round the axles, the ribs shellacked, the fabric dope dried, the radiator water purified. All the rivets, the split pins, the stitches are checked and rechecked. The pump control handles. The magnetos. The batteries to warm their flight suits. Their shoes are polished. The Ferrostat flasks of hot tea and Oxo are prepared. The carefully cut sandwiches are packed away. Lists are carefully ticked off. Horlicks Malted Milk. Bars of Fry's

Chocolate. Four sticks of liquorice each. One pint-sized bottle of brandy for emergencies. They run sprigs of white heather on the inside of their fur-lined helmets for luck, and place two stuffed animals – black cats, both – one in the well beneath the windscreen, the other tied to a strut behind the cockpit.

Then the clouds curtsy in, the rain kneels upon the land, and the weather knocks them back a whole day and a half.

AT THE POST office in St John's, Lottie Ehrlich skips across a cage of shadow on the floor, steps to the three-barred window where the clerk tips up his black visor to look at her. She slips the sealed envelope across the counter.

She buys the fifteen-cent Cabot stamp and tells the clerk that she wants to get a one-dollar overprint for the transatlantic post.

– Oh, he says, there aren't no more of them, young lady, no. They sold out a long time ago.

AT NIGHT BROWN spends a lot of his time downstairs in the lobby of the hotel, sending messages to Kathleen. He is timid with the telegraph, aware that others may read his words. There's a formality to him. A tightness.

He is slow on the stairs for a man in his thirties, the walking stick striking hard against the wooden floor. Three brandies rolling through him.

An odd disturbance of light falls across the banister and he catches sight of Lottie Ehrlich in the ornate wooden mirror at the top of the stairs. The young girl is, for a moment, ghostly, her figure emerging into the mirror, then growing clearer, taller, red-headed. She wears a dressing gown and nightdress and slippers. They are both a little startled by the other.

— Good evening, says Brown, slurring a little.

— Hot milk, says the young girl.

— Excuse me?

— I'm bringing my mother hot milk. She can't sleep.

He nods and tips at an imaginary brim, moves to step past her.

— She never sleeps.

Her cheeks are flushed red, a little embarrassed to be caught out in the corridor in her dressing gown, he thinks. He tips the nonexistent hat again and pushes the pain through his bad leg, climbs three more steps, the brandies jagging his mind. She pauses two steps below him and says with more formality than it requires: Mr Brown?

— Yes, young lady?

— Are you ready for the unification of the continents?

— Quite honestly, says Brown, I could do with a good telephone line first.

She takes one step farther down the stairs, puts her hand to her mouth as if about to cough. One eye higher than the other, as if a very stubborn question got lodged in her mind a long time ago.

— Mr Brown.

— Miss Ehrlich?

— Do you think it would be a terrible imposition?

A quick eye-flick to the floor. She pauses as if she has just propped a number of stray words on the tip of her tongue, odd little things with no flow to them at all, no way to get them out. She stands, balancing them, wondering if they will topple. Brown imagines that she, like everyone in St John's, would like a chance to sit in the cockpit if there is another practice run. An impossibility, of course; they cannot bring anybody up in the air, least of all a young woman. They have not even allowed the reporters to sit in the plane while it waits in the field. It is a ritual, a superstition, it is not something that he will be able to do, he wonders how he will tell her, he feels trapped now, a victim of his own late-night strolls.

— Would it impose greatly, she says, if I gave you something?

— Of course not.

She negotiates the stairs and runs down the corridor towards her room. The youth of her body moving in the white of the dressing gown.

He tightens his eyes, rubs his forehead, waits. Some good-luck charm perhaps? A memento? A keepsake? Silly that, to have allowed her a chance to speak at all. Should have just said no. Let it be. Gone to his room. Disappeared.

She appears at the end of the corridor, moving sharply and quickly. Her dressing gown exposes a triangle of white skin at her neck. He feels an acute and sudden pang of desire to see Kathleen and he is glad for the desire, the errancy of the moment, this odd curving staircase, this far-flung hotel, the too-much brandy. He misses his fiancée, pure and simple. He would like to be home. To nudge up against her slim body, watch the fall of hair along her clavicle.

He holds the banister a little too tight as Lottie approaches. A piece of paper in her left hand. He reaches out. A letter. That is all. A letter. He scans it. Addressed to a family in Cork. To Brown Street of all places.

— My mother wrote it.

— Is that so?

— Can you put it in the mail bag?

— No imposition at all, he says, turning on the stairs once more, slipping the envelope inside his tunic pocket.

IN THE MORNING they watch as Lottie emerges from the hotel kitchen, her red hair askew, her dressing gown fixed to the neck, tightened high. She carries a tray of sandwiches wrapped in waxed butcher paper.

— Ham sandwiches, she says triumphantly, placing them down in front of Brown. I made them especially for you.

— Thank you, young lady.

She crosses the restaurant floor, waving over her shoulder as she goes.

— That's the reporter's daughter?

— Indeed.

— They're a little cuckoo, eh? says Alcock, pulling on his flight jacket, looking out the window at the fog.

A STRONG WIND arrives from the west in uneven gusts. They are twelve hours late already, but now is the time — the fog has lifted and the long-range weather reports are good. No clouds. The sky above seems painted in. The initial wind velocity is strong, but will probably calm to about twenty knots. There will, later, be a good moon. They climb aboard to scattered cheers, secure their safety belts, check the instruments yet again. A quick salute from the starter. Contact! Alcock opens the throttle and brings both engines to full power. He signals for the wooden chocks to be pulled clear from the wheels. The mechanic leans down, ducks under the wings, armpits the chocks, steps back, throws them away. He raises both arms in the air. A cough of smoke from the engines. The propellers whirl. The Vimy is pointed into the gale. A slight angle to the wind. Uphill. Go now, go. The waft of warming oil. Speed and lift. The incredible roar. The trees loom in the distance. A drainage ditch challenges on the far side. They say nothing. No *Great Scott*. No *Chin up, old sport*. They inch forwards, lumbering into the wind. Go, go. The weight of the plane rolls underneath them. Worrisome, that. Slower now than ever. Up the incline. She's heavy today. So much petrol to carry. One hundred yards, one hundred and twenty, one hundred and seventy. They are moving too slowly. As if through aspic. The tightness of the cockpit. Sweat accumulating behind their knees. The motors strike hard. The wingtips flex. The grass beneath them bends and tears. Bumping along on the ground. Two hundred and fifty. The plane rises a little and then sighs again, jarring the soil. Good God, Jackie, lift her. The line of dark pine trees stands at the end of the airfield, looming closer, closer, closer still. How many men have died this way? Pull her back, Jackie boy. Skid her sideways. Abort. Now. Three hundred yards. Good Jesus above. A gust of wind lifts the left wing and they tilt slightly right. And then they feel it. A cold swell of air in their stomachs. We are rising, Teddy, we are rising, look! A slow grade of upwards, an ever so faint lift of the soul, and the plane is a few feet in the air, nosing up, the wind whistling through the struts. How tall are those trees? How many men died? How many of us fell? Brown converts the pines to possible noise in his mind. The slap of bark. The tangle of stems. The *ack-ack* of twigs. The smash-up. Hang on, hang on. The throat still tight with terror. They rise a little in their seats. As if that might unloosen the weight of the plane beneath them. Higher now, go. The sky beyond the trees is an oceanic thing. Lift it, Jackie, lift it for godsake, lift her. Here, the trees. Here they come. Their scarves take first flight and then they hear the applause of branches below.

– THAT WAS a little ticklish! roars Alcock across the noise.

THEY HEAD STRAIGHT into the wind. The nose goes up. The plane slows. An agonizing climb over treetops and low roofs. Careful now not to stall. Keep her rising. Higher up, they begin a slight bank. Take her easy, old chum. Bring her around. A stately turn all beauty, all balance, its own sort of confidence. They hold the altitude. Banking tighter now. Until the wind is behind them and the nose dips and they are truly leaving.

They wave down to the starter, the mechanics, the meteorological officers, the other few stragglers below. No Emily Ehrlich from the *Evening Telegram*, no Lottie: mother and daughter have already gone home, early, for the day. They have missed takeoff. Pity that, thinks Brown. He taps the inside of his jacket where the letter still sits.

Alcock wipes the sweat off his brow, then waves to the shadow of themselves on the last of the ground and steers the plane at half-throttle out to sea. A line of golden strand. Boats bobbing in St John's Harbour. Toys in a boy's bath.

Alcock picks up the rudimentary telephone, half-shouts into it: Hey, old man.

– Yes?

– Sorry about this.

– Sorry, what?

– Never told you.

– Never told me what?

Alcock grins and glances down at the water. They are eight minutes out, at one thousand feet, with a wind strength behind of thirty-five knots. They lurch over Conception Bay. The water, a moving mat of grey. Patches of sunlight and glare.

– Never learned to swim, me.

Brown is momentarily taken aback – the thought of ditching at sea, of flailing at the water, floating for a moment on a wooden strut, or clinging to the rolling tanks. But surely Alcock swam to safety after he was shot down over Suvla Bay? All those years ago. No, not years. Just months. It is odd to Brown, very odd, that not so long ago a bullet pierced his thigh and now, today, he is carrying that fragment over the

Atlantic towards a marriage, a second chance. Odd that he should be here at all, this height, this endless grey, the Rolls-Royce engines roaring in his ears, holding him aloft. Alcock can't swim? Surely that's not true. Perhaps, thinks Brown, I should tell him the truth. Never too late.

He leans into the mouthpiece of the phone, decides against it.

THEY RISE EVENLY. Side by side in the open cockpit. The air rushing frigid around their ears. Brown taps out a message on the transmitter key to the shore: *All well and started.*

The telephone is a series of wires wrapped round their necks to pick up speech vibration. To listen, they have earpieces tucked beneath their soft helmets.

Twenty minutes into the flight, Alcock reaches under his hat and rips the cumbersome earpieces out, throws them down into the blueness. Too bloody sore, he mimics.

Brown gives a simple thumbs-up. A shame that. They will have no other means of communication now – just scribbled notes and gestures, but they have long ago mapped their minds onto each other's movements: every twitch a way of speaking, the absence of voice a presence of body.

Their helmets, gloves, jackets and knee boots are lined with fur. Underneath, they wear Burberry overalls. At any height, even behind the sloping windscreen, it is going to be freezing.

In preparation, Alcock has spent three evenings in a walk-in fridge in St John's. One night he lay down on a pile of wrapped meat and failed to sleep. A few days later Emily Ehrlich wrote in the *Evening Telegram* that he still smelled like a freshly cut side of beef.

SHE STANDS WITH her daughter at the third-floor window, hands on the wooden frame. They are sure at first that it is an illusion, a bird in the foreground. But then she hears the faint report of the engines, and they both know they have missed the moment – no photograph either – yet there is also a strange exaltation about seeing it from a distance, the plane disappearing into the east, silver, not grey, framed by the lens of a hotel window. *This is a human victory over war, the triumph of endurance over memory.*

Out there, the blue sky lies cloudless and uninterrupted. Emily likes the sound of the ink rising into her fountain pen, the noise of its body being screwed shut. *Two men are flying nonstop across the Atlantic to arrive with a sack of mail, a small white linen bag with 197 letters, specially stamped, and if they make it, it will be the first aerial post to cross from the New World to the Old.* A brand-new thought: *Transatlantic airmail.* She tests the phrase, scratching it out on the paper, over and over, *transatlantic, trans atlas, transatlantic.* The distance finally broken.

FLOATING ICEBERGS BELOW. The roughly furrowed sea. They know there will be no turning back. It is all mathematics now. To convert the fuel into time and distance. To set the throttle for the optimum burn. To know the angles and the edges, and the spaces in between.

Brown wipes the moisture from his goggles, reaches into the wooden compartment behind his head, grabs the sandwiches, unwraps the waxed paper. He passes one to Alcock who keeps one gloved hand on the yoke. It is one of the many things that brings a smile to Alcock's lips: how extraordinary it is to be munching on a ham-and-butter sandwich put together by a young woman in a St John's hotel more than a thousand feet below. The sandwich is made more delicious by how far they have already come. Wheat bread, fresh ham, a light mustard mixed in with the butter.

He reaches back for the hot flask of tea, unscrews the cap, allows a wisp of steam to emerge.

The noise rolls through their bodies. At times they make a music of it – a rhythm that conducts itself from head to chest to toes – but then they are lifted from the rhythm, and it becomes pure noise again. They are well aware that they could go deaf on the flight and that the roar could lodge itself inside them for ever, their bodies carrying it like human gramophones, so that if they ever make it to the other side they will still, always, somehow hear it.

KEEPING TO THE prescribed course is a matter of genius and magic. Brown must navigate by any means possible. The Baker navigation machine sits on the floor of the cockpit. The course and distance calculator is clasped to the side of the fuselage. The drift indicator is fitted in under the seat, along with a spirit level to measure bank. The sextant is clipped to the dashboard. There are three compasses, each of which will illuminate in the dark. Sun, moon, cloud, stars. If all else fails, he will have dead reckoning.

Brown kneels on his seat and looks over the edge. He twists and turns, makes calculations using the horizon, the seascape and the position of the sun. On a notepad he scribbles: *Keep her nearer 120 than 140,* and as soon as he shoves the note across the tiny cockpit, Alcock adjusts the controls ever so slightly, trims the plane, keeps it at three-quarter throttle, keen not to push the engines too hard.

It is so much like handling a horse, the way the plane changes over a long journey, the shift in her weight from the burn-off of petrol, the gallop of her engines, her rein-touch at the controls.

Every half hour or so Brown notices that the Vimy is a little heavier in the nose, and he watches Alcock exert backward pressure on the yoke to level the plane out.

At all times Alcock's body is in contact with the Vimy: he cannot lift his hands from the controls, not even for a second. He can already feel the pain in his shoulders and the tips of his fingers: not even a third of the way there and it has lodged itself hard in every fibre.

AS A CHILD, Brown went to the racecourse in Manchester to watch the horses. On weekdays, when the jockeys were training, Brown ran on the inside of the Salford track, round and round, widening his circle the older he got, pushing the circumference outwards.

The summer he was seven the Pony Express riders came from America and set up their Wild West show along the Irwell River. His people. From his mother and father's country. Americans. Brown wanted to know who exactly he was.

Cowboys stood in the fields, swirling their lassoes. There were broncos, buffaloes, mules, donkeys, trick ponies, a number of wild elk. He wandered around the huge painted backdrops of prairie fires, dust storms, tumbleweeds, tornadoes. But most amazing of all were the Indians who paraded around the tea shops of Salford in ornate headdresses. Brown trailed behind, looking for their autographs. Charging Thunder was a member of the Blackfoot tribe. His wife, Josephine, was a sharp-shooting cowgirl who wore elaborate leather coats and six-shooter holsters. Towards the end of summer their daughter, Bessie, came down with diphtheria, and when she got out of hospital they moved to Thomas Street in Gorton, right beside Brown's aunt and uncle.

On Sunday afternoons, Brown cycled out to Gorton and tried to stare into the window of the house, hoping to see the shine of the headdress coins. But Charging Thunder had cut his hair short and his wife stood in an apron making Yorkshire pudding on the stove.

A COUPLE OF hours into the flight Brown hears a light snap. He puts on his goggles, leans over the fuselage, watches the small propeller on the wireless generator spin uselessly for a second, shear, then break away. No radio now. No contact with anyone. Soon there will be no heating in their electric suits. But not just this. One snap might lead to another. One piece of metal fatigue and the whole plane might come apart.

Brown can close his eyes and see the chessboard of the plane. He knows the gambits inside out. A thousand little moves that can be made. He likes the idea of himself as a centre pawn, slow, methodical, moving forwards. There is a form of attack in the calm he maintains.

An hour later there is the chatter of what sounds to Alcock like a Hotchkiss machine gun. He glances at Brown, but he has figured it out already. Brown points out towards the starboard engine where a chunk of exhaust pipe has begun to split and tear. It glows red, then white, then almost translucent. A flock of sparks flares from the engine as a piece of protective metal breaks away. It flies upwards a moment, almost faster than the plane itself, and shoots away into their slipstream.

It is not fatal, but they glance at the severed pipe together and, as if in response, the noise of the engine doubles. They will have to live with it for the rest of the trip now, but Alcock knows how the engine roar can make a pilot fall asleep, that the rhythm can lull a man into nodding off before he hits the waves. It is fierce work – he can feel the machine in his muscles. The sheer tug through his body. The exhaustion of the mind. Always avoiding cloud. Always looking for a line of sight. Creating any horizon possible. The brain inventing phantom turns. The inner ear balancing the angles until the only thing that can truly be trusted is the dream of getting there.

WHEN THEY ENTER the layers between the clouds, there is no panic. They tug on their fur helmets, reposition their goggles, wrap their scarves around their mouths. Here we go. The terror of a possible whiteout. The prospect of flying blind. Cloud above. Cloud below. They must negotiate the middle space.

They climb to escape, but the cloud remains. They drop. Still there. A dense wetness. Can't just blow it away. I'll huff and I'll puff. Their helmets, faces, shoulders are soaked with the moisture.

Brown sits back and waits for the weather to clear so he can guide the plane properly. He looks for a glint of sun on the wingtip, or a breakout into blue, so he can find a horizon line, make a quick calculation, shoot the sun for longitude.

The aircraft swings from side to side, fishtailing in the turbulence. The sudden loss of height. It feels as if their seats are falling away from them. They rise once more. The ceaseless noise. The bump. The heart skip.

Light fading, they come upon another gap in the upper layer of clouds. The sun falling red. Down below, Brown gets a brief glimpse of sea. A split-second curve of beauty. He grabs the spirit level from the floor. Tilts it, straightens. A quick calculation. *We're at 140 knots approx, on general course, a bit too far south and east.*

Twenty minutes later they come upon another huge bank of cloud. They rise to a gap between layers. *We will not get above the clouds for sunset. We should wait for dark and stars. Can you get above at, say, 60 deg?* Alcock nods, banks the plane, curls it slowly through space. Red fire spits through the fog.

They both know the games the mind can play if caught in cloud. A man can think a plane is level in the air, even if laid on its side. The machine can be tilted towards doom and they might fly blithely along, or they could crash into the water, no warning. They must keep a lookout for any sight of moon or star or horizon line.

So much for the bloody forecast, scribbles Brown, and he can tell from Alcock's response, in the gentle pull-back of the engine, the slight caution in the movement, that he is worried, too. They pull their collars up into the wet slap of weather. Beads of moisture slide upwards along the open windscreen. The battery in the seat between them still sends faint pulses of warmth through the wires in their suits, but the cold is shrill around them.

Brown kneels on his seat, leans over the edge to see if he can find any gap, but there is none.

No range of vision. 6500 feet. Flying entirely by dead reckoning. We must get through the upper range of cloud. Heating fading fast, too!

THE BONES IN their ears ring. The racket is stuck inside their skulls. The small white room of their minds. The blast of noise from one wall to the other. There are times Brown feels that the engines are trying to burst out from behind his eyes, some metal thing grown feral, impossible now to lose.

THE RAIN COMES first. Then the snow. A prospect of sleet. The cockpit has been designed to keep most of the weather at bay, but hail could rip the cloth wings asunder.

They lift into softer snow. No light. No relief. They hunker down as the storm thuds around them. More snow. Harder now. They drop once more. The flakes sting their cheeks and melt along their throats. Soon the white begins to drift around their feet. If they could rise above and look down, they would see a small open room of two helmeted figures pelting through the air. Stranger than that, even. A moving room, in the darkness, in a screech of wind, two men, the top of their torsos growing whiter and whiter.

When Brown shines his torch at the control behind his head he sees that a layer of snow has started to obscure the face of the petrol-overflow gauge. Not good. They need the gauge, to guard against trouble with the carburettor. He has done this before, turned in the cockpit, reached dangerously high above his head, but never in weather like this. Still, it has to be done. Nine thousand feet above the ocean. What form of madness is this?

He glances at Alcock as they ride a small bump of turbulence. Just keep her level. No use telling him now. Can't swim, old boy. Would hardly bring a smile to his lips.

Brown adjusts his gloves, pulls his earflaps tight, hikes his scarf high around his mouth. He swivels in his seat. A throb in his bad leg when he moves. Right knee against the edge of the fuselage. Then the left knee, the bad one. He grabs hold of the wooden strut and pulls himself up into the blast of air. The chloroform of cold. The air pushing him back. The sting of snow on his cheeks. His soaking clothes stuck to his neck, his back, his shoulders. A chandelier of snot from his nose. The blood backing off his body, his fingers, his brain. Abandoning the five senses. Careful now. He extends himself into the thrashing wind, but can't quite reach. His flight jacket is too bulky. He loosens the zip, feels the whoosh of wind at his chest, stretches backwards, knocks the snow off the glass gauge with the tip of his knife.

Good God. This cold. Almost stops the heart.

He hunkers quickly back in the seat. A thumbs-up from Alcock. Brown reaches immediately for the battery wires to warm himself up. He doesn't even need to write the note to Alcock: *Heating is entirely dead*. On the floor, at his feet, lie the maps. He stamps his feet, careful not to sully the charts. The tips of his fingers sting. His teeth chatter so much he thinks they might break.

Over his left shoulder, in the small wooden cupboard, is the flask of tea and the emergency brandy.

IT TAKES AN age to get the lid off the flask, but then the liquor stuns the wall of his chest.

THEY REMAIN IN the hotel room, the table still positioned at the window in case the plane returns. Mother and daughter together, watching, waiting. There has been no news. No radio contact. No stirrings at the makeshift aerodrome. The field has been silent for twelve hours.

Lottie finds herself gripping the window frame. What might have happened? It was, she thinks, a bad idea for her mother to have written to the family in Cork. To have distracted them, maybe. She feels complicit now. Brown didn't need another thing to worry about, no matter how small, why stop him on the stairs, why give him the letter? What was the point of it anyway? Perhaps they fell. They must have fallen. They have fallen. I gave him a letter. He was distracted. They fell. She can hear them falling. The whistle through the struts of the plane.

She puts her fingers against the cold of the windowpane. She doesn't like herself at moments like this, her strange bearing, her shrill self-consciousness, her youth. She wishes she could walk outside of herself, out the window, into the air, and down. Ah, then, but that's it, maybe? That, then, is the point of it all, surely? Yes. A salute to you, Mr Brown, Mr Alcock, wherever you might be. She wishes she could take a photograph of the moment. Eureka. The point of flight. To get rid of oneself. That was reason enough to fly.

DOWN BELOW, IN the lobby, the other reporters crowd round the telegraph machine. One by one they link back to their editors. Nothing to report. Fifteen hours gone. Either Alcock and Brown are approaching Ireland now, or they are dead and gone, casualties of desire. The reporters begin the first paragraphs, writing in both styles, the elegiac, the celebratory – *Today, a great joining of worlds* – *Today, a great mourning of heroes* – keen to be the first to finger the pulse, keener still to be the first to get a hold of the telegraph when any real news comes through.

IT IS CLOSE to sunrise – not far from Ireland – when they hit a cloud they can't escape. No line of sight. No horizon. A fierce grey. Almost four thousand feet above the Atlantic. Darkness still, no moon, no sight of sea. They descend. The snow has relented but they enter a huge bank of white. Look at this one, Jackie. Look at her coming. Immense. Unavoidable. Above and below.

They are swallowed.

Alcock taps the glass of the airspeed meter. It doesn't budge. He adjusts the throttle and the front end of the plane lifts. Still the airspeed meter remains the same. He throttles again. Too sudden, that. Darn it.

Good God, Jackie, put her in a spin. We'll take our chances now.

The cloud grows tighter around them. They both know full well that if they don't break it now they will spiral-dive. The plane will gain speed and shatter in an immensity of pieces. The only way out is to maintain speed in a spin. To have control and lose it, too.

Do it, Jackie.

The engines throw out a taunt of red flame and then the Vimy hangs motionless a second, grows heavy, keels over as if it has taken a punch. The slowest form of falling at first. A certain amount of sigh in it. Take this weary effort at flight, let me drop.

One wing stalled, the other still lifting.

Three thousand feet above the sea. In the cloud their balance is shot to hell. No sense of up. No down. Two thousand five hundred. Two thousand. The slap of rain and wind in their faces. The machine shudders. The compass needle jumps. The Vimy swings. Their bodies are thrown back against the seats. What they need is a line of sky or sea. A visual. But there is nothing but thick, grey cloud. Brown jerks his head in every direction. No horizon, no centre, no edge. Good God. Somewhere. Anywhere. Keep her steady, Jackie boy.

One thousand feet still falling, nine hundred, eight hundred, seven fifty. The pressure of their shoulder blades against the seats. The whirl of blood to the head. The heaviness of the neck. Are we up? Are we down? Still spinning. They might not see the water before they smash. Undo the belts. This is it. This is it, Teddy. Their bodies are still pinned to their seats. Brown reaches downwards. He tucks the log journal inside his flight jacket. Alcock catches him out of the corner of his eye. Such glorious idiocy. A pilot's last gesture. Save all the details. The sweet release of knowing how it happened.

The dial turns steadily still. Six hundred, five hundred, four. No whimpering. No moaning. The scream of cloud. The loss of body. Alcock maintains the spin in the endless white and grey.

A glimpse of new light. A different wall of colour. It takes a split second for it to register. A slap of blue. A hundred feet. Strange blue, spinning blue, are we out? Blue here. Black there. We're out, Jack, we're out! Catch her. Catch her for godsake. Christ, we're out. Are we out? Another line of black looms. The sea stands soldier-straight and dark. Light where the water should be. Sea where the light should crest. Ninety feet. Eighty-five. That's the sun. Christ, it's the sun,

Teddy, the sun! There. Eighty now. The sun! Alcock gives the machine a mouthful of throttle. Over there. Open her. Open her. The engines catch. He fights the jolt. The sea turns. The plane levels. Fifty feet to spare, forty feet, thirty, no more. Alcock glances down at the Atlantic, the waves galloping white-edged beneath them. The sea sprays upwards onto the windscreen. Not a sound from either of the men until the plane is levelled again and they begin to rise once more.

They sit, silent, rigid with terror.

> *Oh go 'way man*
> *you just hold your breath a minit*
> *for there's not a stunt that's in it*
> *with the Maple Leaf Rag*

LATER THEY WILL joke about the spin, the fall, the rollout over the water – *if your life doesn't flash in front of your eyes, old boy, does that mean you've had no life at all?* – but climbing upwards they say nothing. Brown leans out and slaps the flank of the fuselage. Old horse. Old Blackfoot.

THEY LEVEL OUT along the water, at five hundred feet, in clear air. A horizon line now. Brown reaches for his drift-bearing plate, corrects his compass. Almost eight o'clock Greenwich Mean Time. Brown scrambles around for his pencil. *Ticklish?* he scrawls, with a series of exclamation marks. He catches the sideways grin of Alcock. It is the first time in hours they have had a run without fog or layers of cloud. A dull, chewy grey out over the water. Brown scribbles down the last of the calculations. They are north, but not so far as to miss Ireland altogether. Brown reckons the course is 125 degrees true, but allowing for variation and wind he sets a compass course at 170. Ruddering south.

He can feel it rising up in him, the prospect of grass, a lonesome cottage on the horizon, perhaps a row of huddled cattle. They must be careful. There are high cliffs along the coast. He has studied the geography of Ireland: the hills, the round towers, the expanses of limestone, the disappearing lakes. Galway Bay. There had been songs about that during the war. The roads to Tipperary. The Irish were a sentimental lot. They died and drank in great numbers. A few of them for Empire. Drank and died. Died. Drank.

He is screwing back the lid on the flask of hot tea when he feels Alcock's hand on his shoulder. He knows before turning round that it is there. As simple as that.

Rising up out of the sea, nonchalant as you like: wet rock, dark grass, stone tree light.

Two islands.

The plane crosses the land at a low clip.

Down below, a sheep with a magpie sitting on its back. The sheep raises its head and begins to run when the plane swoops, and for just a moment the magpie stays in place on the sheep's back: it is something so odd Brown knows he will remember it forever.

The miracle of the actual.

In the distance, the mountains. The quiltwork of stone walls. Corkscrew roads. Stunted trees. An abandoned castle. A pig farm. A church. And there, the radio towers to the south. Two-hundred-foot masts in a rectangle of lockstep, some warehouses, a stone house sitting on the edge of the Atlantic. It is Clifden, then. Clifden. The Marconi Towers. A great net of radio masts. They glance at each other. No words. Bring her down. Bring her down.

They follow their line out over the village. The houses are grey. The roofs, slate. The streets unusually quiet.

Alcock whoops. Shuts the engines. Angles in, flattens the Vimy out.

Their helmets applaud. Their hair roars. Their fingernails whistle.

FROM OUT OF the grass a flock of long-billed snipe rises and soars.

IT LOOKS TO them like the perfect landing field, hard and level and green, yet what they don't notice coming down are the nearby slabs of peat that lie like cake, the sharp cuts in the brown earth, the lines of wet string that run along the banks, the triangular ricks of earth off in the distance. They miss, too, the wooden turf carts that lie weathered and rainpocked at the side of the road. They miss the angles of the slanes, leaning up against the carts. They miss the rushes grown long on the abandoned roads.

They bring the Vimy towards the ground. A flawless trajectory. Almost as if they could lean out and scoop the soil in their hands. Here we are. The plane suspends itself a foot from the ground. Their hearts thump in their shirts. They wait for the moment of touch. Skim the top of the grass.

They hit and bounce. We are down, we are down, Jackie boy.

But they know straightaway they are slowing too suddenly. A wheel maybe? A burst tyre? A snap of tail fin? No cursing, no shouting. No panic. A sinking feeling. A dip. And then they realize. It is bog, not grass. The living roots of sedge. They are skidding across a green bog. The soil holds the weight of the plane a moment and they skid along fifty feet, sixty feet, seventy, but then the wheels dig.

The earth holds, the Vimy sinks, the nose dips, the tail lifts.

It is as if they have been yanked backwards by surprise. The front of the Vimy slams into the soil. The back end flips. Brown smashes his face on the front of the cockpit. Alcock pushes back against the rudder control bar, bends it with pure force. A shot of pain through his chest and shoulders. Good Jesus, Jackie, what happened there? Have we crashed?

The silence, a noise in their heads. Louder now than ever. Suddenly doubled somehow. And then a relief floods up through them. The noise filters down into the rest of their bodies. Is that silence? Is that really silence? The racket of it. Slipping through their skullboxes. Good God, Teddy, that's silence. That's what it sounds like.

Brown touches his nose, his chin, his teeth, to see if he is intact. A few cuts, a few bruises. Nothing else. We're alive. We're perpendicular, but we're alive.

The Vimy sticks out of the earth like some new-world dolmen. The nose is buried at least two feet in the bog. The tail in the air.

– Crikey, says Alcock.

He can smell petrol somewhere. He switches off the magnetos.

– Quick. Out. Down.

Brown reaches for the logbook, the flares, the linen bag of letters. Pulls himself up over the edge of the cockpit. Throws down his walking stick and it hits like an arrow in the bog below, stuck sideways in the soil. A burn in the leg as he lands. Hallelujah for the ground: it almost surprises him that it isn't made of air. A living dolmen, yes.

In the pocket of his flight suit, Brown has a small pair of binoculars. The right lens has fogged, but through the good lens he sees figures high-stepping across the bog. Soldiers. Yes, soldiers. They seem for all the world like toy things coming, dark against the complicated Irish sky. As they get closer he can make out the shape of their hats and the slide of rifles across their chests and the bounce of bandolier belts. There's a war going on, he knows. But there's always some sort of war going on in Ireland, isn't there? One never knows quite whom or what to trust. Don't shoot, he thinks. After all this, don't shoot us. *Excuse me. Nein, nein.* But these are his own. British, he is sure of it. One of them with a camera bobbing at his chest. Another still in his striped pyjamas.

Behind them, in the distance, horses and carts. A single motorcar. A line of people coming from the town, snaking out along the road, small grey figures. And look at that. Look at that. A priest in white vestments. Coming closer now. Men, women, children. Running. In their Sunday best.

Ah, mass. So, they must have been at mass. That is why there was nobody on the streets.

The smell of the earth, so astoundingly fresh: it strikes Brown like a thing he might eat. His ears throb. His body feels as if it is still moving through the air. He is, he thinks, the first man ever to fly and stand at the exact same time. The war out of the machine. He holds the small bag of letters up in salute. On they come, soldiers, people, the light drizzle of grey.

Ireland.

A beautiful country. A bit savage on a man all the same.

Ireland.

1845–46

f r e e m a n

Dawn unlocked the morning in increments of grey. The rope tightened hard against the bollard. The water slapped against Kingstown Pier. He stepped off the gangplank. Twenty-seven years old. In a black greatcoat and a wide grey scarf. His hair worn high and parted.

The cobbles were wet. Horses breathed steam into the September mist. Douglass carried his own leather trunk to the waiting carriage: he was not yet used to being waited upon.

He was brought to the home of his Irish publisher, Webb. A three-storey house on Great Brunswick Street, one of the better streets in Dublin. He relinquished his trunk. He watched a footman struggle with the weight of it. The servants stood in a line and greeted him at the door.

He slept through the morning and afternoon. A maid ran a warm bath in a deep iron tub. It was filled with a powder that gave off a fragrance of citrus. He fell asleep again, woke panicked, could not tell where he was. He climbed quickly from the water. The print of his wet feet on the cold floor. The towel touched, coarse, at the back of his neck. He dried the sculpt of his body. He was broad-shouldered, muscled, over six feet tall.

He could hear church bells ringing in the distance. A turf smell in the air. Dublin. How odd it was to be here: damp, earthy, cold.

A gong sounded from downstairs. Dinnertime. He stood at the hand basin, before the looking glass, and shaved closely, shook the creases from his jacket, mounted his cravat tight.

At the bottom of the stairs, at the end of a corridor, he stood for a moment disorientated, unsure which door to go through. He pushed one open. The kitchen was steam-filled. A maid was loading plates onto a tray. So very pale. The proximity of her sent a shiver along his arms.

— This way, sir, she muttered, squeezing past him in the doorway.

She led him along the corridor, bowed as she opened the door. A fire leaped orange in the ornate mantelpiece. A whirr of voices. A dozen people had gathered to meet him: Quakers, Methodists, Presbyterians. Men in black frock coats. Women in long dresses, aloof and elegant, the mark of bonnet ribbons still on the soft of their necks. They applauded quietly when he walked into the room. His youth. His poise. They leaned in close as if to secure his immediate confidence. He told them of his long travel from Boston to Dublin, how he was forced into steerage on the steamer *Cambria* even though he had tried to book first class. Six white men had protested his presence on the saloon deck. Threats of blood were urged against him. *Down with the nigger.* They had come within a whisker of blows. The captain stepped in, threatened to throw the white men overboard. Douglass had been allowed to walk the deck, even delivered a speech to the passengers. Still, at night, he had to sleep in the underbelly of the boat.

The listeners nodded gravely, shook his hand a second time, said he was a fine example, a good Christian. He was guided into the dining room. The table was laid with fine cutlery and glassware. A vicar stood to give grace. The meal was exquisite – lamb with mint sauce – but he could hardly eat. He sipped from the water glass, found himself faint.

He was called upon to give a speech: his days as a slave, how he slept on a dirt floor in a hovel, crawled into a meal bag to stave off the cold, put his feet in the ashes for warmth. How he had lived with his grandmother for a while and had gone, then, to a plantation. Was taught, against the law, to read, write and spell. How he read the New Testament to his fellow slaves. Worked in a shipyard with Irishmen as companions. Ran away three times. Failed twice. Escaped Maryland at twenty years of age. Became a man of letters. He was here now to convince the people of Britain and Ireland to help crush slavery through peaceful moral persuasion.

He was well practised – he had spent more than three years giving speeches in America – but these were respectable men of God and empire, in a new land altogether. The obligation of distance. The necessity to say precisely what he meant. To clarify without condescending.

The nerves unbuttoned the length of his spine. His hands grew clammy. His heart hammered. He did not want to pander. Nor did he want to obscure. He was, he knew, not the first black man to land in Ireland to lecture. Remond had been here before him. Equiano, too. The Irish abolitionists were known for their fervour. They came from the land of O'Connell, after all. The Great Liberator. There was, he'd been told, a hunger for justice. They would open themselves to him.

The guests watched as if a carriage were galloping along, but might suddenly overturn in front of their eyes. A bead of sweat rolled down between his shoulder blades. He found himself faltering. He rounded his fist, coughed into it, dabbed at his brow with a handkerchief. He had made himself free, he said, but remained property. Merchandise. Chattel. A commodity in law. At any moment he could be returned to his *master*. The word itself was vicious. He wanted to smash it, ruin it. *Massah*. He could be whipped, his wife defiled, his children bartered. There were still churches in America that supported the system of ownership: an indelible stain on the Christian mind. Even in Massachusetts he was still chased down the street, beaten, spat upon.

He was there, he said, to raise just a single hat, but eventually that hat would raise the heavens. He would go forth as a slave no more.

– Bravo, called an elderly man.

A tentative round of applause rang out. A young cleric rushed forwards to shake Douglass's hand.

– Hear, hear.

The approval sallied round the room. The maid in the black dress lowered her eyes to the ground. After tea and biscuits in the living room, Douglass shook hands with the men, politely excused himself. The women were gathered in the library. He knocked at the door, entered cautiously, bent slightly at the waist, bid them good night. He heard them murmuring as he moved away.

Webb guided him up the curving staircase by the light of a glass-fluted candle. Their shadows spread haphazard against the wainscoting. A washbasin. A writing table. A chamber pot. A bed with a brass frame. He opened his trunk and took out an engraving of his wife and children, set it alongside the bed.

– It's an honour to have you in my house, said Webb from the door.

Douglass leaned across to blow out the candle. He could hardly sleep. The sea was still moving in him.

IN THE MORNING Webb drove him around in a horse and carriage. He wanted to show him the city. Douglass sat alongside him, up front, on the wooden boards, exposed to the weather.

Webb was short, thin, narrow, proud. He used the whip judiciously.

At first, the streets were clean and leisurely. They passed a tall, grey church. A row of small, neat shops. The canals ran straight and true. The doorways were brightly painted. They doubled back and went into the city, past the university, the Houses of Parliament, along the quays, towards the Customs House. Farther along, the city began to change. The streets narrowed. The potholes deepened. Soon the filth was staggering. Douglass had never seen anything quite like it, even in Boston. Piles of human waste slushed down the gutter. It sloshed its way into fetid puddles. Men lay collapsed by the railings of rooming houses. Women walked in rags, less than rags: as rags. Children ran barefoot. Specimens of ancient ruin glared out of windowsills. Windows were dusty and broken. Rats darted in the alleyways. The carcass of a donkey was left bloated in the courtyard of a tenement. Dogs went forth, lean-shouldered. There was a reek of porter about the streets. A young beggar sang a melody in a tired voice: a police boot sank savagely into her rib cage and moved her along. She fell at the next railing, lay against it, laughing.

The Irish had little or no order about themselves, he thought. The carriage went corner unto corner, turning, always turning, grey unto grey. It began to drizzle. The streets were muddy and even more deeply potholed. The sound of a fiddle was rent through with a scream.

Douglass was unnerved by what was unfolding around him, but he stared out eagerly, absorbed it all. Webb cracked the whip down on the horse's back. They clopped back up Sackville Street, past Nelson's Pillar, towards the bridge, across the river once more.

The Liffey was dimpled with rain. A low barge made its way down from the brewery. The wind ran raw and unstoppable along the quays. Vendors of fish moved over the cobbles, pushing barrows of stinking shells.

A tribe of boys in rags jumped onto the side of the carriage. Seven or eight of them. They used the moving wheels to propel themselves on, then hung perilously by the tips of their fingers. Some of them tried to open the carriage door. Laughter and puddle-fall. One monkeyed across and landed softly on the wooden board, nestled his head against Douglass's shoulder. A series of raw red welts ran along the boy's neck and face. Webb had implored him not to give away coins, but Douglass slid the boy a ha'penny. The child's eyes grew slick with tears. He kept his head on Douglass's shoulder as if welded there. The other boys leaned in from the side of the carriage, shouting, pushing, cajoling.

– Mind your pockets! said Webb. No more coins. Don't give them any more.

– What are they saying? said Douglass.

The din was extraordinary: it sounded as if they were chanting in rhyme.

– No idea, said Webb.

Webb pulled the carriage up near a laneway, one wheel on the footpath, shouted at a policeman to scatter the boys. The whistle was lost in the air. It took three of the constabulary to dislodge them from the carriage. The gang ran through the laneway. Their shouts ricocheted.

– Thanks, mister! Thanks!

Douglass took a handkerchief to his shoulder. The child had left a long stream of snot along the arm of his coat.

HE HAD NOT imagined Dublin this way at all. He had envisioned rotundas, colonnades, quiet chapels on the street corners. Porticoes, pilasters, domes.

They passed through a narrow arch into a chaos of men and women. They were gathered for a meeting in the shadows of a theatre house. A red-headed man stood on top of a silver keg, barking about Repeal. The crowd swelled. Laughter and applause. Someone responded with a shout about Rome. The words volleyed back and forth. Douglass couldn't understand the accents, or was it the language? Were they speaking in Irish? He wanted to descend the carriage and walk amongst them, but Webb whispered that there was trouble brewing.

They continued down a havoc of backstreets. A woman carried a tray of kale on a string over her neck, trying in vain to hawk the exhausted green leaves.

– Mr Webb, sir, Mr Webb, y'r honour!

Webb broke his own rule, handed her a small copper coin. She ducked away into her headscarf. She looked as if she were praying over the coin. A few coils of hair escaped, damp and coarse.

Within seconds they were surrounded. Webb had to force the carriage through the crowd of stretched hands. The poor were so thin and white, they were almost lunar.

A LADY ALONG George's Street gripped her umbrella as the carriage passed by. A newspaperman who happened to glimpse him wrote afterwards that the visiting Negro looked rather dandy. An audacious whore on the corner of Thomas Street shouted that she would laugh at his best and whistle for more. He caught sight of himself in a shop window and froze the picture in his mind, stunned at the opportunity for public vanity.

THE STORM MADE the carriage list sideways. Douglass looked for a crack of light in the clouds. None came. Rain fell more steadily now. Grey and unrelenting. Nobody seemed to notice. Rain on the puddles. Rain on the high brickwork. Rain on the slate roofs. Rain on the rain itself.

Webb entreated him to sit below where he could dry off. Douglass descended. The seats inside were made of soft leather. The handles were brushed bronze. He felt foolish, cowardly, warm. He really should sit outside, bear the brunt of the weather, like Webb. He stamped his feet, opened the neck of his coat. His body steamed. A puddle grew at his feet.

Up near the cathedral, there was a break in the rain. The city opened with afternoon sunlight. He climbed out and stood on the pavement. Children were jumping rope, calling rhymes to one another. *One-eyed Patrick Walker, met a girl, begat a daughter, the girl she turned to dirty water, one eye 'tain't your fault, sir.* They crowded around him, touched his clothes, removed his hat, pushed their fingers through his hair. *Magpie, magpie, sitting on the sty, who oh who has the dirty greedy eye?* They laughed at the feel of his hair: tall, bushy, wiry, uneven. A young boy shoved a twig in the mass of curls, ran off, whooping. A girl tugged on the end of his coat.

— Mister! Hey, mister! Are you from Africa?

He hesitated a moment. He had never been asked the question before. His smile tightened.

— America, he said.

— *Christopher Columbus sailed the ocean blue, he won't pick me and he won't pick you!*

The youngest amongst them was no more than three years old. His chest was bony. Leaves were tangled in his filthy hair. A fresh wound underneath his eye.

– Come on and jump with us, mister!

The rope twisted and twirled in the air, slapped in a puddle, rose again, kicked up water drops as it twirled.

– Give us sixpence, will ya?

He was wary of the mud that already dotted his overcoat. He glanced down at his shoes: they would have to be cleaned.

– Please, mister!

– Ah, come on.

A boy spat on the ground and ran off. The girl coiled the rope, gathered the other children together, stood them at attention, instructed them to wave goodbye. A few stray youngsters followed the carriage until they fell away, hungry, tired, sopping wet.

The streets grew quieter the closer they got to Webb's house. A man in a peaked blue hat walked along, firing up the streetlamps until they glowed, a small row of halos. The homes looked warm and soft.

The cold had insinuated itself into him. The damp, too. He knocked his boot against the seat to warm his toes. Douglass longed to be inside.

Webb sounded the horn on the front of the carriage. Within seconds the butler had opened the door and was running down the steps with a brolly. The butler splashed through a puddle and went towards Webb, but Webb said: No, no, our guest first, our guest, please. There was an odd smell in the air. Douglass still couldn't figure out what it was. Sweet, earthy.

He walked quickly up the steps with the butler in attendance. He was brought to the fireplace in the living room. He had seen the fire the night before, but had not noticed what it was: clods of burning soil.

HE CRAWLED OUT of bed to write Anna a note. He needed to be judicious. She could not read nor write, so it would be spoken aloud to her by their friend Harriet. He did not want Anna embarrassed in any way. *My dearest. I am in polite and capable hands. My hosts are witty, convivial, open. The air is damp, yet there is something about it that seems to clarify my mind.*

A loosening was taking place in his thoughts. Just the fact that he was not pursued, did not have to look over his shoulder, could not be whisked away.

On occasion I have to pause, astounded that I am not fugitive any more. My mind unshackled. They cannot place me, or even imagine me, upon the auction block. I do not fear the clink of a chain, or crack of whip, or turn of door handle.

Douglass laid aside his pen for a moment, opened the curtains to the still dark. No sounds at all. On the street, a lone man in rags hurried along, hunched into the wind. He thought then that he had found the word for Dublin: a *huddled* city. He, too, had spent so many years, huddled into himself.

He pondered the possibility of his own living room: Harriet reading the letter aloud, Anna in cotton dress and red head wrap, her hands folded in her lap, his children at the edge of her chair, poised, eager, confused. *I send you my unceasing love, Frederick.*

He tightened the curtains, got back into bed, stretched his feet out over the end of the mattress. His toes extended beyond the bed. It was something humorous, he thought, to include in his next letter.

ON A TABLE, in neat piles, was the Irish edition of his book. Brand new. Webb stood behind him, shadowed, hands folded behind his back. He watched Douglass intently as he flicked through and inhaled the scent of the book. Douglass paused at the engraving at the front, ran his finger over his likeness. Webb, he thought, had endeavoured to make him look straight-nosed, aquiline, clear-jawed. They wanted to remove the Negro from him. But perhaps it was not Webb's fault. An artist's error maybe. Some fault of the imagination.

He closed the book. Nodded. Turned to Webb, smiled. He ran his fingers once more along the spine. He did not say a word. So much was expected of him. Every turn. Every gesture.

He paused, took a fountain pen from his pocket, let it hover a moment and signed the first book. *For Richard Webb, in friendship and respect, Frederick Douglass.*

A measure of humility lay in one's signature: it was important not to flourish the pen.

I was born in Tuckahoe, near Hillsborough, and about twelve miles from Easton, in Talbot county, Maryland. I have no accurate knowledge of my age, never having seen any authentic record containing it. By far the large part of the slaves know as little of their ages as horses know of theirs, and it is the wish of most masters within my knowledge to keep their slaves thus ignorant.

AT THE BOTTOM of his travelling trunk he kept two iron barbells. Made for him by a blacksmith in New Hampshire: an abolitionist, a friend, a white man. Each of the barbells weighed twelve and a half pounds. The blacksmith told him that he had melted them from slave chains that had once been used in the auction houses where men, women, and children were sold. The blacksmith had gone round and bought all the chains, melted them, made artefacts from them. In order, he said, not to forget.

Douglass kept the barbells a secret. Only Anna knew. She had lowered her eyes to the floor when she had first seen them, but she soon grew used to them: first thing every morning, last thing at night. There was a part of him that still missed the days of carpentry and caulking: fatigue, desire, hunger.

He turned the key in the bedroom door, pulled the curtains across, locked out the light of the Dublin gas lamps. He lit a candle, stood in his shirtsleeves.

He lifted the barbells one after another – first from the floor and then high in the air – until sweat dripped down onto the wood. He positioned himself to watch himself in the oval looking glass. He would not become soft. It was exhaustion he wanted – it helped him to write. He needed each of his words to appreciate the weight they bore. He felt like he was lifting them and then letting them drop to the end of his fingers, dragging his muscle to work, carving his mind open with ideas.

He was in the fever of work. He wanted them to know what it might mean to be branded: for another man's initials to be burned into your skin; to be yoked about the neck; to wear an iron bit at the mouth; to cross the water in a fever ship; to wake in another man's field; to hear the jangle of the marketplace; to feel the lash of the cowhide; to have your ears cropped; to accept, to bend, to disappear.

It was his work to capture that through the nib of his pen. His billowy white shirt was covered in ink stains. At times, searching for words, he would hold the blotting paper to his forehead. Later, dressing himself for dinner – cravat, smoking jacket, cufflinks, polished shoes – he would glance in the mirror and find blue spots of ink smudged on his face. He was told by Webb that the Irish words for a black man were *fear gorm*, a blue man. He scrubbed his face, his hands, his fingernails. He looked at himself again in the mirror, lashed out, stopped short, his knuckles trembling at the glass.

He descended the curved staircase, stopped, bent down, shone the front of his shoes once more, using the wetted edge of a handkerchief.

The butler greeted him in the hallway. He could not for the life of him remember the man's name, Charles or Clyde or James. A terrible thing, to forget a man's name. He nodded to the butler, moved through the hallway, into the shadows.

Webb had hired a pianist to accompany the evenings. Douglass could hear the notes colliding in the air as he approached. He was fond of the standard fare – Beethoven, Mozart, Bach – but he had heard there was someone new, a Frenchman called Édouard Batiste who was said to be coming to Dublin to play. He would have to enquire: his life these days was much about having to enquire without exhibiting a lack of knowledge. He could not seem ignorant, yet he did not want to be strident either. A fine line. He was not sure where he could show weakness.

The essence of intelligence was to know when, or if, to expose even the heart's deep need for instruction.

If he showed a chink, they might shine a light through, stun him, maybe even blind him. He could not allow for a single mistake. It was not an excuse for arrogance. It was a matter of defence. Webb, of course, could not be expected to understand. How could he? He was an Irish Quaker. Good-hearted, yes. But he saw all his efforts as pure benevolence. It was not Webb's freedom that was at stake. It was Webb's *ability* to be free. Webb himself had his own ideas about who was slave, who was not, and what it was that lay between them.

Small matter, thought Douglass. He would not let it poison him. The Irish had been so friendly. He was a guest. He had to remember that.

The butler pushed the door open for him. Douglass entered the drawing room with his arms behind his back, his hands clasped. He felt it best to enter a room this way. Equal amounts of deference and aloofness in it. Not haughty. Never haughty. Just tall, full, solid.

It struck him: the sheer surprise of being here. A carpenter, a caulker of ships, a man of the fields. To have come such a distance. To have left behind his wife, his beloved children. To hear the sound of his shoes striking the floor. The only moving shoes in a roomful of men. His voice had now become his hands: he understood what it meant to be made flesh. An energy moved through him. He cleared his throat, but held back a moment. These were, he remembered, the members of the Royal Dublin Society. Creatures of high collars and groomed moustaches. They had an air of antiquity about them. He gazed out at them. The sort of men who had hung their swords above the fireplaces of their minds. He would wait to unleash his fury.

He stepped forwards to shake their hands. Marked their names. Reverend Archibald. Brother Harrington. He would write them in his diary later tonight. These were the small matters of etiquette that he had to remember. The pronunciation. The spelling.

— It's a pleasure to meet you, gentlemen.

— An honour, Mr Douglass. We have read your book. A remarkable achievement.

— Thank you.

— There is much to learn from it. Much to admire in its style, even more in its content.

— You're very kind.

— And is Dublin to your liking?

— It is livelier than Boston, yes.

There was laughter all around and he was grateful for it, the manner in which it allowed him to ease his body out of his stiffness. Webb guided him towards a deep chair in the centre of the room. He glanced across to see Lily, the maid, pouring him a cup of tea. He liked his tea with an extraordinary amount of sugar. His weakness: a sweet tooth. Lily's face, half carved in light as she poured, sharp, pretty, alabaster. She glided across to him. Her cool white wrists. The china cup was very thin. It was said that this made the tea taste better. He could feel the cup trembling in his hands. The thinner the china, the louder the rattle.

He hoped his manner of holding the teacup did not appear crude. He shifted slightly in his seat. He could feel his hands grow clammy again.

Webb introduced him. Even in America, Douglass had seldom listened to the introductions that others made. They embarrassed him. Sometimes they made of him a caricature: the coloured conquistador, the gentleman slave, the American Orpheus. In the course of the introductions they would remark, invariably, that his father was a white man. As if it could not be otherwise. How he was taken from his mother, his siblings, whisked away, brought for a spell under the guidance of white benevolence. Douglass found the descriptions monotonous. The words dissolved in his head. He did not listen. He scanned the faces of the men. He could sense their uncertainty, a little hint of confusion around their eyes as he watched them, watching him. A slave. In a Dublin drawing room. So remarkably well-kept.

He looked up to see that Webb had finished. A silence. The teacup shook in his hands. He allowed the quiet to edge up against the uncomfortable. He had found that being nervous made him tighter with his words, stronger, more careful.

Douglass brought the saucer up to the bottom of the cup.

I prefer to be true to myself, even at the hazard of incurring the ridicule of others, rather than to be false, and incur my own abhorrence. From my earliest recollection I date the entertainment of a deep conviction that slavery would not always be able to hold me within its foul embrace. Now, in the long curve of this journey, I find myself spinning a new strand and I appeal to you, gentlemen, to strive against the despotism, bigotry and tyranny of those who might refuse me entry to this very room.

AT THE END of his second week he wrote to Anna that he hadn't been called a *nigger* on Irish soil, not once, not yet anyway. He was hailed most everywhere he went. He wasn't yet sure what to make of it, it baffled him. There was something crystallizing inside him. He felt, for the first time ever maybe, that he could properly inhabit his skin. There was a chance that he was just a curio to them, but something in him felt aligned to those he met, and in all his twenty-seven years he hadn't seen anything like it. He wished she could be there to witness it.

It was a cold, grey country under a hat of rain, but he could take the middle of the footpath, or board a stagecoach, or hail a hansom without apology. There was poverty everywhere, yes, but still he would take the poverty of a free man. No whips. No chains. No branding marks.

He was, of course, travelling in high company, but even on the roughest streets he had not heard any vitriol. He attracted a ferocious stare or two, but perhaps it was also because of the rather high cut at the back of his coat: Webb had already told him that he could perhaps afford a tad more modesty.

THE BELL ON the door sounded out long and lazy. The tailor looked up but the shop continued its business. That's what surprised Douglass the most: the absence of alarm. No shock. No scurry. He walked along the rack of coats. The tailor finally came from behind the counter and shook his hand: You're welcome to my establishment, sir.

– Thank you.

– You're the talk of the town, sir.

– I'm interested in a new jacket.

– Certainly.

– And a longer cut of coat, said Webb.

– I'm quite capable of dressing myself, said Douglass.

They glared at each other across the gulf of the room.

– Gentlemen, said the tailor. Come this way.

Webb stepped across but Douglass put his hand on his chest. The air froze. Webb lowered his eyes and gave the faint hint of a smile. He took out a wallet of morocco leather and rubbed the length of it, inserted it back in his jacket pocket.

– As you wish.

Douglass stepped, large and loud-footed, with the tailor towards a rear room. Scissors, needles, cut-outs. Dusty ells and bolts of cloth spooled out across the tables. What fields did the cloth come from? What fingers had spun it out?

The tailor whisked a looking glass across the room. The mirror was on a stand, mounted with wheels.

He had never been measured by a white man before. The tailor stood behind him. Douglass flinched a moment when the tape was put around his neck.

– Sorry, sir, is the tape cold?

He closed his eyes. Allowed the measurements. His rib cage, his chest, his waist. Raised his arms in the air to see how deep the armpit of the waistcoat could go. Breathed in, breathed out. Allowed the tattered yellow tape along his inseam. The tailor scribbled the measurements down. His handwriting was fine and exact.

When he was finished, the tailor wrapped his fingers around Douglass's shoulders, gripped him hard.

– You're a fine broad man, sir, I'll venture that.

– To tell the truth . . .

He glanced at Webb in the front of the shop. The Quaker was standing at the window, looking out, an overseer. The Liffey seemed to want to carry him away on its continuous sleeve of grey.

– I'd be rather grateful, said Douglass.

– Yes, sir?

He looked out at Webb again.

– If you'd also fit me for a camel's-hair vest.

– A vest, sir?

– Yes, a waistcoat I believe you call it.

– Indeed, sir.

The tailor turned him round once more, busied himself with a measurement of Douglass's rib cage, brought the ends of the tape together at his navel.

– You can put it on Mr Webb's bill.

– Yes, sir.

– He's always been fond of a surprise.

THE CROWDS CAME, eager, hatted, earnest. A balloon of perfume about them. They lined the front of the Methodist churches, the Quaker meeting halls, the front drawing rooms of mansions. He stretched up on his toes, put his thumbs in the pockets of his new waistcoat.

In the afternoons he took tea with the Dublin Anti-Slavery Society, the Hibernian Association, the Whigs, the Friends of Abolition. They were well-informed, clever, audacious in speech, generous with their donations. They thought him so very young, handsome, debonair. He could hear the ruffle of dresses in the queue waiting to meet him. Webb said that he had never seen so many young ladies attend the events. Even one or two Catholics from good families. In the gardens of well-appointed houses the women spread their dresses on wooden benches and posed for portraits with him.

Douglass was careful to make sure that he mentioned his wife, his children at home in Lynn. It was odd, but at times the talk of Anna drew the women closer. They hovered. There were giggles and para-sols and handkerchiefs. They wanted to know what fashions the free Negro women in America wore. He said that he had no clue, that one dress looked much like the other to him. They clapped their hands together in a delight he could not understand.

He was invited to dinner with the Lord Mayor. The chandeliers in the Mansion House sparkled. The ceilings were tall. The paintings majestic. The rooms led into one another like fabulous sentences.

He met with Father Mathew, joined forces with the temperance movement. The streets of Dublin were full of the demons of alcohol. He took the Pledge. It might, he thought, enamour him of a whole new audience. Besides, he never drank. He did not want to lose control. Too much of the master in it: its desire to sedate. He walked with the Pledge badge worn prominently on the lapel of his new coat. He felt himself to be taller somehow. He drew the grey Dublin air into his lungs. He was seldom left alone. There were always one or two who volunteered to accompany him. He found rhythm in the dips and swerves and repetitions of the Irish accent. He had a penchant for mimicry. *Grand day, y'r honour. For the love of God, wouldya ever gi'us sixpence, sir?* It delighted his hosts to hear his impersonations. There was a deeper intent there, too: he knew that something so simple could hook a crowd. *I am pleased to be in aul' Ireland.*

He was five weeks in Dublin. His face appeared on printed bills around the city. Newspaper reporters met him for high tea in the Gresham Hotel. He was *leonine*, they wrote, *feral, an elegant panther*. One paper dubbed him *the Dark Dandy*. He laughed and tore the paper up – did they expect him to dress in rags of American cotton? He was taken to the Four Courts, brought to the finest dining rooms, asked to sit under chandeliers where he could be properly seen. When he was guided into a room to speak, the applause often extended a full minute. He removed his hat and bowed.

Afterwards they lined up to buy his book. It amazed him to raise his gaze from his fountain pen and see the row of dresses awaiting him.

On certain days he grew tired, thought of himself as an elaborate poodle on a leash. He removed himself to his room, took out the barbells, worked himself into a frenzy.

One evening he found the bill for the waistcoat neatly folded on his bedside table. He had to laugh. They would eventually bill him for every thought he ever had. He wore the camel's-hair waistcoat to dinner that evening, casually slipping his thumbs into the pockets as he waited for dessert.

EVERY DAY HE found another word: he wrote them in a small notebook he carried in his inside pocket. *Rapacity. Enmity. Phoenician.* Words he recognized from The Columbian Orator. *Assiduous. Declarative. Tendentious.*

When he had first found language, in his boyhood days, it had felt to him like carving open a tree. Now he had to be more careful. He did not want to slip up. He was, after all, being watched by Webb and the others: root, blossom, stem. It was essential to hold his nerve. To summon things into being by the mysterious alchemy of language. Atlantic. Atlas. Aloft. He was holding the image of his own people up: sometimes it was weight enough to stagger under.

IN RATHFARNHAM HE thundered forth. He talked of womanwhippers, man-stealers, cradle-plunderers. Of fleshmongers and swine-drovers. Of sober drunkards, thieves of men. Of limitless indifference, fanatic hatred, thirsty evil. He was in Ireland, he said, to advance universal emancipation, to exact the standard of public morality, to hasten the day of freedom for his three million enslaved brethren. Three million, he said. He held his hands up, as if he cupped every single one of them there, in his palms. We have been despised and maligned long enough. Treated worse than the lowest of low animals. Shackled, burned, branded. Enough of this murderous traffic in blood and bone. Hear the doleful wail of the slave markets. Listen to the clanking chains. Hear them, he said. Come close. Listen. Three million voices!

After his speech, the Gentleman Usher from Dublin Castle took a hold of his arm and breathed whiskey and amazement into his ear. He had never heard such a speech, such fine words put together. For any man to speak in such a way! It was profound, he said, insightful, weighty beyond anything he had experienced before.

— You're a credit to your race, sir. An absolute credit.

— Is that so?

— And you did not go to school, sir?

— No. I did not.

— And you took no formal lessons?

— No.

— And if you'll forgive me . . .

— Yes?

— How do you possibly explain such eloquence?

A hard knot cramped Douglass's chest.

— Such eloquence?

— Yes? How is it . . .

— You'll excuse me?

— Sir?

— I have to run away.

Douglass crossed the room, his shoes clicking loudly on the wooden floor, a smile breaking out as he went.

IN THE AFTERNOONS he caught sight of Lily when she cleaned the upstairs of the house. Just seventeen years old. Her sandy-coloured hair. Her eyes ledged with freckles.

He closed his door, sat to write. He could still see her shape. On the stairs he allowed her to pass. A whiff of tobacco came from her. The world was made ordinary again. He walked quickly down to the drawing room where he sat to read the literary journals to which Webb subscribed, the reams of books, the journals. He could lose himself in them.

Lily's footsteps sounded above him. He was glad when they ceased. He went back upstairs to write. His room had been made spotless and the barbells remained undisturbed.

IN THE BANK on College Green they sent instructions back to Boston to lodge 225 pounds sterling in the accounts of the American Anti-Slavery Society. It amounted to 1,850 dollars. Douglass and Webb emerged in their crisp woollen coats and white linen shirts. There were gulls out over Dublin: as numerous as beggars. In the back of the chanting crowd he saw the young boy with the raw red welts along his neck and face. Hey, Mr Douglass! the boy screamed, Mr Douglass, sir!

He was sure, as the carriage turned the corner by the university, that the boy volleyed out his first name.

HE HEARD IN the newspapers that O'Connell was due to speak to a giant crowd along the Dublin docks. The tribune of the people. Ireland's truest son. He had spent his life agitating for Catholic emancipation and parliamentary rule, and had written on abolition, too. Brilliant essays, fervent, impassioned. O'Connell had adventured his life for proper freedom, was known for his speeches, his letters, his rule of law.

Douglass cancelled a tea in Sandymount to get there on time. He arrived along the teeming docks. He could not believe the size of the crowd: as if the whole sponge of Dublin had been squeezed down into a sink. Such a riot of human cutlery. The police herded the crowds along. He lost Webb and pushed his way through, made his way to the stage as O'Connell emerged. The Great Liberator looked portly, tired, out of sorts: he had apparently been so since his release from jail. Still, a giant roar went up. *Men and women of Ireland!* The din was extraordinary. O'Connell held a speaking trumpet, and when he spoke into it the words shot up out of him, huge, fearsome, brimming. It astounded Douglass, the logic, the rhetoric, the humour.

O'Connell held the crowd in the well of his outstretched arms. He swayed forth. Slowed down. Pivoted on his heels. Paced the stage. Adjusted his wig. Allowed silences. The speech was relayed by others who stood on tall ladders and passed the word along the dockside.

— Repeal is Erin's right and God's decree!

— Withersoever we turn, England has reduced our nation to bondage!

— The employment of force is not our object!

— Associate, agitate, stand by me!

The hats went up in the reeking air. The cheers stepping in rhythm along the crowd. Douglass stood, transfixed.

Afterwards, a huge mob surrounded the Irishman. Douglass forced his way through, excused himself past dozens of pairs of shoulders. O'Connell looked up, knew immediately who he was. They shook hands.

– An honour, said O'Connell.

Douglass was taken aback.

– Mine alone, he said.

O'Connell's hand was pulled away. There was so much Douglass wanted to speak of: repeal, pacifism, the position of the Irish clergy in America, the philosophy of agitation. He reached forwards to grasp the Irishman's hand again, but there were already too many bodies between them. He felt himself pushed back, jostled. A man shouted in his ear about temperance. Another wanted his signature for a petition. A woman curtsied in front of him: a smell of filth rolled off her. He turned away. His name rang out at all angles. He felt as if he were spinning in eddies. O'Connell was being guided down off the stage.

When Douglass turned again, Webb had his arm, said they had an appointment in Abbey Street.

– Just a moment.

– I'm afraid we must go, Frederick.

– But I must talk with him –

– There'll be more chances, I assure you.

– But –

Douglass caught eyes with O'Connell. They nodded to each other. He watched the Irishman move away. Slumping within his bright green coat. Wiping his handkerchief on his brow. His wig shifting slightly on his head. A slight sadness there. But to have that command, thought Douglass. That charm. That energy. To be able to possess the stage in such an extraordinary way. To stir justice without violence. The way the words seem to enter the very marrow of the people who still hung around the dockside, bits of refuse floating on the water.

TWO DAYS LATER, in Conciliation Hall, O'Connell brought him on stage and he thrust Douglass's hand in the air: *Here,* he said, *the black O'Connell!* Douglass watched the hats go up into the rafters.

— Irishmen and Irishwomen . . .

He looked out over the tip heap. All muck and adulation. Thank you, he said, for the honour of allowing me to speak with you. He held out his hands and calmed the crowd and spoke to them of slavery and commerce and hypocrisy and the necessity of abolition.

An energy to him. A fire. He heard the ripple of his words move through the crowd.

— If you cast one glance upon a single man, he said, you shall cast a glance upon all humanity. A wrong done to one man is a wrong done to all. No power can imprison what is good and right. Abolition shall become the natural thought of the world!

He paced the stage. Tightened his jacket. It was a different crowd than any he had seen before. A low rumbling amongst them. He allowed a silence. Then punched up his sentences. Stretched his body towards them. Sought their eyes. Still, he could feel a distance. It troubled him. A bead of moisture lay at the base of his throat.

A shout came up from the rear of the hall. What about England? Would he not denounce England? Wasn't England the slave master anyway? Was there not wage slavery? Were there not the chains of financial oppression? Was there not an underground railroad that every Irishman would gladly board to get away from the tyranny of England?

A policeman moved into the back of the crowd, the pointed helmet disappearing. The heckler was soon quietened.

Douglass allowed a long silence: I believe in Erin's cause, he said. A wave of nodding heads crested below him. He had to be judicious, he knew. There were newspaper reporters scribbling down every word. It would lead back to Britain and America. He paused. He lifted his hand. Turned it slightly in the air.

— What is to be thought of a nation boasting of its liberty, he said, yet having its people in shackles? It is etched into the book of fate that freedom shall be universally delivered. The cause of humanity is one the world over.

A relief poured through him when the crowd applauded. O'Connell walked on stage and raised his hand in the air once more. *The black O'Connell!* he said again. Douglass took a bow and glanced down to see Webb near the front row, chewing the stem of his eyeglasses.

AT DINNER ON Dawson Street he sat alongside the Lord Mayor, but leaned his chair back so he could talk with O'Connell.

Later that evening they strolled together in the garden of the Mansion House, moving solemnly among the pruned winter rosebushes. O'Connell hunched over slightly, with his hands clasped behind his back. He wished, he said, that he could be of more direct help to Douglass and his people. It burdened him terribly to hear that there were many Irishmen among the slave owners in the South. Cowards. Traitors. A discredit to their very heritage. He would not let their shadow fall upon him. They brought a poison with them, a shame on their nation. Their churches should be shunned. They had taken an oath of false supremacy.

He took Douglass by the shoulders. He had killed a man once, O'Connell said. In a duel in Kildare. Over a point of Catholic pride. Shot him in the stomach. Left a widow behind, a child. It haunted him still. He would not kill again, but he would still die for his true belief: a man could only be free if he lived in the cause of liberty.

They talked gravely about the situation in America, about

Garrison, Chapman, the presidency of Polk, the prospect of seces-
sion.

There was something encyclopedic about O'Connell, yet Douglass could sense in the great man a hidden exhaustion. As if the very
questions he carried were too heavy to hold and they had eased their
way into his flesh, lodged themselves in his body, bound him down.

He felt O'Connell's arm upon his and he could hear the laboured
breathing in the silence between steps. A thin man stalked the far side of
the garden, tapping at a timepiece that hung down from his waistcoat.

O'Connell sent the man away, but Douglass thought he recognized, for the first time ever, the small defeat of fame.

*It is said that history is on the side of reason, but this outcome is by no
means guaranteed. Obviously, the suffering of the past will never fully be
redeemed by a future of universal happiness, if indeed such a thing is ob-
tainable. The evil of slavery is a constant ineradicable reality, but slavery
itself shall be banished! The truth cannot be deferred. The moment of truth
is now!*

THE CARRIAGE WAS ready: it was October, time to bring his lecture
tour south. His clothes were brushed. His writing papers were
wrapped in oilskin. Webb had the servants feed and water the horses.
Douglass bent down to pick up the travelling trunk himself. New
books, new clothes, his barbells.

— What in the world have you got in here? asked Webb.

— Books.

— Let me, said Webb.

Douglass grabbed for the trunk himself.

— Looks rather heavy, Old Boy.

He tried to fake ease. He could feel a hard pull of muscle along his
back. He saw Webb smirk ever so slightly. Webb called for the driver,

John Creely. He was a small man, sparely built, with the emaciated face of a serious drinker. Together the three men lifted the trunk high onto the ledge at the back of the carriage, tied it with rope.

Douglass wished he had not brought his barbells. A rash decision. He feared that Webb would deem him vain.

In their familiarity, they had developed a dislike for each other. There was a bombast to Webb, thought Douglass. He was intolerant, easy to offend, devout to righteousness. He had been annoyed when he got the bill from the tailor. He had taken the cost of the waistcoat out of Douglass's earnings for his books. A stinginess to him. He felt Webb watching him much of the time, waiting for him to stumble. He was afraid that he might become a specimen. Pinned. Observed. Dissected. Douglass hated to be called *Old Boy*. It brought him back to fields, to whips, to spiked anklets, to barnfights. And there was the money – Webb was collecting it to donate it to the cause back in America. Each night he asked Douglass if he had received any private donations. It rankled him. He emptied his pockets with exaggerated formality, yanked the cloth tongues out, shook them.

– See, he said, just a poor slave.

Still, Douglass was not unaware of his own shortcomings. He found himself curt at times, quick to judge, imprudent. He needed to learn tolerance. He was aware that Webb didn't want financial gain, and it was true that Webb seemed apologetic for the slightly rancorous tone he sometimes took with the black man.

They tightened the rope on the trunk. The servants came out to bid him goodbye. Lily blushed a little when he came to shake her hand. She whispered that it had been an extraordinary honour to meet him. She hoped one day that she would meet him again.

He heard a cough behind him.

– Only so much light left in the day, Old Boy, said Webb.

He shook their hands one more time. The servants had never seen anything like it from a guest before. They remained watching until the carriage disappeared beyond the college, down the length of Great Brunswick Street.

THERE WERE RUMOURS of a potato blight, but the land outside the city seemed healthy, green, robust. Near Greystones they stopped on a hill to watch the magnificent play of light on the last of Dublin Bay. There were rainbows in the distance, iridescent over the dulse-strewn strand.

WEBB AND HE took turns sitting up on the boards, up front with Creely. The land was stunning. The hedges in bloom. The gallop of streams. When it rained they sat in the carriage, opposite each other, reading. Occasionally they leaned across to tap one another on the knee, read a passage aloud. Douglass was rereading the speeches of O'Connell. He was amazed by the agility of the mind. The nod towards the universal. He wondered if he would get another chance to meet the man, to spend proper time with him, to apprentice his own ideas with the Great Liberator.

The carriage bounced along rutted roads. It was only slightly faster than a stagecoach or jaunting car. Douglass was surprised to learn that there were as yet no railroads south of Wicklow.

The afternoons spread in a great rush of yellow across the hills. Shutters in the sky, opening and closing suddenly. A swinging brightness and then a darkness again. There was some raw innocence about the land.

When he sat up front, on the boards, crowds came out of their houses just to look at him. They clapped his shoulder, shook his hand, blessed him with the sign of the cross. They tried to tell him stories of landlords, of absentees, of English atrocities, of loved ones far away, but Webb was impatient to get along, they had a schedule to keep, lectures to give.

Small children ran after the carriage, often for a mile down the road, until they seemed to seep down, brittle, into the landscape.

WICKLOW, ARKLOW, ENNISCORTHY: he charted the names in his diary. It struck him that there truly was a suggestion of hunger over the land. In the boardinghouses at night the owners apologized for the lack of potato.

IN WEXFORD HE stood on the top stairway of the Assembly Hall. He was hidden from view, but he could see down the staircase to the next floor where a table was set up; his poster on the wall, rippling in a small breeze.

It was the local gentry who came to see him. They were finely dressed, curious, patient. They sat quietly in their chairs, removed their scarves and waited for him. His words stirred them – *Hear hear!* they shouted, *Bravo!* – and after his speech they made out promissory notes, said they would organize bazaars, fetes, cake sales, send the money across the Atlantic.

But when Douglass stepped out into the street he felt a sharpness move along his skin. The streets were thronged with the poor Irish, the Catholics. An energy of doom to them. There was talk of Repeal Rooms, clandestine debates. Houses being burned. Whenever he moved amongst them he was disturbed and thrilled both. The papists were given to laughter, revelry, high sadness, their own clichés. A street performer danced in the bell-tipped lappets of a clown's outfit. Children went along the street hawking ballad sheets. Women sparked clay pipes. He wanted to stop in the streets and deliver an impromptu word, but his hosts moved him along. When he glanced back over his shoulder, he felt he was looking into a ditch that was only half-dug.

He was driven down a long laneway of majestic oak trees towards a huge mansion. Candles in the windows. Servants in white gloves. He had begun to notice that he was surrounded mostly by English accents. Magistrates. Landlords. They were melodic and well informed, but when he asked of the hunger that he had seen in the streets they said there was always a hunger in Ireland. She was a country that liked to be hurt. The Irish heaped coals of fire upon their own heads. They were unable to extinguish the fire. They were dependent, as always, on others. They had no notions of self-reliance. They burned and then poured the empty buckets down upon themselves. It had always been so.

The conversation swerved. They engaged him on matters of democracy, ownership, natural order, Christian imperative. Wine was served on a large silver tray. He politely declined. He wanted to know more about the rumours of underground forces. Some of the faces around him smarted. Perhaps he could be told more of Catholic emancipation? Had they read O'Connell's fervent denunciations? Was it true that Irish harpists once had their fingernails plucked so they could not play the catgut? Why had the Irish been deprived of their language? Where were the votaries of the poor?

Webb took him out onto the veranda by the elbow and said: But Frederick, you cannot bite the hand that feeds.

The stars colandered the Wexford night. He knew Webb was right. There would always have to be an alignment. There were so many sides to every horizon. He could only choose one. No single mind could hold it all at once. Truth, justice, reality, contradiction. Misunderstandings could arise. He had one cause only. He must cleave to it.

He paced the veranda. A cold wind whipped off the water.

– They're waiting for you, said Webb.

He reached out for Webb's hand and shook it, then went back inside. A chill went around the room from the open door. They took their coffee in small china cups. The women were gathered around the piano. He had learned how to play Schubert on the violin. He could lose himself in the adagio: even in the slowness, they were thrilled by the deftness of his hands.

THEY CONTINUED SOUTH. Just over the River Barrow they took a wrong turn. They entered wild country. Broken fences. Ruined castles. Stretches of bogland. Wooded headlands. Turfsmoke rose from cabins, thin and mean. On the muddy paths, they glimpsed moving rags. The rags seemed more animate than the bodies within. As they passed, the families regarded them. The children appeared marooned by hunger.

A hut burned at the side of the road. The smoke looked like it was issuing from the ground. In the fields, near stunted trees, men stared balefully into the distance. One man's mouth was smeared with a brown paste: perhaps he had been eating bark. The man watched impassively as the carriage went by, then raised his stick as if bidding goodbye to himself. He staggered across the field, a dog padding at his heels. They saw him fall to his knees and then rise again, continuing on into the distance. A dark young woman picked berries from the bushes: there was red juice all down the front of her dress as if she were vomiting them up one after the other. She smiled jaggedly. Her teeth were all gone. She repeated a phrase in Irish: it sounded like a form of prayer.

Douglass gripped Webb's arm. Webb looked ill. A paleness at his throat. He did not want to talk. There was a smell out over the land. The soil had been turned. The blight had flung its rotten odour into the air. The potato crop was ruined.

— It is all they eat, said Webb.

— But why?

— It's all they have, he said.

— Surely not.

— For everything else they rely on us.

British soldiers galloped past, hoofing mud up onto the hedge-rows. Green hats with red badges. Like small splashes of blood against the land. The soldiers were young and frightened. There was an air of insurrection about the countryside: even the birds seemed to howl up out of the trees. They thought they heard the cry of a wolf, but Webb said that the last wolf had been shot in the country a half century before. Creely, the driver, began to whimper that perhaps it was a banshee.

— Oh, quit your foolishness, said Webb. Drive on!

— But, sir.

— Drive on, Creely.

At an estate house they stopped to see if they could feed the horses. Three guards stood on the gate. Stone-carved falcons at their shoulders. The guards had shovels in their hands, but the handles of the shovels had been sharpened to a point. The landlords were absent. There had been a fire. The house smouldered. Nobody was allowed past. They were under strict instructions. The guards looked at Douglass, tried to contain their surprise at the sight of a Negro.

— Get out of here, the guards said. Now.

Creely pushed the carriage on. The roads twisted. Hedges rose high around them. Night threatened. The horses slowed. They looked ruined. A gout of spittle and foam hung from their long jaws.

— Oh, move it, please, called Webb from the inner cab where he sat knee to knee with Douglass.

Under a canopy of trees the carriage came to a creaking stop. A silence pulled in around them. They heard a woman's voice under the muted hoofshuffle. It sounded as if she was invoking a blessing.

– What is it? called Webb.

Creely did not answer.

– Move it, man, it's getting dark.

Still the carriage did not budge. Webb snapped the bottom of the door open with his foot, stepped down from the inner cab. Douglass followed. They stood in the black bath of trees. In the road they saw the cold and grainy shape of a woman: she wore a grey woollen shawl and the remnants of a green dress. She had been dragging behind her a very small bundle of twigs attached to a strap around her shoulders, pulling the contraption in her wake.

On the twigs lay a small parcel of white. The woman gazed up at them. Her eyes shone. A high ache tightened her voice.

– You'll help my child, sir? she said to Webb.

– Pardon me?

– God bless you, sir. You'll help my child.

She lifted the baby from the raft of twigs.

– Good God, said Webb.

An arm flopped out from the bundle. The woman tucked the arm back into the rags.

– For the love of God, the child's hungry, she said.

A wind had risen up. They could hear the branches of the trees slapping each other around.

– Here, said Webb, offering the woman a coin.

She did not take it. Bent her head instead. She seemed to recognize her own shame on the ground.

– She's not had a thing to eat, Douglass said.

Webb fumbled in his small leather purse again and held out a six-penny piece. Still, the woman did not take it. The baby was clutched to her chest. The men stood rooted to the spot. A paralysis had swept over them. Creely looked away. Douglass felt himself become the dark of the road.

The woman thrust the baby forward. The smell of death was over-powering.

— Take her, she said.

— We cannot take her, ma'am.

— Please, y'r honours. Take her.

— But we cannot.

— I beg you, a thousand times, God bless you.

The woman's own arms looked nothing more than two thin pieces of rope gathering upwards towards her neck. She flopped the child's arm out again and massaged the dead baby's fingers. The inside of its wrists were already darkening.

— Take her, please, sir, she's hungry.

She thrust the dead baby forwards.

Webb let the silver coin drop at her feet, turned, his hands shaking. He climbed up onto the wooden board beside Creely.

— Come on, he called down to Douglass.

Douglass reached for the muddy coin and placed it in the woman's hand. She did not look at it. It slipped through her fingers. Her lips moved but she did not say a thing.

Webb hit the reins hard on the shiny dark back of the horse, then drew back just as sudden, as if he was moving the carriage and yet not moving it at the same time.

— Come on, Frederick, he called. Get in, get in. Hurry.

THEY GATHERED PACE. Through bogland, shoreside, long stretches of unbelievable green. The cold spread its arms. They stopped to buy more blankets. They drove, then, silently, through the dark, along the coast. They hired a man to run a lantern in front of them until they reached an inn. The small globe of light cast the trees in relief. The man fell after eight miles: there were no open inns on the road. They huddled in the carriage together. They did not mention the dead child.

It rained. The sky did not seem at all surprised. They passed a barracks where soldiers in red uniforms were guarding a shipment of corn. They were allowed to feed and water the two horses. An old man stood on the road near Youghal throwing stones at a dark-winged rook in a tree.

There was nothing they could do about the hunger, said Webb. There was only so much a man could achieve: they could not give health to the fields. Such a thing happened often in Ireland. It was a law of the land, unwritten, inevitable, awful.

THEY ARRIVED ALONG the quays of Cork in the autumn chill. The evening was clear. There was no breeze. A great damp stillness. The cobbles shone black.

They pulled the carriage in to 9 Brown Street where the Jennings family lived. A beautiful stone house with rose gardens along the tight walkway.

Douglass swung open the door of the carriage. He was exhausted. He moved as if some axle inside him were broken. All he wanted to do was go to bed. He could not sleep.

Negro girl. Ran away. Goes by name Artela. Has small scar over her eye. A good many teeth missing. The letter A is branded on her cheek and forehead. Some scars on back, two missing toes.

For sale. Able colored man, Joseph. Can turn himself to carpentry. Also for sale: kitchen appliances, theological library.

Available immediately: Seven Negro children. Orphans. Good manners. Well-presented. Excellent teeth.

HE CAME DOWN the staircase, carrying a lit candle on a patterned saucer. The stub of candle threw his shadow askew. He saw himself in several forms: tall, short, long, looming. He slid lightly on the stairs. In the arc of stained glass above the front doorway he could see the stars.

He contemplated walking outside a moment, but he was still in his nightclothes. He continued barefoot instead along the wood-panelled corridor and entered the library. The room was all books. Long stretches of argumentative intent. He ran his hands along them. Beautiful leather covers. Rows of green, red, brown. Gold and silver imprinted along their hard spines. He held the candle aloft, turned slowly, watched the way the light flickered from shelf to shelf. Moore, Swift, Spenser. He set the candle on a circular table, moved to the ladder. Sheridan, Byron, Fielding. The wood was cold against the sole of his foot. The ladder was set on wheels and attached to a brass rail. He climbed to the second rung. He found that if he reached for the shelf with his hand he could propel himself along. He pushed himself slowly at first, back and forth. A little quicker, more recklessly, and then he let go.

He would have to be quiet. Soon the house would begin to stir.

Douglass pushed again, off the shelf, along the row of books. Climbed another rung. Higher now. There was a whiff of tallow in the room. The candle had extinguished itself. His mind swung to his young children. They would allow this, he thought. They would not judge it, their very serious father guiding himself on the ladder past the window, the sun coming up over the quays of Cork, the stars almost gone now, dawn a gap in the curtains. He tried to imagine them here, in this house of high bookshelves.

He dropped from the ladder, retrieved the stub of candle, made himself ready to tread the stairs when the door creaked open.

– Mr Douglass.

It was Isabel, one of the daughters of the house, in her early twenties. She wore a plain white dress, her hair pinned high.

– Good morning.

– A fine morning, yes, she said.

– I was just looking at the books.

She flicked a quick look at the library ladder as if she already knew.

– Can I get you breakfast, Mr Douglass?

– Thank you, he said, but I think I'll return to sleep now. The journey from Dublin got the best of me, I'm afraid.

– As you will, Mr Douglass. You do know there are no servants in this house?

– Excuse me?

– We fend for ourselves, she said.

– I'm happy to hear that.

He could already tell these friends of Webb were unusual. Owners of a vinegar factory. Church of Ireland. They did not display their wealth. The house had a humility to it. Open to all visitors. The ceilings were low everywhere but the library, as if to force a man to bend down everywhere except near books.

Isabel glanced towards the window. The sun was making itself apparent above the small line of trees at the end of the garden.

– So how do you find our country, Mr Douglass?

Douglass was surprised at the forthrightness of her question. He wondered if she was interested in the courage of honesty – that the countryside had shocked him, that he had seldom seen such poverty, even in the American South, that he found it hard, even now, to understand.

– It's an honour to be here, he said.

– An honour for us to receive you. And your journey was pleasant?

– We travelled the back roads. There was much to see. Some beautiful places.

In the silence she drifted towards the window. She looked out to the garden where the light continued to climb, agile against the trees. He could tell there was something more she wanted to say. She fingered the edge of the curtain, wrapped one of the threads around her finger.

— There is a hunger afoot, she said finally.

— Certain parts of the journey were bleak, I must admit.

— There is talk of a famine.

He looked at Isabel again. She was thin and ordinary, certainly not pretty. Her eyes were a sharp green, her profile plain, her bearing natural. No jewellery. No fuss. Her accent was genteel. She was not the sort of woman likely to open the windows of a man's heart, yet there was something about her that daubed the air between them bright.

He told her of the dead child he had seen on the road. He noticed the words move into her face, inhabit her: the road, the raft of twigs, the dropped coin, the roof of trees, the way the light had fallen around them as they drove away. The story weighed her down. She wrapped the fringed thread so tight that the top of her finger was swollen.

— I will send someone out to see if they can find her. On the road.

— That would be kind of you, Miss Jennings.

— Perhaps they will help her bury the child.

— Yes.

— In the meantime, you should rest, Mr Douglass, she said.

— Thank you.

— And later you must permit my sisters and me to show you around. There is much in Cork to be proud of. You'll see.

He could hear the rest of the house stirring, the floorboards above them creaking. He bowed slightly, excused himself, went into the hallway. He was tired, but there was work to do: letters, articles, another attempt at a preface. His book was going into a second printing. It was an exercise in balance. He would need to find the correct tension. A funambulist. He would not pander any longer. He trod the stairs, entered his room, unfolded his pages to edit them. Took out the barbells. Rested his head against the side of the writing desk. Lifted the barbells. Began, all at once, to lift and read, lift and read.

Within moments he heard a clicking of hooves outside the window. Isabel was riding out the gravel road. From his high window he watched her go until her coat of royal blue became a speck.

THE CARPETS WERE lush. His pillows freshly laundered. His hosts had cut new flowers and put them in the window where they nodded in the breeze. A Bible had been placed on the bedside table. *The Crace and Beunfeld Bird and Wildlife Guide. Charlotte, A Tale of Truth. The Vicar of Wakefield. The Whole Booke of Psalmes, with the Hymnes Evangellical, and Songs Spirituall.* At the roll-top writing desk, he found an inkwell, blotting paper, blank journals.

It was a relief to be back to privilege again: the journey through the countryside had agitated him.

Famine. The word had not occurred to him before. He had seen hunger in America, but never a countryside threatened with blight. The smell still clung to him. He poured himself a deep bath. Soaped his body. Put his head in under the water, held his breath, sunk deeper. Even the noises of the house itself were a balm: he could hear laughter echoing up through the rooms. He climbed from the water, wiped the steam from the window. It was still a surprise to see the rooftops of Ireland. What else lay out there? What other ruin?

The sound of leaves falling.

Quieter than rain.

He finished his writing, put the barbells away, lay on the bed with his arms behind his head, tried to doze, couldn't.

The call to dinner came from downstairs. He wiped his hands in the washbasin, dressed himself in his cleanest linen shirt.

THE FAMILY'S FOOD was served in a country style: rows of plates, bowls, soups, vegetables and breads were placed on a giant wooden table and the diners walked along to choose what they wanted. There were, it seemed, many among the Jennings family who did not eat meat. He spread a thick sardine paste upon his bread, ladled the salad. At the table the guests jostled and laughed with one another. The Waring family. The Wrights. Other guests came: a vicar, a taxidermist, a falconer, a young Catholic priest. They were delighted to meet Douglass. They had read his book and were eager to talk. It seemed the house was open to all denominations and ideas. An extraordinary volubility of speech. The situation in America, the position of the abolitionists, the possibility of war, the pandering to southern trade laws, the terrible deeds that had been perpetrated upon the Cherokee Indians.

Douglass found himself happily besieged. None of the formality of the Webb household. The talk spun into incredible tangents. Seldom before had all the vectors of the conversation gone through him alone. Webb watched from the far end of the table.

Part of Douglass wondered if they were laying a trap for him, but, as the hours went on, his ease deepened.

He was surprised to see that the women remained at the table alongside the men. Isabel stayed quiet most of the time. She ate sparingly. She wet her finger and picked the crumbs from her plate. There was a shyness about her, but whenever she entered the conversation she seemed to do so on the tip of a knife blade. She was

quick to draw blood and then retreat. Douglass had never seen anyone quite like her before. He found himself discombobulated when,
in a conversation about Charles Grandison Finney, she turned
towards him and asked how exactly Mrs Douglass felt about the
issue of public prayer.

He felt a rush of warmth to his collar.

— Mrs Douglass?

— Yes, she said.

— Her position is quite clear on all such matters.

He saw Webb move slightly in his chair. The Irishman was chewing at the edge of his dinner napkin.

— She would no doubt be aligned, said Douglass.

He was sure Isabel had not meant to embarrass him, but the heat
seared him. A seep of sweat at the brow. He balanced a cup of tea on
the saucer without it rattling, then pronounced the meal delicious, excused himself, moved towards the stairs, touching Webb's shoulder as
he went.

He had not written to Anna or his children in a few days. He would
do so straightaway.

Upstairs, he caught sight of himself in the looking glass. His hair
had grown higher, thicker, more Negro. He would let it be.

There was no lock on the door. He wedged a chair against the
door handle. He unwrapped the barbells from the shirts in which
he hid them. There were times he was still walking into a church
in Tuckahoe. The wooden crossbeams. The singular plane of light
sloping east to west during morning services. The glimpse of a
red-tailed hawk arcing out through the window. The high sound
of the organ. The smell of grass carried in through the wide white
doorway.

Anna might cherish hearing the letters read to her for an evening
or two, but soon enough they would be burned. It gladdened him,

really, that the letters would become smoke: it was so much of what happened to one's own history.

THE CITY WAS dark, yet it didn't press down on him quite like Dublin had. He began to feel that, even in the gloaming, things had opened up. The church bells rang high and brassy. The markets on Saint Patrick's Street hummed. Swans glided under the footbridges that crisscrossed the city. Shandon Steeple stood out against the sky. Even the slums seemed more forgiving. It was a city that gave alms. The poor were still legion, but he could walk with the Jennings sisters along the quays and the beggars would leave them alone. Men carried pieces of lit clay in their hands. They offered Douglass a pull of their pipes, clapped him on the shoulder.

There was something in the music of the accent that Douglass liked: it was as if the Cork people put long, lazy hammocks in their sentences.

He was happy when Webb announced, after six long days, that he would leave Cork on urgent business. Both men were glad to be rid of one another. Douglass watched the carriage move away and felt a bolt of freedom. It was the first time in ages that he felt truly alone. At ease in the ornate looking glass.

It must be said that in my time here in Ireland my heart feels stirred. Instead of the bright, blue sky of America, I am covered with the soft, grey fog of the Emerald Isle. I breathe and lo! the chattel becomes a man! Though I have seen much that would make my own people tremble, I am encouraged to exercise my true and proper voice. I breathe the sea air freely. And while there is much I observe to make the heart heavy, I am at least temporarily without chains.

HE WALKED ALONG the River Lee, his hands clasped behind his back. A new walk for him. Large and public. The attitude of a thinking man. He enjoyed the pose, found it conducive to the idea of himself. He heard the clopping of a horse behind him on the cobbles, the soft sound of a harness creaking. Isabel descended the horse, walked alongside him, her hand careful at the horse's neck. The sheen of sweat on the animal's body.

Barges plied along the river. Corn barges. Barley barges. Cattle barges. Salt barges. Pig barges. Sheep for the slaughterhouses farther downriver. Firkins of butter. Oatmeal. Flour bags. Egg boxes. Baskets of turkeys. Canned fruit. Bottled soda and minerals.

They watched the river of food in silence. Gulls busied themselves behind the boats, swooping every now and then to claim what they could.

They walked along by a merchant-marine shop, a bookseller's, a tailor shop. Farther down the quays she pulled the horse close to her. As if it might offer protection.

— I could not find her.

— Excuse me?

— That woman you met upon the road.

For a brief moment he was not sure what Isabel was talking about, an incidental skim of words across the surface of the day, but then he caught himself, said it was a great shame, but he was sure the child was buried by now.

— You did what you could, said Isabel.

He knew it was not so: he had done nothing at all. He had borne witness and stayed silent.

— There's nothing worse, she said, than a small coffin.

He juggled the words in his mind for a moment. He nodded. He liked her. He thought of her, increasingly these past few days, as a younger sister. It was odd to think so – her green eyes, her awkward walk, the rustle of her humble dresses – but, that's what she was: sisterly. Hovering. Curious. Intrusive. She explored new ideas with him. There were few limits. What did he think of the notion of Liberia? What was the gulf between revenge and justice? Did he have a plan with Garrison to send the money back from churches that embraced slave-holders?

She was quieter when the talk returned to what was happening around them. She stopped midsentence. She worried the bracelet on her left arm. She gazed into the distance. Her voice caught.

There was enough food in the land to feed Ireland three or four times over, she said. It was being shipped across to India, China, the West Indies. The exhaustion of empire. She wished there was something she could do about it. The truth could not be preserved by silence. Her own family had warehouses full of food farther down the river. Bottles of vinegar. Stocks of yeast. Malting barley. Even crates of fruit jam. But it could not just be given away. There were laws and customs and issues of ownership. Other complexities, too. Business alliances. Extended contracts. Taxation. The demands of the poor. The creation of moral illusions.

It struck him that Isabel carried the wounds of privilege. Perhaps, then, he did also? He leafed through the New Testament. *From everyone who has been given much, much will be demanded.* And yet if he himself spoke out on behalf of the poor Irish, what would happen? What language could he create for this? To whom would he speak?

The politics still confounded him: who was Irish, who was British, who was Catholic, who was Protestant, who owned the land, whose child stood rheumy-eyed with hunger, whose house was burned to the ground, whose soil belonged to whom, and why? The simple way to see it was that the British were Protestant, the Irish were Catholic. One ruled, the other lay underfoot. But where did Webb fit in? And where did Isabel fit in? He would gladly have allowed himself to align with the desires of freedom and justice, but it was to his own known cause that he had to remain entirely loyal. Three million voices. He could not speak out against those who had brought him here as a visitor. There was only so much he could take upon himself. He had to look to what mattered. What was beyond toleration was the ownership of man and woman. The Irish were poor, but not enslaved. He had come here to hack away at the ropes that held American slavery in place. Sometimes it withered him just to keep his mind steady. He was aware that the essence of proper intelligence was the embrace of contradiction. And the recognition of complexity was to be balanced against the need for simplicity. He was still a slave. Fugitive. If he returned to Boston he could be kidnapped at any time, taken south, strapped to a tree, whipped. His *owners*. They would make a spectacle of his fame. They had tried to silence him for many years already. No longer. He had been given a chance to speak out against what had held him in chains. And he would continue to do so until the links lay in pieces at his feet.

He thought he knew now what had brought him here – the chance to explore what it felt like to be free and captive at the same time. It was not something even the most aggrieved Irishman could understand. To be in bondage to everything, even the idea of one's own peace.

His body, his mind, his soul, had, for years, served only for the profit of others. He had his own people to whom he was pledged. Three million. They were the currency of his freedom. What weight would he carry if he tried to support the Irish, too? Their agonies, their ambiguities. He had enough of his own.

The barges passed.

A river of food afloat.

The sun went down over the slate rooftops of Cork.

THERE WAS A story he sometimes told his audiences. The slave masters in America used barrels. Bourbon mostly. Olive oil. Wine. Any sort of barrel that could be found. They drove large six-inch nails into the wood. Sometimes they placed crushed glass inside the barrel, too. Or thorny bushes. Then, he said, they would bring their *slave* – he always invoked this word on a deeper pitch – up to the top of a hill. For the most minor of offences. Maybe she had forgotten to lock the stable door. Or perhaps she had dropped a piece of crockery. Or maybe she had looked askance at the mistress of the house. Or maybe she had left a dishcloth dirty. It did not matter. She was to be punished. It was the natural order of things.

Halfway through his story he would give the slave a name: Mary. He would hear a silence come over his Irish listeners. Mary, he said again.

And then the *owners* – this word volleyed savagely from him – forced Mary to take the barrel from the barn. It was rolled out into the dust, along the dirt road, to the top of a small nearby hill. They gathered the other slaves together and brought them, too, to the hilltop. To witness. The owners would often shout verses from the Holy Book. They forced Mary to step inside the wooden barrel. They pushed her head down, crushed her shoulders into it. The protruding nails ripped her body. The glass penetrated her feet. The thorns encircled her shoulders. Then the masters put the lid on and hammered it shut. They rocked it back and forth a few minutes. They read again from the Holy Book.

Then the barrel went down the hill, tumbling.

THE CROWDS WERE enormous. He had spoken alongside Father Mathew. He found a language in the temperance movement. The papers still called him the black O'Connell. Posters were pasted up all round the city. His fame spread, day by day. He picnicked with twenty-four women from the Cork Ladies Anti-Slavery Society: they delighted in the large lounge of him underneath a spreading oak tree, a dainty blue napkin at his throat, the gurgle of a brook behind him. The women unloosened the bonnets at their necks and raised their faces towards the sun. They hung on his every word. Later, the group walked together, carrying picnic baskets and parasols, out over the long grass and back towards a wooden bridge. Douglass dared to take off his shoes and socks and waded briefly in the cold water. The women turned away and giggled. The water darkened the cuffs of his trousers.

Newspaper reporters clamoured to see him. Whole pages were devoted to his lectures. He had collected hundreds of pounds to be shipped back to Boston. He had sold over two thousand books. He would go on to Limerick next, then to Belfast. From there he would go to England where he would negotiate his freedom, buy himself back, return to America, a freeman.

There was a great welling inside him. His voice had always come from others, but when he stood to speak now, it felt more distinctly his own. There were times he wished he had a thousand voices and could throw them in so many directions, but he had just one, and it served a single purpose: to annihilate slavery. He was almost glad one afternoon when, walking past an ale house on Paul Street, he heard someone say that a *nigger* had just walked past, a filthy *niggerboy*, did he not have a home to go to, he wouldn't find bananas in that direction, did he not know there were no trees to swing from in Cork, Cromwell had taken them all already, go on now, *nigger*.

He stopped, swelled his chest, held his ground, almost a fake fury, then walked on in his camel's-hair waistcoat. *Nigger. Filthy nigger.* For the first time, the word felt strangely welcome. An old shirt that he would have to wear in the future. Something to unbutton and tear off and rebutton again and again and again.

A FEW DAYS before he left Cork – a day that would stay with him quietly, a flag, a kite, a remnant – he heard a knocking at the door on Brown Street. He was in the midst of writing. His forearms were splattered with ink. His back ached from the bend over the desk. He pushed back in the chair and listened to the voices drifting up from below, then leaned into the work of writing once more.

Later that evening he bathed and dressed and descended the stairs for dinner. A young woman sat at the end of the table, next to Isabel. She seemed at odds with the manner with which she had been seated. Hunched, awkward, but pretty. With fair hair. Her skin so very pale. He thought he knew her, but he did not know from where. She stood up and said his name.

– Good evening, he replied, still confounded.

A hush came over the table. It was obvious to him that some other response was needed. He coughed into his fist.

– Such a pleasure to see you, Madame, he said.

He could feel the embarrassment swell the room.

– Lily is leaving for America, said Isabel.

It was then that he recognized her. She seemed so very different out of her uniform. Younger even. He remembered her shape on the stairs. She had, it seemed, left the employ of Mr Webb and journeyed from Dublin.

– She will leave from Cove in a few days, said Isabel.

– That's wonderful, said Douglass.

— She walked here.

— Good Lord.

— Lily was inspired by you. Isn't that right, Lily?

— By me?

A small panic seized him. He could see a blush come over the young woman's face. She seemed to want to vanish. He wondered if she had left Webb's house without rancour. He certainly had not meant to cause consternation. He nodded politely, tried to avoid her gaze. He recalled with a sharp pang the way she had whispered goodbye. He was glad nothing more had come from his presence in Dublin.

— Your speeches, said Isabel. They were a great inspiration. Isn't that right, Lily?

The maid didn't look up.

— Boston? said Douglass. Is that your intention?

She nodded and by degrees lifted her head: a surprising shine to her eyes.

— Perhaps I'll try New York, she said.

A murmur of approval went round the room. Douglass ate quickly, quietly. He kept his gaze on his plate, but glanced upwards every now and then to see Isabel and her sisters lavish attention on the young maid. They served her and poured her a ginger mineral from a pitcher.

The maid seemed to balance a weighing scale about her eyes: she seemed at any moment as if she could easily launch into a volley of words, or just as easily burst into tears.

When Douglass stood to excuse himself — he had more writing to do, he said — he raised a glass to Lily and said that he wished her well, that she would have Godspeed on her adventure, that he, too, hoped to return to his native land and to his wife and family soon.

The toast was taken up around the table. A clinking of water glasses. The maid flicked a brief glance at him: he was not sure if it was one of fear or anger. He made his way up the stairs. Her appearance had unnerved him. What exactly was he expected to do? How should he have reacted? He did indeed wish her well, but what more could he have said? Perhaps tomorrow he could recommend a prominent family for her to work with? Maybe Garrison or Chapman might know someone? Or he could suggest an area of the city where she would be at ease? Why, he wondered, had she come all the way to Cork by foot? And in such weather, too?

He sat at his writing desk, buried the nib of the pen in the inkwell. He had much to do, but he could not write. He tossed and turned beneath the covers.

The birds woke furious with dawn. A blanket of dark had been lifted from Brown Street. He heard his name called from below. He parted his curtains. Isabel stood in the puddled yard at the rear of the house.

— Lily left in the middle of the night, she said.

He could feel the cold against the pane of the window. A rooster crowed in the yard and a young hen rose in the air and scrambled away.

— Can you come with us, Mr Douglass? she said.

An alarm in her voice.

— One moment, please.

There were letters to write. Correspondence to sign. Meetings to arrange. A debate to prepare with the clergymen of the North Cathedral.

He closed the curtains and placed his washbasin upon the windowsill. He removed his nightshirt and dampened a towel. The water was cold to the touch. It tightened his skin. He heard his name called from below once more. Then the high whinny of a horse from the stables. The clop and splash of hooves. Two of the Jennings sisters, Charlotte and Helen, came from beneath the archway. They wore wide hats and green rain clothing. Isabel appeared again seconds later, holding a sturdy nag by the reins.

Douglass leaned out the window. He had forgotten for a moment that he was shirtless. He saw the two younger sisters turn away and giggle.

Isabel rigged a series of leather harnesses around the horses: she left the tallest horse for him.

He cursed himself. A maid. A simple maid. So, she had left early. And so what? It was hardly his fault. Yet he was eager to please. The inability to say no. He stepped back from the window, bumped his head on the frame. Perhaps it was a foolish desire on behalf of the young woman. It was not as if – not as if – surely not, no. He had not shown any impropriety. None at all. Certainly not.

He went to his writing desk, shuffled the papers. Weighed them up. Stacked them, then turned to pull on his shirt and boots. He had been given an oilskin slicker by Mr Jennings. A fishermen's coat. That, and a black hat, wide-brimmed and shapeless. He hadn't yet worn it during his visit. He caught sight of himself in the swivel mirror. Preposterous. But he was not beyond laughing at himself. He clomped down the stairs, poked his head into the kitchen. Mr Jennings slapped his teacup down and spurted tea across the thick wooden table. Douglass gave an exaggerated bow and said he was off for a few hours, he had been taken hostage, it seemed they were hoping to overtake the young maid from Dublin, if he didn't return by nightfall could they please send a search party and perhaps a Saint Bernard? The elderly Jennings sat back in his soft chair and laughed.

Douglass opened the latch on the back door, stepped outside and under the archway to the front of the house where the women sat on their horses, waiting. They smiled at the sight of him: the coat, the wide hat.

He had not been on a horse in a long time. He felt foolish as he swung up onto it. The stirrup bit hard into his foot. The animal was dark and muscled. He could feel its rib cage through his own body. He was surprised when Isabel got off her own mount and deftly readjusted the underbelly strap of his horse. A strength in the young woman that he had not seen before. She moved forwards, patted the horse's neck.

— We'll take the Cove road, she said.

They went south along the quays, beyond the gaol, past the poorhouse. Her sisters rode dainty and high-backed. Isabel was cruder in her style. She galloped up behind stagecoaches, glanced in, reared up, rode on. Looked around as she rode, calling out Lily's name.

The streets were draped in an October grey. The wind pulsed wintry along the river. Rain spat down in flurries. Outside the fever hospital a man moaned with hunger. He stretched out his arms to them. He had a long, loping, simian stride. They rode past. He started hitting himself, like a man beset with bees and madness. They rode faster. A woman came out from an alleyway and begged for a penny. Her face was bearded, splotched with fever. They hurried again. If they stopped to give alms they would never get beyond the city.

Douglass was glad now of the green slicker and the hat. He realized after a few miles that the hat shaded his face almost completely, that nobody on the roadside could discern who was underneath.

The city seemed to stop at a brick warehouse and then suddenly there were trees. The road curled and whipped out into parcels of green. They passed a stagecoach, waving at the passengers arrayed along the side. The coach was piled high with boxes and suitcases. It looked as if it might totter over. They enquired after the maid but nobody had seen her.

Douglass remained shaded beneath the brim on his hat.

— Fine weather, he said through the light rain.

He could not shake the American out of his accent.

— Indeed, sir, for a Yankee.

The Jennings sisters smiled as they pulled away from the stage-coach. He tried to gallop ahead of them, but the sisters were more than capable: they braided round him, spurred him on.

In the countryside small ribbons of smoke curled up in the air. He was amazed the way the poor Irish lived underground. He could see their hovels from the road, built from turf and sticks and mounds of grass. Their fields were tiny. So many hedges. An occasional run of stone wall. The children looked like remnants of themselves. Spectral. Some were naked to the waist. Many of them had sores on their faces. None had shoes. He could see the structures of them through their skin. The bony residue of their lives.

He cast his mind back to Dublin and the little boy who had welded himself to his shoulder. It seemed so long ago now. The people didn't frighten him anymore. It was not so much that he had become immune, it was more that he knew he would not be harmed. He wondered what might happen if this road ran into a road in Baltimore, or Philadelphia, or Boston, how the people might meld into each other.

He wanted now to find Lily, to wish her a truly safe journey. He spurred his horse on. They found shapes on the road, shadows, but none of them were the maid.

In the small villages the rain kept curiosity at bay. They rode out into the beauty of the dripping fields. The sound of the hooves like pistol fire. A rainbow hung on the sky. They halted their horses under a hazel tree where someone had built a low bench. Isabel unwrapped the sandwiches and took a flask of tea from her saddlebags. She had even brought cups. Her sisters sat on the bench. They melded well with Isabel: they were prettier and quieter, as if required by some strange law to balance her out. It was, the sisters agreed, a daring adventure, but they should not go too much farther. It was already near lunchtime. They would never find Lily now.

— We have plenty of time, said Isabel. It's early yet.

— My sister has a mind of her own. Unfortunately she lost it a few years ago.

— It's ten miles to Cove. And ten back, said Helen.

— We'll lose the light.

— Oh, please do come. Please.

The road had become busier with stagecoaches and jaunting cars loaded with cases. The families had their eyes set on the distance. Their children were bundled into grim strips of blanket. The wooden tongues of the cars groaned. The carriages swayed in the ruts. The horses looked bound for the yard. They were bent over with the work of keeping to the road.

The Jennings sisters galloped west, then south. It was, said Charlotte, a prettier journey, and quieter, too. The road rambled and turned. Still, there were families upon them, all heading south, gathering, small rivers.

They asked in vain for any sighting of the young maid. The closer they got to the sea, the more the roads thickened with leaving. Vendors had set up stalls against the hedges. Families were hawking the last of their possessions. Douglass and the sisters had to slow their horses down to get through the crowds. All manner of things for sale. Fiddles, inkwells, pots, hats, shirts. Paintings strung on the hedges. Curtains hung from the branches of trees. Pieces of cloth with half-moons, the once-gaudy colours faded with time. A beautiful silk dress, embroidered with thin strips of gold, draped sadly over the seat of a jaunting car.

They pushed their horses on through, towards the cliffs that overlooked the harbour.

A man came towards them. He wore two boards draped across his shoulders, tied with a string. On it were the prices to Boston, New York, Newfoundland. He called out the prices in a singsong. Some children tugged at his pockets. He slapped them away.

The crowd grew so thick that they had to dismount to guide their horses.

A young priest walked among the crowd, looking for the sick. To administer the Last Rites. He was fingering rosary beads as he went. He glanced at Douglass. They had never seen each other before, but for a brief moment they both thought they recognized one another and they stopped to say something, but nothing came, no words between them.

The priest stepped away, under the overarching green branches of a tree where a child's clothes hung limp.

– Father, said Isabel. Excuse me, Father.

The priest turned and stepped towards them. His eyes were huge and tired. He pulled the rosary beads tight round his fingers. His face sharpened. His voice was bitter. No, the priest said, he had not seen anyone answering to Lily's description. He toed his foot into the mud, as if he might find her there. He turned then and spat into his hands. No, he said again, sharply.

The priest went on, calling to the people around him in the Irish language.

Isabel shivered and touched the neck of her horse. Douglass pulled his hat down further and guided his horse away by the reins. The sisters, too, had fallen into a reverent silence. The wind came off the sea and rose up to meet them. The harbour curved like a question mark. A dozen or more wooden ships were dotted on the water below. A small, sad flotilla of masts and tightened sails. Their names scrubbed off by the waves.

They walked their horses to within ten yards of the edge of the cliff. The town itself lay below them like a twitching thing. The thatch of the roofs. The bend of the trees. Carriages moving like small insects along the waterfront towards the square. Douglass knew what chaos lay down there, what desires, what fevers. Yet it was immense with beauty. The town of Cove genuflected to the water. Birds flew ravenously around the cliffs, weightless on the updraughts.

He wrapped the reins around a tree and walked to the edge of the cliff. He took off his hat. The wind and rain rang fierce around him. It took him a moment to realize that Isabel was at his side. The two sisters remained behind, perched now on their horses. The pale of the waves came upon the shore below.

Isabel twined her arm around his. Her face against his shoulder. He was aware of the sisters watching. He wished he could gently prise her from him, but she stayed there, looking down over the town.

Soon the sun would fall and the sea darken and all the land about them would go cold.

IT WAS LATE afternoon by the time they found Lily. Rainsoaked and shivering on the pier. Her head shawled, her body mummied into a coat. She had bought her ticket and was waiting for the morning boat. She would not look at them, her face drawn in some private anguish.

Douglass and the two sisters stood apart. They watched as Isabel bent down in front of Lily. A supplicant. They looked as if they were praying together.

Isabel had brought a few days' worth of food. Wrapped in a blue teacloth. Bundled and tied. She pressed it gently into the young girl's arms. She reached inside her coat, brought out a number of folded bills that she quickly stuffed into Lily's palm. Douglass felt a chill. He watched as Lily moved her mouth but did not seem to say anything. What words went between them? What silence? There was a howl from a nearby shop. The screech of a woman. The thump of a fist. A din of laughter from a public house. From somewhere distant came the sound of a mandolin.

Isabel peeled her gloves off, and pressed them, too, into Lily's arms. Then she reached inside her own coat and fumbled at her neck. A brooch of some sort. She handed it to Lily. The girl smiled. Isabel leaned forwards and embraced the maid, whispered something in her ear. Lily nodded and pulled the shawl tight down over her head. What thoughts trembled there? What fierceness had brought her here?

Douglass felt rooted to the ground. It was as if he could not even pick up his feet. He longed for the warmth of a fire. He pulled his collar up and coughed into it. He felt his breath bounce back towards him. *Negro girl. Ran away. Goes by name Artela.*

Isabel glanced over her shoulder and called out to her sisters. They brought her horse forwards. Her long dress was muddied at the hem. She wiped her feet against the cobbles and climbed demurely to the saddle, spurred the horse through the thronged streets. They moved through the town, past an auctioneer's shop, and away.

THE PRIEST WATCHED them crest the hill. There was a long scar of dark mud along the side of his soutane where he had slipped and fallen. He still held the rosary beads in his fist, though they were looser now, they jangled at his hip. Isabel raised her hand in parting, but the priest did not respond. He followed them metronomically, his head turning, the rest of his body clamped in place. Then he strode away through the wet grass towards the fires.

THE HORSES DRIPPED with exhaustion. Skittishly they moved through the dark. It was already well beyond midnight when they got home. Mr Jennings was waiting in the yard. He had prepared food and hot drinks and blankets. The yard was a commotion.

When Douglass put his foot to the cobbles his knee half-buckled underneath him. He was given a candle and a blanket. He trudged indoors. His shadow multiplied upon the stairs.

That night he could not sleep. Towards daylight he went downstairs to the quiet of the library. His knees ached. His shoulders felt welded to his neck. He entered the room quietly. Isabel was sitting in the corner, in the gloom. She looked up to see him come in: it was his ritual to use the ladder to move himself along the bookshelves. He waited a moment in the doorway, stepped across, took her in an embrace. Only that. He held his hand at the back of her hair. He hesitated a moment. She sobbed. When he pulled away, the shoulder of his shirt was wet.

ON HIS LAST morning in Cork, Frederick Douglass took a jaunting car, alone. The horse seemed to yield to him. The reins felt soft in his hands. He went south-west of the city and strolled the strand. Quiet here. No emigrant ships. The tide was out and the beach was pencilled by a series of soft sand ripples. Perfect echoes, one after the other, stretching out to the shadowfold of the horizon. No sea any more. Just cloud. He felt a pang of homesickness: it reminded him so much of Baltimore.

When he placed his foot down, the water squelched beneath the sole of his boot. A brief imprint. The ground felt mobile beneath him. He lifted his foot and watched the water leak away, the sand rebound. It was a thing to do over and over again, footprint after footprint.

The sand apparently stretched for miles, but Isabel had told him to be careful, the area was renowned for its swift, quiet tide. The water could insinuate itself secretly, rush in, turn, surround him, and he would be trapped. He found it hard to imagine. It looked, to Douglass, so very peaceful.

He bent down and in the rippled layers noticed a number of tiny crabs pedalling their legs in the sand. He lifted one onto the palm of his hand. The creature was almost translucent, its eyes high and unwieldy. A fiddler crab, perhaps. It ran to the edge of his fingers, hesitated, returned. He moved his arm in the air and the crab scuttled to the high part of his wrist. Douglass dropped it down into the sand again where it burrowed and hid. How quickly it disappeared.

He noticed a number of women farther out on the strand, stooping to collect shells. They wore long headscarves and carried straw baskets on their backs. Searching for food. He had read in the newspapers that the blight was worsening, that the price of flour had doubled within a few days, that stocks of corn were lower than ever. It was only hoped that the next year's crop would not fail.

Douglass walked along the shore. A tall-masted ship clung to the horizon. He watched it go. When he looked back towards the strand again, the women seemed to have disappeared into the earth. Only their dark overcoats could be seen. Every now and then they bent downwards, stooping in rhythm for whatever it was they might find.

1998

para bellum

HE EMERGES FROM THE BRIGHT ELEVATOR. MOVES THROUGH the marbled lobby towards the revolving door. Sixty-four years old. Slender. Greying. A slight strain of yesterday's tennis in his body.

A dark blue suit jacket, slightly rumpled. A pale blue sweater underneath. Trousers creased. Nothing brash, nothing showy. Even the way he walks has a quiet to it. His shoes sound clean and sharp against the floor. He carries a small leather suitcase. He tilts his head towards the doorman who leans down to take the case: just a suit, a shirt, a shaving kit, an extra pair of shoes. Under his other arm he keeps his briefcase tight.

Through the lobby quickly. He hears his name from several angles. The concierge, an elderly neighbour on the lobby couch, the handyman cleaning the large glass panes. It is as if the revolving door has caught the words and begun to let them spin. Mr Mitchell. Senator. George. Sir.

The black saloon car sits idling outside the apartment building. A little shiver from its exhaust. A relief floods through him. No press. No photographers. A hard New York rain, so different from the Irish kind: hurrying itself along, impatient, dodging the umbrellas.

He steps out into the afternoon. Beyond the awning, an umbrella is held aloft for him and the car door is opened.

– Thank you, Ramon.

There is always a moment of dread that there might be someone waiting inside the car. Some news. Some report. Some bombing. No surrender.

He slips into the rear seat, lays his head against the cool leather. Forever an instant when he feels he can turn round, reinvent. That other life. Upstairs. Waiting. He has been the subject of many newspaper columns recently: his beautiful young wife, his new child, the peace process. It stuns him to think that he can still be copy after so many years. Captured on camera. Pulled through the electronic mill. His caricature on the op-ed pages, serious and spectacled. He'd like a long sweep of silence. Just to sit here in this seat and close his eyes. Allow himself a brief snooze.

The front door opens and Ramon slides into the seat, leans out, shakes the umbrella, glances over his shoulder.

– The usual, Senator?

Almost two hundred flights over the past three years. One every three days. New York to London, London to Belfast, Belfast to Dublin, Dublin to DC, DC to New York. Jetliners, private planes, government charters. Trains, town cars, taxis. He lives out his life in two bodies, two wardrobes, two rooms, two clocks.

– JFK, yes. Thank you, Ramon.

The car shifts minutely underneath him, out onto Broadway. A familiar sudden loss, a sadness, the sorrow of a closed vehicle, moving away.

– Just a moment, Ramon, he says.

– Sir?

– I'll be right back.

The car eases to a stop. He reaches for the door handle, climbs out, perplexing the doormen as he hurries quickly through the marbled lobby, into the elevator, his polished shoes clicking, carrying the rain.

THE NINETEENTH FLOOR. Glass and high ceilings. The windows slightly open. Rows of long white bookshelves. Elegant Persian rugs. An early lamp lit in the corner. He moves quietly over the Brazilian hardwood. A collision of light, even with the rain coming down outside. South to Columbus Circle. East to Central Park. West to the Hudson. From below he can hear the Sunday buskers, the music drifting up. Jazz.

Heather stands in their son's bedroom, hunched over the changing table, hair pulled high to her neck. She does not hear him enter. He remains at the door, watching as she pulls together the velcro of the nappy. She leans down and kisses their son's stomach. She undoes her dark hair and leans again over the child. Tickling him. A giggle from the baby.

The Senator remains at the bedroom door until she senses him standing behind her. She says his name, unlatches the child from the changing table, swaddles the boy in a blanket. She laughs and steps across the fine carpet, still carrying the soiled nappy.

– You forget something?

– No.

He kisses her. Then his son. He pinches the boy playfully on the toes. The roll of soft skin at his fingers.

He takes the nappy – still warm to the touch – and drops it in the bin. Life, he thinks, is still capable of the most extraordinary quips. A warm nappy. At sixty-four.

Heather walks him back to the elevator, takes the flap end of his suit jacket, draws him close. The scent of their son on both their hands. The elevator cables pitch their mourn.

WHAT SHE WORRIES most of all is that he will become the flesh at the end of an assassin's bullet.

SO MANY MURDERS arrive out of the blue. The young Catholic woman with the British soldier slumped over her child, a hiss of air from the bullet wound in his back. The man in the taxi with the cold steel at his neck. The bomb left outside the barracks in Newtownards. The girl in Manchester thrown twenty feet in the air, her legs separating from her as she flew. The forty-seven-year-old woman tarred and feathered and left tied to a lamp post on the Ormeau Road. The postman blinded by the letter bomb. The teenager with a six-pack of bullet holes in his knees, his ankles, his elbows.

When she was with him in Northern Ireland, last July, it chilled Heather to see wheeled mirrors being slid in under the car before they drove off. George said it was just a formality. Nothing for her to worry about. He had an air about him, a mid-century dignity that dismissed most danger.

She liked to watch him in a crowd. The way he could forget himself, dissolve and allow everyone else a sense of their own importance. He believed in people, he listened well. Nothing false or politic about it. It was simply the way he went about things. He disappeared amongst them. His tall hunch, his glasses. Even the fine cut of his suit would vanish. Sometimes she could find herself looking for him, and he would be tucked in the corner, talking with the most unlikely of people. He was given to sudden, close leanings. A touching of arms.

An unexpected laugh. It unnerved his bodyguards no end. It didn't matter whom. It was his failure, too, of course: the inability to say no. So hard for him to turn away. An old-fashioned politeness. His New England air. She would watch the party drift: a small pool of water, unknown to itself, shifting sideways. More and more people gathering round him. At the end of an evening she would watch him try to row himself out: that hopelessly surrounded swimmer, bashful now, ready to leave, tired, trying to pull himself up from the deep end, eager not to disappoint.

She holds her foot in the elevator door for a moment longer than she should. But then it closes and he is gone, and all she can hear is the electronic pulleys as he descends through the heart of the building. He will be home in two weeks. By Easter Sunday. He has made a promise.

She hears the faint ting of the elevator bell below.

THE LINCOLN CENTER traffic. The merge of the avenues. The bustle. Dancers hurrying across the plaza. The buskers beneath the awning, tromboning the raindrops down.

He likes it here on the West Side, though sometimes he wishes they could live farther east, just to make it easier to get to the airport. A simple, sharp practicality: to save half a travel hour, to be with her and Andrew just a moment or two longer.

Out onto Broadway. Left onto Sixty-Seventh Street. They turn onto Amsterdam and head uptown. If Ramon catches the lights properly they can go all the way, transform it into an avenue of yellow awnings. Past the cathedral. East, through Harlem. The whirl of faces and umbrellas. Onto 124th Street. The Bobby Sands mural on the wall near the police station. He has been meaning to find out who painted it, and why. Odd to have a mural in New York. *Saoirse* painted in bright letters above the hunger striker's face. A word he has learnt over the past few years. The streets of Belfast, too, are covered in murals: King, Kennedy, Cromwell, Che Guevara, the Queen painted huge on gable-ends and walls.

A quick merge and swerve. Onto the Triborough Bridge. A glimpse of water. In the distance, somewhere up the river, is Yankee Stadium. He is all of a sudden back at Fenway Park, thirteen years old: the great swell and hush of green as he steps into the top tier of seats, his first flash of ballpark, Birdie Tebbetts, Rudy York, Johnny Pesky at shortstop. A country boy. First time in the city. Watching Ted Williams step up to the plate. The Kid, the Thumper, the Splendid Splinter. He can hear the crack of the first ball cut across the floodlights. Good days, those. Long ago, not far away.

He leans against the cool of the seat. He has travelled in all manner of cavalcades, processions, parades down through the years, but what he likes most of all is this silence. To travel under the radar. If even just for an hour or two.

He opens the briefcase. They cross the bridge at a clip. Ramon has a badge that he flashes at the tollbooth. Sometimes the police try to peer inside, past the dark glass, as if they are looking beneath the surface of a river. To gauge the importance of the catch. Only me, I'm afraid. His staff is already in Belfast and Dublin. And he has refused security while at home in New York, Washington, Maine. No need. They will hardly strap a bomb beneath his lawnmower anyway.

There is much to catch up on. A report from Stormont. An internal memo on decommissioning. A file that came through from MI-5 on the prisoner release. All the secret histories. The ancient longings. The violence of feeble men. He is weary of it all, tired of the permutations. What he wants is a clear, fine skyline. He puts the files aside a moment, looks out the rain-hammered window at the riffle of New

York. All the greys and yellows. The concrete cubes of Queens. The broken neon signs. The leaning water towers with their rotting wood. The spindlework of the elevated trains. It's a primitive city, aware of its own shortcomings, its shirt stained, its teeth plaqued, its zip open. But it is Heather's city. She loves it. She wants to be here. And he has to admit that there is something grudgingly attractive about it. It is not quite Maine, but nothing is ever Maine.

He has heard once that a man knows where he is from when he knows where he would like to be buried. He knows his spot already, on the cliff, looking out to sea, Mount Desert Island, the deep green, the curve of horizon, the angled rock, the waves spindrifting upwards. Give him a small square of grass over the cove, a low white fence around it. A few sharp rocks to dig into his back. Sow my soul in the rugged red soil. Let me rest there, happy, watching the lift of the lobster pots, the slow saunter of seacaps, the curl of the gulls. But have some patience, please, Lord. Another twenty years at least. Thirty, even. Thirty-five, why not? Many mornings yet left. He might as well crawl up towards the full century.

The hiss of rainwater sounds underneath the tyres. Ramon has a heavy foot when it comes to highways. Onto the Grand Central Parkway. From lane to lane. The brief *thwap* of dryness beneath the underpasses. Out towards the Van Wyck. No going back. The light fading through the slender shoulders of afternoon rain.

Easter two weeks away.

Last chance.

Si vis pacem, para bellum.

YESTERDAY, IN CENTRAL Park, in the yellow sunlight, she reached for a backhand, caught it perfectly, sliced the racquet so that the ball floated a moment and dropped just over the net, and he lurched forwards, laughing at the audacity of the shot, the perfect backwards spin, as he went crashing into the net. All round, the applause of the city, in the leaves and trees and buildings, and a red-tail hawk shooting over the courts, and some clouds skilful overhead in the blue, and the babysitter in the background, rocking the carriage, and he had the fleeting desire to make the phone calls to Stormont, leave it all at deuce.

AT THE KERBSIDE he quietly slips Ramon a gift. Three tickets for Opening Day. The Mets. Second deck. Not far from home plate. Bring your boys, Ramon. Teach them well. Tell Bobby Valentine to let loose the cowhide.

THEY KNOW HIM so well at JFK that it almost feels as if he should stand at the counter and negotiate from there. Your air rights. Your refunds. Your delays.

The stewardesses have a fondness for him, his quietness, his humility. From a distance he looks like a man who might shuffle through a constant grey, but up close he is fluid and sharp. His shyness carries a form of flirt.

At the British Airways desk he is taken by the arm and brought beyond check-in to what they call the Vippery. No metal detectors. No search at all. He wishes he could go through the channels, like a normal traveller, but the airline insists and they always whisk him through. This way, Senator, this way. The corridor to the Vippery is rutted and stained. Odd how badly painted the walls are. A sickly mauve colour. The baseboards broken and scuffed.

He is brought through the back entrance into the gold-plated shine. Two lovely beaming smiles from the front desk. Girls in silk scarves of red, white and blue. Their perfect English accents. As if serving all their vowels on a fine set of tongs.

— Wonderful to see you again, Senator Mitchell.

— Good afternoon, ladies.

He wishes they weren't quite so loud with his name, but he nods to them, glances at their name badges. Always a good idea to have a first name. Clara. Alexandra. He thanks them both and he can almost hear the noise of their blushes. He glances over his shoulder, the slight rascal in him, and is guided towards the back of the lounge. He has met movie stars here, diplomats, ministers, captains of industry, a couple of rugby players up to their broad shoulders in wine. The minor figures of public glory, their Rolexes peeping out from beneath their cuffs. It doesn't much interest him, the spotlight. What he looks for is a seat where he won't be disturbed, yet can get up and stretch his legs if needs be. He has taken to yoga in recent times, on Heather's insistence. Felt rather stupid at first. Downward dog. Dolphin plank. Crane pose. But it has loosened him up enormously, untightened all the bolts. In his younger years he was far less supple. A certain mental agility in it, too. He can sit and close his eyes and find a good meditative point.

He spots a likely place, in the far corner of the lounge, where the rain rolls decoratively down the darkness, shifts his weight towards the window, allows the young lady to shepherd him along. As if she is the one to have chosen the seat. Her hand at the small of his back.

He keeps the briefcase between them. For distance and decorum.

— Can I get you a beverage, Senator?

He has become a man of tea. He never would have believed it. This unasked-for life, it always surprises. It began in the North. He couldn't get away from it. Tea for breakfast, tea for lunch, tea in the afternoon, tea before bedtime, tea between the tea. He has learned the art of it. Choosing the right kettle. Running the tap water until

cold. Boiling it beyond the boil. Heating the teapot with a swish. Dol-
ing out the leaves. Timing the brew. Wetting the tea, the Irish call it.
He is not a man for alcohol, and it is the tea that has dragged him
through many a late evening. With cookies. Or biscuits as they say.
Every man with his own peculiar vice. His will hardly rock heaven or
hell. McVitie's Digestives.

– Milk and three sugars, please.

He is careful not to watch the swish of her as she moves away
through the lobby. He leans back against the seat. But Lord, he is
tired. He has, in his briefcase, a few sleeping pills prescribed by a doctor friend, but he is not fond of the idea. Perhaps in an emergency. A
newspaper wag said: *Some calm in the Stormont.* He can already feel
the weight of the days ahead, the changed minds, the semantical shuffling, the nervous search for equilibrium. He and his team have given
them a deadline. They will not go beyond it. They have promised that
to themselves. A finishing line. Otherwise the whole process will drag
on for ever. The rut of another thirty years. Clauses and footnotes.
Systems and subsystems. Visions and revisions. How many times has
it all been written and rewritten? He and his team have allowed them
to exhaust the language. Day after day, week after week, month after
month. To roil in their own boredom. To talk through the vitriol
towards a sort of bewilderment that such a feeling could have existed
at all.

It has been, on occasion, like playing hide-and-seek with oneself.
Open the door and there you are. Count to twenty yet again. Ready
or not. Run and hide. Pretend you don't know where you are.

He used to play that game with his brothers when he was young,
in the small house in Waterville. He hid in the closet beneath the stairs
where his mother kept the jars of figs. A familiar smell. The jars were
ranged high on the shelves: his own small Lebanon, cramped and tidy.
A tiny glint of light came from the hallway, leaked in, clarified the

dark. He tucked himself away in the corner, at the base of the wooden shelves, waiting to be caught. His brothers got so used to him hiding in the same place that once they left him for hours, just to rile him, and to rile them back he just stayed completely still, remained beneath the stairs until after dinner when they finally came to get him out, cramped, sore, vaguely victorious.

The old days, they arrive back in the oddest ways, suddenly taut, breaking the surface, a salmon leap. The Waterville house backed onto the wide Kennebec River. The smoke from the mill drifted downstream. Huge logs arrived and were winched, dripping wet, from the grey river. The wood saws whined. Sawdust whipped across the wind. Railway whistles pierced the air. The town had a vigilance about it. He worked the newspaper route. Rode a bicycle with fringed handlebars. Hopped across the railway trestles. Learned the back roads and the byways. The coins in his pockets clanged. He liked the days when the river iced and he wondered about what it carried underneath: water beneath water. He watched the men coming home from the factories after long days of giving up their flesh. Mornings of fresh blue snowfalls. By the end of the day the snow was dark with grit.

He grew up in his brother's clothes. It used to make his mother smile to see the shirts slide from one shoulder to another, as if youth were just a thing that would always be passed along the line. When he was finished with the clothes, she would load them up and drive them to the Salvation Army store down on Gilman. *Ya hadi* she would say. Give us grace.

He was aware of the Horatio Alger quality that hung around him. His mother was Lebanese, a textile worker. His father, an orphan, a janitor in a college. An American boyhood. The newspapers sometimes mocked it. He walked out of college into an unquiet life. Torts, contracts, deeds, the gavel. He could quite easily have been a lawyer in a bow tie, or a small-town judge living on the outskirts of town. He thrived on Webster and Darrow. *A Plea for Harmony and Peace. Resist Not Evil.* Mysteries dissolving into facts. As a lawyer, he hated to lose. No virtue in second place. He took his chances. Attorney, candidate for governor, federal judge. Fifteen years in Washington. Majority leader for six years. The second most powerful man in America.

He knew how to flip a coin in the air and listen to the language of how it was made to land: what amazed him was that there were times when a coin could land sideways. Vietnam. Grenada. El Salvador. Kuwait. Bosnia. Mexico. All those times when logic was perched on a rim. Health care. NAFTA. The Clean Air Act. The occasional dividend of change.

He retired then, ready to pursue his own route, practise law, breathe easy, leave the flashbulbs behind. Even turned down the Supreme Court. But then the President phoned again. Clinton's casual charm. The ambitious ease. A favour, George, he said. Two weeks in Northern Ireland. It's just a trade convention. That's all. An escape across the water. The Senator was drawn in. He would go for a fortnight, that was all. Before he knew it, it was a year, then two, then three. The shadows of Harland and Wolff falling over Belfast. Where the *Titanic* had once been built. The vague hope of helping to turn the long blue iceberg, the deep underwater of Irish history.

He glances out the window now at the rows of planes, the moving carts, the men on the runway waving their neon sticks. All the world, always going somewhere. Everyone in a rush. The fatal laws of our own importance. How many aloft at this very moment? Looking down on ourselves in the hazy and confused landscape below. How odd to glimpse the reflection of himself in the window, as if he is both inside and outside at the same time. The young boy looking in at the man in his late years, a father again, surprised to be here at all. The manner in which life deals the unexpected. So constantly unfinished.

He has been asked many times by reporters if he can explain Northern Ireland. As if he could whisk a phrase out of the air, a sound bite for the ages. He is fond of Heaney. *Two buckets were easier carried than one. Whatever you say, say nothing.* Brief breakthroughs, intermittent calm, large ruptures in the landscape. He has never even been able to get all the political parties together in the same room, let alone the whole situation in a single phrase. It is one of their beauties, the Irish, the way they crush and expand the language all at once. How they mangle it and revere it. How they colour even their silences. He has sat in a room for hours on end listening to men talk about words and yet never mention the one word they want. The maniacal meanderings. The swerves and sways. And then, all of a sudden, he has heard them say, *No, no, no,* as if the language only ever had one word that made any sense at all.

Paisley. Adams. Trimble. McGuinness. Throw a word in their midst and watch them light the fuse. Ahern. Blair. Clinton. Mowlam. Hume. Robinson. Ervine. Major. Kennedy. McMichael. A fine cast. Shakespearean almost. And he sits in the wings, with de Chastelain and Holkeri, waiting for the moment for the cast to bring out their spears. Or not.

There has been, he must admit, a thrill to his days in the North. An edge. A recklessness he enjoys. Another boyhood. Under the stairs. Ready to emerge, in suit and tie, with hands raised high in false surrender. Strand One, Strand Two, Strand Three. He dislikes the praise, the glad-handing, the false backslaps, the gestures to his patience, his control. It's the tenacity of the fanatic that he wants to pitch himself against. There is, he knows, something akin to his own form of violence in the way he wants to hang on and fight. The way the terrorist might hide himself in a wet ditch all night. Cold and the damp seeping down into the gunman's boots, right up into the small of his back, along his spine, through his cranium, out his pores, so cold, so very cold, watching, waiting, until the stars are gone, and the morning chatters with a bit of light. He would like to outlast that man in the ditch, outwait the cold and the rain and the filth, and the opportunity for a bullet, remain down in the reeds, underwater, in the dark, breathing through a hollow piece of grass. To stay until the cold no longer matters. Fatigue conquering tedium. Match him breath for breath. Let the gunman grow so cold that he cannot pull the trigger and then allow the silhouette to trudge dejected over the hill. To filibuster the son of a bitch, and then watch him climb out the ditch and to thank him and shake his hand and escort him down the high-brambled laneway with the senatorial knife in his back.

– Your tea, sir.

He touches his palms together in grateful thanks. She is carrying a silver tray: small neat sandwiches, biscuits, cashews.

– Some nuts, Senator?

– Ah, yes.

He tries hard to hold back the blatant grin, if not outright laughter. He would like to tell her that he's had too many of them in recent times, but she might misunderstand, or take it rudely, so he simply smiles and takes the tea, allows her to place the cashews on the table. Indeed, they have been many and legion, the nuts. The paramilitaries, the politicians, the diplomats, the civil servants, too. The polygon of Northern Ireland. He can see six, seven, eight sides to it all, even more. A firefly flashing forwards at regular intervals. Context crossing context. There is nothing to gain from the North: no oil, no territory, no DeLoreans anymore. He is not even paid for the work: just his expenses, that's all. No salary. Some political traction, of course, for him, for the President, and for posterity, maybe even history itself, but there are easier ways to get that, simpler vanities, more approachable conceits.

He is well aware that there are some out there who think they have him on an endless looping string. The judicial puppet. Peace and Judy. But it doesn't bother him one bit, even when they draw him, glum and dangling, in one of their crude newspaper cartoons. Or their backhanded jibes. There is something fierce about him: he has earned the right to part the darkness slightly, to go with them into the corners.

What the Irish themselves worry about is that they will somehow keep on delaying, but he will not allow it, the endless riverrun, riverrun, riverrun. He will be over eighty when Andrew goes to college. The father mistaken for the grandfather. The distant ancestry. All those ancient ghosts. There were sixty-one children born in Northern Ireland the day Andrew was born. Sixty-one ways for a life to unfold. The thought slides a sharp blade of regret down the core of his spine. His son is just five months old now, and he can count on just four hands the amount of days he has spent with him. How many hours has he sat in the stark chambers listening to men argue about a single comma, or the placement of a period, when all he wanted was to return to the surprise of his very young child? Sometimes he would watch them as they talked, saying very little or nothing at all. Kites of language. Clouds of logic. Drifting in and out. Caught on the moving wave of their own voices. He heard certain phrases and allowed them to take him out over the treetops, into what the Northern Irish called the yonder. Immersed in the words. Sitting at the plenaries, waiting. The brittleness in the room. The cramped maleness. A relentless solicitude about them, they would hold up a hand and tell people they did not deserve the reverence, but it was plain to see that they needed it.

Some days he wishes that he could empty the chambers of the men, fill the halls instead with women: the short sharp shock of three thousand two hundred mothers. The ones who picked through the supermarket debris for pieces of their dead husbands. The ones who still laundered their gone son's bed sheets by hand. The ones who kept an extra teacup at the end of the table, in case of miracles. The elegant ones, the angry ones, the clever ones, the ones in hairnets, the ones exhausted by all the dying. They carried their sorrow – not with photos under their arms, or with public wailing, or by beating their chests, but with a weariness around the eyes. Mothers and daughters and children and grandmothers, too. They never fought the wars, but they suffered them, blood and bone. How many times has he heard it? How often were there two ways to say the one thing? My son died. His name was Seamus. My son died. His name was James. My son died. His name was Peader. My son died. His name was Pete. My son died. His name was Billy. My son died. His name was Liam. My son died. His name was Charles. My son died. His name was Cathal. My son's name is Andrew.

THE RAIN OUTSIDE still hammers down. Luggage carts hurry to and fro. He lifts a biscuit, blows the tea cool. Sunday nights to Ireland. Wednesday nights to London. Thursdays to Washington DC, at his law firm. Friday nights to New York. Sundays back out to England and Ireland again.

Sometimes it feels as if there is no motion at all: thousands of miles in the decompression chamber, the same cup of tea in the same cup in the same airport lounge, the same city, the same neat car.

He wonders what might happen if the plane were delayed, how easy it would be to go home, ascend in the elevator, to turn the key, flick on the lamp, become that other man on whom he is equally intent.

HE IS GUIDED last onto the plane. A special privilege. As if he could be unseen. A nice thought: to be truly unseen. To own an influential anonymity.

He was always recognized in Washington. The push, the shove, the backslap. The corridors of power. What he disliked were the galas, the garden parties, the red carpets. Flashbulbs, press briefings, TV cameras. The irksome necessities. He was recognized in New York, too, but nobody seemed to care. The city was so brash that it was obsessed only with itself. In Maine, he felt at home, amongst his own people.

Out here, in this nation of cloud and air, they all know him, too. They are quick to hang his suit jacket, place the small bag in the overhead bin. He glances across and is glad to see that the seat beside him is free. No need for the kind nod, or the apologetic half-grin. He has his routine down firmly now. The window seat. Briefcase tucked down beside him. Shoes gently lifted, though not fully taken off, not yet. Something vaguely rude in the idea that you remove your shoes before lift off.

The stewardess moves along the aisle. A tray, a tongs. He reaches for the white towel, holds it to his brow and then cleans in the depths between his fingers. How quickly the towel grows cool. For once he wishes he had one of those confounded portable phones. What is it they call them? Cellulars. Mobiles. Handhelds. Just to call home. But his refusal to get a phone has become a point of honour now. He clings to the idea, an old-fashioned beating of the chest. He has spent sixty-odd years without one: no point in beginning now. Ridiculous, really. All his aides have them. His negotiating team. All the reporters. There have even been times, just before take-off, when he borrowed one from his fellow passengers, just to make a quick call to Heather. His hand over the mouthpiece so as not to appear rude.

A menu is slipped into his lap, but he knows this month's choices by heart: lobster bisque, garden salad, chicken cordon bleu, Asian noodles, beef tenderloin, mushroom risotto. The British are working on their culinary reputation, it seems. Their best, their brightest. They are a tough, intransigent lot, though they have softened a good deal in the past year or so. Embarrassed by what they have done for centuries in Ireland. Ready to leave. To hightail it out of there. They would wipe their hands clean in an instant, if only they didn't have to do it in front of the world. They seem stunned that Northern Ireland somehow exists. How did they possibly ever believe that the country could have been good for them? What it all came down to was pride. Pride in the rise, and pride in the fall. They want to be able to leave with a measure of dignity. Tally-ho. Ta-ra. Voyeurs to their own experience. Living at an angle to the moment. And the Irish, down south, with almost the exact opposite dilemma. Embarrassed by the fact that it was taken away. Centuries of desire. Like the longing for a married woman. And now suddenly she is there, within your grasp, and you're not quite sure whether you want her at all. Second thoughts. Other dowries. The mildew in the room where the past is stored. The Unionists, the Nationalists, the Loyalists, the Republicans, the Planters, the Gaels. Their endless gallery of themselves. Room after room. Painting after painting. Men on tall horses. Flags into battle. Sieges and riverbanks. The alphabet soup of the terrorists.

At first he couldn't understand the accents. The spiky consonants. Angular and hard-edged. It seemed to him like an altogether different language. They came to the microphone. He had to lean forward to try to decipher it. The small punctuations of grief. Ach. Aye. Surely. Not our fault, Mr Chairman. Six into twenty-six won't go. They kicked the bloody door in, so they did. They pushed wee Peader out the helicopter. All due respect, Senator, we don't talk to murderers. If Mr Chairman would like to know what it's like why don't you come, for once, to the Shankill?

They were dumping out the contents of endless drawers on the floor. But he soon caught on. He began to tell the difference between a Belfast and a Dublin accent, between Cork and Fermanagh, between Derry and Londonderry even. All the geography that went into words. The history behind every syllable. The Battle of the Boyne. Enniskillen. Bloody Sunday. There was a clue in every tiny detail. Gary was a Prod. Seamus was a Taig. Liz lived on the Shankill Road. Bobby on the Falls. Sean went to St Columba's. Jeremy to Campbell. Bushmills was a Protestant whiskey. Jameson for Catholics. Nobody drove a green car. Your tie was never orange. You went for holidays in Bundoran or you went to Portrush. Fly your flag. Pick your poison. Choose your hangman.

Lord, it was a tangled web. One he would do well to sleep upon. One that needed an eternity of rest.

Still, he had grown to like them: the politicians, the diplomats, the spin doctors, the civil servants, the security men, even the loudmouths outside the gates. All of them with their own particular music. A certain generosity to them. All the dirty laundry somehow made eloquent. He was told once that any good Irishman would drive fifty miles out of his way just to hear an insult – and a hundred miles if the insult was good enough. The self-deprecation. The effacement. The awareness. There was something about the endless wrangling that has caught him in the glue pot and kept him there. The confounded intricacies. The edges of endeavour. The fascination with the impossible. He wanted to stay alert to what might be learned. And there was always a key in the anonymous moment. The women in the canteen. They nodded at him and caught his eye. The sad smile. The generous delusion. The lean forwards. *God bless you, Senator, but it's a fool's errand.* Well, be that as it may, but I'll still take the part.

HE WAS NOT beyond knowing that they thought him – when he first arrived – a quiet patsy. The Arab. The Yank. The Judge. Your Harness. Mohammed. Mahatma. Ahab. Iron Pants. They even called him, for some reason, the Serb. He wasn't interested in playing himself Irish or Lebanese. Not for him the simple ancestral heart: he wanted to make himself the smallest continent possible.

Still, he was sure some of them wanted a slice of anger from him. To stumble somehow. To say the wrong thing. So they could apportion the blame away from themselves. But he figured out ways to fade into the background, stuck to silence, looked over the rim of his glasses. He disliked his own importance in the process. It was the others who had brought the possibility here: Clinton, Reynolds, Hume, Major. He just wanted to land it. To take it down from where it was, aloft, like one of those great lumbering machines of the early part of the century, the crates of air and wood and wire they somehow flew across the water.

A RED EYELID of sun out the window. The vaguely scattered morning clouds. London below. The hum and flood of plane lights. His feet have swollen during the flight. In the overhead locker he reaches for his sweater.

He is vaguely embarrassed that Heather dresses him these days. She knows a Persian tailor who double-breasts his suits. It took a little while to step into the crease. Even the very word *bespoke*. The sweaters are from Cenci or some such place. Something comforting in them. A small surrendering to memory. Odd that desire is made true by distance. He can pull on the sweater and almost be back on Sixty-Seventh Street. Odd, too, how a life can so easily reshape itself. Perhaps the failure that irks him the most is the original marriage. It simply didn't work out. They tried, he and his first wife, they hung on, they failed, what was broken was broken. Ashes do not become wood. What he feared early on was the idea that his grown daughter might see him in his new suit and ties, and that she would say nothing at all, that the silence would go right to the core of failure.

He hitches his jacket up on his shoulders. Onwards. Away. He is sixth off the plane. He allows the others to go ahead. His body still vaguely belonging to the cabin. That air in the back of his calves.

Halfway down the corridor he is surprised by a hand on his elbow. Bombing? Murder? Broken ceasefire? But it's a young man, blue-eyed with a nose ring. Must have been sitting at the front of the plane. Vaguely familiar. Maybe a pop star of sorts. Or someone from the movies. *Good luck, Senator, we're praying for you.* In an English accent. Odd to think of the young man praying at all. Mostly it was the older women of Northern Ireland who said that to him. Adjusting their hairnets. Wrapping their fingers white with beads.

He shakes the young man's hand and strides along the corridor. But Lord, he hates this walk. Who will be there to meet and greet him? What sort of security detail? It always gets heavier on this side of the pond. Simply to walk him to another terminal. He can make out their shapes at the end of the walkway. A young woman with short blonde hair lifts her hand in greeting: he recalls her name though he has only met her twice. Lorraine. And two new security men. Coming towards him briskly. No news on their faces, no sudden collapses. No apparent grief. Thank God for that.

– How was your flight, sir?

– Wonderful, thank you.

A small lie of course, but why whine? She'll hardly whisk out a pillow for him. They move swiftly down the stairs, out to the waiting car, towards Terminal Two.

– Sorry, sir, but your next plane's delayed thirty-five minutes, she says.

Lorraine has, on her belt, space for three phones. She juggles them with style and grace, hooks her fingers under the belt: the Wild West of telecommunications.

In the British Midland lounge they have reserved an area for him. Tea, pastries, yoghurt. She hands him a memo and he scans it quickly. A report on Ahern and Blair. Concessions on the proposed North-South bodies. A clause in the Framework Document from three years ago. The status of the Council and the source of its authority. They are, it seems, approaching a tentative agreement on Strand Two.

For a moment he allows himself the luxury of a smile. Two o'clock in New York. Heather and Andrew will be sleeping.

THE NORTH, BELOW, is stunned with morning sunlight. Patches of bright yellow on the mud flats. The fields so wide and grassy. Lake and water-meadow. A silver estuary and a huge lake. One small cloud, cast out by the herd, limps away to the west. The plane banks and the city of Belfast appears, always smaller than he expects it to be. The high cranes of the shipyards. The maze of side streets. The football pitches. The flats. The fretful desolation. Then out over the fields again, the incredible depth of green. He has never quite seen the land so bright before: a clear day through the morning clouds. He is used to its grey edges, its laneways, its high walls. They pull in over Lough Neagh. A vague sadness on touchdown, a tensing of the throat.

On the grass below, the shadow of the plane is squeezed down to its own size, then is gone. *Welcome to Belfast International. Contents in the overhead bin may have shifted during flight.* The stewardesses fuss with his jacket. He is whisked through security once more, out past the small café and the newsagent's where he takes a quick glance at the newspaper headlines on the small metal racks. Nothing of damage. A good sign.

Outside, the vague smell of farmland manure hangs on the air.

Three cars waiting. Gerald, his driver, greets him with a nod and a lift of the case.

In the car Gerald passes back a sheet of numbers. A small jump in his chest that it might be bad news, but it's the baseball scores, copied from Reuters, handwritten. He scans them quickly. Opening day. Ah, yes. Hail and hallelujah. The Sox have won.

– A good start, he says.

– Aye, Senator. Oakland? Where's that now?

– Way, way out there. California.

– Out in the sunshine.

– Keep the good news coming, Gerald.

– We'll see what we can do, Senator.

The convoy pulls out through the airport, towards the M2, a wide motorway. Fields and hedges and scattered farms. Not much traffic until they get closer to the city. He could, quite possibly, be in any large American town, until he looks out to see the flags fluttering over the housing estates, sketching the skyline, claiming it, colouring it. The Unionists go for the Star of David, the Republicans fly the flag of the Palestinians. Small wars, large territories.

Written on a wall on the road out near Ballycloghan, in large white letters against the grey, a new piece of graffiti: *We will never ever forget you, Jimmy Sands.*

Which brings a wry smile to even Gerald's face as they drive past, since it was of course *Bobby* they would never forget.

IN THE EARLY days – when the process was fresh – he would drive to the Stranmillis Tennis Club along the banks of the Lagan.

Nine or ten outdoor courts, all artificial turf. Sprinkled with gritty sand. Tough on his ankles. But he liked to get out and knock the ball back and forth: he played with the younger civil servants.

They were careful at first not to try to beat him until they learned that there was a sort of unbeatability about him. He was relentless, he hung on, a backcourt player, he slid along the rear line, returning the ball safely over the net, time after time. The photos belied it, but he was sprightly.

The luxury of age was the giving up of vanity: he could play for hours on end in the Irish drizzle. He wore white shorts and long tube socks and a blue tracksuit top. Afterwards he would take the opportunity to laugh at himself in the changing-room mirror.

He was surprised early one morning to come off the northernmost court to see a group of women gathered together on the courts at the front of the club. He wandered quietly in amongst them. Signs were hung on the rear of the benches: ALL IRELAND WOMEN'S TOURNAMENT. He liked that notion. At least in tennis they could play together. He was taken by the sight of an elderly woman who piloted her wheelchair along the back of the courts. A thick-boned woman with striking grey hair. She must have been ninety, but she carried herself quite well in the chair. A generosity to her. She stopped at the back of each court and marked the clipboard with a pencil, then called out to the players and the umpires. She had a singsong voice. He thought he heard an American accent, but wasn't sure.

He came back later that day after a series of plenaries in Stormont. The usual bickerings. The day had sapped the fire from him. The tournament was still in progress. He loosened his tie and took off his jacket and slid in amongst the crowd to watch the final match.

The woman in the wheelchair was positioned at the back of the court. She wore a tartan wool blanket over her lap. She nodded at each point, and clapped at the end of the games: large, loud, animate. He couldn't tell what side she was supporting, if any. Every now and then she let out a long laugh, and put her head on the shoulder of a younger woman alongside her. Small ripples of applause slipped across the evening.

These were the moments he liked the most. The refuge of the anonymous. The ordinary bits and pieces. Ireland unwarred.

The match ended to a round of polite applause and the elderly lady was wheeled away from the back of the courts. He saw her reach out for a small plastic glass of champagne.

She was left alone a moment and he noticed the edge of her wheelchair catch on the artificial turf.

— Lottie Tuttle, she said, stretching out her hand.

— George Mitchell.

— Oh, we know who you are, Senator, we saw you this morning with that awful backhand.

He reared back and laughed.

— You're American? he asked.

— Lord, no.

She finished the small glass of champagne.

— Canadian. Sort of.

— Sort of?

— Newfoundland.

— Beautiful place.

— Lottie Ehrlich was the name. Once. Long ago.

— I see.

— I go back to the Druids, really.

She laughed and pushed the right side of the chair and it spun gracefully. He could hear elements of Irish in her accent.

— I live out by the peninsula. Strangford.

— Ah, he said. I've heard of it. The lake.

— Indeed. The lough. You should come visit, Senator. You'd be most welcome. We've a small cottage on the water.

— Well, I'm rather tied up now, Lottie.

— We're hoping you're going to sort out this mess for us, Senator.

— I'm hoping that, too.

— After that you can return to your backhand.

Lottie smiled and made her way round the back of the court to talk with the tournament winner. She pushed the wheelchair along entirely by herself, but then she turned round with a grin.

— Really, Senator, your problem is that you're not planting your back foot properly.

HE SAW HER a few times after that. She was a regular at the club. She had, by all accounts, been a handy player once. She had lost her grandson to the Troubles years ago. The Senator never enquired how the boy died: he did not want to get himself in the business of having to choose sides, whose fault, whose murder, whose bomb, whose rubber bullet, whose bureaucracy.

What he liked about Lottie Tuttle was the manner in which she insisted that she still push herself along in the wheelchair.

He saw her early one morning guide the chair out to the middle of one of the courts. She wore a wide white skirt and white blouse. Even her racquet was ancient, a great wooden frame with red-and-white catgut. A younger woman set up on the opposite side of the net and lobbed a few shots at her. They played for half an hour. Lottie hit only three or four balls, and afterwards she sat at the back of the court, exhausted, her swollen arm wrapped in ice, until she fell asleep and dozed under a blanket.

HE RUNS THE gauntlet of the offices at Stormont. Rows of low squat buildings. Hardly palatial. The Gulag, they call it. A good name. Appropriate.

His car pulls up slowly. The crowds are gathered outside the gates. Candles on one side, flags on another. He keeps his head down, inhabits the backseat. But in the rear of the crowd he spies a man carrying a sign, and a bolt of joy moves through him: *The incredible happens.*

Hallelujah to that, he thinks, as the gates open up, and the car nudges through, flashbulbs erupting at the windowpane.

He walks from the car park and takes the steps two at a time: even jet-lagged, he wants to carry an energy into the building.

THEY ARE ALL here now: the North, the South, the East, the West. The Unionists at one end of the corridor, the Republicans at the other. The Irish government downstairs. The British upstairs. Young diplomats plying the middle ground. Moderates scattered about. Pretty young observers from the European Union walking through with clipboards. The hum of the photocopy machine. The pattering of keyboards. The smell of burnt coffee.

His walk is careful but energetic: handshakes, eye-flicks, nods, smiles. Tim. David. Maurice. Stewart. Claire. Seamus. Charles. Orla. Rory. Françoise. Good morning. Great to see you. We'll have that report ready at noon, Senator.

A bounce in his step. Along the drab grey corridor. Into the small bathroom. A quick change of shirt. He shoves his arms briskly through the sleeves. He would hate to be caught shirtless. He leans into the mirror. The hair greyer than it should be. And a little more scattered on top.

He whisks a quick comb through the hair, parts it sideways, splashes a bit of cold water on his face. A river comes back to him, he does not know why: the Kennebec. There is a song he heard once, at a dinner in Dublin. *Flow on lovely river, flow gently along, by your waters so clear sounds the lark's merry song.* The Irish are great for their tunes, but all their lovesongs are sad and their warsongs happy. He has heard them often, late at night, singing in the hotel bars, notes drifting up to his room.

His staff is waiting in the outer office. Martha. David. Kelly. They, too, are dark-eyed with lack of sleep.

They phone down the hall to bring in de Chastelain and Holkeri. Followed by their own staff, Irish and British both. A long trail of the weary.

— How was your flight, Senator?

— Wonderful, he says.

They grin and nod: of course it wasn't. Their own war stories. Delayed flights. Forgotten anniversaries. A burst water pipe on Joy Street. A missed wedding in Newcastle-upon-Tyne. A flat tyre on the road from Drogheda. A sick niece in Finland. Something in their separateness has bound them together. They are all entirely sick of the process, but the deadline has jolted them awake.

— So tell me, he says, where do we stand?

What they have is a sixty-page draft, two governments, ten political parties, little less than two weeks. Strand One. Strand Two. Strand Three. None of the strands yet set in stone. The incredible weave of language. All the little tassels still hanging down. The tiniest atoms. The poorly tied knots. There is the possibility of an annex. The rumour of a rewrite. The suggestion of a delay. Where are they in London? Where are they are in Dublin? Where are they in the Maze? Or is that Long Kesh? There has been a call for transcripts of the plenaries. What exactly does *substantive negotiations* mean? Did the security team check the political background of the canteen staff? There is talk of a farm on the Tyrone border where whole crates of rocket-propelled grenades have been hidden. Someone has leaked the MI-5 report to the London *Times*. Could anyone please decommission the *Sunday World*? Paisley is cooking up a protest outside the gates. Did you hear that Mo Mowlam took off her wig again? Can you believe that they tried to smuggle a tape recorder into the Stormont inside a sofa? There are whispers of assassination attempts from within the prison walls. A 440-pound bomb was defused in Armagh. Someone threw a Molotov cocktail into the grounds of a Catholic kindergarten. The Women's Coalition has called for calm and decency. The light in David Trimble's office was on until four thirty in the morning. Someone should make sure that the Sands graffiti in Ballycloghan is scrubbed off. The one thing that should be working flawlessly are the photocopy machines. Make sure the word *draft* is stamped clearly across every page. Was there absolute clarification yet on the North-South ministerial council?

Everyone jumping off their own ledges, sailing out into the middle of the air, developing patterns of flight on the way down.

LATER IN THE morning, alone in his back office, he turns the desk lamp on. A small tilted urn of light. His desk has been cleaned. His photos dusted. The pile of papers stacked high. The red light on his private message machine blinks. He skips through the messages: seven in all. The second to last from Heather. She must have called in the middle of the night. *Listen*, she says. The sound of his son sleeping. *Listen*. The small intake of Andrew's breath. He plays it twice and then a third time.

Sixty-one children.

He flicks the buttons open on his sleeves, rolls the cuffs back, phones downstairs to see if they'd bring him another pot of tea.

ONE SUMMER IN Acadia he learned chess. Move after move. Swap. Remain. Stay. The incredible switch of the king and the castle amazed him. You had to touch the king first and then bring the castle across.

He was fascinated by the edge of the board. There was a saying: *The knight on the rim is grim.*

He learned to keep the knight over at the edge, safe until, late in the game, he could come inside and there was a whole board with eight sudden squares.

FOR THREE DAYS he and his staff stay in the Europa. In downtown Belfast. The Hardboard Hotel, they call it. The Piece Palace. Bits of it blown up twenty-seven times over the past few years. The most-bombed hotel in Europe. It is still, for some reason, the hotel of choice for the journalists, most of whom he knows on a first-name basis. They hang out in the piano bar, all times of the day. He has seen them often, the first drink placed down in front of them, practising their posture, their casual disregard, their unreadability. They sit at the back as if the act of drinking has been forced upon them. Its obligation. And then all of a sudden the first drink is gone, and they are half a dozen towards obliteration. Stories of Sarajevo, no doubt. Srebrenica. Kosovo. As if Northern Ireland is a slight melancholy demotion. The very idea of a peace process is sentimental to many of them. A mysterious part of them needs an epic failure. They are out most nights, looking for the burning barrels and the kneecapped girls. Or else they are looking for a leak, some shred of scandal, some sexual sectarianism. When he enters the lobby, they try to cadge a quote. He understands it, the base desire at the core of a story. To put their own version of events into the world. It is the tabloids that he avoids the most: the *Sun,* the *Mirror,* the *News of the World.* He is careful whom he is seen stepping into the lift with, just in case they take a candid shot of him.

They see him as a man who had stepped out from another century, polite, reserved, judicial, an ancient American, yet it is also a form of disguise: underneath they intuit that he is cast for the very end of the twentieth century, biding his time, waiting for his moment. No one has ever quite fully figured him out, if he is driven by the fear of evil, or spurred on by the prospect of what is good, or if he lies in the complicated in-between. Mystery. Silence. Sleep.

Upstairs, the suite is small and dark. The bed narrow. The bedcovers shiny with use. But there is at least a bowl of fruit on the table and flowers on the credenza. Easter lilies: a gentle nudge.

Bags on the floor. Jacket. Shirt. Belt. Trousers. No Heather to tidy him up. He lies down, exhausted, the day's work still trilling in him. He feels bad for the two security men who have to guard his door. He would like to invite them in, have them put their feet up, pour a soda from the minibar. They are good men, one and all, but what a job, to stand outside a door all night with only the silence of a man who has learned to sleep anywhere, anytime.

Hotel rooms sharpen his loneliness. The hum of others who were here before.

One of his aides once dropped a contact lens on the floor near the window in the downstairs dining room. She got to her knees and searched around by the baseboards. Bits of dust, stray edges of the carpet. She found the contact lens clinging to a piece of wallpaper. But when she fingered the lens, she noticed, for the first time, that the slice of wallpaper was newer than the surroundings. A perfect square, but the paper had been badly applied. A bit of the wallpaper had begun to peel. She noticed a scorch mark beneath, the blackness faded to red. Most likely a petrol bomb thrown years ago. The old hieroglyphics of violence.

He has heard that the women of Belfast used to keep wet blankets by the door, just in case.

He pulls back his own blanket, prepares himself for bed. He has a mobile wardrobe that accompanies him from place to place, a set of lurking ghost clothes. He finds the pyjamas, gruffs his way into them. It's easy then to fall asleep, if even just for a few hours.

HUME. TRIMBLE. ADAMS. Mowlam. Mallon. McMichael. Cooney. Hill. Donoghue. McWilliams. Sager. One by one they visit his office. The air of worried men and women. Everyone with something to lose. This – he has discovered – is part of their generosity. The ability to embrace failure. The cost of what they might leave behind.

They are at ease with him now. They know his ways. He does not like to sit behind his desk anymore. He has broken that territory. He comes out, instead, and sits by the small table that he has set up near the window with four wooden chairs.

With each visitor there is a new set of biscuits and a warm teapot. He pours the tea himself. One of his small gestures. He is not sure if it's a trick or not, but he likes the ritual. The trays are stacked upon his desk. That, too, is part of his routine. He does not want the meetings disturbed. Showmanship or decency: he is not sure which.

He brings the trays downstairs to the canteen where the ladies in the hairnets hurry out to meet him, all fuss and apology.

– What about ye, Senator?

– Leave those trays be, Senator.

– Ach, don't be doing that. What're ye like?

– If ye weren't married, I'd kiss ye.

– Ye wouldn't come home and clean *my* kitchen, would y'now, Senator? That'd be some peace process, let me tell ye.

If the canteen is empty he will take a seat in the corner to watch them a moment. He likes their singsong, their bustle. They remind him of the ladies of Maine. The waitresses in the diners. The women in the tollbooths, leaning out their fume-darkened windows.

One of the tea-ladies, Claire Curtain, has a scar on the left side of her forehead in the exact shape of a horseshoe. One afternoon she caught him looking at it, and she blithely told him that it was a result of a bombing – she was on her way to a concert in a bandstand, there was a horse regiment standing nearby, the blast went off, she was walking by along a tree-lined avenue, and she was hit in the head, left with an almost perfect shoe mark on her forehead, and what she remembered most of all was waking, concussed, confused by the sight of horse hooves dangling in the trees.

THE CORRIDORS BUZZ. A faint chanting coming from the crowds outside. The nervous whirl of helicopters overhead. He climbs the rear stairs towards his office, a packet of McVitie's Digestives tucked under the flap of his suit jacket.

He was driven last summer, by Gerald, out to a farmhouse on the Plantation Road in Derry. He had been at a conference in Coleraine and it was still early: he was not expected back in Belfast until midnight.

He thought at first that he might get Gerald to drive to the sea and take the coast road up around the headlands, but they swung south instead, out into a tangle of backcountry where Gerald had grown up.

Chestnut trees arced the roads. Sheep and cattle paraded in the fields. The light lengthened, stretched the shadows of the hedges and trees. It reminded him of lower Maine: that lush, rained-upon feel.

They drove along a length of carefully planted forest. Gerald pointed out his old school, the fields, the boxing club. It was nine or ten in the evening, but the sky was still bright, birds out over the haystacks.

– You ever been this way, Senator?

He shook his head, no. They crested a small hill and Gerald pulled the car in towards a blue gate. Down below, in the half valley, there were wide brown steppingstones across a river. Enormous oak trees bent to the water. A series of hedgerows slumped towards a distant farmhouse. Rough tractor tracks ran along the riverbank.

Gerald stepped out of the car and leant against the gate, his chin cupped in his hands. A summertime smoke drifted across the air: a wood fire, an odd thing on such a warm evening.

— I lived over yonder when I was a child, Gerald said.

He pointed to the small farmhouse tucked into the grove of high oak trees.

— My sister's there now.

He knew what Gerald was asking. No harm, the Senator thought. It was late in the evening, but he could allow an hour to slip away.

— You should give her a call, Gerald.

— Ach. She's there with her wee uns. Sure, she'd have a heart attack.

The driver shifted in the silence, as if waiting for another response. Nothing more was said. The light fell slowly across the fields. The Senator reached for the blue gate. When he pushed the bar, the gate groaned and returned. The hasp was rusty. A few blue flakes fell down into the grass.

— Just stretching my legs, he said.

It was odd how uneven the field was: from the gate it had looked perfectly flat and smooth. Clods of earth. Old mounds of manure. Tough, thorny weeds. He stepped towards the enormous stillness of the trees. His good shoes squelched underneath him.

Gerald called from behind him and then he heard the dull closing of a car door, the quiet hum of an engine. He glanced back to see the car crawling along, the roof just visible over the hedgerow.

The car beeped again. He raised his hands in salute, but kept walking through the field. His shadow slanted in the evening light. The northern sky took on colours now, in the distance, the aurora borealis.

Reds, greens, purples. He could feel the hem of his trousers against the grass. Small splashes of mud rising up on the back of his heels.

At the river he thought for a moment that he would just turn around and go back the way he came. A loud beeping. No car. He was out of sight. He unloosened his tie. The steppingstones were slick. He peered down into the water. The evening sun fashioned wheels of light on the surface. He thought he saw the dart of minnows. He held on to a tree branch and hunched a little to prepare for the fall, but landed safely on the middle riverstone.

Leaves stirred about him. Odour of moss and reeds and trout. It thrilled him to think there were still moments like this. He looked up through the enormous trees. A ray of sky. He grabbed the long grasses on the far side of the riverbank, pulled himself up. His foot trailed behind him and splashed in the water. A cold swell around his ankle. He ran up the steep bank. The back of his shoe chafed against his heel. In the distance, again, a loud beeping.

Fifty yards from the farmhouse, he saw her in the rear courtyard. At the washing line. Amid grey stonework and a couple of abandoned cars. She was young and aproned. Her hair was stretched into a dark bun at the base of her neck. The washing line ran for thirty yards along the courtyard. White rope between two tall poles. A large straw basket of laundry lodged in against her hip. She was taking giant white bed sheets from the line. Gerald's sister.

She walked along the length of the clothesline and unclipped the wooden pegs one by one, then put them in her hair.

The sun appeared large on the western horizon now: the bed sheets were magenta.

He heard the house phone ring from a distance: it carried through the air. Gerald's sister stooped and put the laundry basket on the cobbles. She walked wearily towards the house. She seemed to sigh into the doorway. The ringing stopped.

Moments later he heard a shriek from the house and saw her emerge in a rush of hair and apron and clothes pegs. She ran towards the washing line, and yanked the last of the sheets, looked wildly about.

Gerald's car was pulling along the laneway, beeping. The Senator stepped out from among the trees. Gerald had rolled down his window and was grinning now.

— Meet the Senator, he said.

— Ach, sure, look at his shoes, she said. What've ya done to the poor man?

— My fault entirely, said the Senator.

— I'm Sheila.

— Pleasure to meet you.

— He let you walk through the field?

— Not exactly.

— He's never had any sense, our Gerry.

She took him by the elbow and guided him towards the house. He cleaned his shoes carefully on the dark mat, then stepped through the scullery and along a tiled corridor in his stockinged feet. A warmth rolled from the large red stove. A smell of recent cooking. Simple crockery on shelves on the wall. In the front room, three quiet children gathered around a television set. A game show. They wore their pyjamas. Sheila called out to them. Her voice was high and sharp. The children snapped the television off and stood up to attention, reached out to shake his hand. Freckled. Towheaded. He got down on one knee in front of them and knuckled their shoulders.

He asked their names: Cathal, Anthony, Orla. A sharp absence flooded through him: he showed them a picture of Andrew but they couldn't comprehend it; they glanced at the picture, said nothing.

He was guided to the kitchen table and he could hear the high whistle of the kettle already going. Gerald sat across the table from him, his hands folded, his face in a generous grin.

Moths crossed the mouth of a lamp on the far side of the room. The wallpaper was patterned with flowers. On the sideboard sat a row of photographs. In several of the photos there was a young man, long-haired, handsome. He seemed to disappear from the photographs: the man reached a certain age and then was gone. A sudden worry flooded the Senator: perhaps Gerald's brother-in-law was involved with the Troubles somehow? Maybe there had been a murder. Perhaps a conviction somewhere. A shooting. An internment. He felt a rod of fear stiffen his shoulders. Perhaps he had done the wrong thing entirely, walking through this field, entering this farmhouse, taking off his shoes. Perhaps others would claim he had an allegiance. He wasn't sure now how he could possibly extricate himself. All his time here, a series of careful choices. How simple it was to put a foot wrong.

A set of headlights swept across the ceiling. The darkness had fallen so very quickly. Cars on the outside road. Maybe they had been followed. Someone taking photographs perhaps. There was a gap in the curtains, for sure. He turned his body sideways to the window. He put his hand up to his face. Another sweep of headlights went through the room. He cursed himself, knotted his hands tight.

He saw Gerald's sister step out from the kitchen towards him. Her figure was small, slim, lithe. Her face clarified when she stepped beyond the doorway. Something hard about her eyes. He was surprised by a body odour that rolled from her. Sheila ran her hands along the sideboard. Then she stopped a moment and touched one of the photo frames.

– We lost him about six years ago now, she said.

– Excuse me?

– My husband.

– I'm sorry.

– The North Sea, she said.

Sheila flicked a quick look at the children who were gathered on the carpet near the bay window.

— He was working in the oil fields.

She lowered her voice again.

— We don't talk about it much in front of the wee uns, she said.

He felt a surge move through him. A gust of thanks. Sheila had intuited his brief terror. He wanted to grasp her hand. The happiness of being wrong. The affirmation of it. But what could he say? He had assumed the worst. Ireland. Always the worst.

He flicked another look out the window.

— Do you mind if we close the curtains, Gerald?

He wanted to sag back in the chair and relax. Amid the teacups and the crockery. He could be cynical tomorrow: always time for that.

He brought the cup to his lips. Already a small skin of cold had formed on the surface of the tea. He glanced at the mantelpiece clock. It was almost ten thirty. Sheila put the kettle on again. The Senator stretched his legs out in front of him. He heard the children moving about on the carpet, whispering amongst themselves. There was something funny at hand, it seemed. Their famous visitor. His American accent? His bearing? The way he dunked his biscuits in his tea perhaps? They were giggling now and he saw a sternness move across Sheila's face. She glared at her children. They fell quiet. A small curtain seemed to cross her eyes, too.

She cut another slice of fruitcake. Gerald plugged in the electric fire. He had yet another story to tell. The Senator glanced at the clock on the mantelpiece. At eleven in the evening he stood to say goodbye. Again the children giggled.

He reached across to shake hands, but instead she pulled him towards herself in the manner of someone familiar. He thought she was going to kiss him on the cheek.

— You want me to darn that? Sheila asked quietly in his ear.

— Excuse me?

Another whisper.

– Ye'll not be taking your shoes off in Stormont, now, will ye?

He glanced down to see the hole in the heel of his right sock. She was laughing now, her face tilted up at him.

– It'll only take me a wee minute, she said.

Later that night on the phone to Heather all he could hear was the laughter down the wire from his wife, and three days later, in an express package that had to be opened and examined by the secret service, five new pairs of plain grey socks, none for Saturdays or Sundays, simply because she wanted him home.

HE SHIFTS HOTELS on the fifth night. There have been rumours and bomb scares. Another strong hint at an assassination attempt. In the morning, he packs his pyjamas, his toothbrush, his extra clothes, and in the evening the security team move him across to the Hilton at the waterfront. From there he will go to his favourite, the Culloden.

Little matter. All his time is in the Stormont offices now. Those dark corridors.

On the phone he talks to Blair and Ahern. President Clinton, too. A letter of best wishes arrives from Nelson Mandela. A handwritten note from Václav Havel. Late in the evening, he and Holkeri pace the halls. Light leaks from under doors. Whispers in the back shadows. Waiting for new drafts of sentences, paragraphs, whole documents to come their way. He is reminded of salmon moving the wrong way up against the water. The Kennebec. Its intricacies. The swift curl at the mill. Patches of light in the eddies, standing waves.

WHEN THE DIPLOMATIC pouch arrives from London on Sunday night – two days late – his heart falls through his chest. Strand Two. From Ahern and Blair. He knows the very moment he reads it that it will not work. He gathers with de Chastelain and Holkeri and their staff. A chill coming in on the weather. There is a Frost poem from school days. *Whose woods these are I think I know.* He hears it again, distantly, brokenly. *Miles to go before I sleep.* There are times he wishes he could knock an absolute simplicity into the process. Take it or leave it.

He has read whole volumes on the philosophy of nonviolence. How peace had to be understood in all its moral dimensions. The proper coexistence of all existents. The excluded middle ground. The surpassing of personality. The vanity of cultural superiority. The tension between individual conscience and collective responsi- bility. The need to proclaim again and again what has already been said.

Later, at the press conference, he holds up his hands in a gesture of calm. He has practised this. There is an art to it: keep the hands open enough not to frame the face, spread the fingers wide in a gesture of appeasement. The ability to deflect a question without swatting it away. He allows a long silence before answering. Speaks evenly, calmly. Moves his gaze around the room. Slowly. Judicially. He tries not to adjust his glasses on his nose – too much a gesture of fabrication. He already knows he will absorb the blame. It is his delay, his fault, his carelessness. No matter. They must go on.

He thanks the prime ministers and government officials. They deserve a lot of praise. Tremendous effort. Energy. Concentration. Ardour. Grace. We urge everyone to proceed. Common sense dictates. Discussions are ongoing. Can you rephrase your question? That assertion, sir, is incorrect.

Flashbulbs pop. A mobile phone rings. A frisson of nervous laughter skitters around the room. He keeps his answers vague. Tiptoes around the truth. He is careful not to let the politeness reel off into anger. His job is to tamp the confusion down. Return again to the moment of simplicity. Reiterate what they came for. The people of Northern Ireland have waited long enough.

What they need are the signatures. After that, they will negotiate the peace. Years of wrangling still to come, he knows. No magic wand. All he wants is to get the metal nibs striking against the page. But really what he would like now, more than anything, is to walk out from the press conference into the sunlight, a morning and evening jammed together, so that there is rise and fall at the same time, east and west. It strikes him at moments like this that he is a man of crossword puzzles, pyjamas, slippers. All he really wants is to get on a plane to New York, enter the lobby of the apartment on Sixty-Seventh Street, step into his own second chance, that proper silence of fatherhood.

HE WRITES HEATHER an email to say that he will be home soon. Easter Saturday at the latest. He is careful with the note, in case it is intercepted. No flourishes. No professions of love. He clicks *Send*, and then goes for a walk in Lady Dixon Park in the middle of the night, amongst the roses, rolling a pebble along at his feet, his security detail behind him, matching him step for step.

It is a photo that's used in the newspapers a few days later. For the Easter editions. The Senator rolling a stone with his foot. In the gloom. Away from a cave of light. On Good Friday itself.

Nothing, in Northern Ireland – not even the obvious – ever escapes attention.

IT IS AS if, in a myth, he has visited an empty grain silo. In the beginning he stood at the bottom in the resounding dark. Several figures gathered at the very top of the silo. They peered down, shaded their eyes, began to drop their pieces of grain upon him: words. A small rain at first. Full of vanity and history and rancour. Clattering in the emptiness. He stood and let it sound metallic around him, until it began to pour, and the grain took on a different sound, and he had to reach up and keep knocking the words aside just to get a little space to breathe. Dust and chaff in the air all around him. From their very own fields. They were pouring down their winnowed bitterness, and in his silence he just kept thrashing, spluttering, pushing the words away. A refusal to drown. What nobody noticed, not even himself, was that the grain kept rising, and the silo filled, but he kept rising with it, and the sounds grew different, word upon word, falling around him, building beneath him. And now – at the top of the silo – he has clawed himself up and dusted himself off and he stands there equal with the pourers who are astounded by the language that lies below them. They glance at each other. Three ways down from the silo. They can fall into the grain and drown, they can jump off the edge and abandon it, or they can learn to sow it very slowly at their feet.

A RUMOUR OF morning hangs faint on the sky. He wears his thick grey overcoat, his scarf, a plain wool hat. He does not wear a flat one for fear he will appear partisan. The confounded demands of peace. He drives towards Stormont, taps Gerald on the shoulder just as they pull in.

– You sure, Senator?

He sees security men scurry into position the moment he gets out. The cold stings his cheeks. The dawn holds the prospect of rain. He leaves the car door slightly open, just in case. The men and women are ranged around barrels, warming their hands. They raise their heads at the sight of him. They have gathered so many candles, burning all night. Against the wall, rows and rows of flowers. How is it possible to speak of the dead? He has imagined the troubles of these people. A sort of ghosthood. How many nights have they sat outside these gates, waiting? Shopkeepers. Plumbers. Musicians. Butchers. Tinsmiths. Professors. Their blights and difficulties. He is at home amongst them. A teenage girl with a shine of sadness in her eye. A man pulling down the shabby hood of his coat to speak. Aye, Senator. What about ye? Frosty enough for ye, hai? Reporters jostling their way through the crowd. A Muslim woman in a headscarf: even she with an Irish desire. A longing spreading through the raw cold. Murmurs moving amongst them.

At the edge of the crowd, he stops. He is not quite sure if it is she or not. Her face in the distance. He peeks over a row of shoulders. The movement of the crowd. The sway. At the edge of the barricades. In a wheelchair. Wrapped in a couple of blankets. He gently parts the crowd and moves towards her.

— Morning.

— Hello, Senator.

Her name, briefly, escapes him. From Stranmillis. Lost her grandson.

— No tennis today?

— Thought I'd come for the final set.

— Oh, well, we hope it's that, he says.

— Game and set, anyway, Senator.

— So far.

— Make it happen for us, she says, and she pauses a moment: Please.

He nods. The tartan blanket pulled up to her neck. Ninety years old at least. How can she possibly be out in such weather? It strikes him how easy it is to say yes, yes, he will make it work, he will do everything in his power to make it work. But it is out of his hands now. It does not belong to him: it is the property of others.

— Thanks for coming out, Lottie.

— Good luck, Senator.

— Thank you.

– Senator. My daughter. Hannah. Have you met her?

– Yes, of course.

A younger version of Lottie, really. Late fifties or sixties. An energy to her, a flair.

– We can't thank you enough, Senator, says Lottie.

– It's nothing, he says.

– Oh, it's something, it surely is.

Lottie turns in her chair, pulls off her glove and extends her hand towards him and says: You don't know what this means, Senator.

– I'll do what I can.

He is guided back towards the car and for some odd reason – he is not sure why – he slides into the front seat beside Gerald and he puts his hand on the dashboard as if this is a border to cross, a place he will not come back from. The car eases through the gates and the barrier is pulled down behind him. *You don't know what this means*. Perhaps she is correct – he has spent all this time not truly knowing what it means. Now, it means everything. He will see this through now. To the bitter end. He will not back down. He hears another shouting behind him, a chant and the bash of a lambeg drum.

He is dropped off in front of the building. He tells Gerald to go home and get some rest, but he knows full well that his driver will remain in the car park, the seat of the car extended backwards, the radio clicked on, steam from the heat gathering on the windscreen, turning and squirming in the small space.

Up the steps he goes, into the drab office block. A heaviness in the corridors. He walks along, shaking hands, touching shoulders. He knows every single one of their names. They are polite, deferent – scared, too. If they are to own it, they are also the ones to lose it. A valuable thing. Once in a thousand years. Peace.

He takes the stairs to the third floor. The stairwells reek of cigarette smoke. In his office he cracks open his window.

News comes later in the morning. A murder in Derry. A member of the paramilitaries. The statements are out. The press releases. The men of violence. Pointless retaliation. Trevor Deeney. Sitting in a car beside his wife. Shot point-blank. For what reason? Is there ever a reason? There will be retaliation. Already promised. This murder, too, is retaliation. Murder the murderers. Deeney's brother opened fire in a bar called The Rising Sun. No end to the ironies. He leans his forehead against the desk. Strapped to a wheel, we shall not break.

Si vis pacem.

He reaches for the phone. We cannot let this happen, he says. We must make a sharp statement. Draw a line. Show no fear.

Para bellum.

He walks from office to office. Works on the press release. They are all in agreement: nothing will derail us now. We have come too far. Enough is enough. No surrender. We own that dictum now. It is ours. No. Surrender.

Later the news reaches him that Bertie Ahern's mother, in Dublin, has died. Still, the Taoiseach will arrive by helicopter later tomorrow. Blair, too, will arrive with his convoy. The power brokers. The figure-heads. The men who have inherited it. All of them will be in one place. In the one building. Primed. There is talk of a thousand journalists now, too. A thousand. It stuns him. From all corners of the globe. He must co-ordinate it now, this endgame. No matter what. He sits at his desk, uncaps his fountain pen. *There can be no discussion of a pause or break. I intend to tell the parties that I won't even consider such a request. There's not going to be a break, not for a week, not for a day, not for an hour. We'll either get an agreement or we'll fail to get an agreement.*

He cracks the window further. A sea-wind. All those ships out there. All those generations that left. Seven hundred years of history. We prefigure our futures by imagining our pasts. To go back and forth. Across the waters. The past, the present, the elusive future. A nation. Everything constantly shifted by the present. The taut elastic of time. Even violence breaks. Even that. Sometimes violently. You don't know what this means, Senator.

For the next two days he will hardly sleep, hardly eat. No hotels even. He refuses to leave the office. He will sleep at his desk. He will wash at the hand basin in the small bathroom. Run the water. Tap the soap dispenser. Wash his hands thoroughly, methodically. Splash water on the back of his neck. Walk back along the corridor. Meet with Hume and Trimble. Listen carefully to their every word. Good men, both. The linchpins of the process. And he will spend hours on the phone with Clinton. Examining the very minutiae of the process. The dream of it all. The parade of footsteps along the corridor. Draft and redraft. He will beg the civil servants not to leak the documents. He will stand at the photocopy machine himself. Just to guard the memos. He will even number the copies. Walk up and down the stairs. From the canteen to his office, and back. Visitor after visitor. Party leaders. Representatives. Diplomats. Civil servants. He will feel as if he has had the same conversation a dozen times, two dozen. He will catch himself in midtalk, wondering if he has said this same thing just seconds before. A flush of blood to his cheeks. An embarrassment. Searching for new ways to say the exact same thing. He will listen for a riot, another murder, a bomb blast. On the radio. The television. At the gates even. None will come. Just the constant knocking on his door. Trays of sandwiches. Pots of tea. He will hear the sirens roar out the window. The cheers and the booing. The letters slipped in under the door. The whispered moan of prayers. The uneaten trays of food. Claire Curtain. Lottie Tuttle. Sheila Whelan. All the bits and pieces of his days. His desire for sleep nearly as powerful as his desire for peace. He should call her. Has he called her? Her voice. His breath. Andrew. Sleep.

THE CANTEEN WORKERS finish at ten in the evening, but then his own staff trundle downstairs to light the stove, boil the water, stir the leaves. He will lift and pour, lift and pour. This whole memory, it will taste of tea.

THERE IS A swerve to Blair. The neat suit, the tie. A dishevellment to Ahern. A busy grief. Both of them sweeping in, taking over their offices. Second floor. Third floor. Meeting after meeting. Phone call after phone call. Blair says to him that he feels as if he is entering a caisson. The pressure slowly building. Beginning to swell. A common feeling, that, but what is the word for it? There is, surely, a word for it, a phrase. The Senator cannot recall. So tired now. The ache in his shoulders. Searching for the word, but he cannot find it.

FOUR IN THE morning. Blair's office. The desk neat and meticulous. A pen balanced on the rim of a coffee cup. The Prime Minister's shirt open to the second button. They are stuck now on a point of language. The British and their words. The Irish and their endless meanings. How did such a small sea ever come between them?

He watches Blair run his hands through his hair. Strange, that. The Prime Minister's hair is wet. And the cheeks are glistening. Somehow freshly shaved? Did he manage a shower? Where, then, and how? Surely there is no shower in the building? There cannot be. All these months he has been here, the Senator has never seen one, nor heard of one. No need, back then, with hotel rooms. But a shower? He craves one now. Just the idea. The pourdown. The cleansing. He should ask straight out, but, then again, there is the matter of decorum. Etiquette.

Impolite, probably, to tread upon the personal with the Prime Minister? Focus now. Focus. The issue is prisoners. And remand. And language. Eight hundred years of history. How is it now that they can manipulate the words? What is the right way to force the Unionist hand? Will Adams play along? Can Ahern have a word in McGuinness's ear? What last words? Where is Hume? There is a leak of light, still, from under Trimble's door. The intrusion of the ordinary. Tired. So very tired. He still cannot shake the idea that Blair's hair is wet.

He leaves Blair's office at five forty-five, and at six in the morning, he sends his staff searching. They arrive back, triumphant. There is indeed a shower. Unknown to them all this time. On the third floor. The only one in the building. Incredible, really. A closet hardly big enough to step inside. The Senator goes upstairs, undresses, steps in, leans his head against the tile. Slick and grimy. He doesn't care. The water pounds down upon his shoulders. Warm and hard against his face. A caisson indeed. *The bends.* That's it. That's the phrase he was looking for. The bends.

He dries himself off with his shirt and walks out into the corridor, a little bounce in his step, his socks wet from where he has padded on the floor.

EARLY ON GOOD Friday afternoon Gerald hands him an envelope. He unfolds the sheet of paper. Sits back in his chair. He had forgotten altogether. Well, there you have it. The Sox. Bottom of the ninth.

He hears a cheer from downstairs, an applause along the corridor, as if the whole country has heard the news.

A FEW TAPS on the pane make him turn. It is lightly raining outside. Falling diagonally against the glass, catching a moment, as if surprised to be stopped. Rolling downwards. Accumulating and dropping farther. He crosses the room and leans across to lift the latch, opens the window wide. Damp air enters the office. Sounds from the street. A beeping of car horns. A cheer from the front gates. A distant sound of traffic and then a silence. He would like to hold this moment, suspend it, to surround himself with only this, to be bounded by it. He leans his hands against the frame. The small touch of rain against his wrist.

The Senator hears the ringing of the telephone and a gentle knocking on the door, slowly more insistent.

The cheers along the corridor growing louder.

He leans his palms against the window. Perhaps to contemplate such happiness is to diminish it. Sixty-one children. He knows, now, that there will be an ordinariness to that he will return to, other days of tedium and loss, and the Troubles will most likely crash into him from behind, when he least expects it, but for now, for the very briefest moment, this suspended instance, the impossible has happened.

The Senator touches his head against the cool of the glass.

— Come in, he says.

HE LEAVES FOR the airport at dawn on Easter Sunday morning. A bright day. As if it were designed for this somehow. He emerges from the Culloden Hotel, down the stone steps, towards the car. The tiredness in his eyes, his jaw, his shoulders. His whole body belonging elsewhere.

A helicopter hovers on the skyline. The distant trees sway. Fragments of white cloud slide on a layered blue sky.

A couple of journalists wait for him in the driveway of the hotel. *The Irish Times. The Independent. Die Zeit. Le Figaro.* They are already calling it the Good Friday Accords. He wanders over. Hands in his pockets. Still wearing his blue suit, but his shirt open, the small vee of sunburn at his neck, the rest a paleness. He has only ten minutes. He knows their trade: they will want to talk to him one on one. Fintan. Dirk. Lara. Dominique. Always their first names. He walks along the gravel, side by side. The grey dust scuffing his shoes. He is astounded by the calm of his answers. Yes, we must maintain a sense of composure. The real work is only just beginning. I am quietly optimistic. Hopeful in fact. We sensed all along that something could be achieved. We turn it over now to the people of the North and South. The true nature of a democracy is its ability to say yes when even the powerful say no. There were times when I thought we were teetering on the edge.

He would like for a moment to tell one of the journalists that there was a giddiness in the hallways of Stormont, that he could hear the champagne corks being popped downstairs in the canteen, that he leaned his head against the shower stall and wept with joy. Still, there is decorum to maintain. A need for parsimony. A careful tread. We have all been caught out before.

The true verdict, he says, will belong to history. The ordinary people own it now. We could not have found peace unless the desire for it was already here. Nothing could have been achieved unless it was, first, wanted. The collaboration was across the board. No, it doesn't take courage to shoot a policeman in the back of the head. What takes courage is to compete in the arena of democracy. But let's not pretend it's finished. Yet let's not pretend that it has only just begun either. It was not an expectation, no. It was a conviction. Generations of mothers will understand this. I do not find it sentimental at all, no, never, not that. Cynicism is easy. An optimist is a braver cynic.

A catch in his voice now. Think about it, he says. It's simple enough. We're forced to change because we're forced to remember. And we're forced to remember when we're forced to confront. Sixty-one children.

He watches the hovering helicopter. It dips sideways an instant, disappears behind the angle of the treetops. He feels a dull thump in his chest, but the sound of the rotors dwindles and the helicopter turns and fades off.

The journalists thank him. Shake his hand. He makes his way across to Gerald who leans against the car, grinning ever so slightly. The driver has a sheet in his hand. The Senator takes it, tucks it away. He will leave it for the plane.

The car rattles out onto the road. The blur of green hedges. The distant warehouses. The rooflines. The flags. The skirling flutes, the bright sashes, the echo of the lambeg drums. Enough now. The crossed armalite, the morose songs, the black berets. Gone, all gone. Whosoever brought me here is going to have to take me home.

It will be morning now in New York. He will fly to London, then home. He will get there by noon. First off the plane. He will leave, for a moment, all decorum behind. He will emerge through customs to see her there, leaning forwards, over the barrier, waiting. Dark hair with a ray of grey. Sunglasses on her head. The most eloquent of welcomes. He will take Andrew in his arms. Lean down towards him. Fasten both of them in an embrace.

Or he will call ahead and talk to her and have her waiting downstairs. In the marbled lobby. Her hands against the glass. With his son in the papoose against her chest. The quick kick of her heel backwards in the air. Like women from other wars. She will spin out through the revolving doors, four quarters, provinces of desire.

Or he will surprise her entirely. Arrive without a word. Make his way through the airport, walk quickly along the corridor, out the door into the brief light, Ramon waiting by the overhang in his flat cap. The highways. The bridges. The green signs. The crush of yellow traffic. Through the arc of the tollbooth. Over the bridge. Ramon will dip down through Harlem, speed west, swing south along Broadway. The families out walking in the hard yellow sunshine. Young women with dogs. Children in baseball caps. Near Lincoln Center, they will slow down, ease across the lanes. Ramon will pull sharply into the curved driveway. The Senator will leave the briefcase in the back of the car. No reporters please. No cameras. No notebooks. He will push open the revolving door. A series of nods and smiles. Ask the doormen not to call up. No warning. He will want to surprise her. At least for an instant. He will hope that she doesn't hear the elevator bell. He will softly key open the door and ghost through the room, across the carpet, into the bedroom, catch them sleeping, a noontime nap. He will pause a moment, watching. Her hair askew. Her body long and slim and quiet against the sheets. The baby against her. Slip off his shoes, his suit jacket, his sweater. Lift the bed sheet. Easter Sunday. Crawl into bed beside them. The cool of the pillow. The sheer slice of sunlight through the room. Waken them to laughter. The pinch of his skin. Hers. The slow curve of her hip.

A walk, then, to Sheep Meadow. The grass cool to the touch. The skyscrapers grey and huge against the trees. To be allowed to feel small again. To embrace that insignificance. The sun over the west side of Manhattan. Falling. The dark rolled backwards.

The car drives on. Beyond Belfast now, into the countryside. The light on the slant of the fields. Fenced here, unbounded there.

There is always room for at least two truths.

Book Two

But this is not the story of a life.
It is the story of lives, knit together,
overlapping in succession, rising
again from grave after grave.

— WENDELL BERRY, FROM 'RISING'

1863–89

i c e h o u s e

SHE STOOD AT THE WINDOW. IT WAS HER ONE HUNDRED AND twenty-eighth day of watching men die. They came down the road in wagons pulled by horses. She had never seen such a bath of killing before. Even the horses seemed incredulous. Kicking up dust behind them. Their eyes huge and sad. The wheels screeched. The line of wagons stretched down the path, into the trees. The trees themselves stretched off into the war.

She came down the stairs, through the open doors, into the wide heat. The wagons were already backed up on the road. A curious quiet. The men had exhausted their shouts. They were left with small whimperings, tiny gasps of pain. The ones sitting appeared to be asleep. The ones lying were packed so close together, breathing in unison, that they appeared as one mass. A contortion of blood and limbs. Rotting leather breeches. Stinking flannel shirts. Flesh ripped open: cheeks, arms, eye sockets, testicles, chests. The beds of their wagons were black with blood. It had fallen on the wheels, too, so that their lives seemed to circle and turn beneath them.

One soldier wore sergeant's stripes on his sleeve, and a gold harp stitched on his lapel. An Irishman. She had tended to so many of them. He was wounded in the neck. It was covered with a filthy gauze. His face was various shades of dark from the blown-back powder. His teeth were blackened from biting cartridges. He moaned and his head lolled sideways. She swiped the wound as clean as she could get it. His windpipe made a sad low noise. He would be dead within minutes, she knew. Small black strips of shadow moved over him. She looked up. Vultures flew overhead. They did not strike a wingbeat. Soaring on the thermals. Waiting. She had a brief thought that she should smother the injured man.

She touched his eyes. She could feel his life fall shut beneath her fingers. No need to stop his breath. It was much like drawing a small red curtain across. So many of them waited until they were in a woman's hands.

SHE WAS TAPPED on the elbow. The doctor was small and rotund. They would have to lift the men from the wagon, he said, get them onto the grass. He wore a bow tie splattered with blood. A rubber apron over his tunic. There were twelve other nurses working the wagons: four women.

They lifted the soldiers as gently as they could and placed them in the grass in the imprints of others who had been there just hours ago. All around, the grass was exhausted by the shape of the war.

The doctors paced along the length of the dying. They chose which ones they might possibly save. The soldiers groaned and stretched out their arms. She wanted immediately to wash them clean. The other nurses had lined up wooden pails of water, with sponges at their heads. She thrust a towel down into a bucket.

Lily herself had crossed more water than she cared to remember. She had often thought that she could use all the wide Atlantic to wash them.

THEY CARRIED THE living inside on stretchers. Slippery with blood. The injured sat, vacant, in their beds. The hospital had been a glass factory once. Some of the men had rescued pieces of glass and ranged them around their beds. Intricate vases, coloured tumblers. There had been a small amount of stained glass made for the churches of Missouri, but most of it had been taken away and sold.

Occasionally a loud shattering went through the hospital when a soldier stumbled out of bed, or lost his mind, or thrashed his way out from the sheets, or knocked over his bedside table. In the basement below, large glass sheets were still kept. There had been dozens of mirrors, too, but they had been hidden away so the men couldn't see what had become of them.

LILY HAD LEFT St Louis in the same week as her son. To be near his regiment. He was seventeen years old. A head of chestnut-coloured hair. A shy boy once, he had left, swollen with the prospect of war.

She had walked for days, found the hospital among a series of small buildings not far from the battlefields. At first she was given the laundry room to work in. They had set up a little makeshift hut out back. The hut was a collection of logs with a sloping tarpaulin roof. Under the snapping tarp sat a row of six wooden barrels, four to be filled with hot water, two with cold. She wore long gloves and thick boots. Mud splashed up on the back of her dress. Her hem was dark and thick with blood. She washed bed sheets, towels, bandages, medical uniforms, torn blouses, forage caps. She stirred the clothes around a wooden drum. Another barrel rolled two drums together to squeeze the dirt from the fibres. The handle circled endlessly. Her hands blistered.

When the water was finished, she sprinkled lime in the barrels. It was said to kill the smell of blood. She hung the clothes high on a washing line. At night coyotes trotted out high-legged from the nearby forest. Sometimes they leaped and ripped the clothes from the line. She could see strips of white scattered through the trees.

After eighty-six days a Negro woman had taken over the washing. Lily was brought inside to help the nurses. She donned a black Zouave jacket and a thin cotton dress. Her hair was tied in a bun at the nape of her neck and kept in place with a bonnet. A Union badge was pinned to the front of the bonnet.

She cleaned the bedpans, changed the sheets, stuffed the mattresses with clean straw, soaked cotton balls with camphor. Scrubbed the bloody operating tables clean with sand. Still, the smell was intolerable. The reek of excrement and blood. She longed to be outside with the filthy clothing once more, but she proved to be a good aide and the surgeons liked her. She did basic stitching and fever-soothing. She refilled their bedside basins and slopped out their chamber pots. Put her arms under their shoulders and shifted their weight. Patted their backs while they hacked up lungfuls of dark phlegm. Slopped up the mess from their terrible diarrhoea. Held cups of cool water to their lips. Fed them oats, beans, thin soup, yellow horse fat. Gave them rhubarb for the fever. Ignored their desires, their catcalls. Ice baths were prepared for the soldiers who had gone mad. They were plunged down deep into a freezing tub until they were unconscious. She held their heads underwater and felt the freeze move up her wrists.

Some of the soldiers whispered obscenities when she approached. Their language was vile. Their erections were angry. To quieten the men, she told them that she was a Quaker, though she was nothing of

the sort. They begged forgiveness from her. She touched their fore-
heads, moved on. They called her Sister. She did not turn.

Lily helped the surgeons with emergency operations: she had to
sharpen the edges of saws to hack off limbs. The saws had to be sharpened twice a day. The men were given rubber clamps to put in their
mouths. She held down their shoulders. They spat the rubber clamp
out and she shoved it back in. She held bags of chloroform over their
noses and mouths. Still, they screamed. Huge wooden tubs were kept
under the tables to collect the blood that leaked down. Limbs sat in the
buckets: arms next to thighbones, sawed-off fingers next to ankles.
She mopped the floor and scrubbed it with carbolic soap and water.
Rinsed the mop out in the grass. Watched the ground turn red. At the
end of the evening she walked to the rear of the building to vomit.

Few of the soldiers stayed around for more than a day or two.
They were sent to another hospital in the rear, or back to the battlefield. She had no idea how the men could fight again, but off they
trudged. Once they had been engineers, quartermasters, butlers,
cooks, carpenters, blacksmiths. Now they went off wearing the boots
of the already dead.

Sometimes they returned just days later and were dumped into the
long burial trench in the forest floor. She put camphor in her nose to
temper the stench.

Lily enquired after her son, but tentatively, as if probing the flesh
of a wound. She knew that if she saw him, she would, most likely, not
see him for very long. Thaddeus Fitzpatrick. His short stocky body.
His freckled face. His very blue eyes. She described him this way to
strangers: it was as if his whole body had been built around his eyes.
His father, John Fitzpatrick, had long ago disappeared. She had been
forced to take his name. New names didn't mean all that much anyway. They belonged to the namers. In St Louis, where she had worked
as a maid, she was known as Bridie. *Change the sheets, Bridie. Sweep the*

ashes, Bridie. Comb my hair, Bridie, dear. A woman's name could swerve. She was Lily Fitzpatrick now. At times, Bridie Fitzpatrick. But she thought of herself, still, as Lily Duggan: if she carried anything, she carried that. The sound of Dublin in it. A name that belonged to the Liberties. The greyness, the cobbles. In America you could lose everything except the memory of your original name.

Thaddeus was named after her own father, Tad. She had raised him by herself, first in New York and then St Louis. A small hand- some boy. He had learned to read and write in school. He showed an interest in numbers. At twelve, he began an apprenticeship as a fence- builder. Her very own son, sinking fence posts. She had a dream of him moving out on the prairies. Going west. Deep snowfalls. High cedar trees. The broad meadows. But the war kept him rooted. He was going to fight tyranny, he said. Four times he had lied about his age in order to join up. Four times he had been returned in his hand- sewn uniform. Each time a little more cocksure than before. A vitriol to his gallantry. As if he didn't understand it himself. Once, he had hit her. With a closed fist. He turned on her and opened a deep cut above her eye. His father's son. He sat brooding at the kitchen table. Never said sorry, but quietened down for a week or two, until the anger pushed him out the door again. His shoulders tightened out the uni- form. The trousers were so long that he dragged them in the mud.

There was music in the streets of St Louis. Trumpets. Mandolins. Tubas. Fifes. Men in bow ties along the Mississippi, beckoning boys to war. Other men decked out in ceremonial swords and sashes. Glory. Manhood. Duty. *Break this stranglehold. Awaken this nation to its proper Destiny. Out to Benton Barracks with the Boys!* They offered seventy- five dollars for enlisting. He somehow thought that it would be a fort- night's war, a young man's lark. He put on his haversack and thrust himself amongst the Union soldiers. Right face. Left wheel. Right, oblique, march.

Drummer boys beat a pace. Regimental pennants flew. The First Minnesota. The Twenty-Ninth Iowa Volunteer Infantry. The Tenth Minnesota Volunteers. Snatches of a song were heard on the air. *The sun's low down the sky, Lorena, it matters little now, Lorena, life's tide is ebbing out so fast.*

She had never put much faith in God, but Lily prayed for her son's safety and so prayed never to see him in the wagons. And in praying never to see him, she wondered if she was dooming him to the battlefield for ever. And in praying to bring him home, she sometimes dwelt on whatever terrors he would carry back with him, if he came back at all. Circles within circles. Patterns on a cross.

She stepped out from the ward, down the staircase, into the night. She disliked the immensity of the dark. It reminded her too much of the sea. She listened to the call of the katydids. Their repetition seemed a better form of prayer.

SHE HAD COME, in the early days of 1846, all the way from Cove. Seventeen years old. Eight weeks on the water. The sea wallowed and heaved. Lily stayed in her bunk most of the time. With the women and children. Their beds were stacked close together. At night she heard the water rats scuttling in the hold. The food was rationed, but she was able to eat courtesy of Isabel Jennings, the twenty pounds sterling she had been given. Rice, sugar, molasses, tea. Cornbread and dry fish. She kept the money elaborately stitched in the heel edge of a bonnet. She carried a shawl, a calico dress, one pair of shoes, several handkerchiefs and thread, thimble, needles. Also the blue amethyst brooch that Isabel had slipped into her hands that late afternoon of rain. Pinned beneath her waistband so that it could not be seen. She huddled in her bunk.

The wind was demented. Gales battered the ship. She was terrified by the pitch of wave. Her head was bruised from the bunk frame. Fever and hunger. She wandered up on deck. A coffin was being slid from the side of the boat. It landed and broke in the water. A leg disappeared. Her stomach heaved. She went down below again into the stinking dark. Days piled into nights, nights into days. She heard a shout. A sighting of land. A heave of joy. A false alarm.

New York appeared like a cough of blood. The sun was going down behind the warehouses and tall buildings. She saw men on the wharfside in the ruin of themselves. A man barked questions. Name. Age. Birthplace. Speak up, he said. Speak up, goddamnit. She was sprayed with lice powder and allowed entry. Lily jostled her way along the waterfront among the stevedores, police officers, beggars. A stench rose up from the oily harbour. The brokenness. The rawness. The filth. She had met only a few Americans in her life – all of them in Webb's house in Dublin, specimens of great dignity, men like Frederick Douglass – but in New York the men were adherent to shadows. The sloping Negroes were bent and huddled. What freedom, that? Some still wore the branding marks. Scars. Crutches. Slings. She passed by. The women along the docks – white women, black women, mulattos – were rude with lip paint. Their dresses rose above their ankles. It was not at all what Lily had wanted the city to be. No fancy carriages pulled by drays. No men in bow ties. No thumping speeches along the waterfront. Just the filthy Irish calling out to her in all manner of disdain. And the silent Germans. The skulking Italians. She wandered amongst them in a haze. Children in rags of unbleached cotton. Dogs on the corner. A mob of pigeons descended from the sky. She moved away from the cries of teamsters and the cadenced call of peddlers. Pulled her shawl around her shoulders. Her heart shuddered in her thin dress. She walked the streets, terrified of thieves. Her shoes were filthy with human waste. She clutched her bonnet tight. Rain fell. Her feet blistered. The streets were a fever. Brick upon brick. Voice upon voice. She passed dimly lit lofts where women sat sewing. Men in top hats stood in the doorways of dry-goods stores. Boys on their knees set cobblestones. A fat man wound a music box. A young girl made paper cut-outs. She hurried on. A rat brazened past her on the pavement. She slept in a hotel on Fourth Avenue where the bedbugs concealed themselves beneath a flap of wallpaper. She woke, her first morning in America, to the scream of a horse being beaten with a truncheon outside her window.

THERE WERE STILL sheets of glass in the basement downstairs, made of the finest, clearest sand. She caught sight of herself in the reflection: thirty-six years old now, slight, still fair-haired but an edge of grey at the temple. Her eyes were lined and her neck deeply striated.

ONE EVENING SHE spied a dark-haired soldier in the basement: he had broken the lock on the door and rearranged the sheets of glass into a standing box around him. He sat inside the glass coffin, a sharp laughter rolling from him. He was, she knew, full of laudanum.

In the morning, the sheets of glass were perfectly rearranged, neatly stacked in the corner, and the soldier was in line to go back to the battle. He was one of the ones, she thought, who would survive.

– Look out for my son, she said to him.

The soldier stared beyond her.

– His name is Fitzpatrick. Thaddeus. Goes by Tad. He wears a harp on the lapel of his uniform.

The soldier finally nodded, but his gaze settled behind her. She was quite sure he hadn't heard a word of what she said. A shout rang out and he moved away, among the harrowed. They rolled their ponchos, scrubbed their tin cups, muttered their prayers, went off again.

It had become for her a very ordinary sight, the way these soldiers disappeared beyond the trees, as if they had become mute assistants to their muskets.

SHE REACHED FOR a hanging lamp, struck a match, lit the wick. It guttered blue and yellow. She placed the pier glass around it, went out of the ward, lighting all before her. She waited on the stairs outside. Open to the night. A small breeze in the enormous heat. The trees darker than the darkness itself. Owls screeched their way through the canopy and bats moved from under the eaves of the factory. Distantly she could hear the yips of coyotes. An occasional sound from the hospital behind her: a scream, the rattle of a trolley along the upper floor.

Lily removed a pipe from the pocket of her Zouave, used a small twig to tamp down the tobacco. Hauled the smoke down deep into her lungs. The small comforts. She clamped the pipe between her teeth, draped her arms over her knees, waited.

She recognized the clack of Jon Ehrlich's wagon. He pulled the horses up outside the hospital. He hailed her, pitched her the harness rope so she could tie the horses to an iron ring near the basement door. It had become routine. Jon Ehrlich had fifty years on him, maybe more. He wore a forage cap with a leather visor, a logging shirt, a lumber jacket, even in the middle of summer. The ends of his hair were greying where it had once been blond. His back was stooped by work, but still there was a stealth to him. He was taciturn, but when he spoke he had a soft Scandinavian lilt.

On the back of the wagon he had stacked eight crates of ice. He had made a contract with a doctor in the hospital and floated the ice down from storage sheds far north. The ice was carefully packed.

– Ma'am, he said, tipping his cap. Well, then?

– What's that?

– News? Your boy?

– Oh, she said, no.

He nodded and moved to the back of the wagon, unhitched the ropes and flung them across where they struck the dirt. Underneath the floorboards, there was a small pool of melt.

He took a pin from a hinge, folded down the wooden gate. He used a long iron hook to guide the top crate down. He positioned himself at the back of the wagon, turned, hitched the crate of ice onto his back. Bent his knees and grunted. The weight of the ice deepened his limp.

She lit the way in front of him, a lake of yellow. Down the stairs, past the sheets of glass. They moved through the basement, their shadows multiplying around them. He struggled with the weight of the crate. The size of a sailing trunk. She could hear his breathing, heavy and rapid. She pushed open the ice cellar door. Inside, slabs of meat hung from hooks. Rows of medical supplies lined the shelves. Jars of fruit. The cool blue hit her in a wave. He stepped into the ice-room and stacked the old blocks of ice in the corner. They had melted out of their straight lines. Hard to prop on top of one another. Soon they would disappear.

He pushed the new crate against the wall. Eight times it happened. A silence between them. His lumber jacket wet with ice and sweat.

Jon Ehrlich removed a pair of small pliers from his pocket, carefully opened the crates one by one. Sawdust and straw fell to the floor. He reached in and removed each huge cake of ice, one after the other, wiped them clean with his gloved hands. The new cakes were perfectly planed and straight. A tinge of blue to the edges and then a hard white in the middle. He stacked them in formation. The closer they were, he said, the longer they would last. She sat in the corner and watched him work, then went upstairs to the ward kitchen to fetch him a drink. By the time she returned, he was already sitting on the outside steps, waiting. He had opened a well-worn book. A hard waft of sweat drifted from him. She glanced at the book. The letters meant nothing at all to her.

– That the Bible?

– Yes, ma'am.

She had formed a distrust of men who carried Bibles. It seemed to her that they believed their own voices were somehow embedded there. She had seen them in the churches of New York and St Louis, raining down their loudness upon the world.

– I'm not saying I'm aligned with every word, said Jon Ehrlich, but some of it makes sense.

He folded the book shut, touched his hat, moved to the wagon, and rowelled the horses round. The cart was noisy with its emptiness.

– Good night, ma'am.

– Lily, she said.

– Yes, ma'am.

She slipped back into the cellar and lifted one of the older blocks, three quarters melted. The width of a tea tray now, slippery to the touch. She brought it upstairs to the ward where the two night nurses waited. They placed the old ice in the centre of the table and sliced at it with a sharp knife, little edges and slivers that they could place in the mouths of the injured men.

THERE WERE AFTERNOONS she watched the old Negro woman outside at the hut, washing the blood from the uniforms. The tarpaulin roof flapped as she worked, silently, no cane song, no spirituals, only the slap of the tarp punctuating the heat, the woman looking up every now and then at the rows of men still journeying back and forth, carting their corpses.

SHE RECOGNIZED HIM by his feet. He came in a mass of other men. They lay supine on the wagons, their arms and legs entwined, a hideous needlework. He was near the top of the pile, but his face was obscured. She had no need to turn him over. She knew straight away. He had broken his ankle as a child. The gnarl of the toenails. The curve of the instep. She had massaged that foot. Cleaned the dirt from it. Salved its cuts.

Broderick, the orderly, carried him out of the wagon and laid Thaddeus on the grass. A handkerchief was placed over his face. Flies were already beginning to gather.

– We'll bury him now, nurse.

Instead she shook her head and turned to carry a soldier upstairs. Broderick lifted his cap, joined her. They shouldered another and then another. Lily arranged them in their beds, scissored through their uniforms. Asked them their names. Tended to the awful mess of flesh. They talked to her of the battle, how they had been pinched on either side by the ranks of grey. How horses had come in upon them. The fog that had opened. The thump of hooves. A casual trumpet silenced in midnote. The thud of bullets into tree trunks.

She attended their every need. Her hand dipped in and out of the washbasin.

It was much later, when all the living had been attended to, that she glanced out the window at the row of bodies still waiting in the grass. Mounds of flesh. Only the clothing would march off again. The jackets, the boots, the buttons. She stood a long while in the silence of the stairway, then set her face hard. She walked outside into the grass and knelt beside him and took the handkerchief from his face and touched his cheek and stroked his bare chin and felt her stomach wrench with the cool against her hand. She undressed him. I expect your risen spirit is listening to me now. When you get up to sit with God or the devil you can curse them both for me. This god-awful manufacture of blood and bone. This fool-soaked war that makes a loneliness of mothers. She undid the buttons on his shirt. Put her hand on his heart. He had been shot just shy of his armpit. As if his own hands had been raised in surrender but the bullet managed to sneak in anyway. A small wound. Hardly big enough to take him away.

Lily cleaned the wound with hard soap and a basin of cold water. She dressed it like she would have for the living, and then dragged his body across the grass.

NO MOON. A great darkness. The hoof-clop of the horses. Jon Ehrlich descended the wagon in a narrow-brim hat and boots. She waited for him as always on the lower stairs. When she saw him approach she lit the lamp. The weather was beginning to turn, the hint of a snap in the air.

– Lily, he said, tipping his hat.

She turned to help him take the first crate from the wagon. She pushed the crate forwards and steadied it against his back. He locked his knees and shouldered the burden. Bent into the familiar pose. She walked in front of him, into the basement, the light pooling, a swinging semicircle through the old glass factory. Some rats scurried in the corner, slinking past sheets of glass. Lily halted in front of the ice-room door. She turned her face away.

When he yanked on the cold metal handle and pushed open the door, he saw the boy laid out full-length on the remaining cubes. His uniform neat and washed and mended, his shoelaces tied, the harp badge on his chest. His hair washed and combed.

– Lord, said Jon Ehrlich.

He placed the block on the floor, touched his palm against the book in his jacket pocket. Lily let out the sound of an animal: something cut, arrowed, gutted. She came towards him with her head bent savagely low. He sidestepped her. She turned. She drew her arm back and she thumped him on the chest, powerfully, a push of grief. Jon Ehrlich stepped backwards. A shot of breath moved through him. He planted his feet. Didn't move. She punched him once more. The full force of her fist. She cried out and kept on punching until she was exhausted against him, her head against his shoulder.

Later, almost morning, they buried Thaddeus two hundred yards from the hospital. A chaplain came. There was a drunkenness to his prayers. Some men had gathered at the hospital windows to look down upon them. A faint reef of light climbed up over the east.

She knew she was going with Jon Ehrlich. He didn't even question her when she sat up on the wagon and straightened out the folds in her dress. She looked straight ahead. She could hear the soft rip of grass in the mouths of the horses: the way it moved and crushed.

LILY ACCOMPANIED JON Ehrlich to his home north of the Grand River. She was baptized into the Protestant faith: it didn't seem too different from what she had already chosen not to believe in. Not since Dublin had she been in any manner of church. Even then it had only been through obligation. She sat in the second pew from the front. She was given a Bible and a commemorative piece of lace. The service was short and brusque, some words in Norwegian, most in English. The preacher asked if there was anybody present who was ready to renounce evil and accept the Lord as his or her divine saviour. Jon Ehrlich tapped her on the elbow. Yes, she said, and went to the front of the church. Bowed her head. Waited. One or two scattered hallelujahs rose around the church. She was taken out the back door, towards a small trout stream, where the congregation gathered.

A song erupted from them. *Take me from this darkened valley, wreath me in sheaves of peace.* She was carried through the reeds into the shallows of the river. A heron took off in the air, flapped wildly across the water, its wingtips touching the surface, rippling it. The pastor told her to hold her nose. He put his hand at the small of her back. When she was dunked, she felt little but the chill.

She had no real idea what it meant to be Protestant, it was an absence to her, although she remembered so clearly the Quaker meetings she had seen in the house in Great Brunswick Street, with Webb at the front of the room, hands interlocked, his long rambling ideas on fate, peace, brotherhood. She had not told Jon Ehrlich of those days. She feared, if she did, he might grow silent around her. He was a good soul. He deserved no jealousy. The old life in Ireland was distant to her now: she needed it no more, she had stepped away.

After the baptism she was married immediately and was taken to the cabin by the lake. Lily Ehrlich. She descended the wagon onto the hard dust and looked around.

— I live by small means, he said.

It was a flat land. A quiet lake. Other small lakes stretching into the distance. A series of wooden storage sheds were clumped together near the road. Mosquitoes swirled in great swarms. The horses swished their impatient manes.

— I best get you inside, he said.

He had a clear, still smile. She pulled her dress tight as a bud, curtsied in front of him.

— Get you flat down.

— About time, she said.

It was the first she had laughed in quite a while.

He swung open the cabin door for her. Silver flecks of dust stuttered the sunlight. A bed in the corner made with pine pole and frapped twine. He watched while she undressed before him, then he dropped his boots, unsnapped his braces, and his clothes pooled around him on the floor.

For an older man, she thought him sprightly and enthusiastic. They lay together, panting, her face against his shoulder. She woke him when the darkness was still on the sky. He turned towards her and grinned.

— Even the Good Book says it's no harm.

LILY WAS THIRTY-SEVEN years old when she had her first of six Ehrlich children: Adam, Benjamin, Lawrence, Nathaniel, Tomas and their only girl, Emily, the youngest, in 1872, seven years after the end of the war.

AS SOON AS the cold came, the lake began to freeze. Jon Ehrlich rose and dressed in the faint warmth from the stove and went quietly out from the cabin and tested it every day. When the ice was four inches deep it was capable of holding a man. He walked from one side of the lake to the other, staying close to the shore at first. Lily watched him diminish in the distance, tall and thin, the limp growing smaller.

A fierce wind blew across the bankside snow, kicked small eddies into the air. The trees made a dark run into the flat distance. He brought his oldest sons out to join him.

Father and sons turned and turned, testing the strength of the ice. Falconing, he called it. They circled closer to the centre of the lake. Each time they reached the end of a spiral, Jon Ehrlich raised his boot and stamped to check the thickness. Lily watched the two older boys, Adam and Benjamin, do the same thing. The clean thud of their boots broke the silence. She thought they might disappear under at any time, that the lake would take them and ice over, swallow their scarves, their hats, their face wrappings. But they circled inwards, meticulous in their patterns. They knew the depth of the ice by the sound of their boots.

They went out the next morning to begin sinking the lake. Jon Ehrlich used a long thin auger to bore the holes. Steel with a sharp point. When he turned the handle, it looked to Lily as though he were churning butter. Small sparks of ice rose from the surface. He went across the lake with the boys, sinking hole after hole in the ice, three feet apart. They made a chequerboard of the lake. They stood over each hole and inserted a thin stick to make sure the drill had gone all the way through. The water gurgled up and spread. Layer upon layer. The spill from each drill hole met its neighbour, a spreading sheet of freeze.

As the days wore on, they followed their own footsteps back across the lake and rebroke the mouth of ice on each of the holes. The water rose again. Lily brought them lunch on the lake: hunks of bread and ham, bottles of milk corked with towelling and string. Jon Ehrlich drank and drew his sleeve across his mouth. Adam and Benjamin watched their father and did the same. Soon Lawrence, Nathaniel and Tomas joined them on the lake.

They came inside to the cabin where Lily had built up the fire. Jon Ehrlich washed in the basin, then sat down by the light of a lantern. A man of two lives. He slipped on his spectacles, and read aloud from the Book. Late in the evening, he and Lily walked out together to see how much the ice had deepened. They wore no skates. They did not want to score the ice although Jon Ehrlich knew they would be planing it later on.

They rebored the ice and it deepened, day after day, season after season. When it snowed the process was quicker, and there were nights when the ice could deepen by a full three inches.

The dark of their figures moved over the enormous white. When the lake was thick enough, they drew a heavy wooden frame behind them. The frame was shod with a sleeve of steel. The snow built up and collected in furrows. Row upon row of them appeared on the western edge of the lake. They looked to Lily like so many white eyebrows.

When the snow was cleared, Jon Ehrlich and his sons planed the ice down. They measured out large squares, each the size of a half door. They cut into the lake with an ice plough. The blades were set in grooves and the plough was drawn by the draught horse. Particles of ice shot up in the air. When the lake was deeply scored, they bent into the work of sawing along the ploughed lines. The best ice was the colour of crystal. Hard and pure.

THE FLOORS OF the storage sheds were covered with tanbark. No windows. Double-walled. The spaces between the inner and outer walls were filled with sawdust to insulate what lay inside. The ice cakes were packed high and so close together that they could hardly slide a blade between them.

It was to Lily one of the great mysteries: how the ice could hold out against the weather, even through spring.

The cold fell. They farmed the lake. After a while even the youngest, Emily, went out to help them lift the cubes. They used long-handled hooks to slide the cakes across the lake towards the draught horse waiting, patient for its chores. One quick flick of the wrist could send the cake of ice spinning twenty yards across the lake. Lily liked to watch Emily guide the cakes across the surface, the elaborate motions the young girl made with the cubes.

WHEN THE TRIBUTARIES thawed, they floated the ice all the way to St Louis on a barge that complained under the weight. The cakes were

packed in crates and covered in straw to keep from melting. Elk bu-
gled along the riverbanks. Peregrines soared in the blueness overhead.

Jon Ehrlich guided the barge past the sandbanks into port and
packed the wares in an underground cellar along the riverfront. An
ice dealer from Carondelet Avenue came and inspected the work.
Crisp bills were counted out. It was good business. It was as if Recon-
struction itself knew how to make things work. Hotels. Restaurants.
Oyster shops. Rich men in fancy homes. Even sculptors who wanted
to carve from giant ice blocks.

He bought a new lease on a small upstate lake. Experimented with
new methods of insulation. Developed a toboggan system. Floated
the cakes along a series of intricate canals. He drew up plans for a series of levers and pulleys for the storage sheds. There was a call to
float ice down the Mississippi to cities as far away as New Orleans.
They built a new house on the far side of their lake, open to morning
sunlight. A smokehouse, too. Hanging from hooks were sides of
bacon and cured ham. Medicinal plants: spikenard, snakeroot, senna,
anise. Bins filled with sweet potatoes. Deep barrels of butter. Apple
jelly. Peaches in preserve.

Lily had never seen such stores of food. She moved among the full
shelves in a daze.

On Sundays they loaded their horse cart with spare provisions and
drove them to church, early, so that they could be distributed quietly
amongst others. Jon Ehrlich guided the reins down gently on the
backs of the horses. His breathing was laboured. Age was beginning
to catch him. As if his body had taken on some aspect of the ice. Still,
he unloaded the stores of food. Lily felt little call for the church, except as a moment away from her chores, but it gladdened her to give
food away. She had seen worse hunger before, long ago. She did not
care to see it again. Irish and German and Norwegian families lined

up at the back door. An air of hammered pride about them, as if they would not need it long.

Jon Ehrlich came home one mild evening in the spring of 1876 and parked the horses down by the storage sheds. It had been a long journey. A week on the road. He came up through the newly cobbled yard, carrying a large canvas in an ornate frame. He called her name. She did not respond. He walked in the door and kicked off his boots, called her name again. She came from the kitchen at the back of the house. Shuffling her slippers on the floor.

– What in the name of God is the commotion?

He held the painting up for her to see. She thought at first it was a box of some sort. She stepped closer. She glanced at Jon Ehrlich, then at the box once more. A riverside in Ireland. An arched bridge. A row of overhanging trees. A distant cottage.

Lily did not know what to say. She reached out and touched the framed edge of the painting. Looking into it was like looking out another window. Clouds. Fast water. Geese gunnelling through the sky.

– It's for you.

– Why?

– I bought it in St Louis.

– Why?

– It's your country, he said.

He had bought it, he said, from an artist who was reputed to be famous. They had told him so at the marketplace.

– Your own people, he said.

Lily stood back from the painting. Her hands shook. She turned away.

– Lily.

He watched her walk out the door, towards the lake. The early insects of spring gathered round her. She sat down on the lakeside with her head in her hands. He could not understand it. He placed the painting against the table by the door. Said nothing more about it. He would, he thought, get rid of it tomorrow.

Later that night they lay in bed together, with their children, Emily and Tomas, asleep at their feet. She trembled and turned away from him, then swung quickly back towards him. She had been a child of deviants in Dublin, she said. Drunkards. She had never told a soul before. She had tried to forget it. She expected no judgement and wanted no pity. Her father drank. Her mother drank. Sometimes it seemed that the rats drank, the doors drank, the lintels drank, the roof drank, too. She was brought into bed between them, mother and father. A tenement house. The bedboard rattled. She lost a child. Fourteen years old. She had been sent to work as a maid. Hers had been a life of basements, of rat droppings, of inner staircases, of soup ladles. A half-day off a week. Sloshing through the wet dark streets. To buy tobacco. The only relief.

No part of Ireland had ever vaguely resembled the canvas Jon Ehrlich had brought home. The country he had brought her was unrecognizable except, perhaps, for one journey she had made from Dublin to Cork long ago. She had walked from a house on Great Brunswick Street. Walked and walked and walked. Fifteen, sixteen, seventeen days, south, through Wicklow, Waterford, over the mountains, across to Cork. She was a simple girl then. That was all. She followed a desire. She still recalled the canopies of trees, the shifting light on the fields, the valleys, the riverbanks, the wind whipping a hard low rain into her eyes, the hunger that grew up out of the land, its rotten odour settling over the men, women, children.

Now, a painting. Of all things. A painting. It seemed to say something to her that she had never understood before. A cathedral bell in Dublin sounded out. A horse screamed. Sackville Street. A gull moved over the Liffey. Still, she could not recall the exact sounds of her childhood: they shifted and unshaped in her mind. Why was it that certain moments returned to her? What called them forth? She pressed her face, now, into Jon Ehrlich's chest. She was not sure what to do with such thoughts. She felt sliced open. The Duggan in her — the gone part of her — had never once thought that she could own anything at all, let alone such a painting. Forty-eight years old. She had been in the country now for more than thirty years. She had become American. At what whirling moment had she halted and turned, unbeknownst to herself, the other way? At what time had her life released its meaning? She couldn't locate it. She had been, yes, a simple girl. A maid. In a house of unsimple things. Listening to strange talk. Ideas of democracy, faith, slavery, benevolence, empire. They were things she couldn't quite understand, but they suggested an elsewhere. And so I walked. No idea where I was going. No plan, Jon Ehrlich. I just walked. Look at me now. A painting. You bring me a painting. You place a painting into my arms.

She turned her face into his chest once more. He was not sure what to do with the manner in which she wept. She curled against him then, and fell into a hard, deep, exhausted sleep.

The painting was put on the mantel above the fireplace. At times she thought she could see Isabel Jennings striding along the riverbank, the long elegant swish of her dress. There was Richard Webb standing on the arched bridge, looking down at the fast water, the splash of current, in all his earnest frustration. There were days, too, when she let her mind drift towards Frederick Douglass: he did not enter the painting much, but hovered outside it, waiting to stride in, perhaps from the distant hill or the road behind the cottage. The recollection of him lifting his barbells in his room startled her. His face in the rain on the day she left. The pale of his palms. She remembered the disappearance of his carriage down Great Brunswick Street and, upstairs, the casual way his towel had been left draped over his washbasin. Hunched over his writing desk in his shirts of billowy white.

She had heard that Douglass was aligned now with the party of the late Abraham Lincoln. Making speeches for the proper suffrage for the Negroes. He was a man much admired but reviled, too. They had achieved freedom but at what cost? In Ireland she had thought of him as a gentleman, tall, piercing, commanding, but here he was more of a confusion. It was not that she had anything against the Negroes. Why should she? There was no call for it. They were men and women, too. They starved, they fought, they died, they planted, they reaped, they sowed. Yet there was such an upstirring about them, too. Lily had heard there'd been riots from the Irish in New York. Men strung from lamp posts. Children burned in an orphanage. Savage beatings on the streets. Nothing was simple. So many possibilities. The years had shaded her. Lily's own son had fought for the Union. He had died on the battlefield for the very words that Douglass had spoken of in Ireland all those years ago. And yet Thaddeus had never even once mentioned slavery or darkies or freedom. He had just wanted to fight. That was all. The glorious vanity of dying.

There were times when she went south to St Louis, or north all the way to Des Moines, that she saw Negroes on the streets and she felt a dislike moving through her. She stopped herself. Tried to catch her own falling. Still, it was there, distant and hazy.

In church she lowered her head and prayed for forgiveness. Old prayers. Remembered incantations. She opened the Bible in front of her. She thought that she should learn how to read, but there was a purity in the silence. She tried to recall the words of Douglass in the drawing room on Great Brunswick Street, but instead, her mind drifted towards those men for whom she had pulled the curtain across: the warmth of blue beneath their eyelids as their flesh moved towards grey.

SHE WATCHED EMILY lean into her father, listening. Seven years old, following the rough of his finger across the page. The Book of Job. Revelation. The Book of Daniel. The sight gladdened her. The space by Emily's bed was beginning to fill with books from school. Still, it was odd to watch a child so very different from herself, her own flesh and blood.

Often Lily found the young girl asleep with her long hair inserted in the pages, a sort of bookmark.

A SHOUT ECHOED outside. Lily thought nothing of it. She moved from the smokehouse back to the kitchen. She unscrewed a jar of cornmeal, sprinkled some on the wooden counter, leaned against the stove. The warmth rolled from it. She closed one of the stove doors with her knee. She reached for a jar of buttermilk. Another shout cracked the air.

The shouts had come from down near the storage sheds. She paused. Another series of dull thuds, then a silence. She walked towards the window. The sky a very pale blue. Another sound, hollow and continuous, a groan, a slow surrender. Adam's voice sounding over the snow.

Lily ran out. The cold stung her. The snow kicked up at her feet. No shouts came from the sheds any more. Just a raw quiet.

Past the stables and the toboggan shed. Calling their names as she went. At the sheds she could see shards of sawdust caught on the air. She rounded the corner. The planks had splintered. Nails had popped out from the boards. A large iron hinge lay on the ground. A single ice fork was still stuck in the snow bank. A tangle of pulleys lay forlorn on the ground.

A small run of blood ran between the cakes of fallen ice and the wooden wall. She went to Benjamin first, then to Adam, across once more to Benjamin. The small of the boy entirely crushed by a single cake. She pushed the weight off his chest, put her cheek to his lips. No breath at all. She wiped the sawdust from his eyebrows. She did the same with Adam. She did not cry out. She could hear the other cakes of ice still moving and slipping above her, but quietly now, as if in reverence. She inched across the fallen planks of wood, and bent over her husband.

Jon Ehrlich attempted a nod, but a bubble of blood rose up at his mouth. She pushed the shattered cube off his legs. Don't you go. Don't you dare. He moved his head slightly. His eyes fluttered. Don't you die on me.

She was sure she saw him nod and then she heard the rattle of his throat. Lily could feel the fall of his life away from him, some manner of relief, a melting away. She rose from her knees and put her hands to her head and let out a high keen.

The storage shed still stood, three-walled. The remaining walls yawed and groaned. The lake within the ice. The water eager for movement. She stepped across the shattered planks and leaned down to Benjamin once more.

She put her arms under the shoulders of her youngest son and tried to yank the dead boy out from under the collapse. His boot caught on a piece of beam. She could feel the boot rip as she yanked him from under the rubble. She tugged again. The ice moved.

Some laughter rolled from him. She bent down towards him. Some laughter again. Oh. Benjamin. Oh. She grabbed the back of his head but it lolled. She shook him. Get up, get up, you're alive. His eyes were huge and surprised and unmoving. She rose into a crouch, pawed her way across the hard ground. Reached for Adam. She put her face against his lips. No breath. No warmth. More laughter, she was sure of it. But from where, whom? She heard it again, this time from its proper distance. Her chest heaved. From the house. The other children emerging from the cabin. The high play of their voices. Lily rose and rounded the corner of the sheds. She brandished an ice fork. Go back to the house, she said. Put wood on the fire, Nathaniel. Clean up the cornmeal, girl. Don't come out again. I'll be right home with you. I'll be right back. You hear me? Tomas? Lawrence? Now, I said. Sweet Jesus. Now. Please.

Emily stared at her. Rooted to the ground.

– Go, shouted Lily. Go!

She went back to the work of dragging the bodies from underneath the ruin. The three walls remained. They moved minutely, threatening collapse.

SHE LAID THE bodies out side by side on the ground, her husband and two sons, then went back towards the house. She needed cloths to cover their eyes. Lily pushed open the cabin door. The boys were cowering in the pantry. Emily was at the window, looking out. Lily called her daughter's name. No reply. She called it again. Emily, she said. No movement at all. She stepped across and turned the girl from the window. The child's eyes were remote, vacant.

Lily slapped her daughter hard across the face, told her to get herself dressed, there was work to do. The child did not move, but then she rose and put her forehead against Lily's collarbone. Mother, said Emily.

TWO EVENINGS LATER Lily Ehrlich hired a carpenter to come out and restack the cakes and fix the wooden shed. The weather was mean.

The wind blew bitter. The hammering went all the way through the night.

A thaw would come soon. She would have to learn how to move the ice herself. To get it to the boats and to float it downriver.

She lay in her bed, surrounded by her four remaining children. The boys were old enough now, she thought. Emily could help manage the books. There were ways to survive. She looked out at the lake. The light from the moon sighed upon it. She woke Tomas first, then the other two. They stepped out into the night, down towards the barn, their breath making cloudshapes against the dark. First of all we'll get the wagons ready, she said. Make sure the horses are fed.

THE BOOKLETS CAME from a company in Cincinnati. *The McGuffey Reader. An All-Surpassing Opportunity. Teach Yourself in 29 Days. Money Back Guarantee.* She had no idea what to do with them. The words presented themselves as a series of squiggles. How could she learn to read if she could not, in the first place, read? How could she be expected to learn what was unlearned in the first place? Her eyes swam. Her throat tightened. She tucked the booklets away on the shelf.

She hired a carriage and went south, two days, all the way to St Louis. The buildings seemed so enormously tall. Laundry fluttered from windows. Men in stetsons tied their horses to hitching posts. A railway station whistle sounded out. Lily enquired about the bookshop. A young boy pointed the way. A bell on the door rang. She shuffled among the shelves. Frightened that she might be seen. The words on the spines of the books meant nothing at all.

It was a clerk who found it for her, high on the shelves accessible only by ladder. She knew it was he by the frontispiece engraving. The book was wrapped for her in brown paper and twine.

At home, Emily ran a small finger underneath the marks on the page. This is *I*. This is *W*. This is *A*. This is *S*. This is a *B*.

BY THE THIRD year after Jon Ehrlich's death, Lily had a group of men working with her – two Norwegians, two Irishmen, and a Breton foreman. Her sons, too. Lily was a small thin figure on the ice, a little hunched by age, tapered by sorrow, but her voice carried across the expanse. They bought the newest machinery: broadaxes, cross-cut knives, ice ploughs, harnesses. The saws kicked up white sparks. The horses heaved and steamed. The sheds were rebuilt and reinforced.

After school, Emily helped skim the huge cakes of ice across the surface of the lake.

Lily went to the city once a month. A gruelling journey. Often it took three days each way. Lily haggled across the desk on Carondelet Avenue. She knew the price she was getting and she knew at what price the ice dealer was selling. It galled her to think that there was such a gulf.

She took Jon Ehrlich's fountain pen out of her small silver purse and marked a signature on the page. She had learned this much, a push of the pen into the resemblance, at least, of a name. The ice dealer worked a thumb at the base of his nose. He was thin and sharp, as if he'd been sliced with a fresh saw.

– You can write?

– Of course I can write. What do you think I am?

– I didn't mean anything by it, Mrs Ehrlich.

– Well, I hope not.

She strode away, along the Mississippi. She watched the younger women walk along in their elegant finery: wide hats and swishing dresses. Paddleboats and steamers. The whole river was wide with commerce. Paperboys called out about gold and railways. A hot-air balloon went over the river and drifted off towards the west. A man on a machine rode back and forth near the Opera House. With an enormous front wheel. The onlookers called it an *ordinary*. There were young men in wide cowboy hats who tied their horses outside saloons. They didn't glance at her much any more, but Lily didn't mind. Her back was stiff from the years of ice. She developed a rolling shuffle. She kept three elegant dresses for business matters. The rest of the time her clothing was plain, dark, a touch of mourning about it.

In her fourth year without her husband, she negotiated a price with the foreman from Brittany. She sold him the cabin, the leases, and all the equipment. The first thing she packed was the painting that Jon Ehrlich had given her. All the boxes, the furniture, the chairs, the delph, the books. They loaded four wagons. She kept the painting upfront. They pulled up to their new home on Florissant Avenue. The roadbed was made with crushed limestone. The house was a two-storey redbrick with high ceilings and a wide staircase. A pale blue carpet festooned with threaded roses. At the top of the stairs she hung the painting, then immediately set about her business as a dealer. *Middle Lake Ice*. An English sign writer made a logo on the warehouse doors. She was flustered by his accent. He bowed to her and she blazed red with embarrassment. An Englishman, of all things. Bowing to her. Lily Duggan. Bridie Fitzpatrick. Once the death carts had rumbled. The snowflakes fell.

It amazed her to think that she didn't even have to touch the ice any more. That it was others, farther north, in Missouri, Illinois, Iowa, who did the work of farming. She costed out the business carefully. The wages, the transport, the melt. The astounding logic of money. The ease with which it could appear, and the speed at which it could be lost. In St Louis, she secured a line of credit with the Wells Fargo Bank on Fillmore. She walked up to bank tellers who knew her name. How are you, Mrs Ehrlich? Such a pleasure to see you again.

On the street men and women nodded to her politely. It frightened her. She held the edge of her wide dresses and stammered hello. She was shown the best sides of meat in the victualers. There was a hat shop on Market Street. Lily bought a flamboyant design with an ostrich feather, but when she brought it home she caught sight of herself in the long oval mirror and couldn't bear the thought of being seen in it, put it back in its box and never touched it again.

The demands came. From the hospitals. On the steamers. In the restaurants. Fish stalls. Confectioner stores. There were even some hotels that had begun to use the ice in drinks.

After six years Lily Ehrlich was able to send her oldest surviving boy, Lawrence, to university in Chicago. Then Nathaniel and Tomas, too. In the winter of 1886 Emily turned fourteen years old. She spent most of her time upstairs in her bedroom, devoted to books. Lily thought her daughter, at first, to have been overcome with loneliness, but soon found out that the girl liked nothing more than to shut the curtains, light a candle, read in the flickering dark. The plays of Shakespeare. The writings of Emerson. The poetry of Harte, Sargent, Wordsworth. The room was so full of books that Lily couldn't see the wallpaper.

Her own experiment with books had not lasted very long: she was mother to the daughter. That, in itself, was enough.

Lily divided her ice business in the winter of 1887. Three equal parts to her sons. Lawrence came home from university wearing a grey suit and bow tie, the owner of an eastern-sounding accent. The two younger boys were interested in the puffs of steam that drifted across the rail yards: they sold their portions, tipped their hats, said goodbye. Nathaniel went west to San Francisco, Tomas went east to Toronto. Emily received nothing: not out of spite, but simple convention. It never even crossed Lily's mind. Mother and daughter bought a smaller house on Gravois Road. Out front, they cultivated a garden. They kept to themselves. On Sundays they dressed for church: long gloves, wide hats, white veils that fell over their eyes. They were sometimes seen on the promenade together. There weren't many suitors for Emily's attention. Nor did Emily expect any. She was hardly considered pretty. The books consumed her. There were nights when Lily asked Emily to come to her bed, slip in the covers beside her, settle against the pillows, and read. *I was born in Tuckahoe, near Hillsborough, and about twelve miles from Easton, in Talbot county, Maryland.*

That house on Great Brunswick Street seemed far away to Lily now, remote from her in daily custom and sound. The years themselves seemed to forget what she once had been. The shadows of forty years.

SHE WAS NO judge of fine fashion, but for the occasion she wore a long purple polonaise with a fitted cutaway overdress. The amethyst brooch lay high on her neck. Her grey hair was tucked under the curved brim of a mauve bonnet.

She stepped slowly from the horse-drawn carriage and shuffled arm in arm beside Emily who wore a simple alpaca dress. The evening was cool. Dark had just fallen. She was confused by the movement of the light and the close passing of so many bodies. They entered the hotel. Past the granite columns. The bellmen gave them cursory glances. Inside, high piano notes floated through the lobby. The dull pain was deep in her body now. Her hands, her knees, her ankles.

Lily cast a quick look at the large wooden clock in the corner near the bay windows. Too early by far. All around, women stood in expensive shawls and gowns. A few men in black tie and jackets. The fuss and flux. Small pockets of Negroes, too, in the corners. Mostly men. Everyone so finely turned out.

She edged forward. A gauntlet. She was sure they were watching

her. She skirted the latticed wall, found a row of landscape paintings
to pretend to admire, pulled Emily close.

– Quiet now, she said.

– I didn't say anything, Mother.

– Hush anyway.

On large wooden easels around the hotel lobby she saw his name.
Underneath, the words: *National Women's Suffrage Association.*

Small clusters of women walked around underneath the chandeliers. Their serious chatter. Over by the bar, curls of smoke purpled
the air. A distant clinking of glasses.

The piano player launched into a new tune. Lily turned to Emily
and tucked a stray strand of plaited hair behind the girl's ear.

– Mother.

– Quiet.

– There he is, said Emily.

Across the lobby, Lily saw him. Douglass was seventy-one years
old now. His grey hair still stood in serious abundance. He wore a
black jacket and white shirt with standing collar. In his breast pocket,
a white handkerchief. He filled out his jacket and had developed a
slight slouch, but there was still a heft to him: thicker, wider, yet more
at ease. He was surrounded by a group of eight or ten women. They
leaned in eagerly towards him. He stood at a slight remove, but then
he cupped his hands and made some comment and the women laughed
as if they were all part of some intricate clockwork.

He glanced across the lobby. Lily couldn't be sure, but perhaps his
gaze had remained on her. Maybe some movement behind her, some
human fuss. When she turned to look at him again, he had already
begun walking towards the hotel auditorium.

The room drew in behind him. A gust of air. A wake of light. As if
it were all being funnelled down to follow him. She felt herself falter.
She was seventeen years old again. Standing outside Webb's house.

Bidding him goodbye. The early Dublin light. The shaking of hands. So unusual. The creak of the carriage. Later the butler, Charles, rebuked the staff. How dare you. The smallest moments: they return, dwell, endure. The clack of a hoof against the cobbles. The way he had looked at her as he left. The manner in which he had opened the day. The spectacle of possibility. I have little or nothing here. A small room at the top of a house. A series of back stairs. I as good as belong to them. Owned. She left under darkness. The shame she felt in Cork. At the Jennings' dinner table. He did not recognize her. At the dockside, too. He remained saddled. She was no more to him than a sweeping of papers, a wash of the carpet, a broom of the floorboards, a yard of calico. But what had she wanted? What had she expected? She heard the loud braying of the horses. The swoop of seagulls. The rain. She could not look him in the eye. Sheets of rain across her face. A destiny. Stepping onto the boat and away. It was all a confusion. She had been so very young. The ship horn was a relief.

Lily took Emily's arm and they walked together across the floor. Two policemen stood outside the auditorium door, tapping their truncheons against their calves. They glanced at her, said nothing. The hall was almost full. Rows and rows of women on folding chairs. Their dresses spread out around them.

They took their seats near the back of the hall. She removed her gloves and put her hand upon the back of her daughter's, rubbed her thumb along the inside of Emily's wrist.

Douglass was introduced by a pale woman in a plain black tunic. The applause rippled through the air. He stepped up from the front seats. Climbed the stairs at the side of the stage. A slowness that he disguised well. He strode to the lectern. Put his hands upon it, looked out. He was thankful for the introduction, he said, glad to be in a city that meant so much to the many causes of true democracy that he so fervently espoused. There was a slight tremble in his voice.

He paused a moment, then stepped from the side of the lectern as if to show the full extent of himself. His polished shoes, his dark trousers, his jacket trimmed at the waist. His skin was lighter than she recalled. He spread his arms wide, allowed a silence. *When the true history of the anti-slavery cause shall be written, women will occupy a large space in its pages.* He spoke as if he were saying it for the first time, that he had just found these words in the last few steps across the stage, low now, almost a whisper, a secret to be imparted. *The cause of the slave has been peculiarly Woman's cause.* Immediately there was a stir around the room. A stout lady stood and applauded. Several other women followed. There was a shout from a man in the front seat, thrusting a book in the air. *Send the nigger home!* A scuffle broke out. A flail of arms and legs. The protester was escorted out. Four women left alongside the man. Douglass held his hands in the air and extended the white of his palms. A hush descended. *When a great truth gets abroad in the world, no power on earth can imprison it, or prescribe its limits, or suppress it.* She could see an orchestra in him, a whole range of instruments and sound. His voice was loud and booming. *It is bound to go on until it becomes the thought of the world.* He paced the stage. In and out of a pool of light. His shoes clicking on the wooden floorboards. *Such a truth is a woman's right to equal liberty with man. She was born with it. It was hers before she comprehended it. The rational basis for proper government lies in the female soul.* Lily could feel the grip of her daughter's hand, growing tighter now with each moment. There were motes of dust round Douglass in the air, animate and twirling: it seemed as if the dust itself might constitute something.

He put his hand to his forehead as if trying to summon a new idea. He shut his eyes: close to prayer.

Lily thought that he might remain that way, that she, too, would become fixed forever in whatever occurrence his mind had found. She was back on the staircase. He brushed past her to go downstairs.

She felt her heart lift. All around her now there were women standing, and the applause rang out around the hall, a series of shouts, but Lily stayed seated, and what she felt was incomparable, singular, yet ordinary, too, all the living moments gathered together in this one, the door of his room closed, a tiny rim of light underneath it, growing brighter in the dark. She understood that she had come such a distance, travelled all this way, she had opened a door, and her own daughter was in the room, her own history and flesh and darkness, leaning down by the light of an ancient lantern, to read.

AFTERWARDS, DOUGLASS WAS ushered quickly from the hotel. A carriage waited outside, the horse clopping its hooves against the cobbles. The night had grown sultry. A hangnail of moon perched above St Louis. The gas lamps made the darkness unequal.

A group of protesters had gathered on the far side of the street, men in shirtsleeves and wide braces. A row of policemen stood in front of them, arms linked, nonchalant.

Lily watched as Douglass lifted his head and glanced across as if in amusement. He held the hand of a white lady, guiding her into the carriage. His second wife. The shouts from the street grew louder as Douglass made a show of his manners.

He bowed to his wife and then came around to the other side of the carriage, dipped and turned sideways, then hunched his shoulders, got in. The horse was tall and elegant. It lifted its hooves and snorted.

Lily had the momentary thought that she should stride across, lean in the window, greet him, say her name, ask him to remember, but she stood instead in the shadows. What could she say? What further meaning might she get from saying her name? He might only feign recognition, or perhaps he would not remember at all. She had her daughter. Her sons. The lifting of ice.

Lily heard the jangle of the harness and a wheelcreak across the night. She ruffled the edge of her dress, and put her hand on Emily's arm.

– Time to go home, she said. Come on.

1929

e v e n s o n g

STORIES BEGAN, FOR HER, AS A LUMP IN THE THROAT. SHE sometimes found it hard to speak. A true understanding lay just beneath the surface. She felt a sort of homesickness whenever she sat down at a sheet of paper. Her imagination pushed back against the pressures of what lay round her. Emily Ehrlich survived not by theory, or formula, but by certain moments of ease when she felt herself at full tilt, a sprinting, hurdling joy. Lost in a small excelsis.

The best moments were when her mind seemed to implode. It made a shambles of time. All the light disappeared. The infinity of her inkwell. A quiver of dark at the end of the pen.

Hours of loss and escape. Insanity and failure. Scratching one word out, blotting the middle of a page so it was unreadable any more, tearing the sheet into long thin strips.

The elaborate search for a word, like the turning of a chain handle on a well. Dropping the bucket down the mineshaft of the mind.

Taking up empty bucket after empty bucket until, finally, at an unexpected moment, it caught hard and had a sudden weight and she raised the word, then delved down into the emptiness once more.

THE FIRST-CLASS CABIN was small and white. Two beds. A portside view. Fresh flowers in a crystal vase. A welcome note from the captain. A chandelier that had been designed not to sway.

Announcements shot through the static of the loudspeaker, a steward's nasal whine: dinnertimes, sunburn warnings, club alerts.

THEY HAD NEVER cared much for appearances, but on the first evening mother and daughter helped each other get dressed.

The water was calm, but even in the small pitch and roll it was difficult to comb each other's hair. Emily propped a small round mirror in the porthole window. Her hair had gone grey. Lottie's had been cut fashionably short. Beyond their own reflection, they could see the lines of moving shiplight on the sea.

The weight Emily carried dragged her down to the ground. She was fifty-six years old, though there were times the mirrors suggested a whole other decade on her face. Her ankles were permanently swollen, her wrists and neck, too. She wore her shoes two sizes too big. She walked with a cane. A dark blackthorn wood. A small knob of silver at the handle. A sleeve of rubber at the bottom. It had been fashioned for her by a craftsman in Quidi Vidi. She had a shy walk, conscious of the space she took, as if her body were waiting to acknowledge her discomfort, the space she took up.

Lottie – tall, redheaded, confident – wore a long taffeta dress, a baubled necklace against the curve of her throat. She was twenty-seven, with an air of earliness about her: she seemed to arrive ahead of herself. Mother and daughter were seldom apart. Caught by an orbit. Stitched together in opposites.

They sidled towards the dining room, Emily resting on her daughter's arm. They stopped a moment in the entrance, surprised by the sight of a curving balustrade. Flowers were wrapped round the banister. A spectacle of wealth all round. Young men in dark suits and fly-collar shirts. Thin women with feathers in their hair, their necks strained, their arms outstretched. Businessmen gathered in groups, cigarette smoke swirling above them.

A bell rang and a cheer went up. The boat was far enough out to water. An opera of anti-Prohibition toasts unfolded. The air itself seemed to have already drunk several glasses of gin.

They were led to a table to sit with the ship's doctor. A handsome Canadian with a curlicue of dark hair down the centre of his forehead, his face lean and laugh-lined. In a well-cut shirt and arm garters. He leaned across the table towards them. The talk was of Lomer Gouin and Henry George Carroll, of a slight wobbling in the Stock Exchange, of corn prices, of anarchists in Chicago, of Calvin Coolidge and his fondness for robber barons, of Pauline Sabin and her call for repeal.

The food came out, served on elegant china plates. After a few drinks the doctor began to slur. A jazz note kicked out from the stage. A trumpet swayed. The piano wavered. *Wolverine Blues. Muskrat Ramble. Stack O' Lee Blues.*

Emily scribbled a quick word in her notebook while Lottie returned to her room, searched for her new camera, a silver Leica. Emily hoped that her daughter would take pictures of the small galaxies of smoke through which the whole ship seemed to shimmer.

IT WAS THEIR first journey abroad. A six-month trip at least. Emily would send stories back for a magazine in Toronto, Lottie would take photographs. Europe was ablaze with ideas. Paintings in Barcelona. Bauhaus in Dessau. Freud in Vienna. The tenth anniversary of Alcock and Brown. Big Bill Tilden in the men's tennis at Wimbledon.

They had packed as little as possible in their wooden trunk in the hope that they would be able to move easily from place to place. A few changes of clothes, some weather gear, two copies of the same Virginia Woolf novel, notebooks, photographic film, some medicine for Emily's arthritis.

THE DAYS WERE lengthy. The hours drifted. The sea stretched a round majestic grey. In the distance the horizon curved. Mother and daughter sat on the deck and looked backwards as the evening sun flared red.

They read the Woolf novel in tandem, matched each other almost page for page. *The voice had an extraordinary sadness. Pure from all body, pure from all passion, going out into the world, solitary, unanswered, breaking against rocks – so it sounded.* What Emily liked most of all was the appearance of ease that Woolf brought. The words slid so easily into one another. There was a sense of a full life being translated. It was, in Woolf's hands, a display of humility.

Emily sometimes wondered if she, herself, lacked a true conviction. She had been writing articles for the best part of three decades. Two books of poems had appeared and faded, from a publisher in Nova Scotia. Her articles had created a good deal of interest, but she wondered if she owned a faint idea of many things, and a strong idea of only a few. As if she had developed an immunity to depth. That she only, now, skimmed the surface. That she swam on an elaborate piece of glass. She may have upset the petty canons of expectation – an unwed mother, a newspaper journalist – but it hardly seemed enough. She had spent many years trying to carve out a place for herself, but she was so much older now, tired enough to wonder why it mattered. A heaviness on her.

There was something she wanted, just out of reach, but she was never quite sure what it could possibly be. She had a sense of something more, the turn of a page, the end of a line, the push of a word, a break in the structure of her habits. She envied the young Woolf. The command and promise the Englishwoman showed. Her profusion of voices. The ability to live in several different bodies.

Perhaps the reason for her trip was to unhem herself from routine. To throw an added pulse into her days. She and Lottie had been side by side in the Cochrane Hotel for so many years. The room was tiny but they would have been perfectly able to move around each other blindfolded.

ON DECK, THE badminton matches unfolded. Emily noticed the arc of the shuttlecock from a distance, the way it caught in midflight and hovered as if arrested by some magnetism that lay inside the ship and then, when hit in the other direction, lazed for a moment, woke to the possibility of wind, shot forwards once more.

Lottie came up from the cabin, wearing a long skirt, whisking a borrowed racquet through the air. A live wire. Always had been. No airs, no graces, but shot through with an electricity, a free-floating awe. She was not pretty, but it hardly mattered. She was the sort of young woman whose laughter could be heard round distant corners. She was quickly partnered up for mixed doubles.

A waiter patrolled the deck with a tray of drinks held high over his head. An old Serbian couple walked hand in hand: they were returning, they said, from their experiment of America. Two beautifully dressed Mexican men walked beneath the gloss of their hair. A marching band practised at the bow. Emily watched the progress of the funnel shadow as it moved across the deck, slowly travelling from one side of the ship to the next.

It astounded her to think that her own mother had been on a coffin ship some eighty years before, a floating boat of fever and loss, and here she was, now, with her own daughter, travelling to Europe, first class, on a vessel where the ice was made by an electrical generator.

SHE LEFT THE dining room, her cane striking off the boards. Gradations of darkness over the water. No moon. Starlight skittered on the high waves. The lights seemed to rise from the ocean. In the distance the sea seemed so much blacker than the sky. The deck was wet with spray. Every now and then the engines calmed and the ship took on a running pace and the silence was immense.

She slowly negotiated the staircase towards the cabin. A steward accompanied her. She bid him goodbye, ached her way into bed. Later in the night she heard voices in the corridor. They drifted and merged, faded and reappeared. She could hear a smatter of laughter and then there was silence for a moment, the sound of closing doors, a distant thump that seemed to come from up on deck, like dancing, a smash of a glass and voices drifting on the air. She turned the pillow, tried to find the cool side.

The lock on the door finally turned. The breathing slowed. Lottie had been drinking. Emily heard her dress fall exhausted to the floor. The opening of the trunk. A bare foot righting itself on the floor. A slight giggle.

Emily watched her daughter slip into bed.

SHE HAD NEVER been party to love herself. Not even a husband. Just a man who had come along and eventually disappeared. Vincent Driscoll. A newspaper editor in St Louis. A sheen to his high forehead. Ink on his fingers. He was forty-two years old. He kept a picture of his wife in his wallet. Emily was a secretary in the advertising division. High-buttoned blouses and an amethyst brooch. Twenty-five. She harboured ambitions. She submitted an article about the Women's Christian Temperance Union. She knocked on the editor's door. Driscoll said she had a feminine style. Florid and overwrought. He himself spoke in hard, clean, clipped sentences. He put his hand on the low of her back. He seemed to take some cynical pride in the way she allowed the hand to remain.

He took her to the Planters House Hotel. He ordered fried oysters, saddle of antelope, a Gruaud Larose. Upstairs, straps fell lightly from her shoulder. The damp white loaf of his body shuddered.

She wrote another article and then another. He took a pencil to them. He said he was grooming her. The spring floods of the Mississippi. A boiler explosion on Franklin Avenue. The shooting of a bear in Forest Park Zoo. Tom Turpin and his *Harlem Rag*, the Negro music down on Targee Street. He edited the stories closely. She opened the paper one day in 1898 to see her first-ever article there: a meditation on the legacy of Frederick Douglass, dead three years. She had written every word herself. The byline read: V. Driscoll. She felt hollowed out. She swayed. In the hotel, Driscoll pushed against his expansive white suit. His jacket never buttoned without obvious strain. His bottom lip twitched. The appearance of the article in the paper should have thrilled her. How dare she. She should thank him. He was allowing her his name. Their collaboration alone should have been enough. She wandered along the riverfront under a red sky. She heard the newsboys shouting out the name of the paper. Her own words within. She walked to her rooming house on Locust Street. A tiny room with an enamel washbowl and a wooden towel railing. Her few clothes hung lifeless in a carved wardrobe. A small desk folded down from the wall. She made a table entirely from books. She struck the nib against the paper. She would bide her time.

She climbed the stairs of the newspaper office once more. Slid her copy across his desk. He looked up at her and shrugged. V. E. Driscoll, he said again. His concession. The *E* for Emily. Their secret.

Fireworks shot up over St Louis. The twentieth century was an explosion of colour. In the hotel room she eased her ankles around the back of Driscoll's knees. He raised the bed sheet as if it were a white flag. She attached the word *spread* to his life: his forehead spread, his waistline spread, his fame, too. She waited. She was not sure for what. It sickened her. His control. His bearing. The way she allowed it. On the street the Driscoll name was called out by newsboys. Emily walked away. She felt a stirring. A sickness in the morning. She began to carry. It stunned her. She thought briefly of visiting a doctor, decided against it. There would be no father, she was a woman beyond her times, she had suffered for it but she did not care, convention didn't enthral her. The dampening of love had shed more light on its nature than any actual experience of it. All she wanted, she said, was her name. Her real name. There was no room for a woman writer at the paper, he said, not beyond the society page. Never had been. She touched her stomach. She mentioned a pregnancy. He blanched. The child might, she said, have real lungs for the world. He spread his palm gently on his giant wooden desk, but his knuckles were white. It was, he said, blackmail. She sat demurely. She moved her fingers in the well of her dress. A portrait of his children sat on the desk. He tapped his pencil on the edge of it. Initials only, he said. She would have to continue to write under Driscoll and then she would have a second column, E. L. Ehrlich. It had enough of a male ring to it. She could live with that. It was hers alone. The *L* for *Lily*.

She gave birth to the child in the early winter of 1902. At night, when the baby slept, she wrote again, meticulous with each sentence. She wanted her articles to have the compression and rhythm of poems. She pushed the words towards the edge of the page. Worked and reworked. The cutting contests in the Rosebud Café, where the musicians pounded hard on the piano keys. A meeting of anarchists in the basement of a tenement in Carr Square. The bare-knuckle boxing fights down near the newsboys' home on Thirteenth Street. She was in the habit of writing at tangents so there were times that she would stray into a treatise on the patterns of bird migration along the Missouri, or the excellence of the cheesecake that could be found in the German diner on Olive Street.

She liked her aloneness. At times, over the years, she had met men who showed interest in her. A vendor of Persian carpets. A tugboat captain. An elderly survivor of the Civil War. An English carpenter who was creating an Eskimo village for the World's Fair. But she gravitated to aloneness. She watched the back of their jackets as they left, the creases made by their shoulder blades. She was left walking with her daughter along the riverbank. Their breathing melded. Their dresses moved harmonically. She found herself an apartment on Cherokee. She splurged on a typewriter. It clattered through the evening. She wrote Driscoll's column. She didn't mind. She even enjoyed inhabiting his narrow mind. For her own column she felt as if she were stretching every cartilage. A happiness came over her. She combed her daughter's flare of hair. There were days of great release: she felt as if she was hauling herself from the depths of the well.

In 1904 Driscoll was found slumped over at his desk. A massive heart attack. His third in a row. She thought of him shuddering in his tight white waistcoat. The funeral was held in the bright St Louis sunshine. She arrived in a wide black hat and long gloves. At the back of the mourners, she held Lottie's hand. Later that week she was called into the newspaper offices. Her heart hammering with expectation. She would now be given her full name, her byline, her right. She had bided her time. She was thirty-one years old. This was her chance. So many stories. The World's Fair had made the city shimmer. The skyline was stepping upwards. So many accents on the streets. She would capture it all. She walked the stairs. The newspaper owners sat with hands folded, waiting. One of them absently probed the stem of his spectacles at his earlobe. He grimaced as she sat. She began to speak, but they cut her off. Driscoll had left a letter for them in his desk drawer. She could feel her lip tremble. The letter was read out. He had, he claimed, written her articles all along. Word for word. Every small swerve. It was his parting gift. His face slap.

She was stunned by the industry of his revenge. She would never, said the owners, be allowed to work again. She tried to summon a word. They closed the folders in front of them. One stood up to open the door for her. He looked at her as if she were nothing more than a passing horse.

She walked along the river, her face hidden underneath her wide hat. Her mother had walked along here, too, years before. Lily Duggan. Water carried on water. Emily went home to the apartment on Cherokee. She threw her hat away, packed a bag with their things, left the typewriter behind. They moved out from St Louis to Toronto, where her brother, Tomas, a mining engineer, lived. A room for two months. His wife balked. She did not want an unwed mother around. Emily and Lottie took a train to Newfoundland: the sea did not ice.

They rented a room on the fourth floor of the Cochrane Hotel. Two days later she knocked on the door of the *Evening Telegram*. The first article she wrote was a portrait of Mary Forward, the owner of the Cochrane. Mary Forward walked around under her storm of grey hair. Her bracelets slipped down her forearms as she lifted the hair from her neck. The hotel itself was captured in quick sharp strokes. The newlyweds – farmboys and farmgirls, their fingers thick and nervous – sitting in the breakfast room. The piano that sounded out at all hours. The banisters that curved into a question mark. Mary Forward liked the article so much that she framed the page in the doorway of the bar. Emily wrote another. About a schooner caught on the rocks. Another about a harbour master who had never been out at sea. She was allowed to use her full byline. She slid into the skin of the town. She felt comfortable there. The fishing boats. The small bells sounding over the water. The threat of storm. She caught the palette of colour along the quays. Reds, ochres, yellows. The constant search for the better word. The silences, the blasphemies, the quarrels. The locals were wary of newcomers, but Emily had the texture of old weather and she dissolved amongst them. Lottie, too.

Over the years Emily published poetry with a press in Halifax. The books fell away, but that hardly mattered to her any more; they had existed for a while, found themselves a shelf to rest upon. So, too, with the weekly columns: she might not have been party to love, but it still took a lot of volume to fill a life.

IN THE MORNING Emily swung her feet from the bed. Lottie was still sleeping. A piece of hair had fallen across her face. It rose and fell gently with her breath. A vague scent of gin in the room.

Emily rolled her tights up onto her ankles and struggled into her shoes. She reached for her cane, bent across Lottie, kissed the warm of her forehead. Her daughter stirred, didn't wake.

The corridor was quiet. She walked along its whiteness. She stopped and leaned against the wall to get her breath back. She could not lay her hands on the emptiness of what she felt. The boat pitched and moaned. She thought to herself that she was, perhaps, skirmishing her way around a headache.

She was helped up the stairs by a young steward. The fresh air calmed her a moment. The grey of the water stretched endlessly. It fell into shapes like a child's painting.

The boat hit some choppy water. A loud whistle cut the air. The umbrellas were folded and put away. The deckchairs skilfully stacked.

Somehow a maplewood guitar had been left on the upper deck. A stain of rain on its dark neck. She picked it up and shuffled back to the stairs. She wanted to return it to its owner. A sharp, warm pain moved across her forehead. She was at the point of exhaustion. Her cane dropped and skittered down the stairs. She grabbed the handhold. Slowly eased herself down. She was careful not to clang the guitar against the stairs as the boat rolled.

A reek of vomit came from the corridor. A garbled message shot over the loudspeaker. The last thing she could recall was the falling clang of the guitar as another wave hit.

EMILY WOKE WITH the ship's doctor leaning over her. He held a stethoscope to her chest. Took her pulse. He wore a reflecting mirror on his forehead. When he backed away to look at her, she could see the shimmy of her form in the round mirror. She struggled to sit up and speak. There was a quality of gauze to the world.

Lottie hovered in the background, chewing her nails. Her tall frame, her pale blue eyes, her short bobbed hair.

The doctor ran his hands along the length of Emily's arm, checking for swelling at her neck. A stroke, she thought. She mumbled something. The doctor soothed her, put a hand on her shoulder. He wore a wedding ring on his left hand.

– You'll be all right, Mrs Ehrlich.

She felt her body tighten. She saw Lottie lean across and mention something to the doctor. He shrugged, said nothing, unhinged the stethoscope from around his neck. He turned to the row of cupboards behind his head, reached for a bottle of pills, counted some out in a silver dish, scooped them into a small glass jar.

SHE REMAINED IN the sick bay for three days. A severe dehydration, he said. A possible strain on her heart. She would have to go for tests when they arrived in Southampton. Lottie stayed beside her, morning to night.

A damp cloth was placed on her forehead. She wondered if a part of her had fallen ill precisely because she wanted to dwell for a while longer in the presence of her daughter. The desire not to lose her. To keep her nearby. To live inside that alternative skin.

A DAY FROM England, she was brought up on deck. A little haze of brown in the mist. An indistinct form of dark. Lottie told her that it was the coastline of Ireland. The headlands of Cork disappeared behind them – at the rear of the boat the phosphorescence shone.

IN SOUTHAMPTON SHE gave the porter a few shillings to carry their trunk off quickly. She would not go to hospital. They had already made arrangements for a driver to bring them to Swansea. She couldn't change anything now.

She saw Lottie, on the gangplank, shaking hands with the ship's doctor. So that was it. That was all. She felt a vague sadness.

She took Lottie's arm as they walked down the gangplank together. Her legs felt hollow beneath her. She stopped a moment to gather her breath, adjusted her hat and they walked down to a line of drivers who were waiting on the quayside. An old Ford. A Rover. An Austin.

A portly young man with a clean-shaven face stepped forwards. He extended a soft hand and introduced himself. Ambrose Tuttle. He wore the blue of an RAF uniform, a pale blue shirt, trousers that concertinaed at his ankles. His head came to Lottie's shoulder. He glanced up at her as if she were walking on stilts.

He gestured towards a maroon-coloured Rover with spoked wheels and a tall silver ornament on the hood.

– Sir Arthur is expecting us, he said.

– Is it a long drive?

– Afraid so, yes. We might not get there until nightfall. Make yourselves comfortable. I'm afraid the roads are rather bumpy.

When he bent to pick up the travelling trunk he exposed a wedge of skin at the small of his back. Emily took the front seat. Lottie settled in the back. The car pulled away from the docks. They drove out of the city into a sudden bright sunlight and a tunnel of chestnut trees.

THE ROAD RATTLED through them. On occasion the shadows fretted them as they went beneath an arc of trees. The hedges were long and green and manicured. They seemed to coax the car along.

They were travelling at close to forty miles an hour. Emily glanced at her daughter in the backseat, the wind nibbling at the low of her blouse. The blue of the sky had barely changed since noon. The road was largely empty. She thought the English countryside at ease with its order. Nothing at all like Newfoundland. The fields were angular. They could see a great distance, the ancient highways narrowing towards the horizon, an empire quality to it, regimented, well-mannered. Different from what she had expected. No coal mines, no slag heaps, no grey English slouch.

It was difficult to talk over the noise of the engine. On the outskirts of Bristol they stopped at a small tea shop. Ambrose took off his cap and revealed a head of curly fair hair. He spoke with a curious accent. Belfast, he told them, but Emily figured from the way he said it that he must have been a child of privilege. His accent was more English than Irish. A musical formality to it.

He had been with the RAF for a few years now, in the communications division, but had never graduated to the flying division. He patted his stomach as if to make an excuse.

The sky darkened. Lottie called out instructions from a giant map that gunneled in the wind. Ambrose glanced backwards at Lottie as if she herself might suddenly take flight, a parachute of intrigue.

AS THE LIGHT failed, Ambrose geared the Rover down, banked the corners skilfully, headed into another long stretch of hedges. They neared Wales. A series of small hills, like a sleeping woman silhouetted sideways.

By early evening they were lost. They pulled up to the edge of a field and watched a falconer ply his art: the bird being trained on the end of a string, the long curl of his flight slowly learning its limits. It hovered a moment, then landed superbly on the falconer's glove.

THEY WERE FORCED to stop in Cardiff for the night. A dingy hotel. The air hinted of sea and storm. Emily felt feverish again, lightheaded. Lottie helped her up the stairs and slipped into bed beside her.

In the morning, they drove out along the coast road. The sun rose high behind them, burning off the fog. Children waved from the sides of ditches, boys in grey shorts, girls in blue pinafores. Some were barefoot. A few bicycles came rolling along, mud-splattered and rickety. An old woman waved a walking stick in the air and shouted something in a language they couldn't understand. A line of golden haystacks crossed a field.

The three of them stopped by a narrow stream and shared a flask of hot tea, using just the one cup, shaking the last of the contents into the grass. Emily shuffled along the river. She could hear Lottie's laughter ring high in the air. Down by a bend, at an overhang of trees, Emily saw an older man standing in high wading boots. He had a fishing rod but he made no motion at all, just stood thigh-deep in the water, contemplating. As if rooted in the stream. She raised her hand to wave, but he looked beyond her. She was glad for the anonymity. She was certain now that she would speak to Brown alone.

The man in the river turned, but still he didn't cast his rod. It was as if he was there to hook the light. She raised her hand again and he nodded, more out of obligation than friendliness, she was sure.

When she returned to the stream bank, Ambrose and Lottie were huddled together, sharing a cigarette.

THE HOUSE LAY on the western outskirts of Swansea. At the edge of the water. Down a long laneway of painted white fences. Large, red-brick, garreted. Emily counted three chimneys. The gravel crunched under the tyres. They pulled to a stop. Ravens flew from the eaves. The long limbs of a chestnut tree scratched against the roof of the house.

Brown's wife, Kathleen, came to the doorstep to greet her. She was dark-haired, serious. Pretty in a guarded way. She guided Emily into a wainscoted living room. Tastefully decorated. Long maroon curtains bracketed two French windows, which led into a manicured back garden. The wind seemed interested in the curtains: it came through the parted doors and ruffled the material, sniffed about, toured the room. Photographs on the shelves. One of Alcock and Brown together with the King of England. Another with Churchill. Aviation books ranged the shelves. Large leather-bound volumes in maroon and beige. Some cut-glass awards and framed certificates perched on small wooden frames. A dozen old yellow roses with red-streaked petals sat dying in a large vase on the table.

Emily struggled into a chair by the window. A single cup and saucer had been left on the carpet by the edge of the divan, forgotten. Some forlorn crumbs on the edge of the saucer. She looked all about her, the room, the green lawn out the window, the silvery sea. It had taken many letters to the RAF to track Brown down. There were rumours of whiskey, of brokenness, of failure. That he envied the celebrity of Lindbergh. That he had lost his nerve. In photographs it had struck her that he was on the verge of disintegration.

From upstairs she could hear the creak and moan of footsteps. There was a sound like the dragging of furniture. Doors closing.

Kathleen put her head around the door frame. Her husband, she said, would be down in just a jiffy, he was looking for something, he extended his apologies. Her hair was a sleek curve of water.

Moments later Kathleen came in again, left Emily with a black lacquered tray of tea and biscuits. A pattern on a saucer. A circularity. No beginning, no end. Striding across the fields of St John's ten years ago. Sleeves of ice on the grass. Watching the practice runs at night. The sound of the Vimy throttling in. The rattleroar. The catch of it on the grass. The small spray of muck in the air.

From somewhere came the voice of a child. Emily brought her chair closer to the window, looked down the run of hill towards the sea, grey and corrugated.

She was startled by a low cough. The door was open. Brown stood silhouetted against the light. The shape of a shadow. A young boy stood in front of him, dressed in a crisp sailor suit. His hair was neatly combed. His shorts were pressed. Elastics on his long socks. Brown closed the door. The dark clarified him. He himself was dressed in tweed with a tie firm against his throat. He put his hands to the boy's shoulders and guided him forwards. The boy, well-practised, extended his hand.

– A pleasure to meet you.

– And you. What's your name?

– Buster.

– Ah, that's a wonderful name. I'm Emily.

– I'm seven.

– I was once, too, believe it or not.

The young boy glanced backwards at his father. Brown's hands curled more deeply around the boy's shoulders, then he tapped him twice and the boy turned immediately and ran towards the French windows. He threw the doors fully open and a strong smell of the sea burst into the room.

They watched as the boy ran out past the garden towards a tennis court where he jumped over the sagging net and disappeared behind a row of hedges.

– A sweet boy, Mr Brown.

– He'd run all day if you gave him the chance. Teddy.

– Excuse me?

– Teddy is just fine.

– It's a pleasure to see you again, Teddy, she said.

– Your daughter?

– She'll be along later.

– Quite the girl, if I recall.

– She's taking some photographs along the coast.

– All grown up, I presume.

Brown himself had indeed aged considerably in the decade since the flight. It wasn't simply the loss of the hair, or the weight that had accumulated on his frame. There was an air of hidden exhaustion about him. Slight bags under his eyes. His neck sagged. He had shaved closely – there was still a pink rawness to his cheeks, but he had cut his neck and a small trickle of blood had made its way down to his collar. He had put on a good suit, but his body seemed foreign to the cut of it.

A whiff of disintegration about him, yes, but surely no more, she thought, than her own.

He took her elbow lightly and brought her over to the couch, indicated for her to sit down, pulled up a small wicker chair. He leant to the low glass table and filled the teacups, gestured towards the pot as if an answer might be found there.

– I was rather neglectful, I'm afraid.

– Sorry?

He fumbled in the inside of his jacket, took out a letter, crumpled and water-stained. She recognized it straight away. A blue envelope. *The Jennings Family, 9 Brown Street, Cork.*

– I was so caught up. After the flight. And then for some reason I tucked it away.

She realized that was what he must have been searching for upstairs: the sounds of shifting furniture, opening drawers, closing doors. It was not that she had forgotten about the letter – she had simply assumed that it had found its way to Brown Street, or perhaps it had been lost somewhere along the way: she and Lottie had never received a reply.

– I forgot to post it. I'm dreadfully sorry.

It was still sealed. She glanced down at her own handwriting. The ink had faded slightly. She put the letter to her lip. As if she could taste it somehow. She tucked it, then, in the back flap of the notebook.

— It's nothing really, she said.

Brown was looking at his feet, as if nervously wondering where he might land.

— It's an anniversary piece, said Emily.

— Excuse me?

— What I want to write, it's a tenth-anniversary piece.

— Ah, yes. I see.

Brown coughed into his fist.

— The truth is I haven't done that much. I don't fly any more, you know. I go to lunches. I've made rather a career out of it I'm afraid.

Brown tapped the inside of his pocket: whatever he was looking for was not there. He took out a handkerchief and dabbed it delicately across his brow. Emily extended her silence.

— I'm the best luncher there is. By dinner I start to flag. I could cross the sea on lunch alone. I rather detest these newfangled aeroplanes, though. I heard they plan to serve dinner in them. Can you believe that?

— I've seen photographs, she said.

— The cockpit is enclosed. The pilots say it's like making love with your hat on.

— Excuse me?

— I presume you won't quote me on that, Miss Ehrlich? Rather rude of me to say so. But surely, well, yes, let's just say there are ideal situations in which one should wear a hat.

This was his performance now, she sensed, he brought a breezy irony to his fame. She laughed, drew back a little from him. His days now were an ovation to the past. She knew he had probably talked the Vickers Vimy out of himself, hundreds of interviews over the years. And yet the whole of anything was never fully told. She would have to turn away from the obvious, bank her way back into it.

— My condolences, she said.

— Excuse me?

— Alcock.

— Ah, Jackie, yes.

— A tragedy, she said.

She and Lottie had been in the dining room of the Cochrane Hotel when they had heard the news. Just six months after the flight. Alcock had gone down over France. On his way to an air show in Paris. Lost in a cloud. Unable to pull the plane out from its spin. He smashed into a field. He was found unconscious in the cabin. A farmer dragged him from the wreck, but Alcock died a few hours later. He wore, on his arm, a diamond-studded wristwatch. He was buried with it a few days later.

— Ten years, Brown said, as if speaking out the window, down the lawn, towards the sea.

Emily drained her teacup and adjusted her body in the soft of the couch. The clock on the mantelpiece ticked. Shadows came into the room, slowly dissolved. She liked the play of light at Brown's feet. She wanted to bring him back, brush all the tickertape off his shoulders, return to the moment of raw experience, above the water, to chant the moment alive once more.

— You're a pacifist, she said.

— Of the sort that every man is I suppose. I have done little that is special, and so much that is luck.

— I admire that.

— It doesn't take a lot, really.

— You took the war out of the plane.

Brown glanced at her, looked towards the garden. He ran his hands along his wooden cane, and then tapped it off the side of the table. He looked as if he was weighing up the extent of what he might say.

— Why don't you fly any more?

He gave a half-smile.

– We get older, he said.

She allowed a silence, worked the flesh of her hands into the well of her dress.

– We compromise.

The sound of distant laughter from outside broke abruptly, lingered a moment, then faded.

– I suppose I'm still aloft most of the time.

He fell then into the recollection: the sheer release of being in the air. He told her of his nights in the prison camp, the return home, the thrill of the Vimy, the way the old bomber handled, the vibration of it through his body, the snow stinging his cheeks, the narrow lines of sight, the desire to see Kathleen, the way the plane had landed, the catch in the bog grass, the surprise to still be alive, the crowds in Ireland, the return home, standing on the Aero Club balcony in London, the knighthood, the prize, the day he shook Alcock's hand for the last time. He had written a fair amount, he said, and he still made appearances, but his life was largely quiescent, he was happy at home with Kathleen and Buster. He didn't ask too much, he already had enough.

She saw an ease come over him. She had thought him, at first, sad – earlier, when he stood in the doorway, shielded by his son – but now she detected a vibrancy in him, a return to his original self. It gladdened her. He had a slow smile that started in his eyes and pulled at his lips, until his face was drawn tighter, more intimate.

The tea had grown cold, but they poured the last of it into their cups. The shadows lay long in the room. He absently touched his jacket pocket again.

– One thing, said Brown. If I may.

He meshed his fingers together as if in some small prayer, and glanced at her. He reached out for a biscuit, dunked it in his tea. He held the biscuit a moment until it tumbled and fell. He fished out the soggy wafer with a spoon. For several moments he did not speak.

— If you'll forgive me.

— Yes?

— It wasn't a tragedy.

— Excuse me?

— Jackie, he said. Jackie was in his plane, you see. Exactly where he wanted to be. He would not have thought it tragic at all.

Brown pulled the spoon away from his mouth, but still held the curve of it at his chin. She wished she had brought Lottie so she could photograph him in this pose.

— Up there. Something else takes charge of your freedom. Do you understand what I mean?

She heard him inhale.

— Maybe a child, he said. Perhaps that equals it. Perhaps that is the only thing.

He was gazing out over her shoulder. She turned to see the young boy, Buster, in the garden. He was framed by the edge of the window and looked as if he was talking to someone. She turned farther around and, through the window, saw Ambrose. A cap tilted jauntily on his head. He was picking up the tennis net from the ground. He shook it out as if there were raindrops on it, then he pulled it taut. It fell to the ground once more. The two were laughing, man and boy, though they could only faintly be heard.

Lottie stood at the edge of the tennis court, the camera dangling down by her side. She reached for the other part of the net and tautened it, bent down to pick a tennis racquet off the ground.

— Your daughter, said Brown. Her name escapes me.

— Lottie.

— Ah, yes.

— If you can give her a few moments for a photograph later, we'd be very grateful.

— And who is the young man?

— Our driver. He works at the RAF in London. He drove all night to pick us up in Southampton. Then brought us here.

— We will have to invite him to lunch then.

The china rattled in Brown's fingers as he put the cup and saucer back down on the table.

— Is he a pilot?

— He wanted to be. He works in communications. Why?

— One goes up in a plane knowing, sometimes, that not all of you is going to come down.

The saucer dropped noisily on the glass table, and he put his hand into his pocket. Even through the cloth, his fingers were trembling. He stood and made his way through the room.

— You will forgive me? said Brown, and he went towards the door. He paused a moment, his back still turned. I have something I must attend to.

HE CAME DOWNSTAIRS fifteen minutes later. His tie was firm against his throat once more, and his cheeks were flushed. He came straight towards Lottie and shook her hand.

— Pleasure to see you, young lady.

— And you, sir. If you don't mind? There's good light.

— Ah, yes.

Lottie jiggled the camera from her shoulder. She guided Brown out to the veranda, asked him to sit on the low stone wall, in front of the rosebushes, overlooking the sea. He placed his walking stick along the top of the wall, squinted a little at the camera, took out a handkerchief, wetted it, shone the top of his shoe.

The sky behind him was a spectacle of raincloud, grey shot through with blue. A white rosebush drooped over his shoulder.

— So, Mr Brown. A question.

– Ah, a quiz.

– Do you remember the colour of the carpet in the Cochrane Hotel?

– The carpet? he said.

– On the stairs.

Brown shaded his eyes against the light. For a moment the gesture reminded Emily of that she had seen back in Newfoundland a decade ago.

– Red, he ventured.

– And in the dining room?

– Is that correct, red?

Lottie changed her angle, caught more of the shadow on the side of his face, moved fluidly along the wall.

– And the name of the road you drove along? To get to Lester's Field?

– I see. A photographer's trick. The Harbour Road, if I'm not mistaken. Do they still have those fishing boats?

– People still talk about you there, Mr Brown.

– Teddy.

– They talk of you fondly.

Emily watched her daughter load another roll of film. The exposed roll went into the pocket of her dress. Over the years she had become sharp and skilful: she could reload in seconds.

– I have a shot of you shaving, she said. Do you recall the basin at the end of the field?

– We heated it with a Bunsen burner.

– You were leaning forward into the basin.

– Just in case we were to fly in the evening.

As she spoke she dragged a chair across the veranda. Without asking, she guided Brown into the chair. He moved without complaint. The cloudshapes behind him shifted.

— You made our sandwiches, he said. That morning.

He smiled broadly. She changed her lens, hunkered down close to the ground, shot wide.

— I'm terribly sorry about your letter.

— Mother told me.

— I was awfully neglectful.

— It got across, Mr Brown.

— Indeed, it did.

She lined up another angle, moved him slightly in the chair.

— It was green, by the way.

— Excuse me?

— The carpet, it was green. In the Cochrane.

He threw his head back and laughed.

— I could have sworn it was red.

Moments later a tennis ball shot high in the air and landed in the rosebushes behind Brown.

— Careful, he called out to Buster.

Brown walked across the veranda, and clambered on top of the low wall. He used his walking stick to poke the white ball from among the roses. It took several attempts. A small leaf clung to the edge of the ball.

Brown stepped down off the wall, arched his back and flung the ball through the sky with surprising agility. She shot him midthrow, the leaf in flight behind him.

— Got it, said Lottie.

IN THE EARLY afternoon they took lunch on the veranda: Brown, Emily, Lottie, Ambrose, Kathleen, and Buster. An array of sandwiches with the crusts carefully cut. A dark fruitcake. A teapot kept warm under an embroidered cosy.

Emily was not surprised to detect a faint roll of whiskey coming from Brown. So that was why he had left the room. That was the ease he had felt with the photographs. But why not? He deserved a novelty of sensation, she thought.

She saw him lean close to Ambrose and touch the young man on the arm.

— And how are things beyond? asked Brown. In London?

— Perfectly fine, sir, said Ambrose.

— That's quite an assignment. To drive these pretty ladies.

— Yes, sir.

— You're Irish?

— Northern Ireland, sir.

— Jolly good. I like the Irish.

Ambrose faltered a moment, said nothing. Brown sat back in the chair, nodded, gazed off into the distance. His jacket flap fell open. She saw the peep of a silver flask. Kathleen placed her hand on Brown's forearm to lock him there, to keep him to the ground, as if he might, in alcohol, take off. He nodded to her as if to say, Yes, dear, but just this one time, allow me that.

The afternoon light lapped around the veranda. At the end of lunch Buster bounded off towards the tennis court. He came back holding three racquets and a white tennis ball.

— Play tennis with me, please, please, please.

Lottie and Ambrose glanced at each other, stood up from the table, took the boy's hand, strode across the lawn together.

— Ah, said Brown.

Emily watched from her garden chair. The net had been fixed and tightened. Her daughter bounced the tennis ball up and down on the racquet strings several times, then knocked it across the net towards Ambrose. A fine spray of moisture rose from the ball in the sunlight.

BROWN WAS SLEEPING by the time they left. Curled in a lawn chair with a blanket up at his neck. A caterpillar worked its way, green, across the stonework. Brown's eyelids flickered. Emily reached out and touched his hand, cupped her palm around the edge of his fingers. His body shivered and it looked as though he might waken, but then he turned sideways in his chair and blew air through his lips, exhausted.

Emily stepped away from his chair. She would not mention the alcohol in her article, she knew. No need. No point. She would want, instead, to recall him in the air, between layers of cloud. To give him back that ancient dignity. To hear a whoop as he flew out over the treetops.

She tucked the flap of the blanket around his chin. His shallow breath on her fingers. Small hairs that he had neglected to shave. She turned and shook Kathleen's hand.

– Thank you for your hospitality.

– You're most welcome.

– Your husband is a fine man.

– He's tired, that's all, said Kathleen.

Ambrose cranked the car and put it in gear. He eased forwards. They curved down the road, under the chestnut trees. It would, he said, be a long drive to London.

Emily glanced back and saw Kathleen and Buster standing on the steps of the house. Kathleen had her arms wrapped around her son, her chin perched on his head. The gravel crunched under the wheels.

The trees bent down to the road. The twigs jostled. A small wind shivered the leaves. Buster broke away and Kathleen turned, then disappeared into her house.

WHEN EMILY WOKE hours later – in the car, in the gathering dark – she was not surprised to see her daughter asleep with her head on Ambrose's shoulder. She looked as if she were fitting into something already made to her shape. Lottie's hair spread across the lapel of his jacket.

Ambrose held steady to the wheel, driving as carefully as he could so as not to disturb her.

FOUR MONTHS LATER, they were married. The wedding took place in Belfast, in a Protestant church off the Antrim Road. It was September, but the day was delivered on a coat-tail of summer. Leaves skittered green on the trees. A flock of starlings harried the air.

Emily and Lottie arrived in a white car, the ribbons pulled taut in the breeze. They entered through the black ironwork gates. Emily stepped out carrying the hem of her daughter's lace. For a moment she even forgot her walking cane. Only a tinge of arthritis. She crossed the shadow into the dark of the church. The pews were filled to near bursting point. Dark suits and elaborate hats. Young men in RAF uniforms. Girls in long flapper dresses. Old women with a strategic handkerchief tucked in their sleeves. Ambrose's family owned a mill that specialized in aero-linen. Many of the employees had come along. Hard-looking men in grey suits, flat hats stuffed in their pockets. There were bouquets of flowers from Short Brothers, from Vickers, one in the shape of a Wellington glider. Emily sat in the front pew, conspicuous in her aloneness, but she didn't care: the young vicar began the service by holding his arms high in the air, like a man about to guide a plane towards landing. Emily had not been in a church in many years. She listened closely to the service as it unfolded. She was pleased by the lilt of the northern accent.

A gauntlet was made as the couple walked down the aisle. Ambrose appeared embarrassed at the fuss. His cheeks flushed red underneath his grey top hat. Lottie wore flat heels so as not to tower over him. A rain of white confetti came down outside. The couple kissed on the steps of the church.

In the hotel afterwards, Emily was taken outside to the small garden. Ambrose's father brought her a chair. She sat in a square of sunshine, her cane positioned across her lap. There were a number of ice sculptures on the lawn. The afternoon melted slowly around her. The hard cry of horses, harnessed up in a Missouri dawn. Her mother's overcoat shaped by the wind. Her father's eyelashes frozen together. Ice shard. Prairie storm. It was odd to Emily how life could be so very expansive and still return to the elements of childhood. Lottie in the corridors of the Cochrane Hotel. Walking down along Paton Street on her first day at Prince of Wales. The day Lottie first discovered a camera, a bellowed Graflex. How, at Wimbledon, just four months ago, they sat together at Centre Court, mother and daughter, watching the quarter final, and Lottie turned to tell her what she already knew. The lover's fine sense of crisis. The circumference of Lottie's world had shifted. She would stay now. She had fallen in love. Emily nursed a moment of joy that turned to jealousy and then returned once more to a fascination with the swerve of the world. What was a life anyway? An accumulation of small shelves of incident. Stacked at odd angles to each other. The long blades of an ice saw cutting sparks into a block of cold. Sharpening the blades, seating them, slotting them into handles. Leaning down to make the cut. A brief leap of ember in the air.

She felt suddenly grateful. You wake one morning in the howl of a northern Missouri winter, and moments later you are on the deck of a transatlantic cruiser, and then you are alone in Rome, and a week after that you are in Barcelona, or on a train through the French countryside, or back in a hotel in St John's watching a plane break the sky, or in a hat shop in St Louis watching the rain come down outside, and then, just as suddenly, you sit in a hotel in Ireland watching your daughter across the lawn, moving between the ice sculptures, passing a tray of champagne amongst a hundred wedding guests. Emily could sense the skip in her life, almost like the jumping of a pen. The flick of ink across a page. The great surprise of the next stroke. The boundlessness of it all. There was something in it akin to a journey across the sky, she thought, the sudden shock of new weather, a wall of sunshine, or a pelt of hail, or the emergence from a bank of cloud.

She had a sudden urge to write to Teddy Brown and tell him that she understood entirely now, in this raw moment, why he did not want to fly any more.

Emily rose from the chair and moved across the lawn. Her walking cane sunk into the soft ground. She found herself attended to by a number of Belfast widowers. They leaned in close. She was surprised by their flirtation. They were eager to meet an American, they said. Short, earnest men, well-shaved, teetotallers. She could imagine them easily in their orange sashes and their bowler hats. What would she do now? they asked. What part of the world was she bound for next? They had heard she lived in a hotel in Newfoundland, and not to be rude, but was that any place for a woman? Would she not like to find herself a place to settle down? They'd be quite happy to show her around if she decided to stay in Northern Ireland. There was a fine spot in Portaferry. She should see the glens of Antrim. The windy beaches of Portrush.

The dinner bell rang in the late afternoon. She joined Ambrose's parents at their table. He was a short man with a generous laugh, she a stout woman under a net of tight hair. They were glad to have a Newfoundland girl in their family, they said. Many of their own had gone west over the years: there weren't many came in the other direc-

tion. They grew curiously quiet when Emily told them the story of
Lily Duggan. A maid? From Dublin? Is that so? Her name was Duggan, you say? She thought for a moment that they were interested in
the particulars of the story. The details returned to her, sharply – the
clothes uncracking upon the warm bar of the stove, the groan of the
ice as it was pulled across the lake, a glove slowly blooming with
blood, her mother looking up from the body of her father – until Mr
Tuttle leaned across the table and tapped her gently on the forearm
and asked if this Lily Duggan went to church, and she launched again
into the story, until, finally he leaned again in exasperation: Was this
Lily Duggan a Protestant, then? It sounded as if it were the only question worth asking. Emily thought a moment that she would leave the
answer unsaid, that it didn't deserve the question, but she was on new
turf, and it was her daughter's wedding, and she told them that Lily
had converted to marry, and she saw a quiet relief step into their faces,
and a straightforwardness came over the table again. Later she saw
Ambrose's father at the bar singing *Soldiers of the Queen*. She shuffled
her way up the hotel to go to bed. She was stopped on the stairs by
Lottie and Ambrose. It was hard to believe: Mr Ambrose Tuttle and
Mrs Lottie Tuttle. How odd to think that she and Lottie had spent
virtually every day of their lives together. This, then, was the moment
of release. It was far easier than she had imagined. She kissed her
daughter and turned on the staircase, laboured her way upwards.
Dark drew down. She slept with an abandon, her grey hair splashed
around the sheets.

She was taken the following day south to Strangford Lough. A
small convoy of motorcars. Out into the countryside. Over the years
the Tuttle family had owned a number of islands along the lake.
Among the marshlands and tiny islands that they called pladdies. The
windbent trees. The curving country roads. For a wedding present
Ambrose and Lottie had been given five acres with a cottage that they

could use as their summer home. A beautiful, dilapidated affair with a thatched roof and a blue half-door. An overgrown lawn stepped down to the lake. A small fishing shack sagged on the edge of the water. A crew of magpies perched in the swaying lakeside treetops.

They sat for a picnic in the long grass. A cold wind blew in. She could feel it rifling through her.

She could go now, thought Emily. Return to Newfoundland, alone. She would face the days, alone. She would write. Find a small content. A graceful levity.

The lake was tidal. It seemed to stretch for ever to the east, rising and falling like a breathing thing. A pair of geese went across the sky, their long necks craned. They soared in over the cottage and away. They looked as if they were pulling the colour out of the sky. The movement of clouds shaped out the wind. The waves came in and applauded against the shore. The languid kelp rose and fell with the swells. She could be forgiven the thought that she was already stepping back towards the sea.

1978

d a r k d o w n

He is, in all respects, a pretty good shot. Plenty of power. He can whip a forehand from the back of the court. If he wanted to, he could cover the back line in two or three leaps. But he is more of a loper. His lofty head. His mass of blond curls. An advertisement for ease. His shirt hangs off him, his shorts hang off him, his hangdog features, too. Even his socks have a slouch. Missing their Slazenger. Lord, what she would not give for a gentle cattle prod to wake her grandson for a moment, watch him come to life on the other side of the court. When he returns the ball he does so with a fair amount of accuracy. Can put some sting on a ball when he wants to. Not a bad backhand either. Lottie has seen him slice with artful backspin. A natural talent for the game, but a better one for daydreams. She tried once to engage him in the art of tennis as it related to angles, vectors, trajectories, percentages, any sort of arithmetic she could think of, but he wouldn't take the bait. Nineteen years old and a fine young mathematician, but he will never storm the outer edges of Wimbledon.

She's not exactly Billie Jean King herself, but she can still stand and knock the ball back and forth near the net. Especially on a late-summer's evening with the light still lengthy on the northern sky. Nine in the evening. Sunset still a half hour away.

She can feel the rattle through her bones when she catches one of his returns on the volley. All the way up her fingers, along her wrist, through her elbow, into her shoulder. She is not a fan of these new metal racquets. In the old times they had fishtails, fantails, flattops. Wooden presses. Immaculate workmanship. Now it's all sleek lines and metal heads. One of these days she'll return to her old trusty Bancroft. She leans backwards and scoops another ball from the bucket, eases it along the middle line towards Tomas, a smidgen to his left. He watches it bounce blithely past. She should tell him to wake his carcass up, but it is enough that he has come out here with his ancient grandmother in her white knee-length skirt, to knock a ball around. The sight of him alone is easy on the eye. He's a long handsome drink of water, with Hannah's sweet face and his long-gone father's Dutch stare. A little slice of Ambrose in him, too. The curls. A hint of chubby cheek. The bottle-green of the eyes. All the more so because he does not know it: if she told him he was a heartbreaker, he'd be stunned. He'd rather write a theorem for desire. There's not a young lady around who wouldn't swoon for him, but he's more likely to be found in the university library, leafing about, trilling figures through his head. He wants to be an actuary of all things, a creature of predictions and possibilities, but this evening she would simply like to know the chance of him hitting another forehand.

— Get a grip! she shouts. Only six more left. Bring your left foot into it. Easy with your hip.

— All right, Nana.

– Pretend it's rocket science.

Lottie reaches down for another ball. A slight twinge in her back. A whisper of genetics. A drop of sweat thickens over her lip. She straightens up. She is amazed to see Tomas, at the back of the court, leaning down to pull up his socks, all six foot two of him, beginning to bounce on his toes, the Björn Borg shuffle. She cannot help but chuckle. She rolls the white ball in her fingers, releases it and knocks it gently towards him, the ping off the strings, making sure it has enough of a bounce for him to come in beneath it, and he does, with great gusto. She expects him to miss it altogether, to swing empty, or to balloon it over the fence, but he connects with the ball, and not only that, but he turns his wrist over it, follows through with his shoulder, steps his left foot forwards, brings every long inch of himself into the motion, and it whizzes past her at the net, a perfect height, a proper speed, and she turns to see it land, and although both of them know that it bounces inches outside the line, she shouts rather too loud: In!

ON THE DRIVE back to Belfast they are stopped at a checkpoint on the Milltown Road. A half dozen young soldiers, fresh-faced, camouflaged. Always a tingle of fear at the back of her neck. Tomas rolls down his driver's-side window. They are, they say, checking licences. Not normally a soldier's job, but Lottie says nothing. The young soldiers are no older than Tomas himself. A bit scruffy and open-necked. Once upon a time they dressed smartly: shining brass badges and pipe-clayed belts.

One of them leans in the window and glances at her. A whiff of tobacco from him. She is hardly a vision in her wide white skirt and open cardigan, she knows, but she gives him a full smile and says: Anyone for tennis?

The soldier is not too fond of flippancy – no love, no deuce – and he walks the full length of the car, circles it slowly, checks the R sticker on the back, then touches his hand against the bonnet for heat, to see how far they have been driving. Since when might grandmother and grandson be a suspicion? Where might their rocket launchers be hidden? How likely is it that they are off down the Falls or the Shankill for a spot of punishment beating?

Not a word is exchanged and the soldier flicks his head. Tomas puts the car in gear, careful not to make too quick a getaway, towards the house just off the Malone Road.

IT HAS BECOME somewhat shabby over the years, though it has remnants of Victorian beauty. Redbrick. Bow windows. Three stories. Intricate lace on the curtains.

They step down the narrow path, amid the floribundas, the tennis bag over her shoulder. They stop at the cracked steps and he leans down to kiss her cheek.

— Night, Nana, he says, and his lips brush her ear. He has lived these past few months downstairs in the basement flat. Close enough to the university and far enough away from his stepfather. She watches him descend, a little gusto in his step, his blond curls darkening in the shadow.

— Not so fast, hey.

She has taken on many elements of the northern accent, though it is still bedrocked by her Newfoundland days, so there are times that it catches, and the music mixes, and she is not sure which is which any more. Tomas trundles back up the steps, aware of what is coming. Their Wednesday ritual. She slips the twenty-pound bill into his hand, tells him not to spend it all in one bookshop.

— Thanks, Nana.

Always the quiet boy. Model aeroplanes. Adventure books. Comics. As a child he was always well-kept in his school uniform: shirt, trousers, polished shoes. Even now, in university, his scruffiness has a slight edge of stiff to it. She would like one day for Tomas to come home in one of those ripped-up T-shirts, with safety pins amok, or a bolt of a ring in his ear, show some proper rebellion, but she knows full well he will probably spend the money wisely, put it towards a telescope or a star map or some other such practicality. He might even put it away for a rainy day, hardly a good idea in this sodden city.

– Don't forget to phone your mother and father.

– Stepfather.

– Tell them we'll be out for the weekend.

– Ach, Nana, please.

He loves the cottage out at Strangford Lough, but dislikes his step-father's hunting weekend with a passion, poor boy. Hannah's husband is a gentleman farmer, and he has arranged it for many years, first weekend in September, duck season. More of a Tuttle than the Tuttles themselves.

Tomas darts his eyes heavenward, smiles, ambles down the steps towards the garden flat. Glad now, she's sure, to get away.

– Oh. And Tomas?

– Aye, Nana?

– Find yourself a girlfriend for crying out loud.

– Who's to say I don't already?

He grins and disappears. She hears the basement door close, and she climbs, alone, to the house. A scraggly dog rose runs up along the steps to the house. A city flower. A climber. Yellow with a small red centre. Every bloom with its own little violence.

Lottie stops in the stained-glass doorway. Puts her key in the wobbly latch. The paint is chipping from around the letterbox, and the base of the door has begun to crack. Hard to fathom, but it is almost fifty years since she first stepped through these very doors. Back then it was all fine silverware and high bookcases and shelves lined with delicate Belleek china. Now it's smoke-tarred light bulbs. Water stains. Peeling wallpaper. She shouts out a greeting to Ambrose but there's no reply. The door of the living room is slightly ajar. He is at his desk, the round white of his dome shining. Hunkered down into the chequebook, stacks of papers scattered all around him. Deaf as a post. She leaves him be, steps along the squeaky floorboards, past the gauntlet of her recent watercolours, some of her old photographs, into the kitchen, where she drops her keys, runs the tap, fills the pot, lights the stove, waits for the whistle. Some chocolate biscuits, why not? Four of them on a plate, the sugar, the milk jug, the pair of spoons nestled together.

She elbows the door gently, goes quietly across the worn carpet. A row of tennis trophies on the shelf to the side of the mantel. Mixed doubles, all. She was never one for singles. Always liked the company of a man, though she was tall and strong, known for taking the back court at times. Could whip the backhand down the line. Always loved, afterwards, the dinners in the clubhouse. The champagne toasts, the trill of laughter, cars weaving down the road in a firefly line of head-lights.

Ambrose is startled when she slides the tray onto the edge of his desk, sends a fountain pen rolling towards his lap. A curmudgeonly grunt, but he catches the pen in midflight. She kisses the cool of his temple near a bloom of dark skin. She should bring him to see a dermatologist one of these days. Small isolated continents mottling his scalp.

His desk is an endless stretch of debt. Bank statements. Cancelled cheques. Letters from creditors.

She leans her chin on the top of his dome and kneads the ample flesh of his shoulders until he loosens a little, and allows his head to fall back against her. She can feel his hand stretch the round of her bottom, happy to see he's still capable of adventure.

— So how was Stranmillis?

— He's ready for Centre Court. Any day now.

— A good wee lad.

— We crashed a checkpoint on the way home. A high-speed chase.

— Is that so?

— We lost them in Crazy Prices. Down by the fruit aisle.

— They'll get you yet, he says. You can't escape.

He taps her rump as if to prove his point, then settles back down to the chequebook. Lottie pours the tea, the greatest Irish art of them all. She has learned through the years to get the best of the leaves, to soak, to stew, to pour. Even when she lived in England there was never as much fuss made of the tea. She drags a chair beside him, to peer round his shoulder. The linen business went bust a long time ago. Nothing now but empty halls and broken buckets and the ghosts of some ancient looms. They inherited it all. The curse of privilege. Janitors for the ambitions of the dead.

Still and all, there's just enough in the kitty to get by. His RAF pension. The cottage out at Strangford Lough. The investments, the savings. She wishes Ambrose wouldn't worry so much, that she could coax a longer laugh out of him, that he would rise from the desk and leave it behind, if only for a moment or two, but he is a secret worrier. The crash of '29. They were hardly out of their wedding clothes. The Great Slump. He left the RAF, returned to Belfast. Linen for parachute harnesses and aeroplane wings. Military gliders, light reconnaissance. They soon disappeared. The business took a nosedive. Then it was linen for the war effort. An ill-advised venture into lacy handkerchiefs. Her photography fell by the wayside after the war, dissolving away in the chemicals of the time, a child, a business, a marriage. Lottie even worked in the factory office in the 1950s and early '60s, plied her way amongst the looms and the lonesome pitch of the afternoon factory horn, sad beyond all telling.

She drains the last of her tea and puts her arm around the back of his chair. A clock chime from the hallway.

– Our Tomas might have a girlfriend.

– Is that so?

– Maybe, maybe not.

– Is that a hint?

She laughs, takes his arm and he rises. His cardigan, his open shirt, the sag of his trousers. In every pocket he carries pencils and pads of paper, crumbs of yesterday and tomorrow. The little tuft of grey hair at his chest. Still, there is something impish about him yet. An ability for youth. He caps the fountain pen and shuts the account books, and they move out into the dark of the corridor, towards the stairs.

TWICE BY SHIP, once by plane. They travelled together. The first was to visit her mother, back in the Cochrane Hotel. A vicious wind blew off the Atlantic. They stood on the deck, wrapped in blankets. Lottie leant against the railing. Ambrose stood behind her. He never cared that she was a full head taller than him. There were times she worried that he was just holding some secret grief, burying his head against her shoulder, that they were locked in an interdependence that would someday shatter in sorrow. They docked in Boston and then rode the railway along the Eastern Seaboard. Her mother was virtually immobile then: she lived in a chair in her room, but still wrote – plays mostly. Short, sharp, funny pieces that were performed by a troupe on Gilbert Street. An immigrant theatre. Macedonians, Irish, Turks. Her mother sat in the rear seats in her knit hat, watching, hands folded into one another, white on her dark dress. Theatre was a new form for Emily. She enjoyed it immensely, though the seats were mostly empty. One afternoon they drove together to Lester's Field and paced the length of the overgrown grass. The runway was inhabited now by sheep.

The second visit was in 1934, two months after her mother's death, to clear up her affairs. Lottie couldn't bring herself to throw away the boxes of Emily's papers. She packed them in the trunk of a car and drove all the way to northern Missouri. There were no ice farms any more. She and Ambrose slept in a small roadside motel. She left the boxes on the steps of a local library. She wondered for years what had happened to the papers. Most likely burned, or blown away. When she returned to Belfast she took along her own negatives, watched Alcock climb from a bath of chemicals. She liked the notion of him rising from the dark.

Their last journey was in 1959, on their thirtieth wedding anniversary, when they took a plane from London to Paris, then Paris to Toronto, then Toronto to New York, where Ambrose had business with the linen dealers on White Street. They spent much of their savings on a first-class ticket. They tucked the serviettes at their throats and looked out the window at the shifting cloth of cloud. It amazed Lottie to think that she could get a gin and tonic at twenty thousand feet in the air. She lit a cigarette, nestled close to Ambrose, fell asleep with her head against his shoulder. She took no photographs on that trip. She wanted to see how well it could be put together by memory alone.

THE SKY LIFTS the hem of Belfast. At the window she looks out over the rooftops. The endless slate and chimneyscape. It's a dreary city, but there is something about it that charges her in the early morning.

She knots the belt of her dressing gown. Down the stairs towards the kitchen. Cold rises through the linoleum floor. She finds her slippers at the base of the stove. Lord, but they're still cold. So much for the last of summer. She opens the front panel of the stove to spread the heat, sits down at the wooden counter that looks out into the rear garden, scoots her feet back and forth to warm them up. The roses are in bloom and there is a spot of dew on the grass. There was a legend long ago that if you rubbed the early morning dew on your face you would stay forever young.

She takes two slices from the loaf in the bread bin, pops them in their new silver toaster, fills the kettle for some instant coffee. Mixes the milk in first and whisks it around. A fine frothy concoction. She is wary of bringing the radio to life. It's always a temptation to see how the world itself has frothed up during the night: what riot took place across town, what election was rigged, what poor barman had to broom up the bodies. Seldom a week goes by without some calamity or other. Been that way since the days of the Blitz. One of the things she noticed early on about the women of Belfast, even back during the war, was that they all carried a lace handkerchief in the sleeve of their dresses. An odd fashion statement if ever there was one. A glance at the wrist, a little time capsule of grief. She took to carrying one herself, but the fashion has waned now over the years. Less sleeve, more sorrow. The skies, in those days, were a candelabra of violence. She and Ambrose retreated to Strangford where they watched as the planes turned the night sky into a giant orange bloom.

The pop of the toaster startles her: why such an insistent jump? Out hop the slices, like pole vaulters or prison escapees. One of them even reaches the countertop. She rummages round in the fridge, butters both slices, reaches for the marmalade and spreads it thickly. She spoons her coffee and carries it to the counter.

Her favourite moment, this. Perched on the wooden stool, looking out. The small window of silence. The sky lightening. The roses opening. The dew burning off the grass. The house still cold enough to feel that there is yet a purpose to the day. She has taken to painting watercolours in recent years: a pleasurable pursuit, she rises in the morning, a few strokes of the brush, and soon it is evening. Vast sea-scapes, the lough, the Causeway, the rope bridge at Carrick-a-Rede. She has even taken her camera out to Rathlin Island, working afterwards from photographs. There are times she paints herself all the way back to St John's, the footnote the town made to the sea, Water Street, Duckworth, Harbour Drive, all the little houses propped on the cliff as if in a last-ditch attempt to remember where they came from.

THE TAP OF his cane on the floor. The clank of the water pipes. She is wary of making too much of a fuss. Doesn't want to embarrass him, but he's certainly slowing up these weathers. What she dreads is a thump on the floor, or a falling against the banister, or worse still a tumble down the stairs. She climbs the stairs before Ambrose emerges from the bathroom. A quick wrench of worry when there is no sound, but he emerges with a slightly bewildered look on his face. He has left a little shaving foam on the side of his chin, and his shirt is haphazardly buttoned.

She disappears into the bedroom. The worrywart's dance. Out of her nightdress. Into a pair of trousers and a cardigan. A peek in the mirror. Grey and bosom-burdened. A little bit of weight around the neck now, too.

She peeks her head round the bedroom door to make sure that Ambrose has made it safely down the stairs. His bald head bobs away, around the bottom banister, towards the kitchen. The ancient days of the Grand Opera House, the Hippodrome, the Curzon, the Albert Memorial Clock. The two of them out tripping the light fantastic. So young then. The smell of his tweeds. The Turkish tobacco he used to favour. The charity balls in Belfast, her gown rustling on the steps, Ambrose beside her, bow-tied, brilliantined, tipsy. The music of the orchestra moving in them both. Good days. When the stars were ceilings, or ceilings were stars. She was treated every now and then to songs about Canada. The Irish had a great penchant for singing and could dredge a song from just about anywhere. Some of them even knew the words of the ballad of the First Newfoundland Regiment, doomed to the Bulge, Beaumont Hamel.

Old soldiers from other wars. Captains and colonels. Pilots and navigators. Oarsmen and showjumpers. Elegant men, all. There were times they got together for a gallop of a foxhunt out beneath the Mournes. Summer lawns. Folding chairs. Tennis tournaments. They used to call her the American, much to her chagrin. She even tried to lose her accent, could never quite manage it. She took to stitching the Red Ensign of Newfoundland on the hem of her skirt. The tournaments stretched until sundown. The dinners in the evening. At the big houses of Belfast. Hours of preparation at the dressing table. Leaning into the small oval mirror. Fixing back a strand of hair. Dabbing on the make-up. Not too much rouge on the cheeks. Light on the mascara, but bright with the lipstick. How do I look, honey? Quite frankly, my dear, you look late. His usual answer, but said with a wink and his arm curled tight around her waist. Afterwards she stood naked in front of a mirror, unplaiting the tress of her hair while his white collar fell onto the bed, and the night was kind to them, always kind.

Down the stairs she goes, a spryness in her step. He is sitting by the window with his tea and toast. She leans across to adjust his shirt buttons and manages to swipe away the small patch of shaving foam from his neck without him noticing. He concertinas out yesterday's newspaper, folds it down on the table with a sigh. A bomb scare in the city centre. Seventeen men rounded up in a sweep. A boy kneecapped in the Peter's Hill area. An incendiary device found hidden in the bottom of a baby's pram.

— The great and loyal heroes of Ireland are at it again, says Ambrose.

ON THE WAY to the lough, the car itself seems to relax. An ancient church, a flock of blackbirds in the eaves, auction notes on stone pillars, sheds bulging with fodder, milk cans at gateways, marshland.

They drive past the heritage site and over the small bridge to the island, then around the red gate in the early morning.

The cottage sits on the edge of the lough, hidden by trees. The thatched roof has long been converted to slate, but the rest still nods to the past. The whitewashed walls, the blue half-door, the old copper flowerpots hanging outside the windows, the faded deckchairs, a dinner bell set on a fence post out the back. How many days has she spent out here, hammering nails and hanging doors and painting walls and puttying window frames? A whole new heating system that never worked in the first place. Pumps and pipe work. Rolls of insulation. Wires and water wells. It began as a two-room cottage and made a gentle spread along the lake. She and Ambrose did most of the work together in the years after the war. Days of calm and quiet. Wind and rain. It weathered their faces. Up on the ladder to fix the slates. Cleaning out the drainpipes. Their summer cottage slid over into winter. All those nights, stunned with simplicity, lying next to him in the back bedroom. Facing east across the water. Watching the light drain.

Tomas swings the car into the driveway. A little too quickly. Ambrose stirs in the back seat, but doesn't waken. The tyres slide in the soft ground. Several other vehicles are already parked in the long grass near the barn. Her son-in-law, Lawrence, has invited far too many guests. So be it. It's his weekend. His ritual.

— Leave your grandfather asleep a minute.

Lottie leans over the car seat and tucks the blanket around

Ambrose's neck. He gives the faint hint of a snore. The ground has been turned to mush. Puddles and tyre tracks. She has forgotten her Wellington boots and she slops her way towards the back of the car.

– Give me a hand here, Tomas, good lad.

He slouches against the side of the car and stretches out his arms, his hair down over his eyes.

– Buy yourself some windscreen wipers.

He squints at her, perplexed, until she swipes the curls away from his brow. He laughs and Lottie loads him up with bags, books, blankets, directs him towards the house. She watches him drift through the long grass at the side of the cottage, the stalks brushing wet against his jeans. He still wears large elephant flares. His shirt hanging out at the rear. Never a boy for fashion. He struggles under the load, almost slips, but finds his footing in the gravel near the front door, steadies himself.

He slides towards the half-door – the top portion open, the bottom closed – and leans his way into the cottage. Half in, half out. The load he carries propped on the rim of the door. Even from a distance Lottie can hear the high greeting of her daughter from inside. The spill of happiness out the door. An apron. A few strands of hair over Hannah's blue eyes. A smell of tobacco when they hug.

– Where's Dad?

– Snoozing. Leave him two minutes.

– Did you roll down the window?

– Of course. Are they at it yet?

– They put out the decoys at five this morning.

– They what?

– They began in the dark.

And, as if on cue, Lottie hears her first gunshot of the weekend. Followed quickly by a second. She turns to see a flock of birds bursting their way over the cottage.

AMBROSE WAS, IN his time, a good shot, too. A few of the men from the linen business would get together on the autumn weekends. Headlamps pouring down the road in pale shrouds in the early mist. Boots. Duck-hunting hats. Tweeds. Green slickers. Brownings tucked away in rifle bags, slung over their shoulders. They walked out the island road with the dogs trotting behind them, Labradors, yellow and black. She could hear the heeltaps on gravel as they moved away. They returned in the late afternoon, a faint smell of gunpowder from their clothes. Pochard, tufted duck, goldeneye. They made a ritual of dropping brandy in the boiling water to ease the pellets, they said, from the flesh. She could never taste the meat without thinking of flight.

Arthur Brown. God rest him. She still has the unopened letter from her youth. He is dead now these past thirty years. His own son, Buster, smashed out of the clouds on a mission of war. The second savaging of the century. The failed experiment of peace. She recalls Brown at his home in Swansea, standing on the low wall, his body bent backwards, the ball in midflight and an arc of brief joy on his face.

RANDOM GUNFIRE PUNCTUATES breakfast. She sits in the kitchen, with Hannah at the table, the red-and-white-chequered tablecloth spread out in front of them. Tomas perches by the fire, reading, while Ambrose takes a stroll along the shore between naps.

She is happy to spend some time alone with her daughter: it happens less and less these days. The inevitable teapot, the butter, the scones. The lilies leaning in a tabletop vase. The hard whiff of tobacco: Lottie allows it to drift across her face.

On the windowsill stand a bunch of opened letters and a chequebook. Destiny has given her daughter two things – an agile mind, and a gift, or a curse, for giving away money. It has been that way for years: as a child on the Malone Road she would come home shoeless. Even now, there is always a cheque being dropped in an envelope. Red Cross. Oxfam. Shaftesbury Children's Home.

— What in the world is Amnesty International?

— Just another bunch of Canadians, Mother.

— Does the postman not hate you?

— I'm on their watch list.

Lottie holds the bundle of letters in the air, flicks through them as if they were a moving cartoon: pound notes disappearing over the hill.

— Everything I know I learned from you, Mum.

Not a lie. She was, in her day, hardly a penny-pincher. Still, always a mother. Impossible to escape. She wraps an elastic band around the chequebook, tries to hide it behind the flowerpot.

They weave the hours away, moving fluidly around one another, swapping spoons, handing off bowls, borrowing dishtowels from one another's shoulders. The state of the farm. The pulse of the village. The business Hannah has made with the purebred dogs.

Hannah's hands have aged a little. Thirty-eight years old now, half her life a mother herself. A tilework to her skin. A braid of veins at the base of her wrist. Such a curious thing, to watch your daughter grow older. That odd inheritance.

— Tomas behaving himself up there, is he, then?

— Playing tennis every Wednesday.

— Good on him.

A wistful note in her daughter's voice: Not driving you mad with that new stereo of his, is he?

— Sure the two of us are deaf anyway.

Hannah turns and takes the bread from the stove. With bare hands.

A scorch at her fingertips. She steps to the kitchen sink, runs cold water on the burn.

— I was thinking, Mum. You know. Maybe you'd have a word with him? Maybe he'd go out, just this once? Lawrence has been talking about him all week long.

— You're his mother.

— Aye. He listens to you but.

— He could maybe row out the decoys.

— He could, that.

Through the window, along the shore, she spies Ambrose wandering under the brown of his hat. He has always loved the lake. It stretches beyond him, a wide plash of grey. He will come in shortly, she knows, rubbing his hands together, looking for the warmth of a fire, a small brandy and a newspaper, the ordinary pleasures of an early September.

THE HUNTERS RETURN at lunchtime, trudging along the laneway, shotguns swinging. She doesn't know many of them. Friends of Lawrence. A lawyer, a councilman, an artisan boatmaker.

— Where's Tomas? says Lawrence.

— Beyond in his room.

Lawrence wears his shirt buttoned high. He is big-boned underneath it. He holds, by the neck, two goldeneyes. He drops the birds on the table, turns away, fills his pipe with tobacco, tamps it on the heel of his hand.

— He'll be on then for tomorrow?

— Ach, leave him be, says Hannah.

— Do him the world of good.

— Lawrence. Please.

He shrugs off his cardigan and hangs it by the edge of the fire, mutters. A big man, a small voice. He livens when he joins his friends in the living room.

By late afternoon Lottie and Hannah have their hands in the warm guts of a cooked bird. Hannah pulls her fingers expertly along the bottom of the body and the flesh separates in her fingers. She spreads the meat out on a platter, with some slices of apple and a berry garnish. An extravagant gesture of colour.

The men sit at the table, eating, all except Tomas. Jackets draped over the backs of their chairs. Hats perched on the windowsill. A loud laughter rolling amongst them. An ease to the day. A slow banter. A sliding away.

SHE IS GLAD to see Tomas emerge from his room, darkdown, when the guests have left. He wears an old fisherman's sweater many sizes too big, belonging once to Ambrose. He wanders around, an air of sleep still about him. Nods to Lawrence across the room. A gulf between them, stepfather and son. Always a layer of cloud.

He rows out in the evening, after dinner, to check his star charts. In his long wading boots. Binoculars at his neck. They can see him operate on the lake, a small pinpoint of red flashlight drifting along the shore. There is a low moon, a small rip of wind across the lough.

When he hits the oar against the water, the light jumps and swerves and shifts, then settles down once more.

EARLY ON SATURDAY morning she wakes Ambrose for the hunt. The night is pitch-black outside. The cold stuns her cheekbones. She has prepared his clothes already. A warm undershirt and long johns. A heavy tweed jacket. Two pairs of socks. Folded on the small wooden chair. His toothbrush laid out, but no razor. It is the one day of the year when Ambrose does not shave early.

A sweep of headlights over the ceiling. The other guests coming down the laneway. Three, four, five of them this morning. The squelch of their tyres in the mud. Lawrence's voice already among them. A whisper and a shushing of the dogs. The drift of cigarette smoke from outside.

In the kitchen she and Hannah ready breakfast: just toast and tea, no time for a fry. The men are dark-eyed, gruff, weary. They glance out the window at the early dark. Fixing batteries in their torches. Checking cartridges. Tightening their laces.

His silhouette shows sudden in the hallway. She is quite sure, at first, that Tomas has been up all night. It has happened before. He has often spent the whole evening out on the water with his star charts. He slouches his way through the kitchen, nods to the men at the table, sits down next to Ambrose. The ritual acknowledgements. They eat breakfast together and then Tomas rises with Lawrence – not a word between them – and together they go to the pantry where the bolted silver safe is kept.

Lottie watches as the bare bulb throws a globe of light down upon them. Lawrence spins the dial on the safe, reaches in, turns to Tomas. She watches her grandson hold the unfamiliar weight in his hand. Bits and pieces of the language floating towards her: twelve-gauge, five-shot, 36-gramme load.

— You'll be going out then? says Hannah.

An astonishing calm in Hannah's voice, but her body betrays her: the shoulders tight, her neck cords shining, her eyes a premonition of ill fate. She flicks a look at Lawrence. He shrugs, taps at the pipe in his breast pocket, as if that is the thing that will monitor everything.

— Thought I'd give it a go, says Tomas.

— Better have your woollies on.

The kitchen awhirl now. The rumour of dawn. The guests step outside. Tomas leans down to tighten his hiking boots. Hannah takes Lawrence by the collar, whispers something urgent in his ear. Lottie, too, takes Ambrose aside, beseeches him to look after the boy.

— We'll be back by noon.

She is still in her dressing gown as she watches them go. A regiment. The marks of their bootprints in the mud. The dogs loping patiently behind them. They disappear around the red gatepost and the sky rises up as they grow small.

THE MORNING SOUNDS loud with the retort of the guns. Double blasts. Each one a sharp kick inside her. Lottie finds herself entirely on edge. Just to walk around the kitchen needs the utmost control. She would love to wipe her hands clean of flour and step out the half-door, hurry along the laneway, down to the lakeshore, check on them, watch them, bring them sandwiches, milk, a flask. Her eyes can find no resting place. With each shot she looks out the window. A blankness of grey.

Columns of rain pour distantly over the lake. The branches of the trees knit the wind. Surely, now, the storm will bring them home. She turns to the radio for the ease of noise. Bombs doing what bombs will. She searches the dial and settles on a classical station. On the hour mark even that, too, is interrupted. An incendiary device in Newry. Three dead, twelve wounded. No warning.

She watches the shape of her daughter move from table to stove to pantry to fridge. Hannah fakes unconcern. She kneads the dough and allows the bread to rise. As if the heat from the oven itself might push forwards the hands of the clock on the stove. An occasional chatter between them. Did Ambrose have a proper belt? Was Tomas given the thickest of socks? Would Lawrence be alongside them both? Did everyone take an oilskin? When was the last time they shot a scaup? Did he bring his eyeglasses? Has he ever even pulled a trigger before?

IT IS LATE lunchtime before they hear the bark of a dog. The men come down the road as routinely as one might expect: Ambrose and Tomas bringing up the rear, the width of the grassy median between them. Their jackets dark with rain. Shotguns slung over their shoulders. A hint of fatigue in the walk.

She greets them at the front of the cottage, opens the latch on the half-door, beckons them in.

Tomas shucks his jacket and hangs it on the fire irons, bangs his heels on the floor until his boots come off, pulls his wadded socks from his toes, puts them down by the fire. He sits, long and languid, in the chair, hides himself under a towel. A warm smoke rising from his boots and socks.

– What about ye, Nana?

She stands close to the fire, her back against the mantelpiece. She will hold the moment for a long time, the sight of him in the chair, a small crease of light from the fire flickering at the end of his raindark boots.

– Did you like it, then?

– Oh, aye, I suppose.

– Get anything?

– Granddad bagged himself a couple.

There are times – months later, years later, a decade later even – that it strikes Lottie how very odd it is to be abandoned by language, how the future demands what should have been asked in the past, how words can escape us with such ease, and we are left, then, only with the pursuit. She will spend so much of her time wondering why she did not sit down with Tomas and enquire what exactly it was that brought him out the road in the morning, what guided him along the shore, what strange compulsion led him towards the hunt? What was it like, to walk down by the lakeside and crouch in the grass and wait for the birds and the dogs to disturb the blue and the grey? What words went between him and Ambrose, what silence? What sounds did he hear across the water? Which of the dogs hunkered next to him, waiting? How was it that he had changed his mind so simply? She wished, then, that she had carved open whatever idea had crossed his mind in the early hours that one September morning. Was it just one of those random things, slipshod, unasked for, another element in the grand disorder of things? Perhaps he did not want to see his grandfather stepping out alone. Or he overheard his mother talking of the hunt. Or maybe how his stepfather wanted so badly for him to join. Or perhaps it was just pure boredom.

She would find herself wondering – stuck at a traffic light on the Malone Road, or in the butcher shop on the Ormeau Road, or in the peace group on the Andersonstown Road, or in the shadows of Sandy Row, or at the marches where they carried pictures of their loved ones, or the days she found herself outside Stormont awaiting any news of decency, or strolling the rim of the island, or at the back court of the tennis club in Stranmillis, or simply just walking down the stairs with Ambrose, adding day to day, hour to hour – what it was that brought Tomas to the moment, how it became part of the constant unfolding, what was it that changed his mind.

She never asked. Instead, she watched Tomas lift the towel – scuffing it through his hair – and she returned, then, to the kitchen, lit the flame under the stove, the whole of a happiness moving over her.

YELLOW LEAVES LIE in scattered profusion on the green lawn. The cottage has been touched by the edge of a decaying storm. These are the weekends she likes the most: they drive out from Belfast, down the laneway, pause a moment by the gate, the high-voltage wires singing at the end of the country road.

They park down by the barn, on the high side of the driveway where the ground stands firmer, and they use the leaves for grip as they make their way to the half-door.

TOMAS IS SHOT dead seven weeks into the hunting season. In the early morning dark. In his small blue rowboat. In his new ritual of scattering the decoys out on the water.

She is asleep when she hears the first shot. Ambrose beside her. The rise and fall of his chest. His irregular breath in the back room of the cottage. He shifts slightly in the sheets and turns towards her. His pyjama top open. A small triangle of flesh at his neck. The heavy odour of his breath. Lottie shifts slightly away from him. An air of dust about the room. Sure, at first, that she is mistaken. Not a familiar sound for the dark. A crack of falling brick from inside the chimney perhaps: it has happened before. Or the shatter of an outside slate. She fumbles at her nightstand to check her watch. Brings it close to her eye. Has to turn it in her hand, over and over. Five twenty in the morning. That was not a gunshot. Too early for that. Something falling perhaps in the barn outside, or some disturbance from the living room. She glances towards the window. The rain hard against it. The bare cold of the frame when she touches it.

There is, then, a second shot. She puts her hand to Ambrose's shoulder, allows it there a moment. Maybe she has overslept. The curtains are tight after all. Some trick of the light. She rises from the bed in her nightdress. Finds her slippers on the cold floor. Steps to the window. Parts the curtains. All dark outside. Surely then she is just imagining. She peers out towards the lake. Nothing at all. Only the darker shape of a windbent tree. No moon or starlight. No boat. No small red light. No sign of anyone. Silence.

She closes the curtains and steps back across the room. Allows the slippers to fall from her feet. Lifts the edge of the blanket and the sheet and is halfway into the bed when she hears the sound of the third shot.

That, she thinks, was no slate. That was no tumble of brick.

Book Three

2011

*the garden
of remembrance*

I'VE HAD IN MY POSSESSION, FOR MANY YEARS NOW, AN UN-
opened letter. It travelled by Vickers Vimy over the Atlantic almost a
hundred years ago, the thinnest of letters, no more than two pages,
possibly only one. The envelope is six inches wide, four and a half
high. It was once light blue, though it is now discoloured with patches
of smoke and yellow and brown. The writing on the front has faded
and is just about legible. No postmark. It is crumpled at the edges and
it has been folded over a number of times. For many years it was
thrust in and out of pockets and cupboard drawers. At some stage it
was ironed out and there is a burn in the upper right-hand corner, a
small corruption of black, near the indicia, and there are tiny water
splats across the envelope as if, perhaps, it was once carried out into
the rain. There is no seal, no insignias, no discernible shape to what
may lay inside.

The letter has been passed from daughter to daughter, and through a succession of lives. I am almost half the letter's age, and have no daughter to whom I can pass it along, and there are times I admit that I have sat at the kitchen table, looking out over the lough, and have rubbed the edges of the envelope and held it in the palm of my hand to try to divine what the contents might be, but, just as we are knotted by wars, so mystery holds us together.

I am shamed to admit that I have spent much of my time with no particular purpose, unfaithful to my inner promises – a couple of years nursing, a decade in the Women's Coalition, some farming on the island, a few months selling cosmetics, a couple of years breeding bird dogs. I had a child at nineteen, lost him when I was thirty-eight. The bare truth is that I want nothing so much as to hold my dead son in my arms again – if I knew that I could see Tomas row a boat up to the shore, or walk through the kitchen in his wading boots, or step along the mudflats with his binoculars around his neck, I would tear every last piece of the letter to pieces, scatter the lives across Strangford and beyond. As it is, I cherish it. It is kept in the pantry of all places. On a middle shelf, on its own. Tucked inside a sleeve of archival plastic. I am partial, still, to the recklessness of the imagination. The tunnels of our lives connect, coming to daylight at the oddest moments, and then plunge us into the dark again. We return to the lives of those who have gone before us, a perplexing Möbius strip until we come home, eventually, to ourselves. I have no qualms about taking it out every now and then, and examining it for whatever small clue it might give. *The Jennings Family, 9 Brown Street, Cork, Ireland.* There is a real flourish to the handwriting, a sense of curl and shape, a stylistic swerve. It was my grandmother Emily Ehrlich who wrote the letter, my own mother who brokered its passage, but it began with her mother, my great-grandmother, Lily Duggan, if anything truly begins at all. She was an immigrant maid from Dublin who moved to northern Missouri where she married a man who cut and preserved ice.

I have often wondered what might have happened if the letter had made it to its proper destination in Cork, what random turn of events might have grown out of it, what chance, what accidents, what curiosities. Opened, it could have been burned. Or dismissed. Or cherished. Scrapped. Left to mould in an ancient attic somewhere, the territory of a squirrel or a bat.

Unopened, the letter is even less effective of course, except for its preservation of possibility, the slight chance that it contains a startling fact, or an insight into some forgotten beauty.

But all of this is hardly new, or much of a revelation. There is simply no way to know what would've changed, or how the lives might have touched each other, or parted, or what shape they could have taken with the slice of a knife through an envelope. So many of our lives are thrown into long migratory orbits. The fact of the matter is that I once held my breathing son close to my ear but he was shot dead on a wet October morning, in the fierce dark before dawn, and there are moments that I would like to know what might have happened if it hadn't happened, and why it happened the way it did, and what it might have taken to prevent it from happening. Most of all, I would like him to be here once more, alive and tall and truculent and willing to defend me from this latest storm.

IN THE MORNING — after the news from the bank — a flock of brent geese came gunneling over the lough, bringing with them their own mystery, low over the water. They arrive every year. Regular as clockwork. Swaths of them. I have in years past seen twenty or thirty thousand over the course of a few days. They can momentarily darken the sky, huge clouds, then tuck their wings, and blanket onto the water and grass. Not so much grace as hunger. They arrange themselves among the marshes and the pladdies and the sudden thrust of drumlins.

I went out the back door to the lough in my housecoat and boots. Carrying a mug of coffee. My hair in a net. No morning bath. Very attractive indeed. The tide was out and the shoreside rocks were slippery with kelp. Georgie followed me to the water's edge, but then turned back up the garden, put her head on her paws, ancient and tired. I empathized, and tucked the coat under me, and sat down on a cold rock twenty feet out from shore. Not a soul for miles. The birds flew vast across the sky. They dipped and rose and came in a mass towards the shore, over our roof, and then vanished behind me, only for another group to come along moments later, from out in Bird Island direction.

The geese have, it seems, a perfect memory. They keep returning to the same rocks on the same tidal reefs, year after year. They teach their youngsters the art of the lough. Tomas used to row out in his grandfather's blue boat and catch the tidal drift. He watched the scrawl of the geese in the sky for hours, even in the rain. It seemed to me that it was only his boat, or his green oilskin, floating. He sometimes sat up to turn the oar, or to fix the binoculars on a particular point, and his body appeared to rise out of the water itself. In the evenings we rang the dinner bell on the shore to bring him home. He roamed up the garden with the oar over his shoulder.

The water had come halfway up my Wellingtons. It was too cold to swim, though at seventy-two years of age I still like, on occasion, to pull on a ratty wetsuit and take to the water. I remained another hour, watching the geese, until the rock was as good as submerged and my big unwieldy bottom was freezing even through the tail end of my coat. I hailed my dead son and promised him that I wouldn't let the bank take a single blade of grass or drop of water or broken slate of roof. I rose, stiff with sentiment, and hurried back to the cottage where Georgie waited for me. I fed her some beef, then built the fire with peat and logs, and read a selection of Longley poems.

In the afternoon I prepared a small glass of hot brandy with cloves but I knew myself too well to begin that early, and threw it in the fire where the cloves sizzled. I took the letter from the pantry, propped it up on the mantelpiece where it stood with all the other testaments of flight: photographs and bank demands and a ticking clock.

AN ANCIENT STORY: they desire my land. Five acres of island in an inlet of one hundred other islands. A large cottage, one boathouse, one fisherman's hut, one dilapidated kennel that my gone husband, Lawrence, built. The island was a working farm, bird dogs and bloodhounds, and for a while it was used for duck hunting, but not a single shot has sounded across the land since our Tomas died.

I can walk the land and still find old cartridges and pellet packages and the skulls of birds that fell from the sky. The trajectory of a shot bird is an incredible thing. Caught hard in the air, the sky continues to move behind, but the bird drops straight down, a plumb line of descent. A thump on the ground, a splash in the mudflats or out on the waves. And then the delight of the dogs skelping through the grass or over the water.

We had eight dogs at the best of times. There is only Georgie now, faithful old Labrador. She, too, is a little heavy on her paws but can still raise a ruckus when a mallard appears.

Just across the bridge there are monastic ruins ten times as old as my precious letter. A heritage site. Brass plates and stone stiles and climbing moss. The holy books were written here fifteen hundred years ago. Ink from the land. Parchment from cattle.

Not many visitors come down these narrow back roads to the edge

of the lough, but I am still curmudgeonly enough to swing a stick if
they stray past the ruins and come across the bridge, up the mudflats,
towards the cottage.

Three bedrooms, a large kitchen, a living room, a pantry and a
new sunroom built in the 1980s, built under the supervision of my
mother, as if we could get all that war out of us by looking to the
water. The sunroom is high and wide and full of light. A wooden
bench along the windows. Pillows patterned with Admiralty charts.
The rest of the cottage was built low to keep us humble. Rump-sprung
chairs and faded upholstery. A smoke-charred fireplace. A formal
bookcase of mahogany and glass. My son used to have to stoop
through the doorways. The walls are built thick, but there's a cold
that enters the belly of the cottage and remains. All the doors have to
be closed to seal the heat from the fire in the main room. Give me any
sort of light: preferably tilleys, storm lanterns, the blackened glass of
Victorian lamps.

Shells fall on the roof constantly from the birds overhead. There
are times I feel I am living inside a percussion instrument.

AT THE FIRST gesture of dawn, I pulled on the walking gear, grabbed
Georgie and took her around the edge of the lough, along the shore,
through the damp woods at the back of the ruins. Green boughs on
each side and moss soft underfoot. A stone stile in the wall.

She balked at a tangle of underbrush and barked at the shadows of
windblown trees scuppering through the ruins. Her ears high, her
back arched. The ancient monks used reeds to paint the gospels. Cowhide and wolfskin and the pelt of elk to keep out the weather. They
ground down bone, mixed it with grass and soil and berries and plants.
Bird quills. Leather bindings. Stone huts. Bronze bells. A series of
walls for defence. Round towers for lookout. The fires they lit were

small. The books they wrote were taken then across the lough, across the sea, to Scotland.

A female curlew comes to visit these parts sometimes, sailing over the cottage. The mottled grey and brown of her plumage. Her long slender beak looks like a scissors moving across the sky, following her call, snipping through its solitary grief. I like to catch her through the binoculars, in the mudflats, pecking at the earthworms that come up from down below, though I haven't heard her for quite a while now.

I walked through the ruins of the chapel at the nape of the hill, and picked up the cider cans left by youngsters in the village. *Raves,* I think they call them. They might as well. Better here than some foul little bedroom in a council estate. There were remnants of cigarette butts scattered all about, plastic sleeves, bottle caps, soggy boxes. I left the condoms for another day. Two forlorn little curlicues in the gravel. *She loves me, she loves me not.*

By the ruins of the chapel the wrapper of a chocolate bar sparred against the wind and an empty wine bottle completed the romance.

It was all enormously still and silent until a flock of new geese flew in their high patterns from the lough over the air. They made a noise close to rifle fire, and Georgie leapt up along the wall as if she could catch them in midair.

I dumped the litter in the rubbish bins near the heritage signs, crossed back over the bridge, circled around the island. A one-hour walk. Old woman and her dog. Georgie loped on ahead, flushing birds from the long grass. Broken lobster pots were strewn on a sandy patch near the water. The edges of the lough are never watertight, either to the land or the sea. The tides flow in and out. Boats and memory, too.

The phone was ringing by the time I got home. I pushed open the half-door, dropped the leash, walked through the low rooms, stood over the answering machine in the kitchen. The infernal red blinking as he spoke. Simon Leogue, the bank manager in Bangor, again. So polite and poised, a southern accent laced with some London, all our troubles in one voice. *Good morning, Mrs Carson.* A fine young man if he wasn't what he was, but he is.

The only way to erase a message is to listen to it first. The thought of listening twice was far too much for me, so I picked it up and let it drop midsentence, then yanked the plug from the wall. A brief and merciful silence. It was hardly the smartest move, though I have the BlackBerry in case of emergency.

I brought Georgie out the back to the sunroom. The geese formed against the changing sky. The tides beneath it can carry a body swiftly out to sea. Slewter, slaughter, holy water.

THEY SHOT TOMAS as he pulled up his boat to shore in October of 1978. Nineteen years old. Still in university, his second year, advanced probability. I am still not certain whether it was UVF or IRA or UFF or INLA or whatever other species of idiot was around at the time. In truth, I have a fair idea, but it hardly matters any more. Our ancient hatreds don't deserve capital letters.

They shot him for a bird gun. Within hearing range of the cottage in the dark of early morning so that my mother rushed into my bedroom and said: That's odd, Hannah, darling, did you hear that? Already Lawrence was running across the lawn, ice cracking under his feet, saying, Oh, my God, Tomas, oh, my God. We were sure at first he had shot himself, but it was three shots. He was out early, setting the decoys.

The current took him a long way from us before we caught him, down near the Narrows where he was spinning in relentlessly smaller circles. It's hardly wisdom, but the older I get the more I believe that our lives are built not out of time, but light. The problem is that the images that so often return to me are seldom those I want. The water was silver and black. The wind whipped cold. We waded through the shallows to get him. The boat still circling. A silver light rippled alongside us. His donkey jacket. Wading boots. Binoculars round his neck. So very young. He didn't look shot at all, just slumped over. Some frost on his eyebrows. I will never forget that. A little rime of white collecting there. One hand clenched in anger, the other open and limp. Lawrence reached into the boat and took him in his arms. He carried him to shore where the uniforms came running. Cursing their way through the shallows. Drop him, a voice said. Now. Drop him. Spotlights on the shore, though it was full morning. Sirens sounding. My own mother on the shore with her hand to her mouth. In her housecoat. Someone put a blanket around her shoulders. Her silence. Lawrence laid down my son at the edge of the reeds. The newspapers made it ever so simple: a young man out armed with a gun, besieged by men out armed with more guns. How far from real the truth is. I wanted then to take every murdering bastard in Northern Ireland, and have them sleep for a night in my boy's blue rowboat, out on the lough, in the dark, among the reeds, turning in primal celtic patterns.

I PULLED ON my wetsuit and went out the back door into the dark. The water came right up to the lawn. The low stone wall was green with slime. I zipped the wetboots tight and went down the slipway, waded in the high tide. Georgie barked on the shore and by the time I turned round she was already in the water. A reluctant swimmer, our Georgie, so it was all the more endearing that she paddled out, her brown eyes shining and just a little panicked. I must have looked quite a sight to her: the tight wetsuit, only the chub of my face visible along with a few grey hairs escaping from the side of the hood. I eased in. The small shock of cold, and then the lockdown of warmth.

To allay Georgie's fears I stayed close to shore, floating on my back, looking up at the stars making their claw marks. As a boy Tomas loved the notion that the light hitting our eyes might be coming from a star that had already disappeared. For a period he studied the sky and all its complex configurations. He heard the Alcock and Brown story from his grandmother, and wanted to know what Brown might have known way back then to navigate the Atlantic. Flying on instinct and beauty and fear. It amazed him that Brown had flown without a gyroscope. Tomas took his boat out on the lough and charted the stars on graph paper. He brought a sextant with him, binoculars, a spirit level, an infrared torch. The occasional patrols on the lough shone their lights at him: the Coast Guard were well versed in our family's habits, but the military units were miserable. Searchlights on their boats, they pulled up quick and sudden. Loud hailers. Parachute flares. He was petulant with them and gave them lip, until they figured out he was harmless enough, just a boy with an odd yearning, though once they tipped his boat over, and all his careful charts were ruined. In later years, in university halls, he darkened his windows, painted the walls black, cut luminous stickers out to place on the ceiling, navigated from there. A solitary life.

After he was taken from us — it is still so hard to say *murder* — I found myself obsessing about whether or not Tomas had ever kissed a girl, until I met one he had apparently gone out with for a while, a vulgar little hussy who worked in an insurance office on the Ormeau Road. She cured my illusions of another life for him.

There are times when the past acquires a particular resonance and we grow sensitive to the noises normally beyond the range of hearing. Our Tomas was very much nourished by the tangled skein of connections. He sat with his grandmother in our house on the Malone Road and listened to her stories, and wanted at one stage to create a mathematical model of where he came from: Newfoundland, Holland, Norway, Belfast, London, St Louis, Dublin. A zigzag line all the way back to Lily Duggan. I asked him what the diagram might look like and he thought about it for a moment and said that it could be something akin to a nest in a tree as seen against a background of high-speed cinematography. I had little idea what he meant at the time, though it strikes me now as intricately beautiful, the twigs taken from everywhere, bits and pieces, leaves and branches, crossing and crisscrossing, years of time lapse, Catholic, British, Protestant, Irish, atheist, American, Quaker, all the time the clouds dispersing in the shaped-out sky behind him.

Lord above, I miss my boy. Even more so as the years go by. At my most morose, I have to acknowledge that quite possibly the reason I put pen to paper is precisely because I have nobody left to whom I can tell the story. After Tomas died, Lawrence walked his tweeds towards another farm in Fermanagh, left the cottage to me. He left the guilt in the lough, said I would find my own way out, somehow. The truth of the matter is that the light at the end of the tunnel generally belongs to the pharmaceutical companies. There wasn't much hope I could take, even in memory. Two generations of mothers were still alive when Tomas was taken from us. He was happiest of all with his grandmother. Nana, he called her. They sometimes sat on deckchairs on the edge of the lough. She used to say that she was younger than him, and perhaps in some ways she was. It sounds corny when I strike the nib of the pen against the page, but there are times I think the pendulum has reached the top of its arc.

I SWAM FOR the best part of an hour until every small part of me hurt with cold, then I waddled up the garden with Georgie in tow. I changed into every cardigan I have ever owned and walked, still shivering, to the kitchen. Georgie was shoved up tight against the Aga stove and I joined her, then made a feed of sausages and eggs and beans. She curled up at my feet while I sat at the table, and wiped my feet on moonlight on the floor.

TO GET MY senses back after a night of tossing and turning, I walked Georgie around the island in the cold snap of dawn. Or rather she walked me. My curlew was calling from the eastern pladdies. I was glad to hear her after so long. I used to think that her call was forlorn, but her return makes her so much more than a sound.

Georgie ambled alongside me among the tangle of old ropes and smashed oars and broken orange buoys washed in on the edge of the shore. The tide was returning and I cut up towards the mudflats, pulled myself along by holding on to the long reeds, unsettled a smoky muck from the bottom of the water. I sat still for several minutes, the better to absorb the landscape, or rather be absorbed by it.

When I crested the curve in the road my phone beeped. Somehow the bank had got a hold of the number of my BlackBerry. There were two new messages waiting. Very polite. The suitors to my genteel poverty. The little red light pulsed in my pocket. I erased them without even listening.

I turned the corner and looked at the cottage, low against the lough. It struck me there and then that if I didn't do something quickly, I would not be able to do anything at all.

THE LAND ROVER started first time, ancient horse. Georgie climbed in the back seat, her muzzle to the glass. She needed a bath. I cracked the window. The clutch was tight and it took me a while, out the driveway, along past the pladdies, beyond the ruins, the four miles up to the village.

A handsome young man filled her with diesel and then returned my credit card with a slightly embarrassed shrug. He checked the tyres and put in a litre of oil, put his finger to the front of a backwards baseball hat.

'No charge, Mrs Carson,' he said. 'That's on us.'

He stuffed a rag into the pocket of his overalls, turned away. I called him back, closed his fingers around a single pound coin, and he blushed.

'Mind the road now.'

I pulled out in the light drizzle, my eyes hazy with gratitude.

Cars with their lights on in the middle of the morning blazed up behind me. I waved politely for them to go around me, then adjusted to a victory sign as more and more of them passed. Some of them even had the good humour to laugh. It took almost twenty minutes for me to get onto the main road, only narrowly avoiding a crash, which would have solved all my problems neatly.

I had to chuckle on the stretch near Comber when even a slow boat on a trailer passed me, the driver flashing her hazards.

The traffic in Bangor was backed up along the street. The town was bustling. Cars, lorries, delivery vans, bicycles. I hemmed the Land Rover into an illegal spot that demanded I should use a disabled sticker. The one I used for ferrying my mother back and forth was five years out of date, but I placed it up on the dashboard anyway.

I sat on the back bumper and changed from my Wellingtons into a good pair of shoes. I felt rather crusty in my old green hunting jacket, so I took it off and turned it inside out, draped it over my arm. I wore a cardigan and an old blue dress Lawrence had bought for me decades ago: the back of the dress had been let out several times so that it was a patchwork, but from the front it looked just fine, especially with the cardigan draped over it. I walked Georgie down High Street, her hair wild and unbrushed.

The doors of the bank were equipped with a series of confounding alarms. I was as touchy as a triggered trap. When I finally got inside they told me that I had to leave Georgie outside, that dogs were not allowed. I told the poor young clerk that I was not only deaf, but blind, too, and that Georgie was the only one around who had a Ph.D. in civil engineering, hence the only way I could pass their ridiculous Alcatraz.

'I'll see what I can do, Mrs Carson.'

I could see them conferring in the corner. Their little bespectacled cabal. They bobbed back and forth, little Halloween apples. The manager himself crossed in the glass behind and looked out at me, rather worried. I gave him an enormous wave. He surprised me by reciprocating, and I thought to myself that perhaps we could have a decent battle, he and I, but then I realized that there was nothing safe about a game of brinksmanship when, quite literally, my heritage was at stake.

I was made to wait forty-five minutes. Waves of claustrophobia came at me. The unhealthy illusion that I could deal with them was coupled with a dread that they would somehow lead me away in handcuffs. Georgie's bladder was up to its usual tricks and she let loose a stream over by the fake flowerpots. I was adolescently proud of her and fed her a handful of treats. She lay down and nuzzled against my feet. The afternoon light was fading outside. I watched the to-and-fro of the customers. My mother would never have stood for it. She would have been acutely offended, simply to be called into the bank, let alone to have them question her accounts and threaten her home. She had so loved rebuilding the cottage over the years: new windows, insulation, the sunroom. Even in her last years, pushing herself round in a wheelchair, she still obsessively wanted to make sure the walls were washed, the door handles oiled, the frames waterproofed.

Simon Leogue finally slid across the floor towards me. A grey suit. Sandy haired. Sharp-faced. Thirty-seven or thirty-eight years old, it's increasingly difficult for me to tell anyone's age. He glanced down at where Georgie was lying and said that he'd be happy for one of his employees to take the dog outside for what he called *a wee stroll*. I told him the dog was quite all right, thank you very much, and was tempted to berate his attempt at a northern accent but decided against it.

'Would you like to come to the back office, Mrs Carson?'

'I'd rather conduct my business here, thank you. I have nothing to be ashamed of. You can call me Hannah. I'm not a tombstone.'

'Of course not,' he said.

He had quick eyes. He flicked a look at Georgie. Undid an elastic strap from around a folder. His fingernails were not well groomed. There were red welts at the quick of his thumbs. But his hands disappeared when he went into the rather obvious annihilation of my finances. My mortgage. My overdraft. A spear is a spear – it can be thrown from a distance or slid in slowly, perfectly placed between the ribs. He did both at once, remarkably well. I almost liked him for his cool and aplomb. He said he might have to freeze the overdraft until I sold the house. Otherwise it would be foreclosed. He remained even-keeled, artfully uninformative, said there were a number of wonderful small flats for rent around town, or even out by the *sea* once my finances were properly in order. 'It's a lough, not the sea,' I said, but he shrugged as if there would never be a difference. He didn't mention assisted living or a nursing home, which really would have sent me off the cliff. I said something ridiculous about Mayakovsky and the amortization of the soul, but even I knew it was hopeless. I had to admire the skill and unfailing politeness with which I had been very quickly outmanoeuvred. He sat there, a young hound pleased with himself, and I felt denser than usual. The ancient iconography of the Irish imagination: eviction.

I said I would like to take the figures away with me and have my accountant study them properly.

He sighed heavily and slid his business card towards me. 'Accountant?' He said he would give me as much time as he could, but quite frankly there wasn't much left. 'My home number is on here if it's of any help.'

I was too self-sunken to respond. Strangely, there was a shine of grief in his eye. He blinked and looked away from me. I was terrified for a moment that he might be upset on my behalf.

'You should wash your hands better, Simon,' I said.

Georgie dwelled a little long on the floor and I yanked the lead hard, a savage thing to do, but my fury was welling towards tears, and I was not going to let it happen inside the bank.

Outside, the Bangor light stung my eyes. A surge of self-pity lodged at my breastbone. A farm tractor, of all things, trundled down Queens Parade. They are hardly seen any more these days, but this one had a young boy at the helm, a collie dog at his heels near the gear stick. He actually smiled back and raised a forefinger from the steering wheel when I nodded. Tomas was never the sort of boy who was cut out for work on the farm. He avoided it at all costs. Preferred the boat. Why Tomas took the shotgun out with him that morning, I have no idea. He wasn't even fond of bird hunting; it was simply the done thing, the stuff of his stepfather. In his early teens he never hunted at all. He preferred binoculars. Drifting out on the water. It all came down to vectors and angles. He wondered if there was a way to chart the natural world. There was a laze to him, our Tomas, he was never going to be one who lit up the world, but he was more than enough for me. The stolen gun never resurfaced. Who knows what history it served, or whether it was just thrown away and buried down in the bog to join the ancient elk, the bones, the butter?

I watched the tractor go, then straightened out soon enough with a quick slap of reality. The Land Rover was at the far end of the street, clamped. A pretty yellow boot. I wasn't even about to argue with the parking attendants. They stood, surly and malevolent, at the far end of the street. I went straight back across to the bank and got the cash from the machine in the wall before Simon could freeze the overdraft.

I begged them to let me go for free, but the parking attendants exercised their abundant ability to shrug. I paid the fine, but it still took them an age to remove the boot.

Georgie was sleeping in the back seat by the time I pulled down the laneway. I went digging in the garden out back to burn off the anger, or the fear, of the day. I turned a few sods in the old tomato patch. A drizzle fell across the sky, orange in the ambient light from Bangor. One never thinks the stars will disappear. Our failed attempts at navigation. I kicked the mud off my boots and went inside. How many times do we end up scraping the muck from the mirror? There was a gallery of rogues in the passageway near the pantry where I dropped the shovel. The everyday suspects. My mother in her tennis dress, a full-bodied red wine. My father in his RAF uniform. My grandfather at the gates of a linen factory. My American grandmother on the deck of a transatlantic liner. My Tomas holding up six mackerel on a single string. Jon Kilroyan, the farmhand, outside the fisherman's cottage. My husband in tweeds and knee-high wading boots. Neighbours and old friends from the Women's Coalition. A photo of me out fox hunting when I was very young, a beagle trotting behind me, my whole life so apparently prearranged, the privilege aligned along my spine.

TWO DAYS OF storms. Georgie and I stayed indoors. The weather hacked across the lough. The sky was dark. Branches fell from the trees. Rain fell relentlessly. I got lost in its antiphonies.

On the third day, I left. The letter sat in the passenger seat beside me, sleeved in its archival plastic. Hardly the best way to keep it, I suppose, but short of a humidified bank vault, it would have to do.

The road to Belfast thickened with traffic. Cars behind me flashed their headlights and beeped loudly as they passed. I practised my victory sign again, though it seems that the middle finger is the salute of choice these days. The cars beeped and swerved. I was glad to crawl along.

Roundabouts have always confounded me. Just beyond Comber I somehow discovered myself on the road to Stormont, where my mother and I spent a good deal of time over a decade ago. She cried on Good Friday when the peace agreement was signed. Great fits of happy tears. She slid, like a seal, out of any old sadness she carried. There were still four more months left in her. She wanted to hold out for the full century, but told me shortly before she died that enough was enough. Why does death so catch us by surprise? When Tomas was taken away from her, she said it was as if a hole had been punched through her chest to wring out her ancient heart. Now she was graced by the idea of what she called George Mitchell's peace. She had a fondness too for John Hume, his head of wavy hair. Good men, she said. They had the courage to remain volleying at the net. One of her happiest moments was meeting Mitchell at the tennis club. His grey hair. His tracksuit top. The unfailing politeness of the man. The slight touch of an inner rogue to him. He stood with the racquet behind his back. He bowed to her as she spoke. The wheels turning in his mind, she knew. She told him he needed to work on his backhand.

For her, Mitchell's peace laid Tomas to rest. She went in her sleep. She was cremated and we billowed her out over the western sea. Her whole life defined by water, Newfoundland and beyond. There are times I imagine that she rode in that Vickers Vimy herself, willed it across the ocean. She so loved the story of Alcock and Brown, and often took out the photographs, showed them to us, went over them in intimate detail. So much of it was where her own life began.

My own felt as if it were taking the swinging pendulum down. It was three or four years since I had been in Belfast. Our dreary, shapeless, soot-sullied town. Murals, alleyways, black taxis, high yellow cranes. It has always been so aggressively gloomy. But the university area surprised me – it was brighter, greener, full of spark. I parked and walked a distracted Georgie along, pulling hard at her lead. What marvellous names the city has, perhaps to carry away our grief. Holyland. Cairo Street. Damascus. Jerusalem. Palestine.

I found the office easily enough, above a Spanish restaurant on Botanic Avenue. Up the stairs. Into the dusty light. The philatelist was short, slight, bald, with hanging spectacles and a whiff of disintegration. Belfast is full of odd people who have hidden away from the Troubles: they live inside tiny spaces and enormous imaginations. He put his spectacles on his nose and peered at me with wide eyes. There was something of the raccoon about him. He didn't seem at all perturbed by the presence of Georgie who not so delicately sniffed his crotch.

He wiped my chair with his handkerchief before I sat, then he rounded his desk, folded his hands and said my name as if it were the only punctuation the day deserved.

The library lights cast odd shadows. He was framed by a row of Graham Greene novels, perfectly arranged leather editions. The slightest clue can give us away. He opened the plastic and tut-tutted a little bit, I wasn't sure if in awe or derision. He glanced at me and then back to the letter. He put on a pair of forensic gloves and set the envelope down on a piece of blue felt, turned it over with a pair of tweezers. I tried to tell him the story, but he kept holding up a finger to stop me. He surprised me by clicking on a brand-new computer and deftly scrolling through his files. He looked up to say that there were dozens of instances of Alcock and Brown letters available, he had been to many shows in Britain where he had seen the actual letters himself, they were worth considerable sums especially if they were in fine condition. He said my letter had come from Newfoundland, for sure, that the envelope was correct, the indicia were authentic, but it wasn't a transAtlantic stamp, it was an ordinary Cabot. There was no postmark so it could have been sent any year at all and in all the records there was never any mention of another letter and so there was no form of absolute authentication.

The name Jennings meant nothing to him. Nor did Frederick Douglass. He took his magnetic eyeglasses apart and let them fall at the hollow of his little chest. 'To be frank with you, you'd have to open it, Mrs Carson.'

I told him that he had missed my mother by about a decade and that she could have authenticated it quite easily, she had been in the Cochrane Hotel when the flight took off. Seventeen years old. She had watched the plane – and the letter – leave and go small against the sky. It never got to Cork. Years later she followed the letter to England, met Arthur Brown in Swansea. He had forgotten the letter in his tunic pocket. He gave it to her and Emily, and she tucked it away, not knowing what it might become. I was brief and to the point but still he seemed to disappear into his chair, until finally he said that he couldn't quite bring himself to give an absolute value to what was obviously a family heirloom, though it was worth a considerable amount, perhaps a couple of hundred pounds, though with a postmark it could be several times this.

He rose from his chair and opened the door, pausing to scratch Georgie behind the ears. What had I expected anyway? On Botanic Avenue the light stung my eyes, so I made my way down to the Spanish restaurant where the pretty young owner took pity on me and bought me a glass of Rioja along with some tapas, while her husband played on the piano, ragtime and Hoagy Carmichael tunes. Our own age never ceases to astound us. I am quite sure that Lily Duggan felt something similar once, and Emily Ehrlich, and Lottie Tuttle, too, the succession of women whose lives were folded in the letter I held in my hand.

I am not of the opinion that we become empty chairs, but we certainly end up making room for others along the way.

TWO GLASSES OF wine got the better of me. Dizzy, I eventually found the car, drove a while, but then pulled into the side of the Newtownards Road. I must have dozed for a few moments because Georgie began snarling and there was an impatient knocking on the window. A woman in uniform. I rolled down the window. Dark had fallen.

'You're parked cockeyed,' she said.

The truth was that I hadn't even realized I was parked at all. I could almost see my own thoughts moving through my mind, carp in a pool, obvious and slow. 'Excuse me, officer.' I started the engine, but she leant in across the steering wheel and took the keys.

'Have you been drinking?'

I reached across and stroked Georgie's neck.

'Do you have any family nearby?'

I told her I didn't know a soul, but then she threatened to breathalyze me, and suggested that I might have to spend the night at the police station – she called it the barracks – and I cast around for who might still be around in the city.

I had a sudden recollection of days that still seem agile with laughter. In the 1960s, Lawrence used to belong to a group of gentlemen farmers who got together on Saturday mornings. They wore tweed jackets. Plus fours. Their cartridge belts clanked as they stepped down along the lough. The *wives* – as we were known back then – played tennis. I never quite inherited my mother's passion for the game but I went along with it. We met our husbands in the early evening, drank cocktails, drove our cars into ditches on the way home. There is still, I am convinced, an imprint of our wheels on the mudflats, like the remnants of herons.

It's hardly a hallelujah memory, but I must admit I was rather generous with my affection. Over the years, I had several affairs, most of them hurried and fretful and frankly dreary. A meeting in the car park, snatched moments in a golf-club bathroom, the cramped quarters of a patched-up yacht. The men all seemed to want mulligans with their lives. I went home to Lawrence, steeped in guilt and melancholy, promised myself never to stray again. I'm quite sure he did the same also, but I was never interested in finding out. I hunkered into motherhood. Still there were occasional moments when the world got away from me. The most memorable was a single afternoon with Jack Craddogh, a history professor from Queen's University who owned a small summer house just outside Portaferry, all glass and champagne and seclusion. His wife was a furniture designer who regularly went to London. We approached each other tentatively at first, but then he ripped the buttons off my dress and the afternoon disappeared into ecstasy. How odd to recall the gymnastics we were capable of: it is as if I have taken a photograph of the one moment when my young hand lay across his thumping chest.

I stammered a moment, then told the policewoman that I knew a couple who lived nearby, in the direction of Donegall Square.

'Call them,' she said, thrusting a mobile phone at me, but I surprised her with my BlackBerry. Jack answered after the very first ring. He, too, sounded like he had a little vermouth on his tongue. I asked if I could stay the evening. He was confused and I bawled down the phone that they were going to throw Georgie and me in jail for the night.

'Georgie?' he said, and then he remembered. 'Oh, Hannah.' Some muffled complaints in the background, a complicated sigh.

The policewoman hesitated a moment, then said she would drive behind me to make sure I got where I wanted. I must have wobbled a little bit because she pulled me over again and drove the car herself while her partner continued behind us. She said that it was pathetic at my age to be drinking and driving, and if it wasn't for the dog she would have arrested me there and then. She looked like the sort of woman who had once, long ago, had a steel rod expertly inserted up her backside. It would hardly emerge now. I was tempted to tell her my exact history with Jack Craddogh, just to see if I could coax a smile out of her – he actually bit the very last button off my dress, pretended to swallow it, kissed me – but I sat quietly beside her, properly chagrined and said nothing. We were all young once: my mother used to say we should make sure to drink the wine before it turns.

We pulled up to Jack's large Victorian. He stood framed in the doorway under the stained glass, still a tall elegant man. His wife, Paula, lurked in a dressing gown beside him.

Jack came down the path, carrying his age, and opened the small ironwork gate and shook the hand of the policewoman, assured her that he had it all taken care of, he'd make sure I had a good night's sleep. He seemed a little miffed at the idea of looking after Georgie, too, but I walked her through the renovated house – high ceilings and transoms and rich wallpaper and old paintings – and put her out on the small back patio where she rested her head on her paws and re-signed herself to her fate.

The three of us sat at his kitchen table, surrounded by expensive modern machinery, drinking tea, the past banging its flint against the present. Jack had become a birding enthusiast in recent years, a description which almost made me spit up my tea in laughter. The oystercatcher, the wigeon, the black-tailed godwit. He and his wife had taken to sketching the birds in the area. They had often contemplated calling across to my cottage, they said, but hadn't quite made it, the time slipped away from them. I had to admit that the watercolour sketches were quite beautiful and they made me question my own use of time: out there sitting, swimming, watching, waiting.

The thought of the cottage brought a mawkish mist to my eyes, names washed away by decades of rain, and I stammered something about the idea of sketching flight.

Jack broke the seal on a bottle of brandy, and we warmed ourselves with talk of his other ongoing project: he had largely retired, but was still teaching one course on nineteenth-century history at Queen's. His fascination was what he called the literature of the colonial. He spoke slowly, as if chewing his words. His hands were liver-spotted. He poured the brandy with a slight shake.

After a second glass Paula announced that she would leave us youngsters be – she actually used the word *youngsters* – and Jack stood to accompany her out of the room, and his hand brushed against her rear end, which seemed a tremendous act of bravery in the circumstances. He kissed her flush on the lips as if to reassure her. I heard her clomping up the stairs with another sigh.

'So,' he said, as if everything between us had begun anew, and my hand was still hovering barely above his labouring heart. 'What brings you to these parts, Hannah?'

I had the unpleasant sensation that my life was circling around again, only I was even more unequipped for it than ever. He knew of the letter from years gone by, but had never actually seen it. It was, he said, the first time he had ever come upon an actual *living conceit*. I didn't quite know what he meant, and I was tempted to rip the letter open right there in front of his eyes, just to destroy the assertion. My life and my house didn't seem a *conceit* to me at all: it was an actual, breathing place where gulls dropped shells from on high, and where the doors had to be closed to keep in the heat, and where the ghosts had to duck their heads when they walked through the low rooms. I don't suppose Jack Craddogh was too astounded that I and my family had somehow squandered most of my late grandfather's linen money down over the years.

I was careful how I revealed the details, but he said there was very little hope that the university would be willing to take a chance on an unopened letter no matter what sort of verification could be given.

But the letter clearly piqued his interest. He was aware of the Douglass connection: it had, he said, become fashionable of late for the Irish to think themselves tremendously tolerant. He used the word *they* like a doorway he could open and close. The academic question was when, in fact, *they,* the Irish, had become white. It was stitched in with notions of colonialism and loss. He had studied political figures in Australia, Britain and the Tammany Hall of old New York, and how they braided into the literature of the time, how this whiteness emerged. He was wary of scholars who aligned themselves too closely with what he called the darker edges. It all seemed a little too dust-choked for me. But he knew, he said, a number of scholars who were studying Douglass's time in Britain and Ireland. He could put me in touch with one of them, David Manyaki, from Kenya, who was teaching in university in Dublin.

I felt myself rather dizzy with all the geography and the brandy. He rattled on about some notion of inner colonization and he broke a little smile when I began to yawn. I really needed some rest, I told him. I didn't have the capacity for absorption that I once had. He smiled at me, put his hand upon mine, kept it there a moment, looked me directly in the eye until I glanced away. I could hear his wife pacing the floorboards above: putting towels and a toothbrush and a nightgown on the guest bed, no doubt.

He tried to lean towards me. I have to admit it was somewhat flattering. I said I would file it under fatigue rather than desire. Seventy-two years old: some things remain better off remembered.

THE MORNING BROKE bright and cold. The air snapped. The high gothic towers of the Lanyon Building stood stark against a very blue sky. The students walked brisk and short-haired along the manicured paths.

My own days in the university in the late 1950s were quick and shallow. Literature had not prepared me for pregnancy at nineteen. My sweetheart from Amsterdam returned to his canals. I could hardly blame him. I was, for a long time, the sort of failed Presbyterian girl who sucked her hair into endpoints and spouted on about revolution and justice. He was terrified, poor boy. He sent money every Christmas, until one year the envelopes just vanished altogether, and Tomas never got a chance to see him.

Tomas's days at university were cut short, too. When I dropped him off, in 1976, there were students out along the footpaths with their Martin Luther King posters and Miriam Makeba T-shirts. Eight years since the Troubles began and they were still singing: *We shall overcome*. Tomas drifted among them. A hopeful shine in his eyes. He wore his hair curly and his bell-bottoms wide. He was once part of a student occupation where they took over the arts building and they were foolish enough to release white doves out the window. He grew quieter as the days went on. Put his head in his maths books. He never quite had both oars in the water, but he thought he might become an actuary. The length of lives, the probability of survival. No formula for our ironies. What was it like, that dark morning, when a couple of masked men parted the bushes? What small tremor came upon him when he clutched a bullet to his stomach?

I quit the university grounds and brought Georgie back to the car. She laid her head in my lap as I drove. The small comforts.

When I got home to the island there was another letter from the bank. From the ponderous imagination of Simon Leogue. Simon says, You're broke. Simon says, Pay up. Simon says, Sell or else. Simon says: Now. *Now.*

How was it I had mortgaged and remortgaged everything that had gone before me? From the lough I looked back at the house and the whole kitchen pulsed red, then dark, then red again. I felt that I had passed across to a shore where I did not truly live, but then it struck me it was only the answering machine on the kitchen sideboard. I had thought for a while about blackening it out with a piece of paper and stripping it bare only when I wanted to. *Please leave a message at the tone.* I swam for a half hour, then walked up the garden, towelled Georgie, got dressed, put the kettle on, waited for it to whistle. I had a fair idea that the message was the bank calling once more, but a red light is a red light.

As it turned out, it was Jack's professor friend, David Manyaki, who said that he was intrigued by the idea of a letter that might pertain to Douglass and that if I ever made it to Dublin he would be delighted to buy me lunch.

An African accent. He sounded older, accomplished, careful. Some Harris Tweed in the voice.

EARLY MORNING SHELLS fell from the sky, bouncing on the slate roof. The gulls up there, small ziggurats across the expanse. I walked out into the dew. A couple of stray mussels lay open-shelled in the grass. It was Debussy who said that the music is what is contained between the notes. It was a relief to be home, and my energy had returned despite my bedraggled sleep. I took the pile of bills and burnt them in the fireplace.

In the living room near the fire, some of my mother's old watercolours hung. In her later years, she took up painting as her interest in photography waned. She thought the new machinery took the joy out of the work. She liked to sit in the sunroom and paint: there is one of the cottage itself, the blue half-door open and the lough stretching endlessly behind it.

I sat in the kitchen listening to the radio while a ten-force blew in. The wind began hammering across the lough. Within an hour, huge waves were breaking hard against the seawall. The rain came up the garden and whacked the windowpanes and the storm put its shoulder to the lough.

David Manyaki. An odd name. He would be a widower with an Achebe face perhaps. A ledge of grey hair. A deep brow. A serious stare. Or perhaps he was a white man with an African accent. Silver spectacles and charm. With leather patches on the elbows of his jacket.

I wondered if I should BlackBerry him or Google him or whatever the phrase may be, but my mobile phone was cut off, no signal.

WHEN I EXCAVATE my childhood it is always the journey to the cottage from the Malone Road that I like the most. Sitting in the car with my mother and father. We remember paths as much as we remember people. I wanted to retrace some of the miles for old times' sake. I looped north to Newtownards, then east through Greyabbey and south by Kircubbin, all the way along the loughshore.

There is a beautiful slant to the ancient ferryboat at Portaferry. I queued on the eastern shore and watched the boat come across. Churning a thin line of white. About a dozen cars on deck, the sun shining on their windscreens. A few children on the upper level, looking out over the channel for porpoises breaking the water. The journey across the Narrows is only a few hundred yards, but the boat has to attack the channel at an angle, depending on the strength and direction of the tide. For four hundred years it has gone back and forth. In the distance, the mountains lay purple against the sky. Perhaps they were called the Mournes for another reason: in the face of such beauty it always shocks me that we blew ourselves asunder for so many years.

The ferry negotiated the current, slid into dock. I drove the Land Rover on, rolled down the window, paid the tall young ferryman. He didn't look like the sort of young man who would understand a quip about the Styx. Still, he was good-humoured and smiling. For a moment all sense, even memory, of land disappeared. I put on the handbrake, closed the car door, brought Georgie to the upper deck for a breath of fresh air.

At the far end, a young couple snuggled into each other, speaking Russian. Perhaps a honeymoon. I tugged on Georgie's lead and wandered along to where a family from Portavogie were breaking out sandwiches and a flask of hot tea. Two parents, six kids. They offered Georgie bits and pieces of their sandwiches, rubbed her neck. They were on their way down south, they said, for the Queen's visit. I had been out of the loop, away from what the world thinks of itself. I had neglected the newspaper for many months. No television. My radio was permanently tuned to the classical station.

'The Queen herself,' said the young mother, clearly beaming, as if there might be multiple copies of the monarchy. Her tongue was loose with a little lager. She said with a sniff that President Obama was coming, too, in the exact same week. Strange collisions. It hardly mattered: all I had to do was sell my letter.

The ferry bumped up against the far shore. Gulls wheeled above us. I bid the family good day and shunted Georgie back into the car.

I skirted round the coast road. To hell with the cost of diesel. A large queue of cars gathered impatiently behind me. They overtook, flashing their headlights. One even stopped in the middle of the road, got out of his car, and said: 'Fuck you, you stupid old cow,' and I thanked him for his remarkable eloquence. I enquired if he, too, was on his way to see the Queen. A footman's humour. He didn't laugh.

There was no avoiding the busy road. Large trucks bore up behind. I was going so fast that the steering wheel shook in my hands. A rigid pain in both my shoulders. I passed the border without even knowing it and when I stopped at the first petrol station I could find, I recalled that I needed to get euros. The clerk, a young Asian gentleman, directed me towards the bank machine. A moment of freeze. What message would come up on the screen? How do you explain, at seventy-two years of age, such a stranded life?

The screen flickered an instant, but out came the small sheaf of money, the little rollers of joy.

I bought Georgie a celebratory sausage roll. I thought about splurging on a packet of cigarettes, a habit from the old days, but decided against it. We inched out onto the old road with a full tank of diesel.

I switched on the radio in the car. All the talk was of security and the Queen's visit. They didn't seem so worried about a bullet for Obama. Our complex histories. Inner colonialism indeed. I switched the station. The traffic deepened the farther south I got. It had already taken me four hours from Belfast, largely to do with Georgie's bladder control. Every twenty miles or so I had to pull the car to the side in order to let her relieve herself. She wasn't too fond of the journey and kept whimpering in the back seat until I finally allowed her to sit up front with her head out the passenger-side window.

It was early evening by the time I reached the outskirts of the city. I dawdled along, cursing myself for having booked a hotel in the city centre. It would have been far easier to find a place on the outskirts. Dublin so much like anywhere else. Swerving flyovers. Shopping centres. Streets pepper-sprayed with *For Sale* signs. *Closing Down. Liquidity Blowout.* Empty glass towers. The repetitive strain of what we have all become. The vain show. The status hunger. I took advantage of the bus lanes and made my way along Gardiner Street. A Guard tried to flag me but I just kept going, waggling my northern licence plate like a young girl parading herself along. I wanted to walk across the Beckett Bridge just for the sheer irony of it, *No matter, try again, fail again, fail better,* but got caught up in a vicious series of one-way junctions and traffic roadblocks for the state visits.

It was almost eight o'clock in the evening when I finally pulled up outside the Shelbourne, an expensive treat for myself. The valet, a vile little Spanish snob, looked at the car and then at me with more disdain than I can possibly describe, and then I was curtly told that there were no dogs allowed. Of course not. I had to admit to myself that I had known it all along. No point fooling any longer. Not much beyond a snob myself, of course. I feigned outrage and indignation, then promptly got snarled in the traffic again. The truth was I had hardly any money left at all, certainly not for the luxury of a hotel.

Georgie and I slept in the car park by the beach out at Sandymount. Four other vehicles alongside me. Homeless families, I presumed. There was the vacant thought of how ordinary my own problems were. The families were sandwiched tight in their cars. Blankets and hats pulled up around them. All their possessions piled high on the roof, strapped down with rope. They looked like figures from some of my mother's earliest black-and-white photographs. We seem to have a touching conviction that these things will never happen in our own territory. As if nothing of the past can happen in the present. The Grapes of Wrath. One of the cars even had a bumper sticker: *Celtic Tiger, My Arse.* The Guards paid us a visit in the middle of the night, shone a torch in the window, but allowed us be. I pulled my coat high and huddled into the seat. A chill knifed through the gap in the door. I pulled Georgie into my lap to warm me, but she lost her bladder twice, poor thing.

In the morning the children from the neighbouring car were staring in the window. To distract them while I changed, I asked them to take Georgie for a run along the strand. I slipped them a two-euro coin. Still, one of the little monsters said: 'She smells.' Frankly, I didn't know if she meant me or the dog. A surge of grief in my stomach. The children looked relieved to get away from me. I watched the imprint of their feet in the soft sand dissolve. An enormous stretch of grey towards the green of the headlands.

Later I walked with Georgie to Irishtown for breakfast and found a café where they allowed her to doze at my feet. I washed my coat out in the sink, dabbed my dress clean, stared at myself in the mirror. I combed my hair and put on a line of lipstick. Small matters, ancient pride.

The radio warned of more huge traffic jams. I left the car at the beach and took a taxi, which tried looping its way round towards the area of Smithfield. The driver was a local. 'Keep the dog at your feet for fucksake,' he said. A roll of fat twisted at the back of his neck.

We hit more traffic and found ourselves snared. He cursed the Queen with remarkable dexterity. I had to get out and walk the last quarter mile. The driver asked for a tip. *Throwaway,* I thought, but before I could say anything he cursed and sped off.

Smithfield was a shabby little area of the city that didn't fit my perception of what it might have been, but then again neither did David Manyaki who was waiting for me on the street corner.

I had expected an older man, formal, grey-haired, leather patches on the sleeves of his jacket. With silver spectacles and a gravelly manner. Perhaps he would wear one of those small African hats, I could not for the life of me remember the name of them, small and boxy and colourful. Or maybe he would look more like those tall Nigerian businessmen in their shiny blue suits and tight white shirts and baleful little bellies?

Manyaki was in his early thirties. An elegant jumble sale. He was wide of chest, muscled, with a slight touch of flab about him. His hair was in loose cornrows, but fell into short tubes that swung down to his jaw – I tried to remember the word for the style, but couldn't, my mind wasn't catching. He wore a rumpled sports jacket, but underneath it was a colourful dashiki, yellow with threaded silver. He shook my hand. I felt heavy and frumpy, but there was something about Manyaki that sprinkled a line of salt along my spine. He reached for Georgie and petted her. His accent was more deeply African than it had been on the phone, though there was a lilt of Oxford to it.

'Dreadlocks,' I said to him, rather ridiculously.

He laughed.

We entered a dank little café. The owners had set up a small television on the counter where they were watching the events of the day unfold: the Queen was on her way to the Garden of Remembrance. There were scattered protests in the streets. No riot guns, no rubber bullets, no CS gas. The TV commentators were interested in the notion that she had landed in a green dress. I have never been much for monarchy, and although I grew up nominally Protestant, an ancient part of me still aligned itself with Lily Duggan.

We ordered coffee. The television droned in the background.

When I showed Manyaki the letter, he held the plastic at the very edge and turned it around in his fingers. I explained to him that it was written on behalf of my great-grandmother who had worked as a young girl in the house on this very street, Brunswick, but he corrected me immediately and said that Douglass had stayed on Great Brunswick, which was now renamed Pearse Street.

'I was wondering why you wanted to meet here,' he said.

'This is not Great Brunswick?'

'Afraid not.'

I felt a flood of embarrassment that he might know more about my own great-grandmother's workplace than me, but he was the scholar after all. He, too, seemed chagrined that he had corrected me, and said there wasn't really all that much known about the street, or the house, since it was long knocked down, though Richard Webb greatly interested him. He said we could try to walk down to Pearse Street, but the Queen's visit had put a tourniquet on the city.

The letter was sealed in the archival sleeve. He wasn't perturbed at the idea that he couldn't open it. He said he had no real idea what had happened to Isabel Jennings, though she had quite possibly helped Frederick Douglass to buy his freedom through a woman in Newcastle, an Ellen Richardson, a Quaker long active in the cause.

— He went back to America unslaved.

Unslaved. It was a curious and lovely word, and I liked Manyaki all the more for it. There was no more Brown Street left in Cork either, he said. It had been knocked down, as far as he knew, in the 1960s, to make way for a supermarket. He wasn't sure when the Jennings family had left, though he had an inkling that it might have been during the Famine. There was a good deal of guilt for anyone to carry, he said, English or Anglo. I told him that there had been an amethyst brooch that went down through the decades also, but it had long been lost somewhere in Canada – Toronto or perhaps St John's.

He lifted his glasses and squinted up at the television screen. A helicopter hovered. This remarkable peace that has held so long.

Manyaki held the letter at its edges and turned it over, back and forth, then brought it close to the light until I asked him not to expose it too much as the handwriting was delicate, even inside the plastic.

What I liked most about Manyaki is that he did not ask me to open the letter, nor to borrow it so his colleagues in university could bombard it with protons or neutrons or whatever else they might use to discern what lay inside. I think he understood that I wasn't interested in getting to the endpoint, if there was any, and that the prospect of truth was not especially attractive: for such a young man, an academic, he was still curiously interested in the elusive.

There was a collector in Chicago, he said, who had paid thousands for Douglass memorabilia. The collector had already bought a Bible that had belonged to Douglass, and had made an outrageous bid on a pair of barbells that ended up, instead, in a Washington, DC, museum.

Manyaki ran a finger along his temple: 'Any clue what the letter says?'

'I think it's just a thank-you note . . .'

'Oh.'

'As far as I know.'

'Well, that's our secret then.'

'Nobody's ever opened it. Jack Craddogh calls it a conceit.'

'He would,' said Manyaki, and I liked him all the more for his remarkable candour. He seemed to drift away for a moment, stirring sugar into his coffee. 'My father used to write me letters on that thin airmail paper, the crinkly stuff.' He said nothing more, but pried open the top of the plastic and inhaled the smell and then looked up sheepishly at me. What distances had he come? What stories did he himself carry?

Manyaki took out his phone and began snapping pictures of the letter. He was careful with it but there were a couple of tiny little flakes that had separated from the plastic: no more than bits of dust really. The natural entropy of things. I said something inane about us all falling apart in various ways, and he shut the plastic but a tiny pinhead of the paper had fallen on the table.

'You really think you can get a price for it?' I asked.

'How much do you need?'

I half-laughed. He did, too, but gently.

He held his head at a slight angle, like a man whose face has just been touched by someone he did not yet really know. Why had the letter been kept in the first place? The things we put away most carefully in a drawer might very well be the things we will never, again, find. He reached across as if to touch the back of my hand but drew back and picked up his coffee mug instead.

'I can check it out,' he said, pushing back the archival sleeve across the table. 'I'll email these photos later on today.'

The crumbs from the envelope still lay on the table. He glanced down at them. I'm sure he did it without thinking, but Manyaki absently licked the top of his finger and pressed it down upon one. He was looking beyond my shoulder. A tiny piece of paper. The size of a needlehead. He looked at it a long time, but was clearly off somewhere else in a reverie. He dabbed the crumb onto his tongue, held it there a moment, then swallowed.

When he realized what he had done, he stammered an apology but I said it was all right, it would have been swept away with the dishes and teacups anyway.

I DROVE OUT from Sandymount to Manyaki's house later that night. He lived farther along the coast in Dún Laoghaire. Georgie had taken ill in the car. She was not able to move her hindquarters, and had lost control of her bowels. I tried to carry her. The sheer weight. I staggered up the steps and rang the doorbell.

His wife was a pale Irish beauty with a sophisticated accent. 'Aoibheann,' she said. She took Georgie from my arms immediately and backed into the shadows.

It was a beautiful house with all manner of artwork, small sculptures on white pedestals, a line of abstracts and what looked to me like a Sean Scully painting along the staircase.

She hurried me into the kitchen where Manyaki was sitting at an islanded countertop. Two young boys beside him, in football pyjamas, doing their homework. Their sons. A perfect blend. They would have been called *mulatto* once.

'Hannah,' he said. 'I thought you were going back up north.'

'Georgie's sick.'

'Do you need a veterinarian?' said Aoibheann.

Manyaki spread out a sheet of newspaper near the rear kitchen door, put Georgie down upon it, searched on his mobile phone. It took several calls, but he found one in nearby Dalkey on house-call duty. On the phone his accent was more Oxford than African now, his words more clipped and angular. I wondered what sort of upbringing he'd had, his father a civil servant perhaps, his mother a teacher. Or maybe a small dusty suburb of Mombasa. Swimming pools. Cool white linen. Or a small balcony overlooking a hot street. An imam calling everyone out to prayer. The ample sleeves of his father's robes. The arrests, the tortures, the disappearances. Or perhaps he had grown up wealthy, a housetop on a hill, the radio tuned to BBC, a youth in the swimming pools of Nairobi. A university education, a squalid flat in London maybe? How had he ended up here, at the edge of the Irish Sea? What was it that brought us such distances, rowing upwards into the past?

He snapped the phone shut and went back to working with his children on their homework. I felt rather foolish standing there alone – he had forgotten me for a moment. I was grateful that his wife took me by the elbow, sat me down at the granite island and poured a glass of cranberry juice for me.

The kitchen didn't aspire to a magazine page but it could have – fine cabinetry, elaborate knives in butcher-block holders, a brand-new stove made to appear ancient, a red espresso machine, a small remote-control TV that actually appeared from a panel in the fridge. Aoibheann fussed over me – 'Sit down, sit down,' she said – but then had the grace to allow me to cut some shallots and slice potatoes for gratin. She somehow managed to refill the glass of cranberry without my noticing. The news flickered on the fridge: the Queen with the Irish president, another bank collapse, a bus crash.

The doorbell finally rang. The veterinarian was a young woman who already seemed tired of all the dramas she faced. She clicked open a small black leather case and leaned over Georgie.

'Calm down,' she said to me without even looking me in the eye.

She examined Georgie carefully, caressed her belly, examined her legs, looked at a stool sample, shone a light at her teeth and throat, and told me the dog was old. As if that were a revelation. I was quite sure she was going to tell me that she would have to put Georgie down, but she said that the dog was simply exhausted and a little malnourished, possibly had an intestinal infection, that she could do with a round of antibiotics just in case. There was an element of tut-tut in her manner. Malnourished. I felt myself cringe. She scribbled out a prescription and waved it in the air with a bill. Eighty euros.

I fumbled in my purse but Aoibheann just shook her head, opened her handbag, took out her wallet.

'You'll stay the night with us,' she said, glancing across at Manyaki.

NOTHING EVER FINISHES. Aoibheann came from a wealthy Irish family, the Quinlans, who had made quite a fortune over the years in food processing and banking. Her father, Michael Quinlan, was a regular on the pages of Irish business magazines. Father and daughter were largely estranged it seems, possibly due to the marriage with Manyaki.

She and Manyaki had been married in London in a civil ceremony and some element of mystery shrouded their past, perhaps a child or an immigration scandal, it was unclear to me, though it hardly mattered; they were a good couple, and whatever went on with her father seemed to have bridged them rather than torn them asunder. They moved generously around each other, nothing false or cloying. Their children were loud and obnoxious at the dinner table in the manner of children everywhere. Oisin and Conor. Five and seven years old, as dark as they were light.

Aoibheann ran a bath for me in the claw-footed tub. I put my face under the water. She had left some bath-oil beads in a small jar with a ribbon. I reached for it but the whole jar tumbled. One dissolved in my hand. From a distance I could hear the ship horns, boats moving through Dún Laoghaire. Everyone rushing to get somewhere. The desire for elsewhere. The same port that Frederick Douglass came through all those years ago. The water lapping around me. Travelling the widening splash. Tomas. They shot him for a bird gun. George Mitchell's peace. The Queen had bowed her head at the Garden of Remembrance.

There was a loud banging on the door and Manyaki burst into the room. I spluttered up naked from the water. My body, obedient to the ongoing forces of gravity. He shuffled backwards, embarrassed beyond himself, out of the bathroom.

'I'm sorry, I'm sorry,' he called from the corridor, 'I've just been knocking. I thought you were maybe sick, or something.'

The water was freezing. I must have been lying there for quite a while. I ran the hot water and climbed back in. Aoibheann came up moments later with a cup of tea for me. 'I gave your husband quite an eyeful, I'm afraid.'

She threw her head back and laughed: no derision.

'He might need therapy,' I said.

'Oh, we know all about therapy in this house.'

There was something pure and familiar about her. A device,

perhaps, to help her shuck her father's notoriety. She fanned the hot
water upwards with her hands to warm me, dropped a couple more
soft bath beads in without ever looking at my body.

'I'll leave you be,' she said.

'No, that's all right. You can stay.'

'Oh,' she said.

'Quite frankly, I'd like the company. I really don't want to fall
asleep again.'

She dragged up a chair and sat in the middle of the floor, a strange
privacy between us. I noticed for the first time that her left eye was
just slightly lazy and it gave her the look of a woman who had overcome some distant sadness.

There was a frosted window in the bathroom and she looked
towards it as she spoke. An outdoor lamp brightened the dark. She
had met Manyaki, she said, at university in London. She had been
studying fashion design, he was in the English department. He had
come to one of her shows with a girlfriend of his – one of many, she
said, he was never short in the girlfriend department – and had stood
in front of her thesis project, a line of high-fashion skirts and blouses
supposedly inspired by tribal nomads.

'He snorted at it,' she said. 'Right there in the gallery. Just straight
out snorted. I was mortified.' Aoibheann reached for the hot-water
tap again, fanned a little more water down by my feet. 'I hated him.'
She laughed a little, gathering the folds of her humiliation.

She saw him years later at a publishing party in Soho where he'd
written an essay called 'The Politics of the African Novel.' She tried
to ridicule the article while he was in earshot, but the problem was that
the article was pure irony, head to toe, he had designed it that way.

'There I was, lambasting him, and guess what. He started laughing
again. A real smart arse.'

She knuckled the moisture out of her lazy eye.

'So I told him what lake to jump in. I won't tell you how he replied. I hated myself for it, but I was fascinated by him. So the next week I sent him a Bedouin robe, along with a barbed letter saying how he had embarrassed me, that he was an obnoxious arsehole, a git of the highest order, and I hoped he would rot in hell. He wrote a four-page letter back about my pretentious fashion instinct, and how it might be an idea to learn a culture before I slapped it on a million asses.'

I shifted a little in the bath, the water growing cold again.

'It's hardly a love story, but we're married eight years now, and he still wears that robe as a dressing gown. Just to get a rise out of me.'

We sat a moment in silence. It seemed to me that it was possibly the weight of her family she carried. I had heard that her father had once been arrested, or at least questioned, for some financial irregularities just after the boom years. It was hardly any of my business, and I avoided the temptation. I moved to get out of the bath.

'I'm glad you came to visit,' she said. 'We keep to ourselves a lot these days.'

I put my elbow on the rim, and she guided her arm in underneath me, helped me out. I kept my back to her. There's only so much embarrassment we can bear. She took a heated towel from the hot-water press, and put it around my shoulders. She gripped my shoulders from behind.

'We'll get you a good night's sleep, Hannah,' she said.

'Am I that bad?'

'I have half a sleeping pill if you want one.'

'I'd rather a brandy, to be honest.'

When I came downstairs she had made a hot brandy with cloves in a beautiful crystal glass. The conspiracy of women. We are in it together, make no mistake.

I STAYED FOUR more days. Aoibheann washed my clothes and nursed me back to some semblance of rest. I missed my cottage, but the sea kept me company. I walked along the pier with Georgie. There could always be one last emigrant in my family. A friend of mine once wisely said that suicide only suits the young. I counselled myself to stop sulking and simply enjoy my time there.

On the last day of my visit, I rose from the bed and went down to the small garden at the back of the house. I sat on a deckchair, made patterns out of the wisteria. I heard the door handle turn behind me. A quiet cough. Manyaki was barefoot, still in his pyjamas. He wore wire-rimmed glasses. His dreadlocks were askew.

He dragged up a flowerpot, turned it upside down, sat beside me. I could tell immediately from the hunch of his shoulders. The collector had emailed him back about the letter, he said. He rubbed the white of his feet along the stone. 'He's interested,' he said, 'but only willing to pay a thousand dollars.' I shifted a little in the deckchair. I had known, but did not want to be told. I had to feign a quick happiness: rosin on the bow seconds after the violin has been smashed.

Manyaki cracked his fingers together. He thought perhaps the collector might go as high as two or three thousand, but I would have to give him proof that the letter related to Douglass. There was none that I knew of, short of opening the letter and reading it, which was just as likely to make it worthless.

'I'll consider it,' I said, but we knew full well that it wouldn't happen. I would rather just let the letter go. It was hardly worth a drop in the ocean now.

Manyaki drummed his fingers a moment on the base of the flowerpot. He reached across and petted Georgie on the neck.

'Sorry,' he said.

'There's nothing for you to feel sorry about.'

The light fell slant in the back garden: it was a beautiful bright day. Aoibheann and Manyaki accompanied me out to the road where we said our goodbyes. She had packed me a little brown bag of sandwiches and a yoghurt, along with some biscuits. Days of school lunches. They smiled politely. I pulled out into the road and made my way along the coast. A long drive home.

Obama was, by all accounts, arriving at Baldonnel Airport that very day. Hurrah for Ireland. The sky would keep me company all the way home.

THE DARKNESS DROPPED from the bent limbs of the trees. The lough was perfectly calm. I pushed open the door and smushed the waiting envelopes up against the wall. The cottage was freezing. I had forgotten to bring in any wood. I lit a tilley lamp and put it on the mantelpiece.

I had expected an immense relief at coming home, but the house pushed a sharp cold into my bones. Georgie nudged up beside me. There was a little bit of kindling and a few peat briquettes. I lit a fire starter and shoved the bills in with them.

I searched out the wetsuit. A faint smell of mould off it. I warmed it up by the fire. Georgie watched me, her head on her paws. She seemed to own a strong reluctance, but she came down through the grass and stood at the edge of the wall while I waded into the water. A quiet night. Three stars and a moon and a lone plane travelling the high dark. The wind came off the water as if looking for company, the living and the dead passing into each other. The breeze rattled the large windows and then curled around the gable end, settled down.

DAVID MANYAKI CALLED in the morning to say that I had left the letter behind. I knew perfectly well. I had left it square on the bedside table, placed a glass paperweight upon it.

Lord knows, you can't grow this old without looking for others to shoulder our burdens. I told him he could open it. Excuse me? he said. You can open it, David. He called my bluff almost immediately. The room grew small, the ceiling close. I was breathing through muslin. He had short, stubby hands, I remembered that. The tops of his fingernails were very white. His cuticles were chewed. He asked me again if I was sure, and I said yes of course. I thought I heard the envelope tear but there was the archival plastic surely. He was opening that. I tried to recall what the bedroom looked like. His house. The children's curtains on the windows. An eiderdown with a shellfish motif. He must have had the phone cradled at his ear. He eased the letter out of the plastic. His voice grew faint. He had put me on speaker. The phone must have been lying on the bed. Holding the letter in his right hand, slowly easing under the flap with his left. I was in my kitchen looking out to the lough. The weather was perfectly banal. A low roll of grey. What might happen if it tore altogether? How dare he. There was a silence on the other end of the line. He couldn't do it. He would send it express post. The sky lightened out the window. No, I said, just read it to me please, for godsake. The hollow sound of the phone moving. The ceiling dipped. The letter was open now, would I like now for him to unfold the paper? A bolt of blood to my temple. An attempt at nonchalance. Is the envelope torn? No, he said, it was open, but not torn. A grey carpet on the floor. Children's clothes hanging in the cupboard. A tree outside his window, the branch touching against the frame. He unfolded the paper. The little café in Dublin where the small crumb had fallen from the plastic. Two pages, he said. It was written on headed notepaper from the Cochrane Hotel. Blue paper with a silver embossing at the top. They were small pages, folded over in half. The handwriting was faded but legible. Fountain ink. He took the phone off speaker. The branch maybe touched against the window. It's dated, he said. Exactly what I had expected. June 1919. Emily Ehrlich. *I am sending this letter in the hope that it will make it into your hands. My mother, Lily Duggan, always remembered a kindness shown to her by Miss Isabel Jennings.* The sharp cut of his African accent. Slowly he read. Blue paper. The marks around his cuticles. *It is just as likely that this will be lost at sea, but if they make it, perhaps you will receive this from two men who have knocked the war from a plane.* They ditched in Clifden. Caught in the hard roots. The living sedge. They had carried the letter across the Irish Sea. *We seldom know what echo our actions will find, but our stories will most certainly outlast us.* The foghorns along the pier. The traffic sounding outside his window. The stone tower on the waterfront. *This, then, is just a simple acknowledgement.* Emily Ehrlich's blouse splattered with ink. Tapping the edge of the inkpot with the nib of the pen. My mother, Lottie, standing over her shoulder, watching. Out the window, a shape against the sky. *I send it with deepest thanks.* The grass bent backwards. My son walked in the back door. The world does not turn without moments of grace. Who cares how small. A heavy dew soaked his trouser cuffs. I asked him then to read it to me again. Hold on a moment, Manyaki said. I heard the crackle of paper. It was short enough to commit to memory.

I PUT THE cottage up for auction in the early summer of 2011. The furniture was shifted, the paintings taken down from the wall. The air buzzed with lawnmowers. The green grass ran swiftly down to the lough. The window frames and doors were painted. A fresh air moved through the house. The hinges on the half-doors were oiled. The Aga stove was scrubbed. The cushions in the sunroom were patched and the Admiralty charts dusted off.

The past got up and shook itself loose. I stacked my possessions in cardboard boxes and put them in the shed out the back. A cupboard full of vintage dresses. Wooden tennis racquets and presses. Yards of fishing rods and reels. Old boxes of bullets. Useless things.

Jack Craddogh and his wife, Paula, drove out from Belfast to help me pack. I think she wanted to peer into the last of my possessions. I held up an old pair of jodhpurs and wondered how they had ever fit. Jack folded the last of my husband's clothes into a series of cardboard boxes. They were interested in my mother's final drawings. At the end she used oils like watercolour, making the paint appear raw, layering it with radiating currents of colour. She had a way of distorting or elongating figures: a sort of hunger.

Jack and Paula offered me a small amount for the sketches. They were really after the frames. I didn't want the money. It was not needed any more. The bank had extended my overdraft. I took my favourite ones, gave them the rest. They loaded the paintings up in the rear of their car: birds in flight.

Simon, the bank manager, moped around, hangdog with guilt. He walked from room to room, calculating a price that would eventually be his. A peculiar species of estate agent came with him in lipstick and a pencil-thin skirt. She had a southern accent. I told her that if she used the word *heritage* in my presence one more time I'd peck her liver out. Poor thing, she began trembling in her high heels. She was, she said, only doing her job. Fair enough, I said. I showed her where the tea kettle sat. She ghosted through the cottage, avoiding me.

Whenever a buyer came, it always seemed that it was never to buy, but to probe the ache. I took to walking Georgie around the island. She kept close at my heels as if she, too, knew that she might have to remember some day soon. An island with edges. It was not so much the memories that tied me to the place, as how it might look years from now. The trees were stubborn against the wind, their branches twisted inland.

I sat on the shoreside rocks. Georgie lowered herself in a heap. I was hardly guiltless in all of this. There was once so much I could have done. Ever since my son was murdered – I had finally learned how to say it – I'd allowed things to dissolve. All of it of my own making. Reckless. Sunken. Fearful.

My visitors wanted to talk to me, investigate their own desire, but they reeked of insincerity, and I couldn't bring myself to be anything but an ancient curmudgeon. I swished the blackthorn stick through the long grass and shuffled along. When the visitors left, I went back inside and finished off whatever packing needed to be done.

THREE DAYS BEFORE the auction there was a knock on the windowpane. Georgie rose and loped, animated, to the front.

I opened the half-door tentatively. Aoibheann thrust out a bottle of fine French brandy in my direction. David Manyaki was in the car, his face obscured in shadow, the windscreen shaded by the angle of light. I had just about forgotten. He had promised that he would bring the letter intact. He was rummaging in the back, unloosening his sons from their car seats.

'We'll just air them out a little bit if you don't mind,' said Aoibheann, but the children were already running around. 'We tried calling you. Hope it's no bother. David's on his way to Belfast for a conference tomorrow.'

'It's a bit Mother Hubbard, I'm afraid.'

We made our way through the empty house. Aoibheann wore a long sundress; Manyaki was in one of his bright dashikis. They moved slowly, taking stock of the emptiness. Evidence everywhere. The walls were less faded where the pictures had been. Nail holes in the plaster. Marks of furniture on the floor. A wind came down the chimney and turned the ashes.

They went through the living room, past the fireplace, beyond the kitchen. They were careful enough with their silence. Manyaki put the letter down on the table. I unfolded the envelope and examined the handwriting. It was rather ragged. What mystery we lose when we figure things out, but perhaps there's a mystery in the obvious, too. Nothing but a simple note. I closed it again and thanked him. It was entirely mine, I would keep it now: no university, no philatelist, no need for archives.

We sat in the sunroom where we could watch the boys run around the garden. I made a lunch of tinned tomato soup and soda bread.

A couple of jet skis hummed their savage insectry across the water. Manyaki rattled my tired heart when he stood politely from the chair and went down to the waterfront and waded in the shallows with his boys, shooed the jet skis away with a shout and a wave of his hands. His short dreadlocks bounced about his jaw. He and the boys walked together along the seawall, dipped out of sight, then came up the garden with three oysters. He shucked them with a screwdriver, and placed them in the fridge in a small tray of seawater. An hour later – he had to drive to the village to get milk for his boys, he said – he prepared them in the pan. White wine and chopped garlic and rosemary.

I asked them to stay the night. Manyaki and his sons dragged the old mattresses out from the barn. Small puffs of dust rose when they hit the floor. We fluffed the pillows and put fresh sheets on the beds. I got predictably teary-eyed. Aoibheann poured a little ledge of brandy into my glass, kept me from dropping off the cliff.

Just after dinner the older of Manyaki's sons, Oisin, stamped his little feet and said he wanted to feed the gulls. We had half a loaf of bread left. He took my hand and, along with his young brother, Conor, we scattered it up and down the lawn. A little beyond dusk we looked out the window to a herd of red-tail deer stepping high-legged through the gravel. Oisin and Conor sat at the window with their hands against the cold glass, watching. I didn't have the courage to say anything about how the deer would trample the last of my garden, and I held Conor by the window, until he fell asleep, all five years of him in my arms, and I walked out to shoo the deer away.

I stood in the yard, in the near-dark, listening. The sky was a long scene of silhouettes. The nearest trees seemed blue. The moon appeared, shallow and brittle over the lough. Water lapped up against the shore. The dark descended fully.

When I got back inside, Aoibheann was changing the boys into their pyjamas. They bawled a little, then quietened down. She sat at the foot of the makeshift bed and read them a story from her mobile phone.

Once upon a time, she began. I stood at the door and listened. There isn't a story in the world that isn't in part, at least, addressed to the past.

I lit the oil lamps, then left my guests alone and went down to the lough with Georgie. Out I swam. The water was fierce and cold. It moved through the core of me. I glanced at the house. Tomas rose and his tall thin shape went full across the lawn.

When I came back in, I towelled Georgie by the door. Manyaki and his wife were in the sunroom, shaped against the light. A glint off his wire-rimmed glasses. I caught a snippet of their conversation: his conference, their boys, the upcoming auction. They were leaning close together, across the width of a table, a sheet of paper with some numbers on the table between them. Their reflection in the glass. The water behind them stretched distant and black. I stood in the doorway a long, long time, unsure of what to do or say. I wasn't interested in their mercy. Nor would I stay, if they stayed.

When I sat down beside them, their silence was lined with tenderness. We have to admire the world for not ending on us.

TransAtlantic thanks

THERE IS NO REAL ANONYMITY IN HISTORY. And none, really, in storytelling. Many hands have guided this work, and so it would feel wrong to pretend that I wrote this novel entirely on my own. Of course I accept all its missteps and mistakes as entirely my own, but I would certainly be remiss if I didn't mention the people who have helped me along the way. First of all, as always, and endlessly, Allison, Isabella, John Michael and Christian. Also my colleagues and students at Hunter College, Jennifer Raab, Peter Carey, Tom Sleigh, and Gabriel Packard in particular. My sincere thanks to David Blight, John Waters, Patricia Ferrerio, Marc Conner, Brendan Barrington, Colm O'Grada, Fionnghuala Sweeney, Richard Bradbury and Donal O'Kelly for their help on the section about Douglass. Scholars of Douglass should know that I have sometimes combined, conflated, and on occasion fictionalized quotes in order to create the texture of truth. For the Alcock/Brown section I am enormously indebted to Scott Olsen, William Langewiesche, Cullen Murphy, Brendan Lynch and Andrew Nahum of the Science Museum in London. For the section concerning George Mitchell, I should thank none other than George and Heather Mitchell themselves – they had the great grace to allow me to try to imagine my way into their world. In addition, I must thank Liz Kennedy, Tim O'Connor, Mitchell Reiss, Declan Kelly, Maurice Hayes, Tony Blair and numerous others (especially Seamus and Mairead Brolly) who have tried to help me understand the peace process. The people of Aspen and the Aspen Writers' Foundation were enormously helpful every step of the way: very special thanks to Lisa Consiglio for everything. For the *Transatlantic* crew, Loretta Brennan Glucksman, Gabriel Byrne, Niall Burgess and Eugene Downes, my ongoing thanks, always. Over the past couple of years I have been given access to a roof over my head in rough weathers – deepest thanks to Mary Lee Jackson, Fleur Jackson, Kyron Bourke and Claira Jackson for the house on the edge of Strangford Lough; a word and world of thanks to Wendy Aresty for the shelter in Aspen; thanks to Bruce Berger for use of the most beautiful cottage in the west; to Isa Catto and Daniel Shaw for the peace in Woody Creek; and of course to Rosemarie and Roger Hawke for their support and the room upstairs. For editorial guidance and acuity, sincere thanks to Jennifer Hershey and Alexandra Pringle. To Martin Quinn, a deep, deep bow. Thanks also to Caroline Ast, Thomas Uberhoff and Carolyn Kormann. Thanks always to Sarah Chalfant and Andrew Wylie and all at the Wylie Agency. My appreciation to John Berger, Michael Ondaatje, Jim Harrison and Wendell Berry for their ongoing inspiration. There are many others who have helped all the way, in reading and consultation – John and Anna Cusatis, Joe Lennon, Dr Jim Marion, Terry Cooper, Chandran Madhun, Maurice Byrne, Sharif Abdunnur, Bob Mooney, Dan Barry, Bill Cheng, Tom Kelly, Danny McDonald, Mike Jewell, Tim and Kathy Kipp, Kaitlyn Greenidge, Sean and Sally and the rest of my family in Ireland, and most especially my brother Ronan McCann, who runs my website and without whom I'd be entirely lost. There are others too: I hope I have not left too many out. I will thank them quietly along the way, all of us, together, aloft.

about the author

Colum McCann, originally from Dublin, Ireland, is the author of six novels and two collections of stories. His most recent novel, the *New York Times* best-seller *Let the Great World Spin*, won the National Book Award, the International IMPAC Dublin Literary Award and several other major international awards. His fiction has been published in thirty-five languages. He lives in New York.

www.colummccann.com

This book is set in Fournier, a typeface named for Pierre-Simon Fournier, the youngest son of a French printing family. Pierre Simon first studied watercolour painting, but became involved in type design through work that he did for his eldest brother. Starting with engraving woodblocks and large capitals, he later moved on to fonts of type. In 1736 he began his own foundry, and published the first version of his point system the following year.